Union Street

&

Blow Your House Down

Pat Barker

D0036959

Picador

Farrar, Straus, and Giroux

New York

Picador® is a U.S. registered trademark and is used by Farrar, Straus and Giroux under license from Pan Books Limited.

For information on Picador Reading Group Guides, as well as ordering, please contact the Trade Marketing department at St. Martin's Press. Phone: 1-800-221-7945 extension 763
Fax: 212-677-7456
E-mail: trademarketing@stmartins.com

Library of Congress Cataloging-in-Publication Data

Barker, Pat.
    [Union Street]
    Union street ; &, Blow your house down / Pat Barker.
        p.   cm.
    ISBN 0-312-24089-9
    1. Working class women–England–Fiction. 2. Prostitutes–Crimes against–England–Fiction. 3. Serial murders–England–Fiction. 4. Lesbians–England–Fiction. 5. Community life–Fiction. I. Barker, Pat. Blow your house down. II. Title. III. Title: Union Street ; &, Blow your house down. IV. Title: Blow your house down.
    PR6052.A6488U5 1999
    823'.914–dc21
                                                          99-19836
                                                          CIP

First published in Great Britain by Virago Press Limited

D 10 9 8 7 6 5 4 3

CONTENTS

UNION STREET

CHAPTER ONE
KELLY BROWN

There was a square of cardboard in the window where the glass had been smashed. During the night one corner had worked loose and scraped against the frame whenever the wind blew.

Kelly Brown, disturbed by the noise, turned over, throwing one arm across her sister's face.

The older girl stirred in her sleep, grumbling a little through dry lips, and then, abruptly, woke.

'I wish you'd watch what you're doing. You nearly had my eye out there.'

Kelly opened her eyes, reluctantly. She lay in silence for a moment trying to identify the sound that had disturbed her. 'It's that thing,' she said, finally. 'It's that bloody cardboard. It's come unstuck.'

'That wouldn't be there either if you'd watch what you're doing.'

'Oh, I see. My fault. I suppose you weren't there when it happened?'

Linda had pulled the bedclothes over her head. Kelly waited a moment, then jabbed her in the kidneys. Hard.

'Time you were up.' Outside, a man's boots slurred over the cobbles: the first shift of the day. 'You'll be late.'

'What's it to you?'

'You'll get the sack.'

'No, I won't then, clever. Got the day off, haven't I?'

'I don't know. Have you?'

No reply. Kelly was doubled up under the sheet, her body jack-knifed against the cold. As usual, Linda had pinched most of the blankets and all the eiderdown.

'Well, have you?'

'Cross me heart and hope to die, cut me throat if I tell a lie.'

'Jammy bugger!'

'I don't mind turning out.'

'Not much!'

'*You've* nothing to turn out to.'

'School.'

'School!'

'I didn't notice you crying when you had to leave.'

Kelly abandoned the attempt to keep warm. She sat on the edge of the bed, sandpapering her arms with the palms of dirty hands. Then ran across the room to the chest of drawers.

As she pulled open the bottom drawer — the only one Linda would let her have — a characteristic smell met her.

'You mucky bloody sod!' The cold forgotten, she ran back to the bed and began dragging the blankets off her sister. 'Why can't you burn the buggers?'

'With him sat there? How can I?'

Both girls glanced at the wall that divided their mother's bedroom from their own. For a moment Kelly's anger died down.

Then: 'He wasn't there last night.'

'There was no fire.'

'You could've lit one.'

'What? At midnight? What do you think she'd say about that?' Linda jerked her head towards the intervening wall.

'Well, you could've wrapped them up and put them in the dustbin then. Only the lowest of the bloody low go on the way you do.'

'What would you know about it?'

'I know one thing, I'll take bloody good care I never get like it.'

'You will, dear. It's nature.'

10

'I don't mean that.'

Though she did, perhaps. She looked at the hair in Linda's armpits, at the breasts that shook and wobbled when she ran, and no, she didn't want to get like that. And she certainly didn't want to drip foul-smelling, brown blood out of her fanny every month. 'Next one I find I'll rub your bloody mucky face in.'

'You and who else?'

'It won't need anybugger else.'

'You! You're not the size of twopenn'orth of copper.'

'See if that stops me.'

There was a yell from the next bedroom. 'For God's sake, you two, shut up! There's some of us still trying to sleep.'

'No bloody wonder. On the hump all night.'

'Linda!'

'Notice she blames me. You're getting to be a right cheeky little sod, you are.'

'Did you hear me, Linda?'

'Just watch it, that's all.'

'Linda!'

'I'll tell Kevin about you,' Kelly said. 'He wouldn't be so keen getting his hand up if he knew what you were really like.

'Have I to come in there?'

The threat silenced both girls. With a final glare Kelly picked up her clothes and went downstairs to get dressed. On the landing she paused to look into her mother's bedroom. There was a dark, bearded man zipping up his trousers. When he saw her his face twitched as if he wanted to smile. It wasn't Wilf. It was a man she had never seen before.

She ran all the way downstairs, remembering, though only just in time, to jump over the hole in the passage where the floorboards had given way.

Dressed, she turned her attention to the fire. Since there were no sticks, she would have to try to light it on paper alone, a long and not always successful job. Muttering to herself, she reached up and pulled one of her mother's sweaters from the airing line. There were sweaters of her

11

own and Linda's there but she liked her mother's better. They were warmer, somehow, and she liked the smell.

She picked up the first sheet of newspaper. The face of a young soldier killed in Belfast disappeared beneath her scrumpling fingers. Then her mother came in, barefoot, wearing only a skirt and bra. The bunions on the sides of her feet were red with cold.

She was still angry. Or on the defensive. Kelly could tell at once by the way she moved.

'I see you've nicked another of me sweaters. Beats me why you can't wear your own. You'd think you had nowt to put on.'

She searched along the line and pulled down her old working jumper that had gone white under the armpits from deodorants and sweat. After a moment's thought she rejected it in favour of a blue blouse, the sort of thing she would never normally have worn at work. It was because of him, the man upstairs.

Kelly sniffed hungrily at the sweater she was wearing, which held all the mingled smells of her mother's body. Though the face she raised to her mother afterwards could not have been more hostile.

'You got started on the fire, then? Good lass.'

'I'd've had it lit if there'd been owt to light it with.'

'Yes, well, I forgot the sticks.'

She perched on the edge of the armchair and began pulling on her tights. Kelly watched. She went on twisting rolls of newspaper, the twists becoming more vicious as the silence continued.

At last she said, 'Well, come on, then. Don't keep us in suspense. Who is it?'

'Who?'

Kelly drew a deep breath. 'Him. Upstairs. The woolly-faced bugger with the squint.'

'His name's Arthur. And he doesn't squint.'

'He was just now when he looked at me.'

'Oh, you'd make any bugger squint, you would!'

'Does that mean Wilf's had his chips?'

'You could put it that way.'

12

'I just did.'

'It isn't as if you were fond of Wilf. You weren't. Anything but.'

'You can get used to anything.'

'Kelly . . .' Mrs Brown's voice wavered. She didn't know whether to try persuasion first, or threats. Both had so often failed. 'Kelly, I hope you'll be all right with. . .with Uncle Arthur. I mean I hope . . .'

'What do you mean "all right"?'

'You know what I mean.' Her voice had hardened. 'I mean *all right*.'

'Why shouldn't I be all right with him?'

'You tell me. I couldn't see why you couldn't get on with Wilf. He was good to you.'

'He had no need to be.'

'Kelly . . .'

There was a yell from the passage. Arthur, still unfamiliar with the geography of the house, had gone through the hole in the floor.

He came in smiling nervously, anxious to appear at ease.

'I'll have to see if I can't get that fixed for you, love.'

'Arthur, this is my youngest, Kelly.'

He managed a smile. 'Hello, flower.'

'I don't know what she'd better call you. Uncle Arthur?'

Kelly was twisting a roll of newspaper into a long rope. With a final wrench she got it finished and knotted the ends together to form a noose. Only when it was completed to her satisfaction did she smile and say, 'Hello, *Uncle* Arthur.'

'Well,' said Mrs Brown, her voice edging upwards, 'I'd better see what there is for breakfast.'

'I can tell you now,' said Kelly. 'There's nowt.'

Mrs Brown licked her lips. Then, in a refined voice, she said, 'Oh, there's sure to be something. Unless our Linda's eat the lot.'

'Our Linda's eat nothing. She's still in bed.'

'Still in bed? What's wrong with her?'

'Day off. She says.'

'Day off, my arse!' The shock had restored Mrs Brown to her normal accent. 'Linda!' Her voice rose to a shriek. She ran upstairs. They could still hear her in the bedroom. Screaming fit to break the glass. If there'd been any left to break.

'That'll roust her!' Arthur said, chuckling. He looked nice when he laughed. Kelly turned back to the fire, guarding herself from the temptation of liking him.

'You've done a grand job,' he said. 'It's not easy, is it, without sticks?'

'I think it'll go.'

After a few minutes Mrs Brown reappeared in the doorway. 'I'm sorry about that, Arthur.' She'd got her posh voice back on the way downstairs. 'But if you didn't keep on at them they'd be in bed all morning.'

She could talk!

'Anyway, she'll be down in a minute. Then you'll have met both of them.' She was trying to make it sound like a treat. Arthur didn't look convinced. 'While we're waiting Kelly can go round the shop for a bit of bacon. Can't you love?'

'I'm doing the fire,' Kelly pointed out in a voice that held no hope of compromise.

'Don't go getting stuff in just for me.'

'Oh, it's no bother. I can't think how we've got so short.' Sucking up again. Pretending to be what she wasn't. And for what? He was nowt. 'Anyway, we can't have you going out with nothing on your stomach. You've got to keep your strength up.' There was a secret, grown-up joke in her voice. Kelly heard it, and bristled.

'She won't let you have owt anyway,' she said. 'There's over much on the slate as it is.

Her mother rounded on her. 'That's right, Kelly, go on, stir the shit.'

'I'm not stirring the shit. I'm just saying there's too much on the slate.'

'I'm paying for this, aren't I?'

'I dunno. Are you?'

Mrs Brown's face was tight with rage and shame. Arthur had begun fumbling in his pockets for money. 'Put that away, Arthur,' she said quickly. 'I'm paying.'

The door opened and Linda came in. 'I can't find me jumper,' she said. She was naked except for a bra and pants.

'It'll be where you took it off.'

Linda shrugged. She wasn't bothered. She turned her attention to the man. 'Hello!'

'My eldest. Linda.'

Arthur, his eyes glued to Linda's nipples, opened and shut his mouth twice.

'I think he's trying to say "Hello",' Kelly said.

'Thank you, Kelly. When we need an interpreter we'll let you know.' Mrs Brown was signalling to Linda to get dressed. Linda ignored her.

'Is there a cup of tea?' she asked.

Arthur's hand caressed the warm curve of the pot.

'There's some in,' he said. 'I don't know if it's hot enough.'

'Doesn't matter. I can make fresh.' She put one hand inside her bra and adjusted the position of her breast. Then she did the same for the other, taking her time about it. 'Do you fancy a cup?' she asked.

'No, he doesn't,' said her mother. 'He's just had some upstairs.'

Mrs Brown looked suddenly older, rat-like, as her eyes darted between Arthur and the girl.

Kelly, watching, said, 'I don't know what you're on about tea for, our Linda. If you're late again you're for the chop. And I don't know who you'd get to give you another job. 'T'isn't everybody fancies a filthy sod like you pawing at their food.

'Language!' said Mrs Brown, automatically. She had almost given up trying to keep this situation under control. She would have liked to cry but from long habit held the tears back. 'Kelly, outside in the passage. Now! Linda, get dressed.'

As soon as the living room door was closed, Mrs Brown whispered, 'Now look, tell her half a pound of bacon, a loaf of bread — oh, and we'd better have a bottle of milk, and tell her here's ten bob off the bill and I'll give her the rest on Friday, *without fail*. Right?'

'She won't wear it.'

'Well, do the best you can. Get the bacon anyway.'

Now that they were alone their voices were serious, almost friendly. Mrs Brown watched her daughter pulling on her anorak. 'And Kelly,' she said, 'when you come back. . .

'Yes?'

'Try and be nice.'

The girl tossed her long hair out of her eyes like a Shetland pony. 'Nice?' she said. 'I'm bloody marvellous!'

She went out, slamming the door.

'. . . and a bar of chocolate, please.' Kelly craned to see the sweets at the back of the counter. 'I'll have that one.'

'Eightpence, mind.'

'Doesn't matter.'

'Does to me! Forty pence off the bill and eightpence for a bar of chocolate. I suppose you want the tuppence change?'

'Yes, please.'

Grumbling to herself, Doris slapped the bar of chocolate down on the counter. 'Sure there's nowt else you fancy?'

'I get hungry at school.'

'Get that lot inside you, you won't be.' Doris indicated the bacon, milk and bread.

'Oh, that's not for me. That's for her and her fancy man.'

'But they'll give you some?'

'No they won't.'

'Eeeeee!' Doris raised her eyes to the washing powder on the top shelf. 'Dear God. You can tell your Mam if she's not here by six o'clock Friday I'll be up your street looking for her. And I won't care who I show up neither.'

'I'll tell her. Thanks, Missus.'

After the child had gone Doris stationed herself on the doorstep hoping for somebody to share the outrage with. Her and her fancy man! Dear God!

A few minutes later her patience was rewarded. Iris King came round the corner, bare legs white and spotlessly clean, blonde hair bristling with rollers, obviously on her way to Mrs Bell's.

She listened avidly.

'Well,' she said 'I wish I could say I'm surprised, but if I did it'd be a lie. I saw her the other week sat round the Buffs with that Wilf Rogerson. I say nowt against him, it's not his bairn — mind you, he's rubbish — but her! They were there till past midnight and that bairn left to God and Providence. I know one thing, Missus, when my bairns were little they were never let roam the streets. And as for leave them on their own while I was pubbing it with a fella — no! By hell would I, not if his arse was decked with diamonds.'

'And they don't come like that, do they?'

'They do not!'

Kelly, meanwhile, was eating a bacon butty.

'Time you were thinking about school, our Kell.'

Kelly twisted round to look at the clock.

'No use looking at that. It's slow.'

'Now she tells me!'

'You knew. It's always slow.'

Kelly wiped her mouth on the back of her hand and started to get up. 'I'll get the stick if I'm late again.'

'They don't give lasses the stick.'

'They do, you know.'

'Well, they didn't when I was at school.'

'Well, they do now.'

Kelly was really worried. She tried twice to zip up her anorak and each time failed.

'And you can give your bloody mucky face a wipe. You're not going out looking like that, showing me up.'

'Oh, Mam, there isn't time!'

'You've time to give it a rub.' She went into the kitchen and returned with a face flannel and tea towel. 'Here, you'll have to use this, I can't find a proper towel.'

All this was Arthur's fault. She'd never have bothered with breakfast or face-washing if he hadn't been there. Kelly dabbed at the corners of her mouth, cautiously.

'Go on, give it a scrub!' Mrs Brown piled the breakfast dishes together and took them into the kitchen.

'I'll give you a hand,' said Arthur.

'No, it's all right, love, I can manage. It won't take a

17

minute.'

It had been known to take days.

Arthur sat down, glancing nervously at Kelly. He was afraid of being alone with her. Kelly, looking at her reflection in the mirror, thought, how sensible of him.

'Uncle Arthur?' she said.

He looked up, relieved by the friendliness of her tone.

'I was just wondering, are you and me Mam off round the Buffs tonight?' As if she needed to ask!

'I hadn't really thought about it, flower. I daresay we might have a look in.'

'It's just there's a film on at the Odeon: *Brides of Dracula*.'

'Oh, I don't think your Mam'ld fancy that.'

Why not? She'd fancied worse.

'It wasn't me Mam I was thinking of.'

'Oh.' He started searching in his pockets for money. Slower on the uptake than Wilf had been, but he got there in the end. He produced a couple of tenpenny pieces.

'Cheapest seats are 50p.'

'I thought it was kids half price?'

'Not on Mondays. It's Old Age Pensioners' night.'

'Oh, I see. They're all sat there, are they, watching *Dracula*?'

'Yeah, well. Gives 'em a thrill, don't it?'

He wasn't as thick as he looked.

'Here's a coupla quid. And get yourself summat to eat.'

'Kelly! Are you still here?'

'Just going, Mam.' At the door she turned. 'Will you be in when I get back?'

'Don't be daft. Arthur's meeting me from work. Aren't you, love?' She smiled at him. Then became aware of the child watching her. 'I don't *know* when I'll be in.'

'Doesn't matter.'

'There's plenty to go at if you're hungry. There's that bit of bacon left. And you're old enough to get yourself to bed.'

'I said, it doesn't matter.'

The door slammed.

Kelly stared across the blackening school yard. The windows of the school were encased in wire cages: the children threw bricks. Behind the wire the glass had misted over, become a sweaty blur through which the lights of the Assembly Hall shone dimly.

There was a ragged sound of singing.

> 'New every morning is the love
> Our wakening and uprising prove . . .'

If she went in as late as this she might well get the stick. Safer, really, to give school a miss. She could easily write a note tomorrow in her mother's handwriting. She had done it before.

There was a fair on, too, on the patch of waste ground behind the park. She hesitated, felt the crisp pound notes in her pocket, and made up her mind.

She ran into the railway tunnel, her footsteps echoing dismally behind her.

She wandered down a long avenue of trees, scuffling through the dead leaves. Horse chestnut leaves, she realised, like hands with spread fingers. Immediately she began to look at the ground more closely, alert for the gleam of conkers in the grass.

It was too early though — only the beginning of September. They would not have ripened yet.

The early excitement of nicking off from school was gone. She was lonely. The afternoon had dragged. There was a smell of decay, of life ending. Limp rags of mist hung from the furthest trees.

As always when she was most unhappy, she started thinking about her father, imagining what it would be like when he came back home. She was always looking for him, expecting to meet him, though sometimes, in moments of panic and despair, she doubted if she would recognise him if she did.

There was only one memory she was sure of. Firelight. The smells of roast beef and gravy and the *News of the World*, and her father with nothing on but his vest and pants, throwing her up into the air again and again. If she closed her eyes she could see his warm and slightly oily brown skin and the snake on his arm that wriggled when he clenched the muscle underneath.

She was sure of that. Though the last time she had tried to talk to Linda about it, Linda had said . . . had said . . . Well, it didn't matter what Linda said.

Absorbed in her daydreams, she had almost missed it. But there it lay, half-hidden in the grass. It wasn't open, though. She bent down, liking the feel of the cool, green, spiky ball in her hand.

She had heard nothing, and yet there in front of her were the feet, shoes black and highly polished, menacingly elegant against the shabbiness of leaves and grass.

Slowly she looked up. He was tall and thin with a long head, so that she seemed from her present position to be looking up at a high tower.

'You found one then?'

She knew from the way he said it that he had been watching her a long time.

'Yes,' she said, standing up. 'But it's not ready yet.'

'Oh, I don't know. Sometimes they are. You can't always tell from the outside.'

He took it from her. She watched his long fingers with their curved nails probe the green skin, searching for the place where it would most easily open and admit them.

'Though everything's a bit late this year. I think it must be all the rain we've been having.'

She didn't want to watch. Instead she glanced rapidly from side to side, wishing she'd stayed near the railings where at least there might have been people walking past on the pavement outside.

There was nobody in sight.

When she looked back he had got the conker open. Through the gash in the green skin she could see the white seed.

'No, you were right,' he said. 'It's not ready yet.'

He threw it away and wiped his fingers very carefully and fastidiously on his handkerchief, as if they were more soiled than they could possibly have been.

'I've got some more,' he said, suddenly. 'You can have them to take home if you like.' He reached into his pockets and produced a mass of conkers, a dozen or more, and held them out to her on the palms of his cupped hands. She looked at them doubtfully. 'Go on, take them,' he said.

His voice shook with excitement.

Kelly took them, hoping that if she did as he said he would go away. But he showed no sign of wanting to go.

'What's your name?' he asked. He had a precise, slightly sibilant way of speaking that might've been funny, but wasn't.

'Kelly,' she said.

'Kelly. That's an unusual name.'

Kelly shrugged. It wasn't particularly unusual where she came from.

'And does your mother know you're here, Kelly? I mean, shouldn't you be at school?'

'I've had the flu. She said, Go and get some fresh air.'

Normally she was a very convincing liar. But uncertainty had robbed her of the skill and her words clattered down, as unmistakably empty as tin cans.

He smiled. 'I see. How sensible of her to let you come out. Much better than staying indoors.'

He had accepted the lie without believing it. Kelly shivered and looked longingly towards the road. She would have liked to turn and walk away from him, just like that, without explanation, without leave-taking. But she could not. He had done nothing, said nothing, wrong; and there was something in the softness of his voice that compelled her to stay.

'I've been ill too,' he said. 'That's why I'm not at work.'

And perhaps he had. He looked pale enough for anything. 'Well, I think I'd . . .' She didn't bother to finish the sentence.

'I come here every day,' he said abruptly. 'I come to feed the ducks.' He had been looking away from her towards the lake. Now, heavily — almost, it seemed, reluctantly — he bent his head to her again. 'You could come with me, if you

21

liked,' he said.

And stood breathing.

'I don't think . . .'

'It's near the road.' He smiled faintly, holding out reassurance on an open palm.

He looked at her so intently. Other people — her mother, Linda, the teachers at school — merely glanced at her and then with indifference or haste, passed on. But this man stared at her as if every pore in her skin mattered. His eyes created her. And so she had to go with him. She could not help herself. She had to go.

When they got to the lake she relaxed. It was, as he had said, quite close to the road though screened from it by a long line of willow trees that hung over their own reflections in the water. And there were people going past. You could hear their voices, the sound of their footsteps. There were even people at the lake itself: a youngish man with two small girls. They, too, had come to feed the ducks. Kelly watched enviously as the younger of the two girls leaned out over the water to scatter crumbs while her father held on to her skirt.

'I've got the bread here somewhere. And cake. They like cake.' He produced a greaseproof bag from an inside pocket. 'Only you have to watch the geese don't get the lot. They're very greedy.'

Already, from every corner of the lake, ducks and geese and swans were taking to the water, cleaving its smooth surface, while in their wake the willow-tree reflections rippled and re-formed.

The bread was still in slices. Kelly began tearing it into smaller pieces, scraping the really stale crusts with her fingernails so that the crumbs showered down. She was happy. She had put her fears to one side. The birds began to arrive. Some showed signs of wanting to clamber out of the water on to the path, but Kelly clung to the trunk of an overhanging tree and leaned far out to scatter the crumbs. With the surface of her mind she watched the long thick necks bend and sway as the birds squabbled over the bread, but deeper down she had begun telling herself stories again, fantasies whose warmth eased away the last ache of doubt. Her father had come back. It was her father behind her on the path. When she leaned still further out and felt the man's hand holding on to her skirt it was so much part of the dream that she did not bother to turn round.

But the bag was empty. Kelly shook out the last crumbs and straightened up. The man standing on the path behind her was not her father. The family on the other side of the lake had gone. She started to say something and then stopped, for the geese would not accept that there was no more food. They came hissing and swaying from the water, long necks outstretched, wetting the path with their cracked orange feet. Kelly stepped back but they followed, thick necks thrust out, yellow beaks jabbing at her hands and thighs. She pushed them away, sickened by the feel of wet plumage over bone.

'It's all right. They won't hurt. They're more frightened of you than you are of them.'

He stamped his feet and clapped his hands. The geese swayed and rocked away, heads upraised in a long, sibilant hiss of protest.

'There, you're all right now.'

But she was not. She looked down at the mottled flesh of her thighs and remembered how the yellow beaks had jabbed. Then up at him. All her original distrust had returned.

'I've got to be going now,' she said.

'Oh, dear. I was hoping we might . . .'

'No, I've got to go. Me Mam'll be wondering where I am.'

There was a sudden blast of music that went on for a few bars, got stuck, started up again. Kelly's face lit up.

'Well,' said the man, 'It's been very nice. I've enjoyed it.'

He smiled at her and she smiled back. Now that she was going, now that he was making no attempt to keep her there, she felt again that yes, it had been nice.

Yet, as she walked away, the sense of oppression grew. It was so dark near the pond. The light filtered down through the leaves, staining everything green. Even her skin was green.

She walked more quickly, not daring to look back, while the muscles at the back of her neck tightened. And tightened.

Suddenly she came out on to a field of brilliant, white light. There were seagulls there, hundreds of them, standing motionless in pools of reflected cloud. Kelly watched for a moment, while her knotted muscles relaxed and dissolved into streams of water or light. Then, with a shout of joy, she ran towards them.

One by one with the clapping of wings, and then in a whole flock, they rose up and burst like spray in the air above her head.

By the main gate she turned to look back but could see nothing. She stood, scanning the trees, for a full minute before she could bring herself to leave.

There was a moment of complete stillness. Then in the shadow of the trees, a shadow moved. He was no longer looking towards the gate. He had turned to stare in the direction of the music. The music that had seemed to interest her so much.

At the entrance to the Hall of Mirrors Kelly paused. There was somebody there she knew: Joanne Wilson, who lived only a few doors down. But it didn't matter. Joanne was with her boyfriend and too wrapped up in him to notice anybody else.

She stood with his arms around her waist and looked at their reflections in the glass. Hag and goblin, witch and toad, vampire and crow, and every face their own. They giggled and pointed, and fell silent. Joanne hid her face in the young man's neck.

'Don't reckon this is worth ten p,' Kelly said.

'Oh, I don't know.' Her friend, Sharon Scaife, who was plump and suffered for it, had found a mirror that showed her long and stringy as a bean. 'I quite like it.'

'Well, I don't.' Kelly was watching the young man's reflection in the glass. 'I think it's crap.'

'O.K. We'll go somewhere else. There's no need to stop here if you don't want.'

'What about the Ghost Train?'

'Yeah. All right.'

They stood in the queue for the Ghost Train, eating chips so saturated in vinegar that it leaked out and trickled down their wrists. When the last chip was gone Kelly licked the paper, relishing the grittiness of salt on her tongue, worrying at the corners of the bag to get out the last crumb of burnt and crispy batter.

Ahead of them the Ghost Train rumbled and clanked. A girl's scream sliced the air.

Kelly felt that she was being watched. She looked around, but it was almost impossible to recognise anybody. People's faces were purple under the lights and a lot of the men wore funny glasses with big red noses stuck on to them. They were for sale just inside the gate. They hid so much of the face, you couldn't tell what was behind them.

'What you looking for?' Sharon asked.

'Teachers. Don't forget I nicked off today.'

'I dunno how you have the nerve.' Sharon, a well-behaved little girl, was breathless with admiration.

The Ghost Train burst through its swing doors.

'Try and get up front,' Sharon said. 'It's better there.'

But Kelly was still looking behind her. Even when they were in the front car — Sharon gripping the rail until her knuckles showed white — Kelly still looked back. The train began to vibrate and shudder beneath them. The last carriages filled quickly and there — yes, she was almost sure — there he was, dressed all in black as he had been in the park, standing out, thin and dark as an exclamation mark, against the coloured shirts and funny hats, the laughter and joking of the other men.

The train sprang into life, burst through the swing doors into hot and quivering darkness. Girls screamed as skulls and skeletons and vampires leaped down on them from the ramparts of cardboard castles.

'I thought you were going to pass out in there,' Sharon said, looking at her curiously, without the usual admiration.

'It was too hot.'

Kelly was watching the people leave the train. He was not

among them. Perhaps he had slipped out before, or perhaps . . . perhaps she had just imagined it.

'I'll have to be going,' Sharon said awkwardly. Kelly was no fun at all tonight.

'It's only ten o'clock.'

'I'm meant to be in bed at nine. Me Mam'll go hairless.'

'Tell her you couldn't get on the bus.'

Sharon hesitated, afraid of seeming soft. 'She's got me Dad bad again.'

'Oh, your Dad. He's always bad.'

'It's not his fault, is it? Anyway, you can talk. Where's your Dad?'

If she stayed any longer they would quarrel. It was better to let her go.

At the gate Sharon said, 'Why don't you come with us?'

Kelly thought. 'No,' she said. 'I'll stop.'

She watched Sharon walk away. She felt a moment's fear as Sharon reached the gate, and called out to her. But the moment passed. When Sharon turned round, Kelly said only, 'No, it's O.K. Go on. I'll see you tomorrow.'

Slowly Kelly walked back into the swirl and dazzle of the fairground. She was beginning to feel sick, and as she pushed and jostled her way through the crowds the feeling grew. She was not sure now that she liked the fair. All that screaming, and the smells of oil and sweat and stale beer, and people unrecognisable under funny hats. That woman in the booth, who had looked so fat and jolly before, looked rapacious now as she poured her cascade of pennies from palm to palm, and shouted for people to come up; and the goldfish she handed out — they were only too clearly dying inside their tiny polythene prisons.

Kelly made herself keep going. There was a roundabout, and she stopped to watch. The revolving animals twinkled, blurred, and finally stopped. She looked over their heads and there he was, watching her, a patch of darkness against the lurid brightness of the fair.

She started to run. The buffeting of the crowds and her own gasping breaths increased her fear. She did not dare look back, because she was afraid that he was following. She ran faster across the purple grass until at last she came out into the silence and darkness of the vans where there was only the throbbing of an engine to disturb the stillness.

There were long black passages between the vans. She started to walk down one of them but stopped when she heard a man cough close at hand. She started to run again, tripped over a coil of rope and fell, not into emptiness, but into hands that caught and held her.

'Hey up!' a voice said. 'You're not meant to be around here, you know. I only come here for a pee.'

He was fat and shiny with a black moustache. So much she could see in the glow from a caravan window. Nothing that she had feared, nothing that she had imagined, could have been more terrifying than this entirely ordinary face.

When he stood aside to let her pass she ran and did not stop running until she had reached the gate.

Her stomach was heaving. She hung on to the railings and hoped it would settle down. But it didn't. It got worse.

The pub opposite was just coming out. As Kelly watched, a woman turned suddenly and swung her handbag into a man's face. He backed off, swearing viciously. She thought of her mother sitting in the Buffs with Arthur.

She was so near to being sick that she daren't move. And in spite of her fear of what might lie behind her in the fairground she was in no hurry to move away from the lighted area near the gate. For beyond that was total darkness. And the Moor, by day a sour, brick-strewn stretch of waste land covered with dog shit, newspaper and beer cans, acquired at night a mysterious and threatening immensity. But it had to be crossed if she was to go home through the park.

So she hesitated. Until eventually her stomach took the decision for her. She staggered through the main gate and doubled up in the gutter.

When eventually she was able to look up he was there. Again she had the feeling that he had been there a long time. But he wasn't wearing black: he couldn't've been the man on the Ghost Train. Or the man near the roundabout.

Perhaps there hadn't been a man at all.

She said, slowly, 'It wasn't you.'

He looked surprised. When no explanation came he said, 'I've only just got here. In fact . . .' He looked out over the darkness of the Moor, 'I was in two minds whether to come at all.'

She couldn't reply. A second spasm of vomiting had her squatting in the gutter. When she straightened up again he said, 'But now I'm glad I did.'

He had not been the man in the fairground. That ought to have been reassuring, but somehow it wasn't.

'Do you think that's all?' he asked. 'Or is there more to come?' He was staring at her with a kind of disgusted fascination.

'No, I think that's the finish.'

'I should hope so.'

He was wearing a light-coloured jacket, and fawn trousers. Casual clothes like all the men at the fairground wore. Only on him they looked like fancy dress.

'What have you been eating?'

As he spoke, he drew her towards him and began wiping her mouth with his handkerchief, which he first dampened with his spit. She was too surprised to resist and after a while she found it pleasant to be taken care of.

'Chips. Lolly.' She thought further back. 'Sherbet bomb, candyfloss, ice cream.'

'You *have* been having a good time.' He sounded jealous as another child would have done. But he wasn't a child.

'Do you always come to the fair?'

None of the other men had come alone.

'I usually look in.'

It wasn't the answer she wanted.

'Here,' he went on. 'You'd better hang on to my handkerchief. Just in case.'

'No, I'm all right now.' And she was. She could empty her stomach and be well again in seconds. Only she was shivering with cold.

A fat woman in a flowery dress had stopped to stare at them.

'Been sick, has she?'

'Yes.' His eyes when he looked at the woman were small

and frightened.

'Poor bairn. Eyes bigger'n your belly, love?' She looked again at the man. 'Best place for her is bed.'

'We won't be long out of it.'

The fat woman ambled off to join her husband. The man stared after her.

Then he looked at Kelly again, and smiled. 'I suppose we *had* better think about getting you home.'

But there was something Kelly needed to get straight. 'That woman. She thought you were me father.'

'And I didn't say I wasn't?'

She stared at him.

'Perhaps I wish I was.'

Kelly drew in her breath. At first she wasn't even sure she'd heard properly.

'I don't even know your name,' she said. Nobody was going to con her.

'Lewis,' he said. And stopped, abruptly. He didn't say if it was his first or his last name. It didn't matter. At least he'd told her who he was. She relaxed a little. He didn't seem so much of a stranger now. In fact, when she looked around her at the people streaming in and out of the gate, his was the only familiar face.

'Where do you live?' he asked.

'Union Street,' she said.

'Where's that?'

'You go down Light Pipe Hall Road, past the steelworks, and then under the railway tunnel.'

'The steelworks . . .'

The way he said it, in that light, precise, slightly sibilant voice, it sounded as remote as the Pyramids.

'It's quite a long way then. I don't suppose you've kept the money for the bus fare?'

She hadn't, of course.

'I can go home across the Moor. Through the park.'

'It's shut.'

'There's holes in the railings.'

'You'd go in there? After dark?' He sounded almost frightened.

'I can run, can't I?'

She was scornful, as if he were indeed another child. At the same time it was reassuring. He was saying exactly what any grown-up would have said. It might have been her own mother talking to her.

He said, 'But you mightn't be able to run fast enough.'

He was staring at her intently. For him at that moment she was not one child but hundreds of children, rough, noisy, dirty children, the kind his mother dragged him past at bus stops, the kind he leant against the window pane to watch during the long afternoons of his childhood, those window panes that seemed in retrospect to have been always mizzled with rain. Children who played hard, fast, ruthless games, the girls as tough as the boys and always more humiliating because you were supposed to be able to beat them.

If only we didn't have to live here, his mother said. And sighed. It had been the refrain of his childhood: *if only we didn't have to live here.*

Now he said, 'I don't think you ought to walk all that way by yourself. I'll see you to the bus stop.'

So they set off together, the tall man and the child, while behind them the lights of the fairground shrivelled into darkness. And,

'You'll be safe with me,' he says, the quiet, precise man whom people set their clocks by, and avoid.

'*I know a short cut,*' he says, the small, pale boy, taking the girl by the hand.

'Will your parents be worried about you?'

'No.'

It was the first time he had spoken. At first the silence hadn't bothered her at all: she was tired, and she didn't want to talk. But then, as street succeeded street, as his footsteps continued to ring out over the cobbles, she felt the quality of the silence change. It had become deeper, tense, finally a vortex sucking them both under. She was afraid. She was afraid that if she tried to leave him he might not let her go.

'It's me Mam's night for the club,' she made herself say.
'Oh, I see.'

No words could have broken this silence. They were like
dead leaves that floated across the surface for a second or
two and then were sucked under out of sight.

By now they had left the Moor behind and were walking
through an area of mixed factories and housing. Here and
there a window glowed the colour of its curtains: green, or
yellow or red. But the streets themselves were ashen. More
than once they had passed a row of houses that was
boarded up and waiting for demolition.

'Here we are.' He was standing at the entrance to an alley. On one side was a tall factory. It had no windows at all
on the ground floor and the single window in the upper
storey seemed to be boarded up. 'You can cut through
here. It brings you out into Wellington Street.' When she
hesitated he said, 'You can get the bus from there.'

She could have got a bus from where they'd started from.
'Aren't you coming?'

'No, it's late. I'd better be getting back. But I'll stay a few
minutes. Just to make sure you're all right.' He felt about in
his pockets. 'How much do you think you'll need for the
fare?'

'I don't know.'

'Here's a pound.'

It was far too much.

There was a street lamp at the entrance to the alley, but
its light did not carry far. The light shone directly on to his
head so that his eyes looked like black holes in the shadow
of his brows. She was glad he wasn't coming with her. The
sense of oppression she had felt in the park was back, only
worse. She was aware of the movement of her lungs, sucking in and expelling air.

'Go on, then. And mind you get the right bus.'

She started to walk forward into the darkness. His
shadow cast by the street lamp stretched many yards in
front of her as he followed her to the entrance of the alley.
She was walking on his shadow.

She looked back and realised with a jolt of fear that not

31

only the factory windows but those of the houses on either side were boarded up. The whole place was derelict.

Which meant they must be somewhere down by the river. Wharfe Street. Moat Street. Somewhere like that.

Nowhere near where she wanted to go.

She stopped.

At once the voice called after her, 'Are you all right?'

She turned round. He was still standing at the entrance to the alley, a tall, thin man casting an immense shadow.

'Are you all right?' he asked again.

His voice had changed. It was coarser, thicker. She turned back to stare into the darkness. It terrified her, but she would rather go on than go back and meet the owner of that voice.

'Yeah, I'm all right.'

Soon the alley way opened out on to a yard: the factory yard. She stopped again. There seemed to be no way out. But at least she could see. The moonlight streamed down. The yard look very white and blank, though there was darkness again on the other side, shadows, where the exit must be.

Slowly she stepped out into the yard. She felt herself crawling across that vast expanse of whiteness like an insect over an eyeball. A lifetime seemed to go by before she reached the other side.

But there *was* a way out. Only now when there was no more need for fear could she admit how frightened she had been. She had thought the yard was a trap.

She ran into the alley, her heart pounding with relief after dread. She had gone perhaps thirty feet when she saw the wall. At first her brain simply refused to accept it. She felt all over it with her hands, looking for the opening that must be there, although there was light enough for her to see that there was none.

The bricks were new. Perhaps the wall had been built quite recently. When the factory closed down. Perhaps he hadn't known it was there. Perhaps it was all a mistake.

Then she heard his footsteps crossing the yard. There had been no mistake.

She pressed herself against the wall, until she could feel every knob of her backbone against the brick. She looked around for a way of escape as her heart hammered blow after blow against her ribs. Climb the walls? Too high. Get into the yard and dodge round him there? Yes. She darted forward, but already it was too late. He came round the corner and stopped for a moment, watching her. She backed away until she felt the wall behind her again.

He started to walk towards her. His shirt front shone in the moonlight. Above it his face looked grey. She tried to think of something to say. Incoherent memories of other confrontations, with teachers or policemen, jostled together in her mind. If you thought of the right thing to say and said it quickly enough, sometimes they would let you off. But she couldn't think of anything. Her tongue felt big and furry against the roof of her mouth.

Then, as he closed in on her, deeper memories of childhood punishments choked her so that she cried out, 'Don't, please. I won't do it again. Oh, please.'

He was beyond hearing her. She looked into his eyes and there was nothing there that she could reach.

'Mam!' she screamed, then, with the full force of her lungs, 'Mam!'

His shadow towered over her, cutting off the light.

Don't be afraid, he had said. The words thick, terrifying. *Don't be afraid. I'm not going to hurt you.*

But he had hurt. He was hurting now.

She closed her eyes, because his glazed eyes and hanging face were too terrible to look at.

After the first shock of fear she had not cried out. There was no point: nobody could hear her. He had chosen the place well. And she was afraid that if she screamed again he might kill her.

At first he had just wanted her to touch him. 'Go on,' he whispered. A single mucoid eye leered at her from under the partially retracted foreskin. 'Touch me,' he said again, more urgently. 'Go on.'

But even when he had succeeded in forcing her hand to

33

close around the smelly purple toadstool, it wasn't enough. He forced her down and spread himself over her, his breath smelling strongly of peppermint and decay. At first her tight skin resisted him, and he swore at her until he found the way in.

She stiffened against the pain, but even then did not cry out, but lay still while he heaved and sweated. Then, with a final agonised convulsion, it was all over and he was looking at her as if he hated her more than anything else on earth. He stood up and turned aside modestly until he had got his trousers fastened. After a while, since there was no point in lying there, she stood up too. There was a pain between her legs, a mess of blood and slime on her thighs, but she hardly noticed that. She was watching to see what he would do.

And he *was* tempted to kill her. She watched the thought form in his eyes like a cloud and then slowly dissolve.

They stood and stared at each other. He seemed to sag and shrivel as she watched, like a balloon that before Christmas is big and shiny and full of air and afterwards, when you take it down, is just a sticky, wrinkled bag. His eyes flickered. In another minute he would be gone.

'Don't leave me here,' she said.

'It's in the next street.' he said. 'The bus stop. It's in the next street.'

He was panting with fear.

'Don't leave me here.'

For a moment she thought that he might break away and run. Then, with an odd, wincing, ducking motion of his head, he gave in. 'I'll show you,' he said.

But as they came out on to Wellington Street he stopped as though the roar of the traffic startled him.

'You'll be all right now,' he said. He had got his normal voice back. His upper lip was working overtime as if he was in some sort of competition for speaking properly. 'If you go down here, the bus stop's past the second set of traffic lights. If you keep to the main road you'll be all right.'

The balloon had blown up again.

As she watched he pulled one cuff clear of his jacket sleeve. He was waiting for her to go.

34

'*No,*' she said. '*No.*'

'What do you mean, "No"?' He sounded frightened. Her voice had been loud enough to attract the attention of passers-by.

'I mean I don't want to go home yet.' There were no words for what she meant. 'I'm thirsty. I want something to drink.

'Well, you can't,' he said savagely. 'There's nowhere open.'

There were beads of sweat on his upper lip. She saw them with pleasure.

'They're open, aren't they?' She nodded at the fish and chip bar across the road.

'But . . .'

'There's a place at the back.'

Still he hesitated, wiping sweaty hands on his thighs.

'Or would you rather I yelled?'

'Oh, all right.' Again the odd, wincing, ducking movement of his head. 'But you'll have to be quick.'

They crossed the street together. She thought, I don't have to be quick. I don't have to be anything I don't want. Though in spite of his words he lagged behind until she turned and hauled him on to the pavement. The more he hesitated, the more obviously afraid he became, the greater was her rage, until in the end she seemed to be borne along on a huge wave of anger that curved and foamed and never broke. She pushed him into the shop in front of her.

The woman behind the counter looked up as they entered, but without interest. While he spoke she went on fingering the back of her neck, enjoying a pimple or a boil. When he'd finished she stopped long enough to say 'You can't have a cup of tea this time of night, not without something to eat as well.'

He looked at Kelly. 'You're not hungry, are you?' For the woman's sake he managed a watery smile.

'I'm famished.'

Their eyes met for a moment, and again he admitted defeat. He was too easily defeated. Kelly's anger was turning to contempt: she had to fight to keep it alive. And always there was this dreadful intimacy of knowledge, so that when he blinked she knew how his eyeballs pricked and burned, from the weight of the lids dragging across them. Because her own were doing the same.

They sat down opposite each other at the table in the centre of the room. A single light, harsh and glaring, hung from a cord in the ceiling, so low down that it left the upper part of the room in shadow. The cord swung in the draught from the open door, pulling the shadows after it, until the whole room dipped and swung like a silent bell.

She tried to make the man look at her. She needed him. He was all she had. But he did not want to look. His eyes, small and reddish-brown, skittered about like ants in a disturbed nest.

The woman came in to wipe and lay the table.

Suppose I told her? Kelly thought.

There were red burn-marks on the woman's arms where the fat from the chip pan had splashed them.

She would never tell anybody. Nobody else would understand. It wasn't like falling down, or getting run over by a car. She *was* what had just happened to her. It was between the man and her.

And he was . . . nothing!

She had started to think about what had happened, to try to place it in the context of her life. Half-understood jokes — 'Got to keep your strength up, Arthur!' — drawings on lavatory walls, the time she had gone into her mother's room and seen Wilf having a fit on the bed: all these pieces started to fall into position, began to make sense, though not yet a sense she could use.

This was deep and wordless. On the surface she felt . . . a revulsion from surfaces. The dishcloth had left slimy smears all over the table. The slipperiness disgusted her. Everything disgusted her. Her skin seemed to have flared up into an intense and irritable life of its own. Plastic was too plastic, wool too woolly, and the grains of salt and sugar left behind on the table felt like rocks beneath her wincing fingertips. Most of all she hated the remembered texture of his jacket, the moist, lard-whiteness of his skin. She found herself wiping her hands on her thighs in a gesture that was the mirror-image of his.

She looked away from him again. But it was no use: the room was lined with mirror-tiles. Wherever she looked, their eyes met.

The fish and chips arrived. From sheer force of habit Kelly picked up her knife and fork and started to eat. One mouthful was enough. She said, 'I don't think I'm hungry after all.'

He didn't say anything. He was making no attempt to eat. The fish and chips, steaming up into his face, had opened the pores on his nose: he look coarser than she had seen him look before. But still unlined. There were no laughter or frown lines on his face. It wasn't a grown-up face at all, she thought.

Then, as she continued to stare, she saw a slight movement, a crumbling almost, at the corners of the lids. Something was happening to his face. It was beginning to split, to crack, to disintegrate from within, like an egg when the time for hatching has come. She wanted to run. She didn't want to stay there and see what would hatch out of this egg. But horror kept her pinned to her chair. And the face went on cracking. And now moisture of some kind was oozing out of the corners of his eyes, running into cracks that had not been there a minute before, dripping, finally, into the open, the agonised mouth. She watched, afraid. And looked away. But that was no use.

From every side his reflection leapt back at her, as the mirror-tiles filled with the fragments of his shattered face.

Kelly looked around for help. But the woman had gone. She stood up. It seemed necessary to say something but the words would not come. He went on and on and on crying as if he had forgotten how to stop.

Kelly turned and ran.

Mrs Brown stood in the kitchen, and waited for the kettle to boil. She kept her hand on the handle and couldn't tell whether it was the vibration of the metal or her own distress that made her hand shake. She leaned forward, she was parched for a cup of tea, and her reflection loomed up, ox-jawed and brutal, in the curve of the teapot.

It was past schooltime and Kelly was still in bed. But on this day it didn't matter. On this day there would be no nagging. Linda, pink and moist-eyed, had crept out to work early. Arthur was still asleep.

And Kelly, was she asleep? Or was she lying awake, staring at the ceiling? Mrs Brown didn't know and was afraid to go upstairs and find out. The sight of her daughter's misery would bring her own gushing to the surface again, and it had taken most of the night for her to get it under control. She had asked the doctor to give Kelly a sleeping pill, but he had said, no, let her shout and scream if she wants to. It was better for her to do that than go on bottling it up. Better for who? Mrs Brown had wanted to ask, though of course she didn't. She had wanted Kelly unconscious as fast as possible, as much for her own sake as the child's.

The kettle boiled. She made the tea, but when she tried to lift the tray her hand shook so much that some slopped over the sides of the cups. She dabbed at the mess with a dishcloth, ineffectually, and heard herself start to whimper. The whimpering frightened her; it sounded so lost, so out of control, so unlike her normal self. For she thought of herself as a hard, tough, realistic woman, able to cope with most things. She had had to be, bringing up two children on her own.

She felt a spasm of hatred for her husband whom she had not thought of for years but who was now, momentarily, identified in her mind with The Man. It had been so easy for him to walk out, and he didn't give a bugger, he never even sent them something for Christmas, not even a bloody card; not that she wanted him to, mind, she wouldn't've thanked him for it if he had; they could do without him. Then there was Arthur, who, in spite of all his big talk last night, had fallen asleep as soon as his head touched the pillow, and was still asleep now, his cheeks juddering with every breath. God, what a useless lot!

She needed a woman to talk to, but in all this sodding street there wasn't one of 'em you could trust. They'd all turned against her, because since Tom left there'd been other men in the house. Jealous cows. And how they'd talk! Coo and sympathise, oh, yes. But talk. She could hear them now, 'Well, what can you expect, leaving the bairn alone half the bloody night? You know where *she'd* be, don't you? Out boozing at the Buffs with that Arthur Robson. Eeeee!'

Trouble was, none of them knew what Kelly was like. You'd need eyes in your arse to keep track of her.

She was crying as she carried the tray upstairs. She'd got up because she couldn't stand the warmth of Arthur's body a second longer. He never wore owt in bed and whenever in the night he'd turn over she could feel the fuzz of gingery-pink hairs on his backside. The first night that hair had excited her, though it made her shudder now. The hard, hairy, male bum clenching and unclenching . . . She twitched her thoughts away.

As she put the tray down Arthur started to wake up, bringing his lips together with little contented smacking sounds. It was intolerable. She could not bear to stay and watch it, or see the memory of what had happened in his eyes.

She left her own tea beside his on the table and ran downstairs. On the doorstep she hesitated, but only for a second. Muriel Scaife would be safest but she worked as a cleaner in the mornings and might not be back yet. Iris King, then. Iris, built like the side of a house, seemed to offer the same assurance of shelter.

She knocked on Iris's door and waited, hugging herself, protecting herself as much from the memory of last night as from the wind that whipped whirls of dust along the street. There was nobody about. The men were already at work. The women had not yet got ready to go shopping. Long and grey, the street stretched away into the distance. She shivered, knowing it too well to hate it.

Iris King's eyes widened when she saw who was on her doorstep, but only momentarily. She had seen the police car parked outside the Browns' last night as she was coming home from the Bingo, and had even made a special trip up to the fish and chip shop hoping for news. She had never thought that Mrs Brown would come to her, for she was apt to play her mouth on the subject of women who neglected their children and she didn't care who heard her. Iris saw that Mrs Brown was close to tears. She led her along the passage and into the living room, resting one massive freckled arm on the other woman's thin shoulders, for she was a woman who needed to touch people.

For a long time Mrs Brown could only sob and choke and when she did manage to speak it was only the single word 'Kelly', and then, 'My bairn.'

Iris stood with her back to the fire and waited. She was a formidable sight with her bare arms and massive breasts. Her frizzy blonde hair was in rollers: pink spikes stuck out aggressively at all angles, except where a headscarf pressed them uncomfortably close to her scalp. Her bairn indeed! Pity she hadn't thought of that a bit sooner.

Gradually, Iris got the full story out of her. My God, she thought, unwilling to believe it. She knew Kelly well. When Kelly's own house was empty — which, let's face it, was more often than not — she would go across to watch Iris's telly. She was no bother and the bit of food the bairn ate'ld never be missed.

'They should flog 'em,' she said when Mrs Brown's sobs had died down. 'It's no good mucking around with probation and all that. They should bring the birch back in.'

'I wouldn't flog 'em,' said Mrs Brown. 'I'd get a blowtorch and burn the bugger off. And I wouldn't care how they screamed. It's not even as if she was old-looking for her age. She's not. He could see she was a bairn.'

'No hope of them catching him?'

'No. Well, it's three weeks, he could be anywhere now. If only she'd come straight out with it!' This thought, arousing as it did all Mrs Brown's doubts about her daughter's story, reduced her to silence for a while. But her voice, cracked and bleating with distress, went on echoing all over the room. Both women heard the echoes and were made uncomfortable by them.

Mrs Brown said, 'You know she even tried to wash her own pants out? She was just going to put them away and not tell anybody. Then when she couldn't get the blood out she wrapped them up and put them in the bin. I knew a pair had gone missing, mind.' For a moment she hugged herself and rocked.

'We were just sat there,' she said. 'And suddenly she set on screaming. You know all I could think of was she must be ill. And then it all come out.'

They had been watching *Crossroads*. Even as Kelly screamed there had been a moment of resentment that she should have chosen that time of the day to get appendicitis or whatever it was she had.

'I wonder why she waited that long?'

'I don't know. I've thought and thought and I just don't know.'

'She's mebbe been too frightened, eh?'

'But she must've known he couldn't do anything to her.'

'Aye. But bairns don't think like that.'

It was a comforting line of thought, though Mrs Brown knew her daughter too well to believe it entirely. 'Yes, I suppose that must be it. She's been too scared. But that was what the police said, you know. If only she'd spoke up a bit sooner. Oh, and then there was the doctor messing her about. I mean, I know they have to, but you can't help thinking if they're not going to get him anyway . . . what's the point? And that upset her.'

'What you need is a good strong cup of tea.'

Iris went into the kitchen to make it. Now she was no longer faced by the sight of Mrs Brown's misery she was more inclined to withhold her sympathy and make judgements. Her bairn! Where had she been when it happened?

And Mrs Brown, looking uneasily around the fanatically clean and tidy living room, wondered what on earth had possessed her to come. Iris wouldn't keep any of this to herself — well, you couldn't expect her to. But the version that went the rounds wouldn't be fair on her. And it had been late, and she had been at the club. But then what was Kelly doing wandering around at that time of night when she'd been told to come home? The police had blamed *her* for it. They hadn't said much but you could tell. The one with the moustache had been looking right down his nose . . .

Nobody understood. It was her child, her daughter, and in this extremity so utterly hers that she felt her own flesh torn.

'He didn't just muck around with her, you know,' she burst out as soon as Iris came back. She wanted them all to understand the enormity of what had happened. 'He stuck it right the way in.'

The words felt solid and sticky in her mouth like phlegm, and after she had said them there was nothing else that she wanted to say. She huddled over the cup of tea and rocked herself for comfort.

Iris looked at her closely. Say what you like about her, she was feeling it. In fact, she was bloody knackered. 'Howay,' she said, when Mrs Brown had finished her tea, 'I'll take you back home.'

She led her across the street and saw her settled on to the sofa in the living room, sparing no more than a single glance of disapproval for the messy room and the unwashed hearth.

'I haven't had time . . .' said Mrs Brown.

'No, of course you haven't, love.' Iris replied. There was six months' muck in the room if there was a day's. 'Tell you what, I'll put the fire on. You'll feel a lot better when you're warmed through.' She knelt down and started to rake out the ash. 'Still in bed, is she?'

'Yes,' said Mrs Brown.

'Best place.'

Iris had the fire alight in no time despite the lack of sticks. She waited until the paper she was holding over the fireplace turned bright orange and began to char, then whipped it away in a cloud of acrid smoke. 'There. That should go.'

She was remembering that she'd shown Kelly how to light a fire without sticks. Hanging was too good for the sods.

Arthur shambled in. He stopped abruptly when he saw Iris, for he was wary of her, as many men were.

'Now then,' she said.

42

'Now then.'

Arthur sat down in the armchair to demonstrate his right to be there and immediately wished he hadn't, because she towered over him.

'Well,' she said, 'I'll be away now. If there's owt you need you know where I am. Or Ted. He's on two till ten so he'll be in the house all morning.'

'Right, thanks, Missus,' Arthur said, taking over the role of man of the house. He went to the front door with her and Mrs Brown could hear their voices on the step.

He came back looking furtive. Of course it was difficult for him, not being one of the family. He could neither take part in what was happening nor decently go away. But his creeping about, his attempts to obliterate himself, irritated her more than the most insensitive intervention could have done.

'Have I to stop home?' he asked.

'Oh no, you go to work. Keep everything normal.'

'Right.'

It was the answer she had wanted and yet she resented it. He needn't've sounded so relieved. He stood there looking helpless and the sight of him increased her own feeling of helplessness. She wanted to cry again but she couldn't.

As if reading her thoughts, he said, 'You know, you'd be better if you could let yourself go. It's no use bottling things up.'

'Crying won't help.'

If he thought it might it was not his place to say so.

They sat in silence. She wanted to say something nasty to him but could find no justification. Instead she said, 'Iris doesn't miss much, does she? I saw her looking at the hearth.' Bending down, she started picking up cigarette butts.

'Oh, don't bother with that now,' he said.

One of the cigarette ends had pink smears round it. They always brought a woman with them, they said: to talk to the child.

Her eyes prickled. She might have cried after all if the sound of Kelly's footsteps on the landing had not stopped

43

her.

'She's awake,' Arthur said, looking more than ever as though he would like to bolt for the door. She wished he would. Then was glad he was there. She was afraid of Kelly. Then, again, she wanted him out of the way.

'Pop out and see if I've opened the yard door, love. The bin men won't be able to get in and it's practically overflowing. '

But he sat on, frozen, as she was, by the sound of bare feet slapping across the lino overhead.

'Have you told the school?' he asked. 'I mean, that she's not going in today?'

She shook her head. 'No. They'll know soon enough.'

Kelly was on the stairs now. Mrs Brown tried to think of something to say, but her mind was blank. She half expected the child to look different; but she looked the same, only heavier perhaps, with something clay-like in the colour of her skin. She gave them one glance, cool, almost hostile, and hurried past them into the kitchen. It was hard to believe in the extreme distress of the previous night; but then it had vanished by the time the police arrived. She had been mulish, obstinate by then: not obviously disturbed at all.

She wore a skimpy nightdress. Mrs Brown noticed for the first time that she had outgrown it. It was almost up to her bottom at the back.

'Hadn't you better put something on? A cardigan?'

Mrs Brown reached up and pulled one down from the airing line.

'I'm not cold.'

'I'll get you something to eat.'

'I'm not hungry.'

'Oh, you must be.'

'I see the milk's off.'

By this time Mrs Brown had followed her daughter into the kitchen. Kelly, one eye closed, was squinting down the neck of a milk bottle.

'Oh, it's still usable. I'll put the kettle on.'

Kelly stood aside to let her get to the sink. Her skin, Mrs Brown could not help thinking, was exactly the same shade as the milk: blue-white, slightly 'off'-looking.

'I wish you'd put something on,' she said again.

'I've told you. I'm not cold.' Though the October morning outside the kitchen window looked like the dead of winter.

Mrs Brown had to endure those white, smooth, childlike and yet not sufficiently childlike shoulders. For something to do, she started to butter bread. Arthur hovered uncertainly in the passage between the living room and the kitchen. Everybody seemed to feel that if they moved too suddenly something might break. Mrs Brown found herself taking long, shallow, noiseless breaths.

'Who's all that for?' Kelly asked.

Mrs Brown looked down and realised that she had buttered enough bread for a family of six. Blushing, she pushed the plate aside. She felt a spasm of dislike for her daughter. She said, 'You know, you should make the effort to eat something. You didn't have anything last night.'

Kelly shrugged. She seemed so normal. Her hair fell in a greasy tangle over her face, but even that was usual. She was adept at using her hair to hide her thoughts. Mrs Brown was disappointed. She felt as if she was being cheated of a drama that she had the right to expect. Kelly couldn't scream like that and have police all over the house, and then go back to being normal.

'Did you sleep all right?' she asked.

'Not bad.'

The nightdress was slightly transparent. Although Kelly had nothing that you could call a bust, hardly as much as many men, her nipples seemed to demand attention. Like eyes in her chest. You couldn't avoid seeing them.

Arthur decided he would check that the yard door was open for the bin men. When he came back into the kitchen, Kelly was leaning against the larder with both hands round a cup of tea. He felt shy with her. He said, gruffly, he might have a walk down the town if nobody wanted him for anything? Nobody did. He hunched his shoulders, as if expecting a blow, and hurried out of the house.

Normally when Arthur left the relationship between

45

mother and daughter became easier. Today of all days Mrs
Brown needed that slackening of tension. It didn't come.
Kelly had started picking at a slice of bread. Mrs Brown
tried to catch her eye but her hair was all over her face.
Kelly was determined not to look.

'If I was you I'd have a good wash and brush me hair.
It'ld make you feel better.'

When had soap and water made Kelly feel better? But
her grubbiness in this altered situation was no longer childish dirt. It looked sluttish.

'Later,' mumbled Kelly, through a mouthful of bread.

'I'm only trying to think what's best for you,' said Mrs
Brown, her voice quivering. 'A nice bowl of water in front of
the fire? I'll bring your clothes down.'

'No, thanks. I'm going back up in a minute.' She paused.
'Why aren't you at work?'

The question took Mrs Brown's breath away.

'You will have to go back, won't you?' Kelly sounded indifferent, if not cheeky.

'But not today!'

'Mam, it happened three weeks ago. You've been out
every night since then.'

The remark chafed a raw edge in Mrs Brown's mind.
'Well, what do you expect? If you don't tell people anything. What are we meant to do? You know bloody well if
you'd told us you wouldn't've been left on your own for one
night. And there might have been some chance of catching
the bugger then . . .'

'They won't catch him.'

'No, thanks to you, they won't! He could be anywhere.
Mucking about with some other little lass. I don't know,
Kelly, I just don't understand. He mightn't let the next one
go. Have you thought of that? He could have strangled
you. That's what they do, you know. Why didn't you run
away?'

Kelly screwed up her face with the effort of not listening.
She was off. There was no stopping her now.

For Mrs Brown it was a relief. The questions chased each
other out. Why go with him? Why didn't you run away?

And afterwards, why did you stay with him? Why did you go into the cafe? If he made you go, why didn't you tell the woman? Why didn't you tell me? Why wait three weeks? And after waiting three weeks and nearly screaming the house down, why say so little to the police? Why?

Kelly waited for it to be over.

When her mother seemed to have finished, she put down the half-eaten slice of bread and made towards the door. She had to pass her mother to get to it. They looked at each other. Each at that moment expected, and perhaps wanted, an embrace.

Mrs Brown could smell her daughter. Was it her imagination or was there, mixed in with the smell of unwashed child, another smell, yeasty and acrid? There couldn't be. After all, three weeks! And yet the smell repelled her.

If only she could have reached out and held her daughter. The childish bones jutting through the off-white skin might have reassured her that what she felt was merely sympathy and outraged love, not a more complex mixture of fascination and distaste for this immature, and yet no longer innocent, flesh.

Kelly looked at her mother. If she longed for love she did not know it. She felt only a renewed and more savage pride in her ability to survive alone.

Mrs Brown stood aside to let her pass.

As Mrs Brown had foreseen it was not long before everybody knew, though they were not told by Iris King, who was quite capable of relishing that last refinement of power: to know what others do not know and yet say nothing.

Nobody knew how to react. They all knew and liked Kelly. You couldn't very well ignore it. And yet to come right out with it . . . In the end they behaved as if the child had been ill. They asked after her, they gave comics and sweets, they clucked, they fussed; they even offered to do the shopping.

The women were more open in their sympathy than the men, who felt the outrage if anything more deeply but sidled past the subject, wincing.

The children were told to play with Kelly as usual and not ask any questions. They did play with her, dutifully, for a while, but they knew by instinct what their parents preferred to ignore: she was no longer a child. After a decent interval they left her alone. Which seemed to suit her very well.

Behind the family's back they talked, grown-ups and children alike. The whispering never stopped. Behind closed doors voices spoke out more freely. Mr Broadbent, sparse hair standing up with excitement, spit flying, strode up and down the bedroom floor telling Mrs Broadbent at great length and in some detail how he would punish sexual offenders. Finally, in a burst of civic zeal, he mounted that heap of white and defeated flesh and gave it such a pounding as it had not enjoyed, or endured, for many a long year.

Gradually the excitement died down. Most people in the street regretted that and made sporadic attempts to revive the topic. Only Mrs Broadbent was pleased.

But though the talk died away, Kelly remained alone. The other children avoided her — or she them. Mrs Brown, after the first shock was over, went out every night as she had always done. And Kelly roamed the streets till all hours, as *she* had always done, but alone.

Of course she was not the same. For one thing her appearance changed. People were used to the mane of coarse, dark hair. They were used to the way she hid behind it to avoid awkward questions. Suddenly, it was gone. She cut it off. You could tell she'd done it herself because it stood up all over her head in jagged spikes and chunks. Give the woman her due, Mrs Brown had her round to the hairdresser's the next day, and by the time they'd finished it didn't look too bad, not bad at all.

And yet it was shocking. She could have shaved her head, the effect it had. People took it for what it was: an act of rebellion, at once self-mutilating and aggressive. And they drew back from her because of it. In the past she had avoided their eyes. Now they found themselves avoiding hers, for the short hair revealed eyes of a curious naked amber: an animal's eyes.

The trouble was, she was not enough of a child. Her nipples were bigger than they had been. It was difficult to avoid seeing them. Even the scruffy boy's tee-shirts she'd taken to wearing didn't hide them, but rather made them, by contrast, more painfully apparent. You looked. You couldn't help yourself. And raised your eyes. And when you floundered, not knowing how to express, or hide, your thoughts she didn't help at all: she let you flounder. And always there were those eyes. Cool. Amused. Hostile. Controlled.

They were affronted. They had offered sympathy and been rejected. What they could not know was that in their own eyes when they looked at her she saw not sympathy but an unadmitted speculation.

In the end they let her alone.

Whatever else she was, she was no longer the child they had known. Dimly they sensed an inner transformation that parallelled the one they saw. But they did not try, or hope, to understand it. She was accepted in Union Street as her mother was not. But for the moment at least, she had moved beyond the range of its understanding.

* * *

It was a cold night. Frost glinted on the surface of the cobbles as Kelly ran the few yards from the fish and chip shop to her house. Sometimes she regretted the loss of her hair: it had kept her neck warm better than any scarf. She burst into the house, too cold to feel frightened. She *was* still frightened sometimes, though only of the darkness, and only in the house, when she was alone.

The telly kept her company on the nights her Mam and Linda were out. She watched anything rather than switch it off. Tonight, there was a programme about Northern Ireland. She settled down, expecting to be bored. But then there was this young man, this soldier, and he was lying in a sort of cot, a bed with sides to it, and he was shouting out, great bellows of rage, as he looked out through the bars at the ward where nobody came. What caught her attention was: they'd shaved all his hair off. You could see the scars where they'd dug the bullets out. His head was like a turnip. That was what they'd done to him. They'd turned him into a turnip, a violent turnip, when they shot the bullets into his brain.

The cameras switched to gangs of youths throwing stones. But his eyes went on watching her.

She finished the fish and chips and pressed the bundle of greasy newspaper down on to the fire. Blue flames licked round it, reluctantly, then blazed up. She wiped her mouth on the back of her hand, switched the telly off, and felt her way along the passage to the front door. It was pitch black at first, but then the landing window gave a glimmering of light. She could almost feel her pupils dilate.

The street was her home now. Once over the step she was more herself. She picked her way along the cracked pavements as delicately as the cat that, seeing her, whisked itself into the gutter. There was a square of light cast by the fish and chip shop window. She hurried across it. Outside, in the street, it was not darkness that frightened her, but light.

After a few minutes she passed a woman walking home, alone, in the middle of the road, as Kelly had been taught to do. The idea was that if somebody — a man — leapt out at you, you would have more time to run away. Her lips curled. It was a bit late for that! She looked at the woman with contempt. The real defence was to be one of those who leapt.

Inside the boy's tee-shirt and jeans her skin felt cool and muscular. She was glad it was cold. Cold was clean.

Only once since that night had something happened that might reasonably have made her afraid. There had been a man standing in the shadow of a doorway, his face screened from the light. He had beckoned her to approach. She had stopped at once and gone towards him, cautious, but not afraid.

'Hello,' he had said. 'And what's your name?'

She had smiled. If he could have seen her smile he might have been afraid. But she was standing in shadow. She was

50

part of the shadow.

'Kelly,' she said.

And stood breathing.

'Come here, Kelly. I've got summat to show you. Summat you'll like.'

She went, but without hope. This man's voice was coarse.

'There,' he said. 'That enough for yer?'

She looked with her unblinking eyes. She watched the purple flesh-flower bloom, and wilt. He backed away from her, swearing, his hands clawed together over a shrivelling of flesh.

It didn't surprise her. She knew she had the power.

But tonight no voice accosted her as she slipped silently across the road. She knew what she was going to do because she had done it before. And tonight there was the same sensation of pressure, the same feeling of blood squeezing through narrowed veins.

The school this time.

The gate was easy. She climbed it, hung for a moment poised between pavement and sky, then dropped lightly into the playground on the other side. There was a huge pile of coke against the far wall. It would have made a marvellous slide but you were not allowed to play on it. Now, feeling that anything was permitted, she ran a little way up the slope and slid down again. Pieces of coke peppered down after her. But it was no fun playing that game by herself. And she wanted to get inside.

The window shattered, not at the first, but at the second blow. Despising herself for the timidity of her first attempt, she slipped her hand in through jagged glass and found the bolt. She opened the door and went in. There were the long, silent, forbidden corridors and she passed along them stealthily, noiselessly: the intruder.

But in the end it was disappointing. There was a smell of chalk — an impersonal smell — and the cool sound of water gushing in the boys' toilets. All the cupboards were locked and when you found the keys and opened them it was still no use because the things inside didn't belong to anybody. Nobody cared about this place. There were no private smells.

She went into the Headmaster's study, but even that was impersonal despite the photographs of his wife and children. She was bolder now. She put the light on. There wasn't much danger of its being seen because the window overlooked the playground.

She sat down in his chair. Her bottom slid easily across the black leather which, on closer examination, was not leather at all, but plastic. It creaked, though, when she shifted her weight. He liked the way it creaked. If he was telling you off and it didn't creak enough to satisfy him he would wiggle his bum around until it did.

On top of the cupboard behind the door was the cane. She'd only had that once. Girls didn't get the cane very often. Girls did as they were told.

She wetted her fingers and rubbed them across the plastic, but she couldn't make it squeak as leather squeaks. She swivelled the chair experimentally from side to side. All the time anger and courage were draining away from her. It had been a mistake to come here.

The house. Oh, yes, the house had been better . . .

She had gone to the park. It must have been about the middle of October. A month ago now. It had been her first trip outside since that dreadful day when she had started to scream and the police had come. She had gone to the park. To the exact place. To the same tree . . .

She thought she was being defiant. She thought she was proving to herself that she was not afraid. But in fact when the park was empty, when no shadow moved within the shadow of the trees, she felt . . . What did she feel? Abandoned? Though she told herself that she was glad, and began making up what would have happened if he had been there — what she would have done, or said. Perhaps she would just have run home and told the police and then he would have been caught and put in prison.

She stood alone under the tree, feeling the blood squeeze through her veins. Her whole skin felt tight like a boil which you know is going to burst soon. She started to walk towards the lake.

The area bordering on the park was one of the wealthiest in town; the houses big, substantial Victorian houses that had preserved their air of smug assurance into a more violent and chaotic age. She wondered if The Man lived in one of those houses. He had sounded as if he might.

There was a lane between their long back gardens and the park, muddy and overgrown, a strip of the countryside, expensive in a steel town. One of the houses stood out from the rest, in Kelly's eyes, because it had a slide, a swing and a sandpit in the garden. She was too old for such things but they still caught her eye sometimes, just as she found herself looking at the toy pages in her mother's catalogue.

She felt a sudden need to be inside the peaceful, green enclosure of that garden. A month earlier she would have repressed it. Now she wriggled through a gap in the hedge almost before the thought was fully formed. If anybody caught her she could say she'd lost a ball. Or something. It didn't much matter. The fear of being caught was part of the thrill.

She approached the house, telling herself with every step that she would turn back now. The French windows were open. She stood outside and sniffed. Her nose told her at once that the house was empty. But they could not have gone far. On a long trip they would have remembered to shut the windows.

She stepped inside. When she closed the door behind her and stood in the big hall, everything seemed to stir around her, as if resenting the intrusion. Motes of dust seethed together in a beam of sunlight. She began to go from room to room very quietly, her gym shoes squeaking slightly on the polished wood of the floors. There was a smell of lavender. The living room was gold and white and pink, cool after the sunlight in the hall. There was a bowl of roses on top of the open piano, and a photograph of a girl on a pony. At first she touched things gently, feeling her rough skin catch on the silk of furniture and cushions, reluctant to disturb this peace, though she knew she would have to destroy it in the end.

She went upstairs. Her feet padded on soft carpets, fingernails — or claws — clicked on polished wood. She snuffled her way around like some small, predatory animal. She wanted to touch everything, but she was cautious too: her nerves quivered just beneath the surface of her skin. She could hear the dust settle in empty rooms.

The girl's bedroom bored her in the end. Photographs of school — imagine wanting to be reminded of that! Books about ballet, and ponies; lipstick in a drawer. She looked into the garden, so green, so enclosed, so sheltered. She might have pitied or despised the girl who lived in this room, but she would not have known how to envy her.

The bathroom next. She fingered the towels, she selected a bottle from the rows of bottles on a shelf and squirted aftershave on to her skin. It brought goosepimples up all over her arms. Hidden away in a little cupboard were the nastier necessities: hair remover, acne cream, a long steel thing with a little hole in the end that you used for squeezing blackheads out. Linda had one.

She pulled handfuls of clothes out of the dirty linen basket, shirts and underwear mainly. She could tell whether the pants belonged to a man or a woman with her eyes shut, by the smell alone. She snuffled into armpits and stained crotches, then sniffed her own armpits.

The parents' bedroom was best, though at first she could hardly take it in, it was so different from anywhere else she had been. She looked casually at the big, plump, satiny bed, sniffed the smells of perfume and powder, stood on tiptoe to reach the top of the wardrobe because that was where Uncle Arthur kept the things he put on to go with her mother. There was nothing there.

She turned her attention to the bed, rubbing her hands across the flesh-coloured satin until a roughened flap of skin from a healing blister snagged on one of the threads and tore. There was a pile of cushions at the head of the bed: big, soft, delicately-scented, plump, pink, flabby cushions, like the breasts and buttocks of the woman who slept in the bed. A man slept there too, of course, but you could not imagine him. It was a woman's room, a temple to femi-

54

ninity. And the altar was the dressing-table.

There were so many creams: moisturiser, night cream, throat cream, hand cream, special tissue cream for round the eyes. And so much make-up! Little jars and pots of eyeshadow: green, blue, mauve, gold, silver, opal, amethyst. Even yellow and pink. She opened one of them and rubbed a little on the back of her hand, then thrust her finger deep inside the pot for the pleasure of feeling the cream squirm.

She wanted something else, something more. She felt her skin tighten as if at any moment it might split open and deposit her, a new seed, on the earth. She began clawing at the satin skin of the bed, dragging her nails across the dressing-table hard enough to leave scratches, claw marks, in the polished wood. Was this what she wanted? She thought of all the things she could do — pour powder and nail polish all over the carpet, daub dressing-table and mirror with lipstick. She did none of them. Something was stopping her. She looked around. It was the mirror. It was her own reflection in the glass that caught and held her, and drained her anger away.

She looked as wild and unkempt as an ape, as savage as a wolf. Only her hair, glinting with bronze and gold threads, was beautiful. She dragged it down to frame her face; then lifted it high above her head and let it escape, strand by strand, until it was swinging, coarse and heavy, around her shoulders again. But she looked bad. She peered more closely in the glass and saw that the pores of her nose were bigger than they had been, and plugged with black. When Linda used the blackhead remover little worms of white stuff came wiggling out of the unblocked pores. Suddenly, Kelly hated the mirror. On the man's side of the bed was a heavy ashtray. She picked it up and threw it, hurling her whole body against the glass.

It smashed, as a sheet of ice explodes when you drop a stone on it. Lines and cracks radiated out, trapping, at the centre of the web, her shattered face.

She rocked herself, and moaned, thrusting her fingers deep into her mouth and biting on them to stop the groans.

She got up. In a manicure case in the dressing-table drawer she found a pair of scissors, and began hacking at her hair. But the scissors were too small. She remembered a spare bedroom across the landing, with a sewing machine, and ran across to it. The dressmaking scissors she brought back bit into her hair with thick, satisfying crunches. In no time at all big loops and coils were slipping to the floor. When she was shorn, she looked back in the glass and was comforted a little by the sight of her ugliness.

She listened. In every room of the house there was the sound of clocks ticking, curtains breathing, the minute squeaks and rustles of an empty house. But her ears had caught something. There it was again. A quickening of the silence. They were coming back. A second later, she heard a car turning into the road.

She slipped out through the French windows as they came in the front door, though not before she had felt the house begin to heal itself, to close like water, seamlessly, over the disruption of her presence. From the end of the lawn she looked back resentfully at the smug, bland windows, and wished she had done all the things she had thought of doing. She wished she had written all over the house, in bright red lipstick, the worst words that she knew. She wished she had torn and scattered and smashed, because then nobody could have pretended that nothing had happened.

Now, remembering that day, she twisted and turned in the Headmaster's chair, willing that tiny, impersonal box of a room to be vulnerable, to expose itself to her as those other more intimate rooms had done. She picked up the photograph of the Headmaster's wife and children and smashed it on a corner of the desk. She reached out for the paper knife and held it a second, poised above his chair. She expected the blow to jar her wrist but the knife slid in easily, through unresisting plastic. She ripped and tore at the soft, smooth, phoney skin while little white balls of polystyrene escaped from the cuts and trickled down on to the floor. She was sobbing, her excitement mounting on every breath.

There was nothing bad enough to do.

Yes, there was. She went into a corner of the room, pulled her jeans and pants down, and squatted. A lifetime of training was against her and at first she could do nothing but grunt and strain. But finally there it was: a smooth, gleaming, satiny turd. She picked it up and raised it to her face, smelling her own hot, animal stink.

It reminded her of The Man's cock, its shape, its weight. She clenched her fist.

She began to daub shit all over the Headmaster's chair and desk, smearing it over papers, wood and plastic. When there was no more left, except a bit between her fingers, she scraped it off carefully on the sides of a Register.

She careered down the corridor to her own classroom, the smell of her shit hot above the usual smells of gymshoes and custard. She almost ran at the blackboard, and wrote, sobbing, PISS, SHIT, FUCK. Then, scoring the board so hard that the chalk screamed, the worst word she knew: CUNT. The chalk broke on the final letter and her nails, dragging across the board, were torn down to the quick. She stood, panting, with her back to the board and sucked her fingers, glad of the pain and the taste of blood that soothed in some small measure the aching of her tight, her unappeased flesh.

The night she was raped Kelly had gone home across the park after all. As she stood on the pavement outside the fish and chip shop there had seemed to be nothing else to do but retrace her steps. As though in going back the past could be undone.

She did not look back, though if she had done so she would have seen him, there, in his mirror-tiled cell, moisture still oozing out of his eyes and dripping down his face. She did not need to look back. She would carry him with her always, wherever she went, a homunculus, coiled inside her brain.

It was her first experience of the street at night. Not just late: that she was used to. Real night.

At first she was afraid. She started away from every shadow. She had good reason for fear. And yet, as she walked, the empty streets with their pools of greasy, orange light grew on her. She no longer envied the life that still went on here and there, behind coloured curtains. It was better outside. She walked past the drunks and other late-night stragglers without fear, for tonight her glance could kill; and her skin, where the moonlight fell on it, was as white and corrosive as salt.

She slid through a gap in the railings. Generations of children had made it. Next year she would be too big, next year she would have to use the gate. It was a tight fit even now and she scraped her knee on a jagged edge of metal. Normally she would have bent to examine the cut, even in this moonlight that made all blood look black, but tonight it hardly seemed worthwhile.

She went back to the tree. His face pursued her. In a gesture of defiance she pulled all the conkers from her pocket and threw them on the ground. The action looked, and was, futile. His face remained. And would be there always, trailing behind it, not the cardboard terrors of the fairground, those you buy for a few pennies and forget, but the real terror of the adult world, in which grown men open their mouths and howl like babies, where nothing that you feel, whether love or hate, is pure enough to withstand the contamination of pity.

She had said nothing to anybody that night, though next morning when she woke up the feeling of invulnerability was gone. For three weeks she was afraid. For three weeks she sweated in darkness while his face pursued her in and out of dreams and down the howling corridors of nightmares. Then, with a sensation of splitting open, of pissing on the floor, she started to scream

They came. They sat over her. But the feeling of numbness was back. She tried to tell them about his face. She tried to tell them about that moment in the fish and chip shop when the grown-up man had started to cry. But they weren't interested in that. They wanted her to tell them what had happened in the alley behind the boarded-up factory. And they wanted her to tell it again and again and again.

In the end they went away.

But she was not the same. Thank God, she was not the same. She could step out into the street now and become as quick and unfeeling as a cat. She moved through the empty streets with unnamed purposes at work inside her, and her body, inside its boy's clothing, was as cold and inviolate as ice.

Only she was afraid of herself. Increasingly, she was afraid of herself. And she was afraid of what she might do.

One night in early December Kelly came home to find her mother on her knees cleaning the fireplace. It was an odd time of night for the job and her mother was oddly dressed for doing it: she was wearing her best dress.

Kelly watched in silence. Her mother always turned to housework when she was especially distressed. It was a tribute to her stoicism that so little got done.

Eventually her mother looked round, a question in her eyes that she was too frightened to ask. Kelly found no difficulty in ignoring it. Then, as her mother looked down, she thought, We're alike. It had never struck her before, but it was true. There, in the lines of nose and chin, was her own face, glimpsed in a distorting mirror.

The brief realisation of kinship made her ask, 'Where's Arthur?'

'Arthur didn't fancy the club tonight. I went with Madge.'

So that was it. He'd packed her in.

'All right, was it?

'Oh, yeah. There was a smashing turn on at the finish. Bloke dressed up as woman. We howled and laughed. He ended up sticking pins in his tits.' Her voice shook. 'They were . . . balloons!' The word 'balloons' burst out of her mouth like a cork, ugly sounds and cries came glugging after it. Her red, greasy mouth was square with anguish like an abandoned baby's. Her breasts, only too obviously flesh, shook as she cried. Kelly looked away to avoid seeing them.

'Arthur's not coming back. Is that it?'

59

'Yes.' She bowed her head, so that at least now you did not have to look at that ravaged face. Though the downcast cheeks had tears on them, ruthlessly revealing seams and cracks that make-up had tried in vain to hide.

Kelly looked round, half-expecting to see the ugly little scene reflected in mirrors. But there was only the familiar, untidy room. A bottle of milk going sour on the table.

'I'm going to stand that milk in water,' she said. 'That way we might get a decent cup of tea in the morning.'

On her way back from the kitchen she looked at her mother again. She was still kneeling by the half-washed hearth, but not crying now. She knew there was no point.

Kelly wanted to speak, but was afraid that sympathy would set her mother off again. And anyway she felt no sympathy. She felt, rather, distaste for this woman whose hard exterior had cracked to reveal an inner corruption. Her mother had been the one solid feature in the landscape of her mind, not much attended to, perhaps, but there, a presence on the skyline that you felt even when your back was turned. Now that was gone. Her mother's face, crumbling, reminded her of The Man. She could not allow herself to feel pity.

Kelly now turned her back altogether upon the spurious safety of home. More than ever she haunted the streets by night. She liked particularly the decaying, boarded-up streets by the river. There a whole community had been cleared away: the houses waited for the bulldozers and the demolition men to move in, but they never came.

Grass grew between the cobbles, rosebay willowherb thronged the empty spaces, always threatening to encroach, but still the houses stood. Officially empty, but not in reality. You had only to walk down these streets at night to realise that life, life of a kind, still went on.

Kelly went cautiously. But however carefully you trod sooner or later glass crunched under your feet or a sagging floorboard creaked and threatened to give way, and instantly that hidden life revealed itself, if only by a quickening of the silence. Tramps. Drunks. As she became more skilful she saw them. These were not the drunks you meet wending a careful path home to the safety of hearth and bed. These were the hopeless, the abandoned, the derelict.

It shocked her at first to find a woman among them: a woman who bulged and waddled as if she were pregnant. Though when she took her coat off, it was to reveal only wads of newspaper fastened to her body with string. For the nights were cold now. An old woman could easily freeze to death.

She had the bluest, most muculent eyes Kelly had ever seen. They seemed to have melted and flowed over on to her cheeks, which were furrowed and cracked almost beyond belief. These were not laughter-lines, frown-lines, worry-lines. They seemed to occur at random, like the cracks in parched earth, the outward and visible signs of an inner and spiritual collapse.

Parched in any other sense she was not. Her conversations with Kelly were punctuated by frequent swigs from a bottle whose neck she wiped fastidiously on the palm of an indescribably filthy hand. Her name, she said, was Joan. As a younger woman she had worked at the cake bakery. She produced this fact with some surprise, as if it referred to a time in her life she could hardly now recall.

'They used to think I was mad,' she said, her blue eyes less than ever confined to their sockets. 'But I wasn't mad. It was them buggers was mad, skivvying away for their three-piece suites. They wanted looking at.'

She muttered to herself and became suddenly alert, glancing rapidly from side to side, though her surroundings could not have been more bleak or empty in their desolation.

'They're listening, you know. They think I don't know, they think I can't tell. The buggers is always listening.'

She strained to hear. Eventually, somewhere down the street, a door banged in the wind.

'There,' she said, satisfied, lips pleated over empty gums. 'There. They'll have that nailed down tomorrow.'

She lapsed into silence. Kelly, thinking the conversation was over, got up to go, but Joan was suddenly convulsed with laughter, and caught her arm. 'I used to spit in it, you know. I did! I never let a batch get past without.'

Seeing Kelly look blank, she added, sulkily, 'The cake mixture.'

'You spat in the cake mixture?'

'Aye!'

'What did you do that for?'

'Because I couldn't reach to piss in it.' She rocked herself with laughter or anguish or cold. 'It had years of my life, that place.'

But this was too near reality. Easier to raise the bottle and glug. Kelly watched the wasted throat working as she drank.

The men, Kelly avoided. Not out of fear, but because they became maudlin very easily, wanting to touch her arms or stroke her hair. There was nothing sexual in this. They were too far gone for that. No. She was the daughter they had wanted and never had, or had had and lost. And she could not follow them along that road. She felt no pity. At times her mind seemed to slice through them like a knife through rotten meat. And in those odd flashes of total clarity that occur in alcoholics on the verge of stupor, they were aware of it, and shrank from her as if they had burned their hands on frozen steel.

She went back to Union Street. And there was Blonde Dinah staggering home, her hair daffodil yellow under the drooping light. Earlier that night, under that same lamp, a group of girls had been playing. Hands linked together to form a circle, they had turned slowly through the misty radiance; and their voices, chanting the half-understood words, were passionate and shrill. One of the girls was Sharon Scaife, who had been Kelly's friend and would be so again if Kelly would allow it. But Kelly had gone away. The circle in the lamplight was closed to her forever. She knew it, and she was afraid.

On another night, playing in the rubble of a partially demolished street near her home, she found a baby buried under a heap of broken bricks, a baby as red and translucent as a ruby. She looked at him, at his sealed eyes and veined head, and put the rubble back carefully, brick by brick, guarding this secret as jealously as if it had been her own.

She haunted the park, too. She walked up and down, searching, perhaps, though if she was she did not know it. He never came.

Others came. Even in this weather people came to the park to make love. She watched a couple once. He had actually taken his trousers down. She shivered for him, watching his small hard buttocks bob up and down like golf balls. At first it was funny. Then something mechanical in his movements, a piston-like power and regularity, began to make it seem not ridiculous, but terrible. When he lifted his head, his glazed eyes and hanging face revealed the existence of a private ritual, a compulsion of which he was both frightened and ashamed. The girl who lay beneath him was as much an intruder on it as Kelly would have been, had she chosen to step out of the shadow of the trees.

Christmas came and went. Kelly was given more presents than usual: a doll that wet itself, a hairdressing set, a matching necklace and brooch. She did not play with them or wear them, but arranged them carefully in her room, where they acquired, over the ensuing weeks, an extraordinary strangeness like the abandoned apparatus of a lunar probe.

It was a hard winter; the weather after Christmas was particularly cold. The miners were on strike. That didn't affect Kelly much, except that she was sometimes sent round all the corner shops to look for paper bags full of coal. You could still get those after the coalmen had stopped delivering. The cold weather did not keep her indoors. She still spent her evenings in the streets by the river, where she was expert now at stalking her shambling and shabby prey.

Her mother came in very late and often drunk. There was nobody to take Arthur's place, and if she went on like this there never would be. Linda was going steady. She solved her problems by spending more time at her boyfriend's house than she did at her own. Kelly cut herself off from both of them; but underneath the fear increased. She was more than ever alone. There were days now when she felt trapped inside her own skull.

One morning in late February she went out into the back yard to open the door for the bin men. The centre of the yard was so badly drained that in winter it became a sheet of ice. She had to pick her way across it. And there by the dustbin was a bird, its feathers fluffed out, too far gone to fly away or even struggle in her hand. She felt the thinness, the lightness of its bones; she felt the heart flutter. Its neck rested between her forefinger and her thumb, and she thought, Suppose I squeezed? She could so easily let her fingers tighten. She could watch its eyes glaze, feel the final fluttering of its heart. And why not? Why should there be life rather than death? Then her mother came to the kitchen door to tell her to be quick, she was late for school again; and she put the bird down on the ground where she had found it.

When she came home at tea-time it was dead anyway.

In the end even her nights in the derelict streets lost their savour. She seemed to be drying up, to be turning into a machine. Her legs, pumping up and down the cold street, had the regularity and power of pistons. And her hands, dangling out of the sleeves of her anorak, were as heavy and lifeless as tools.

One dank afternoon at the very end of winter, she left the house. It was too early to go to the streets by the river, so she went to the park instead. It had been raining for days. The ground was covered with sheets of water that trapped the last light of the sky and reflected it back again. As Kelly walked on she was aware of the steely blue radiance gathering all around her. It was disorientating: the leaden, lifeless sky and the radiance of light beating up from the earth. She felt dizzy and had to stop.

The mist that had hung about all day had begun to clear, except for a few small pockets above the surface of the lake. Beyond the chemical works in the far distance the sun was setting, obscured by columns of drifting brown and yellow smoke. A brutal, bloody disc, scored by factory chimneys, it seemed to swell up until it filled half the western sky.

With a sensation of moving outside time, Kelly started to walk forward again. At first, there was total silence except for the squeak of her gym shoes in the wet grass. Then a murmuring began and mixed in with it sharp, electric clicks, like the sound of women talking and brushing their hair at once. The noise became louder. She climbed to a ridge of higher ground and there at the centre was the tree, its branches fanned out, black and delicate, against the red furnace of sky. By now the murmur had become a fierce, ecstatic trilling, and when she looked more closely she saw that the tree was covered in birds that clustered along its branches as thick and bright as leaves, so that from a distance you might almost have thought that the tree was singing.

The singing went on. The tree pulsed and gleamed with light. But she could not break out of that room inside her head where she and The Man sat and stared at each other's reflections in the mirror tiles. She would have liked to scream and beat the air but lacked strength to raise her hands.

She fell back, and found herself standing on a patch of muddy ground.

She wandered on, not knowing or caring where her footsteps were leading her. She was hungry and had nothing to eat except a few crumbs of chocolate biscuit that she dug out of the deepest corners of her pockets. But she would not give in and go home.

In the hollow ground around the lake darkness came early. White birds shone through the dusk, heads tucked in, wings furled, feather upon feather furled. But on the open ground the light had become an electric, tingling gold. You did not walk through it: you waded or glided or swam.

In the big houses around the park lights were already being switched on. Homecomings. She turned into the main avenue of trees and began to walk along it, hoping for nothing.

But there on a bench at the far end was a dark figure, sharply etched against the outpouring of gold. She began to hurry; she broke into a run; she arrived at the bench panting for breath, and alive with hope.

At first there seemed to be nothing there but a heap of old rags. Then the old woman lifted her head. Her face was an ivory carving etched in trembling gold. She peered at Kelly, evidently unable to see her properly. Her eyes, magnified by the thick lenses of her glasses, were milky with cataract. Her clothes were covered with egg and cereal stains where she had aimed for, and missed, her mouth.

'What are you doing here?' Kelly asked. Normally she would not have bothered with the old woman. Only the sharpness of her disappointment made her speak.

'Picking me nose with me elbow.'

Her speech was slurred. Kelly moved closer. The old woman's coat, or dressing gown, was open. Her dress had a lowish neck.

'Why don't you fasten the buttons?' Kelly asked. 'You'll catch your death.'

For the flood of warm gold was deceptive: it was cold enough to make your fingers ache.

'I'll fasten them if I want them fastened.'

Kelly was silent for a while. After a struggle, she said, 'Won't anybody be expecting you back home?'

She felt concern for the old woman: an ordinary, unfamiliar feeling. They had had a talk in Assembly about old people: how the cold could kill.

'Not a living soul.' It ought to have sounded bitter or self-pitying, but it didn't. There was another silence, then the old woman went on slowly, 'They're going to put me in a Home.' She laughed. '*Think* they are! I've got other ideas.' She paused, then added reluctantly, 'They say I can't see to meself.'

Even to Kelly's eyes this was obviously true. The old woman's skin was stretched tight over the bones of her skull.

'They say I'm not getting me proper food.'

'Well, perhaps you're not.' The front of her dress seemed to have got most of it. 'At least in the Home you'd get your meals.' She paused. Then burst out, 'And they'd see you were warm. They'd see you had a fire.'

'Is not the life more than meat and the body than raiment?'

She wasn't quoting. She had lived long enough to make the words her own.

Again silence. The old woman's hands were like birds' claws clasped in her lap.

Kelly said, 'I could take you home.'

'No thanks. You bugger off home yourself! I suppose you have got one?'

'Yes. I suppose I have.'

They sat in silence. The light increased.

'I used to come here when I was a little lass, aye, younger than you.' The old woman looked with dim eyes around the park. Kelly followed her gaze and, for the first time in her life, found it possible to believe that an old woman had once been a child. At the same moment, and also for the first time, she found it possible to believe in her own death. There was terror in this, but no sadness. She stared at the old woman as if she held, and might communicate, the secret of life.

'There used to be a band then,' the old woman said, nodding towards the bandstand that the dead leaves rattled through. 'You used to sit and listen to them on a Sunday afternoon.'

With renewed energy she looked at the child, who, sitting there with the sun behind her, seemed almost to be a gift of the light. 'Don't tell anybody I'm here,' she said. It was the closest she had come to pleading.

'You're crying,' Kelly said. She stared at the tears that were streaming down into the cracks and furrows of the old woman's face. She looked at the throat that in its nakedness was as vulnerable as a bird's. 'There must be another way,' she almost pleaded in her turn.

'There's no other way. They're trying to take everything away from me. Everything.' She smiled. 'Well, this way they can't. That's all.'

In spite of the smile she was still crying. Kelly reached out and touched her hand.

'I won't tell anybody,' she said.

She looked down at their hands: the old woman's cracked and shiny from a lifetime of scrubbing floors, her own grubby, with scabs on two of the knuckles.

They sat together for a long time.

'I feel warmer now,' the old woman said, 'I think I'll have a little sleep.'

Kelly went on watching her. The old woman's tears had dried to a crust of white scurf at the corners of her lids. Which were closed now, in sleep, or unconsciousness, or death.

At any rate, it was time to go. Kelly slipped home through the growing darkness.

There was a sound ahead of her, a sound like the starlings had made. And there, coming out of the cake bakery, was a crowd of women, talking together. She stopped to watch them.

Most of them began to run as soon as they were released, with the peculiar stiff-legged gait that women adopt as they grow up, though it is not natural to them. They were anxious to get home, to cook the dinner, to make a start on the housework. A few lingered. Their hair, which might have caught in the machines or contaminated the food, was bound back under scarves or nets. Their voices as they talked together were shrill and discordant from a day of shouting over the noise of the conveyor belt.

Then a young girl came to the factory gates alone. She hesitated. On the other side of the street a boy dropped the newspaper he was reading, and waved. They ran to meet each other and, oblivious of the crowds around them, kissed.

Kelly stared after them, hungrily. Then she bent her head and followed in their footsteps. She was going home.

CHAPTER TWO
JOANNE WILSON

The Wilsons lived a few doors down from the Browns on the other side of Union Street, but there was a time at the end of October when Joanne did not go home. Instead, she woke up in a strange bed and sweated, remembering the previous night.

She had gone to the Buffs and got drunk and, watched by several people from the street, including two girls who worked at the cake bakery, she had allowed herself to be seen going home with a midget. Even as she thought the word she felt disloyal, for the midget in question was Joss, who had always fancied her, and never got anywhere, and went on being kind.

He still hadn't got anywhere, but who would believe that now?

She could just imagine the jokes. Step-ladders. Everybody the same size in bed. All that. Even her own mother had had a bloody good laugh, but she wouldn't be laughing when she heard about last night.

It was her fault, really, thought Jo. If only she'd leave me alone.

The alarm sprang into hideous life. Jo sat up, her eyes tight shut, and groped for the clock. It skittered away from her across the lino.

Footsteps in the passage. The sound of the door opening.

'Jo?'

No reply.

'Alarm's gone.'

'Never! You should send that bugger round the morgue. Wherever did you get it?'

'Oh, I've had that years. Never fails.'

Joss came further into the room. When he stood at the foot of the bed his head was no higher than the rail. 'Howay, then!'

'I can't get up with you stood there, can I?' She struggled to sit up, dragging the sheet with her. 'I've got nowt on.'

He stepped back. 'Well, how was I supposed to know that? Decent folks wear summat in bed.'

'Is that right?'

'You know it is. You could've had a lend of something, you only had to ask.'

'Oh, I never wear owt.'

The flesh of her shoulders gleamed where the light from the street lamp fell on them. He stepped back again, baffled. 'I'll go and get breakfast started. I don't suppose you've ever boiled an egg in your life.'

As soon as the door closed behind him she got out of bed, too quickly, forgetting that any sudden movement made her sick. She grabbed an ashtray from the dressing-table and retched, but only a little bile came up, tasting bitter. She wiped her mouth on the back of her hand.

Through the door she could hear Joss, still moving around in the next bedroom.

'Anyway, how come you're up so early? I thought you said you were two till ten?'

'I am.'

So he had got up specially to see her off. She felt a stab of guilt and uneasiness, then forgot it as her stomach clenched. She wouldn't've cared if anything ever come up, but it never did. There was just this painful retching on an empty stomach. She straightened up for the second time.

'This is bloody ridiculous, this is,' she muttered, and, turning, caught a glimpse of her reflection in the mirror.

She stood, pressing her hands fearfully against the still flat belly. No sign there at least. But her shoulders, her

70

arms, her breasts! Blue veins showed up all over them, as intricately linked as the branches of a tree; all leading down to the nipples which themselves were bigger and browner than they had been a month ago. Some yellowish stuff had dried to form a crust over the skin. She picked at it with her fingernails.

Her body, from childhood so familiar, had become frightening. It occurred to her that it looked like another face, with nipples instead of eyes, a powerful, barely human face. By comparison, her real face seemed childish and unformed.

She was afraid. 'What the hell am I going to do?' she asked that other, inhuman face, which was aware of no problem.

'Breakfast's ready!'

'Coming!'

With a sense of relief, she turned her back on her reflection and began to dress.

Joss was at the kitchen sink when she got downstairs. The kitchen itself was immaculately, old-maidishly tidy. Of course he hadn't much else to occupy himself with.

'There was no need for *you* to get up, you know,' she said. 'You could've had a lie-in.'

'I never lie in. I can't. Soon as I'm awake, I'm up.'

Joanne sat down at the table, and pulled the plate towards her. Bacon and fried bread. Dear God! Her stomach heaved at the sight of it.

'It was a good night, though, wasn't it?'

'You were knocking it back a bit, weren't you?'

'Only halves.'

'No point in drinking halves if all you do is get through them twice as fast.'

'Oh, shurrup, man. You sound like me Mam.'

'Somebody's got to . . .' He stopped abruptly and turned back to the sink. For a while he concentrated on sweeping breadcrumbs into the sink tidy with the side of his hand. His shoulders were on a level with the draining board. Yet the face above them was handsome — even beautiful, if you could call a man beautiful. He seemed to carry his good

71

looks around with him, like a special form of crucifixion.

Pity made Jo aggressive.

'Somebody's got to what?' she demanded.

He spun round. *'Care* about you!'

She was taken aback by the passion in his voice. There was a brief, uncomfortable silence. Then she said, trying to lighten the atmosphere, 'You promised you'd tell what Joss is short for, but you didn't.'

'I said I'd tell you if you made that drink your last.'

'And I didn't?'

'Not by a long shot. But I'll tell you anyway. It's short for Joyce.'

'That's a girl's name.'

'No, it's not. There were a few lads called Joyce down our way. All about my age. A fella gassed himself. His wife had left him. He just come home from work and found everything gone, all the furniture, everything. Except the gas cooker. So he put his head in it.'

'And that was the end of him. You're sure it wasn't 'cause he was called Joyce?'

'No, it wasn't — it was his wife. And after that all the kids were called Joyce, for a bit.'

He saw her look blank. 'It's lucky, isn't it? Calling a kid after somebody what's gassed themself.'

'I never heard that.'

'Oh, they used to do it a lot down our way. Wharfe Street.'

Wharfe Street was the worst street in the town, or had been until a couple of years ago, when the people were re-housed. Now the houses were empty and boarded up, though not yet demolished. In the hierarchy of streets it came almost as far below Union Street as Union Street came below Buchanan Street, with its bay windows and strips of garden outside the front doors.

Something of what Jo was feeling must have shown on her face.

'Plenty of decent folks down Wharfe Street,' Joss said.

'Gassing themselves to get away from the rest.'

It was true. Suicide, mental illness, crime, incest had

flourished there, as though inhaled with noxious fumes from the river. Those who had lived there, whether they had loved or hated the street, did not find it easy to forget.

'Anyway,' Jo went on, 'you live here now. There's worse places. And you've got the house very nice.'

'It gets lonely. Sometimes.'

They were on dangerous ground again. She remembered last night, how stupidly, sloppily affectionate she had been. She remembered him hauling her upstairs and half-pushing, half-throwing her on to the bed. He could have had her then. But he hadn't. He'd been kind. Responsible. It was like everybody said. He'd be a husband in a million, if only his arms and legs were the normal length. What had made them like that? she wondered.

'Still, if you get fed up you can always have a walk round the Buffs. I've seen you in there many a night with Iris King. And Ted.' Not always with Ted, she remembered.

'Oh, me and Iris are old friends. I've known her since she was a bairn.'

'In Wharfe Street?'

'Yes. '

'Perhaps if I gassed meself they might start naming bairns after me.'

'Well, Jo's better than Joyce anyway. Crack or spout, it'd do.'

He was messing about with the sink tidy again. She watched him for a few minutes then said, impatiently, 'I wish you'd stop fart-arsing about. You're as bad as a woman. Worse.'

'I like things tidy. Anyway, what sort of talk is that? Gas ovens, at your age.'

'Oh, don't worry. I'm a long way off that yet.'

Was she? She thought again about the baby, and her stomach clenched with fear. She pushed the plate away.

'What's the matter with that bacon? Is it too salty?'

'No. It's all right. I'm just not hungry.' She roused herself to lie. 'I never eat much breakfast.'

He set the bacon aside without comment.

'I can't seem to stomach the fat.'

'It's O.K. I'll have it for me bait.'

Silence.

'Oh, what's the use? You've guessed anyway. I'm pregnant.'

He didn't reply at all for a long time. Then, 'There's some digestive biscuits up in that cupboard behind you. You can't go to the bakery on an empty stomach. You shouldn't be going at all.'

'Don't say you hadn't guessed.'

'I wondered.' He watched her nibble the biscuit. 'You should make it up with your Mam.'

'It's gone too far for that.'

'You'll need her.'

'No, I won't. She had no right to carry on the way she did. Moaning and groaning all over the house. You'd 've thought she was having it. And questions . . . "Who is he? I'll kill him when I get my hands on him." '

'She's got a right to know.'

'She's no right at all. Good God, she hasn't told me who my father was yet.'

'She's bound to be worried.'

'Aye. Worried in case she might have to do summat! But I'll take good care she never has.'

'You're talking through the back of your head. If you're not going back to your Mam's, where are you going to go?'

Joanne looked around the kitchen. 'You wanting rid of me, are you?'

'You know I'm not. You can stay here as long as you like. Only . . . people'll talk.' He paused. 'You don't want folks taking a tape measure to its legs, do you?'

She lowered her head while the silence widened and engulfed them.

'So,' he went on, expressionlessly, 'what are you going to do?'

She swallowed. 'I might be getting married.'

He looked at her doubtfully. 'Have you told him yet?'

'No. Well, I couldn't. He's been away on a course. You can't say summat like that over the phone — I can't anyway. And before he went . . . I wasn't all that late. I thought I'd come all right.' She stared at him, defiantly. 'It does come all right sometimes. People can be late without it being . . . that.'

'And when are you going to tell him?'

'Tonight. He's back today. That's one of the reasons I couldn't face going home last night. I felt I just had to have a bit of peace. Get me wits together.'

'Instead of which you've got a hangover.'

'I'm still glad I'm here and not there.'

'You'll have to tell your Mam where you are. You can't just leave her to fret.'

'Oh, I wouldn't worry about that. By ten o'clock, it'll be in every house in the street. You know it will. You'll have it to face when you get to work.'

'So will you.'

'Oh, they mightn't come right out with it. And if they do, I'm ready for 'em.'

She went out the back way, more for Joss's sake than her own, and set off down the alley, picking her path between piles of dog muck.

Further down she came upon a black-clad backside bending over immediately in front of her. Old Mother Harrison. The old lady straightened up. 'Now then.'

'Now then.'

'Your Gran keeping all right?'

'Well . . . her chest's bad.'

'Everybody's is this weather.' She looked around at the dank, soot-laden mist. 'I'm wheezing a bit meself.' Phlegm rattled in her chest as she spoke.

'You should go to the doctor.'

'What? With bronchitis? No!'

It was said that Mrs Harrison had been a very beautiful girl. It was still there. You could see it, even though her cheeks were now red-veined and hung loosely from the bone. Her eyes were startlingly, almost incredibly, blue. 'Keeping all right yourself?' The blue eyes were now fixed on Joanne's coat, which she wore unfastened in spite of the weather.

'Yeah. I'm fine.'

'I'll have a walk as far as the end.'

As they walked, Mrs Harrison scanned the ground closely. After every few steps she swooped down and picked up a french letter with a pair of silver sugar tongs. These were all transferred to a maroon canvas bag. She muttered something under her breath.

'I'm sorry, I didn't . . .'

'I said it's a good day. For them.'

'Oh.'

Further along, and another treasure carefully transferred to the bag.

'I expect you wonder why I do this.'

Bugger-all use denying it. 'Yes.'

'You'd be surprised. They come in very handy . . .' A woman poked her head out of her back-yard door. 'Morning, Mrs Bulmer.'

'Morning, Mrs Harrison. '

They walked past. 'You know, sometimes I wonder why I lower myself to speak to her — she's as common as muck.' A quick glance over her shoulder. 'No, I use 'em to get a good blaze on the Mission fire. We meet at ten, you know, for the Breaking of Bread, but I always go up early to give the place a sweep round, and get the fire going. Only the other Sunday, the Pastor come in a bit early, and there he was, stood over the fire, warming his hands. "Oh, Mrs Harrison," he said, (he talks posh, you know — tries to), "Oh, Mrs Harrison, I don't know how you do it. I don't know how you do it in the time." "Why," I said, "it's man's energy. It's man's energy goes onto that fire!" ' She chuckled wickedly. 'It doesn't half make me laugh, seeing 'em all sat round, praying and singing hymns. Not that I'm not a God-fearing woman. I am.'

'But doesn't it worry you?'

She stopped, while another condom was retrieved and put into the bag. Mrs Harrison shivered: 'Imagine it, this weather. All them cold bums clagged up against some bugger's back-yard door.'

'Aren't you afraid of catching something?'

'The Bad Disorder? No. The Lord looks after his own.

Anyway, I never touch them.' She held up the tongs, and smiled. 'George is the one for sugar in our house.'

They walked on in silence for a while. Then, 'I see you're going round with Joss. Not that it's any of my business.'

'No.'

'You want to watch out for Iris King. He's her fancy man, you know.'

'I don't believe it.'

'She's always going round with him though, isn't she?'

'Well, so what? People can be friends, can't they?'

'She doesn't go round with her husband.'

'You don't go round with yours.'

'And she sticks up for him like a tiger. I was stood outside the Bluebell one night' — a favourite collecting-ground — 'and two young lasses come out, sniggering. One says to him, "What's it like down there?" And mind you, that was all she said. Next thing anybody knew she was sat on her arse in a puddle, and Iris was stood over her. "Right, dear," she says. "Now you know".'

'If it was who I think it was it served her right.'

Mrs Harrison lowered her voice. 'You know what they say, don't you? His mother had him to her father and that's why his legs are so short.'

'The whole family's like it.'

'Aye, but he got a double dose.'

'It amazes me how things like that get out. How the hell could anybody know she had him to her father? She's not going to invite the buggers round to watch, is she?'

'Well, no. But if it wasn't to her father I don't know who it was to, because he never let her over the threshold. He was jealous to death of her, and she was only fourteen. Then after, when she was married, he was brought up by his father's sister. He used to go round to see his Mam but his stepfather'ld never let him eat with the others. He allus had to stop in the kitchen.' She paused. 'Course she had to do as she was told.'

'Why?'

'Well, you did in them days.'

'I wouldn't shove my bairn in the back kitchen for any man.'

Mrs Harrison looked taken aback by the sudden passion of this outburst. 'You don't know married life.'

'It's different nowadays.'

'Aye, is it? You'll find out it's not as different as you think.'

Mrs Harrison parted from her just outside the Bluebell. It was seldom she ventured further than this. The Bluebell on one side and the Mission on the other were the limits of her range. Jo turned to wave, but the old woman had already scuttled back into the shelter of the alley. She had been glad of her company, though the prying irritated her. But anything was better than to be left alone with her thoughts.

Jo crossed the bakery yard. A few young men, waiting around to start loading up the vans, whistled and called out after her. Even this didn't cheer her up. There were none of them she fancied, and anyway in a few months' time they wouldn't fancy her.

She went down the steps to the basement. There was the usual line of women, pushing and jostling to get to the clock.

'Worst one-armed bandit I ever saw,' a woman said, as she pulled the lever. 'Bastard never pays out.'

'Gerraway, one of these mornings there'll be three lemons up there, and we'll all be bloody rich.'

Everybody laughed more loudly than the joke was worth.

In the cloakroom they put on nylon overalls. There was always a smell of sweat in this room. The younger girls peered in the mirror at greasy morning skins and pink eyes, arranging scarves over the rollers they would wear all day. Doris, who was nearly sixty, sucked on a cigarette end. Her scarlet lipstick had bled into the wrinkles round her mouth. When she had finished she ground the butt under her foot and said, 'Well, howay then. Bugger won't go away. We'd best get stuck in.'

The women were lined up facing each other at either side of the conveyor belt. A few women who had been to the Essoldo the previous night continued to talk.

'I was sweating on all the twos. All the threes come up. Then all the eights. Then bugger me, all the fives! At the finish, a woman behind me shouted on eighty-one.'

'Well, at least you had a sweat on. I always think you don't begrudge the money if you get a sweat on. It's when you're twiddling y' thumbs all night.'

At Jo's end of the line, there was silence.

There were four women working together: Lilian, Big Bertha — a West Indian woman, older than the rest — Elaine Watson, and Jo. Lilian's job was to line the cakes up before they went into the slicing machine. Big Bertha and Elaine had to restack the layers of sliced and creamed sponge as they came out of the machine. Jo's job — an easy one by comparison with Elaine's and Bertha's — was to slide a card under the reconstituted cake as it slid past her on its way to the packers.

The trouble had started when Bertha first came to work at the factory. Nobody liked it. She was the first coloured worker there. But Elaine had gone on louder and longer than most: there was 'nigger stink' in the cloakroom; why was she being allowed to use the same toilets when everybody knew what mucky buggers they were; and anyway if she had to be there at all, why sponges? There was chocolate cake upstairs; why not there?

As Bertha continued impassive, Elaine's remarks became ever louder and more outrageous until many of the women who had at first supported her became uneasy. There was a general feeling that Elaine was going too far, a revulsion against the constant persecution of a woman who seemed at least reasonably quiet, anxious to pass unnoticed. Doris gave this movement added impetus. One day as they were all sitting in the tea-room she nodded towards Elaine, who was sitting in the far corner, out of earshot.

'You know what's eating her, don't you?' She lowered her voice. 'It's their Barbara. Her eldest sister. She had three to a nigger.'

'No!'

'She did. As true as I sit here. What's more, he buggered

off and left her, and now she's bringing them up on social security, so we're all paying for that little caper.'

'I don't believe it. I know their mother.'

'So do I,' Doris said promptly. 'And God knows why it had to happen to her, for a nicer or a cleaner woman you couldn't wish to meet. But it did happen. And they're living in Bradford.'

'No wonder she's agin 'em.'

'Still, whatever-her-name-is, Bertha, *she's* not to blame for it, is she?'

'No,' Doris said, deliberately.' 'She's not. Now you all know me,' she leaned forward, 'nobody's more against the coloured people than what I am. That's right, isn't it?'

There was a general murmur of agreement.

'But the way she's been going on this past week — Elaine Watson — it's been scandalous. You make your own minds up, but I'm having nowt to do with it.'

By the end of that week, Elaine was almost as completely isolated as Bertha, though there were two very young girls who followed her round in the tea and dinner breaks. If you were young and defenceless, it paid to be on Elaine's side.

Then one day, it happened. Elaine, taking off her overall at the end of the week, complained as usual about the smell. It was neither more nor less than she had said at the end of every other day, but Bertha's patience was at an end. She was sitting on a bench at the other side of the cloakroom, changing into her outdoor shoes. Her eyes fastened on Elaine. She lowered her head and thrust it forward, bull-like. Elaine grinned, nervously, and started to say something else, but the words died on her lips as the other woman got up and lumbered towards her.

'Hey, now then . . .'

But it was too late for anybody to intervene. The black woman's fist shot out and struck Elaine full in the mouth. She fell back against the wall, half-stunned, the impact squeezing an odd farting sound out of her chest. She opened her eyes and saw Bertha hanging over her, fist drawn back for the next blow. She raised her hands, claw-

80

ing at the air in front of her face. Her mouth hung open with fear, but no sound came out of it. Not for a second did she try to hit back. Another blow crashed down, and then another. Blood and mucus streamed from Elaine's nose.

The other women, stupefied until then, roused themselves to take a hand. One of them took Elaine's arm and hauled her away into a corner. Nobody dared touch Bertha, but somebody said, 'You'll get the sack, you know, if they see you carrying on like that. ' Bertha stared at her blankly for a moment and then slowly nodded her head. Her eyes were bloodshot, giving her a look of bridled ferocity. She went back to the bench and started to put her indoor shoes into a polythene bag. Elaine, sobbing and slobbering in the corner, was in no state to hear what anybody said.

This happened on a Friday night. None of the women seriously expected to see both Bertha and Elaine back in their places on Monday morning. It did not seem possible that normal life should continue after such an event. But they turned up, if anything, earlier than usual, facing each other across the conveyor belt like gladiators.

'You want to get yourself shifted,' several of the older women had said to Jo. 'There'll be trouble up your end before long.

Nobody had any sympathy for Elaine. Even the two young girls who followed her around had wavered in their allegiance, until brought back firmly into line. But neither was there any feeling that Bertha's action had been justified. Many of the women were horrified by it. Men fought, sometimes man and wife fought, but violence between women was unthinkable. Occasionally it happened: usually in Bute Street, usually on a Saturday night. But even then it was a modest affair: a little scratching, a little hair-pulling, accompanied by a great deal of abuse. Bertha's use of her fists, the silent ferocity of her attack, was something quite foreign to their experience. And they hated it. More even than the colour of her skin, it confirmed that she was an outsider amongst them.

So today, a few weeks later, while jokes and laughter flew across other parts of the line, the little group around the slicing machine stood and faced each other in silence.

Then Lilian stepped back and, ignoring Bertha and Elaine, said, 'Jo, I've got some new shoes.' Like all Lilian's remarks it was oddly abrupt and disjointed. Difficult to answer. Fortunately, just at that moment, the machines started up and spared Jo the need to reply. She pointed at Lilian's feet and mimed appreciation. Then she drew the stock of cardboard discs closer to her side and prepared to start work.

The noise was horrific as usual. There was no possibility of conversation. Even the supervisor's orders had to be yelled at the top of her voice and repeated many times before anybody heard. At intervals, there were snatches of music. It was being played continuously but only the odd phrase triumphed over the roar of the machines. Some of the women moved their mouths silently, singing or talking to themselves: it was hard to tell. Others merely looked blank. After a while not only speech but thought became impossible.

The first sponge cake reached Jo. She began the sequence of actions that she would perform hundreds of times that day. It took little effort once you were used to it and, provided the cakes continued to arrive in a steady stream, it could be done almost automatically.

Almost. But not quite. Now that she was alone — for in this roaring cavern of sound each woman *was* alone — she wanted to think about Ken, she wanted to plan the evening, to work out exactly how she was going to tell him about the baby. She couldn't do it. Each half-formed thought was aborted by the arrival of another cake. She was left with a picture of his face floating against a backcloth of sponges: dark-haired and sallow-skinned, the rather prominent Adam's apple jerking when he laughed.

The brief break in concentration had allowed a sponge cake to escape without its card. She chased it down the belt and, by working rather faster than usual, gradually made her way back to her starting place.

When Jo was able to look up she saw the supervisor shouting at Lilian. Perhaps she had been feeding the

sponge cakes into the slicing machine too slowly. Or too
fast. Or not lining them up properly before they went in.
More probably there was nothing wrong and the supervisor just wanted somebody to shout at. If that was it, Lilian
was by far the safest choice.

'Soppy Lil', as she was called, had worked there longer than
anybody else, except Doris. Always, as far as Jo could recall,
on the same job, which was by far the easiest on the line.
Anything else would have been beyond her.

She was now about thirty, unmarried, and distinctly girl-
ish in appearance. She still wore her hair in two greasy
bunches on either side of her head. She had worn it like
that at school. She had gone on wearing it like that when
she started work and spent her dinner-hour hanging
around the men on a nearby building site. Perhaps her
mother had hoped that the childish hairstyle and the
dresses that went with it would help postpone the inevita-
ble. Perhaps they did, but not for long. At twenty, she was
pregnant.

Her mother, a respectable, chapel-going woman, had
stormed and raged throughout the pregnancy, always in-
sisting that the child must be adopted. She changed her
mind abruptly when she saw it and became equally insistent
that it be brought home. Nobody asked 'Soppy Lil' for her
opinion and probably she didn't have one. Her frantic de-
sire to placate her mother seemed to have robbed her of
what little wits she had.

It had been decided that the child should be brought
up to regard its grandmother as its mother, and its
mother as its sister. At first this seemed to work well.
Lilian went to the cake factory to work. Her mother, with
no apparent reluctance, stayed at home to take care of
the child. It was a little girl, very pretty — unlike Lilian
who had never been attractive, even as a child, and who
now became increasingly slovenly. The grandmother
doted on the child. The three of them could often be
seen walking down Union Street together: an elderly
woman with hair crimped into neat, stiff waves like cor-

rugated iron; the child skipping on ahead, her hair worn, as Lilian still wore hers, in little bunches at either side of her head; and Lilian herself, bringing up the rear.

This situation dragged on for some years. It was obvious to everybody that there was no longer a place for Lilian in the home — to everybody, that is, except Lilian herself. She hung on, desperately, fawningly, trying to ingratiate herself. Then, suddenly, she was pregnant again. Nobody knew who by. This time her mother's attitude was entirely different. She refused even to look at the baby. When it became clear that this time she would not accept the child, Lilian gave it up for adoption, almost casually it seemed, and returned home alone. But now her exclusion from the family group became more obvious. The child, without understanding anything of what had happened, knew nevertheless that her 'big sister' was in disgrace. Her little voice could be heard, piping censoriously, whenever Lilian did something wrong, which was certainly not seldom. From the moment that she returned from hospital without the second child, Lilian began to deteriorate.

At work, too, she had exhausted most people's patience. One illegitimate child was accepted easily enough; two was evidence of stupidity or worse. She became, though always in a mild way, the butt for jokes. The younger women, in particular, despised her. The older ones were more tolerant.

So she went on, ageing a little, but always retaining the too-girlish dresses, and the bunches of hair. On Saturday nights, she was said to go round the Buffs, letting men take her out the back, for a port and lemon if they were flush, for nothing if they were skint. There was a rumour that she had been sterilised. At any rate no more babies appeared.

Jo had been familiar with this story for many years, though she had hardly thought about it, merely absorbed it unconsciously as she had absorbed so many others during the years of her growing up. She hardly knew why, suddenly, it seemed important. Lilian herself she did not much like: there was too much of the spiteful child in her, she was too obviously delighted to see somebody else in trouble. When

Elaine had just begun to persecute Bertha, and seemed to be getting away with it, Lilian had been beside herself with glee. The violence when it came had shocked her almost as badly as it had shocked Elaine. She had crept about quietly for days after it.

Meanwhile, the trouble so long forecast seemed to have started. Elaine was leaning across the belt to shout at Bertha, who merely shrugged her shoulders and turned aside. The sponges no longer arrived in front of Jo in a steady stream, but two or three at a time. This difference, hardly perceptible to a casual observer, altered the whole nature of the job. Now, instead of merely lifting each cake with one hand and slipping the card underneath it with the other— an economical movement that used only muscles hardened to it by long practice — she had to lean sideways and forwards over the belt, working, moreover, at many times the normal speed in order to regulate the flow of cakes before they reached the packers at the end of the line. This altered movement, repeated, as it would have to be, hundreds and hundreds of times, would amount by the end of the morning to agonising pain.

When the next pause came she looked at Elaine. She was screaming at Bertha again, screaming until the veins stood out on her head. The lights beat down hard on her, revealing a moustache of sweat on her upper lip.

Bertha's task was to put the upper layer of cake on top of the middle layer as it left the slicing and creaming machine; Elaine's to lift the two layers and put them on the bottom layer. By holding on to the upper layer a fraction too long, or releasing several in quick succession, Bertha could treble the amount of effort Elaine had to put into her job if she were to keep pace with the flow of cakes. She had been doing this for some time, though so imperceptible was the alteration, that even a close observer, unfamiliar with conveyor-belt work, might not have detected the change.

Elaine had to chase the cakes down the line. She jostled against Jo, who yelled at her and was herself forced back. Gradually, Elaine inched back to her normal position, working like lightning, reaching far out over the belt.

If you had to lean out like that to pick them up, the cakes were surprisingly heavy. Jo could see the pain and desperation on Elaine's face as she panted and sweated to keep up. Speed made the job messier too. Jam and synthetic cream oozed out over Elaine's hands until they were coated up to the wrist. Inevitably, Jo found herself trying to do Elaine's job as well as her own, straightening out lopsided cakes before she slipped the cardboard underneath. Even so, some very odd-looking sponges found their way down to the packing department.

This went on until the morning tea-break. Bertha looked blank, Lilian gawped, Jo and Elaine sweated and winced with pain. Once the supervisor walked past, puzzled by the apparent break in rhythm at that end of the line. But while she was there Bertha worked normally, so that after a few minutes she wandered off again. Jo, sweat pouring from her armpits, thighs trembling from the strain, simply prayed for it all to stop.

Yet when the machines were finally switched off the four of them simply stood and stared at each other for a second, all antagonism forgotten in the shock of silence. Gradually conversations started and rose quickly to a babble as the women moved towards the door.

As they all climbed the three flights of stairs to the tea-room, Jo could feel aggression simmering in the air. Elaine had been joined by her two friends from the packing department and marched up the stairs between them, keeping up an unmistakeably vituperative monologue. Jo crawled up, hanging on to the banister for support. She felt terrible. Then, suddenly, as they reached the top, hope flashed into her mind. Backache, belly ache, thigh ache. Stickiness? With all the clarity of an hallucination she saw her pants stained with blood. Glorious, marvellous, wonderful blood. Oh please, God, yes yes . . .

'Where's *she* gone?'

'Taken short by the looks of it.'

'I don't wonder. I'm damn sure these breaks are getting later.'

There were three long trestle tables in the tea-room, with

a fourth table to the right of the door on which were dozens of cups, the tea already poured out, grey and steaming. The women collected their tea and sat down. They sat in much the same order as they worked on the conveyor belt. A woman might move up or down a few places to be near a friend, but in general the order did not change much. If any of them had been asked what they thought of this arrangement, the answer would probably have been 'Terrible'. Yet they continued to abide by it. It was easy; it required no thought. So that when Jo returned it was to sit next to Elaine, and almost opposite Bertha. Lilian sat by herself at the end of the table, because her place was occupied by the two girls from packing. Elaine continued to mutter and to dart vicious glances at Bertha, who smiled and blew out smoke, slowly, knowing that she had nothing to fear. Elaine got out a little manicure set and began jabbing at her cuticles.

The supervisor passed, holding a cup of tea in her hand. Like everybody else, she kept to the routine and seldom sat down from beginning to end of the breaks. The women disliked her for it.

'What's the matter with you?' she asked, stopping opposite Jo. 'You look as if you'd lost a bob and found a tanner. '

'Me back aches,' Jo said, as disagreeably as she could. 'I've been working.'

'Your back aches? My heart aches.'

Aye, and your arse'd ache 'n' all if I got near it.

'If she was doing her job,' Elaine muttered, 'there'd be none of this carry-on.'

Bertha blew out smoke. It drifted across the table and got into Elaine's eyes.

'I saw you round the Buffs last night,' Elaine said, squinting to avoid the smoke.

Lilian gave the odd little wriggle of embarrassment and pleasure that she always gave when somebody noticed her.

'You were with that Wilf Rogerson. Weren't yer?'

Lilian produced a fawning grimace like a dog that doesn't know whether the upraised stick means a beating or a game. 'Yeah, I was there. I didn't see you but. . .'

'Oh, we were over in the lounge part.' Elaine flicked the chewing gum to the other side of her mouth. 'Saw you, though.'

The two girls from packing looked at each other, excited and nervous. They knew Elaine in this mood.

'Smashing dress you had on. It was.' Here Elaine turned to her underlings as if daring them to dispute it. 'It was, it was smashing. Only one thing let yer down and that was yer hair. Can't you do summat with it? She doesn't suit it like that, does she?' Again she consulted the younger girls.

'No, it makes her face look too fat.'

'And anyway, she's too old for it.'

Their names were Barbara and Karen but Jo never succeeded in remembering which was which for long. When Elaine was present, they might just as well have been called Giggle and Squeak.

'You want a good bit of it off,' Elaine concluded.

The three of them stared at Lilian, who grinned nervously, overwhelmed by so much attention.

'Either off or up. One or the other. ' Elaine was smiling pleasantly, but there was a tremor of excitement in her voice. She reached across and pulled the two bunches together on top of Lilian's head. Then she craned her head back and pretended to examine the effect.

'My God, Elaine, rather you than me,' Squeak said.

Elaine ignored her. 'Shows yer dirty neck, mind,' she said to Lilian. 'You'll have to get that washed. Here, give us me scissors. '

Lilian wriggled again, not daring to protest.

'Keep still, will yer?'

Instantly, Lilian froze.

'My God, she is 'n' all!'

Lilian's failure to stand up for herself took away what little self-control Elaine had. She stabbed at the hair, sawing and hacking away almost at random. Lilian sat still, a fixed monkey-grin of terror and incomprehension on her face, as first locks of hair and then whole chunks of it slid down her shoulders and on to the table.

'There you are. Give that lot a bit of a trim and you'll be

all right.' Elaine's voice shook with laughter. 'No, hold on, there's a bit here.' Elaine nearly choked. 'I'll finish it off.'

'What about the top, Elaine?' Giggle suggested.

'I think it's gone far enough,' Jo said.

Elaine stopped what she was doing and looked at Jo. 'What's it to do with you?'

'Nowt. But I think it's gone far enough. Don't you?'

'You want to make something of it?'

'No. But I will if I have to.'

Elaine looked around for support. There was none. Some of the older women at the head of the table were getting reluctantly to their feet.

'She's better off without it.'

'I'm not denying that. But you might've let her make up her own mind.'

'*Mind*? She hasn't got a bloody mind!'

'No reason to pick on her. We all know what's eating you. If you haven't got the guts to speak out you'd best shut up altogether.'

'Come on, girls. Come on.' It was the manager. He stood in the open doorway, angrily consulting his watch. 'These tea-breaks are meant to be fifteen minutes, you know. Fifteen. Not thirty.'

He watched them file past. Looking for trouble, he noticed one of the girls walking along without a hairnet on.

'You,' he said. ' Whatever your name is.'

'Lil—'

He wasn't interested. 'Get your hair under that net. And don't ever let me catch you walking round like that again.'

He watched them down the corridor and out of sight, noticing how many slipped into the cloakroom, although they were already late back for work. That's right, he thought, angrily. Always pee in the firm's time, never in your own. That was the motto with some of these girls. 'Girls' he said, and they were girls. Would never be anything else though some of them were forty, fifty, even sixty years old. You only had to listen to them: nothing but gossip and giggle and rubbish.

He took one final look round and marched out, banging

the door.

On the table where Elaine and Lilian had sat were little coils and crescent moons of hair, lying unregarded among the ashtrays and the dirty cups.

By dinner-time, Jo was exhausted. Instead of going across to the canteen she went back to the tea-room, where at least it would be quiet.

She sat down on one of the benches and let the silence wash over her.

The only other woman in the room, Maureen Sullivan, was over by the cake stands, choosing something to eat. Slices of sponge and chocolate cake were available, free, every dinner-time. 'I wouldn't eat that muck if I was starving,' was the common reaction. Maureen, although not starving, ate it every day.

There were varicose veins on the backs of her legs, standing out thickly like worm-casts on the beach: she wore no stockings. Jo found herself staring at them. She watched as Maureen sat down and started to eat the cake. Her top teeth were missing so that the flesh was pleated over bare gums, making it difficult to manage the cream. She sat, licking it humbly off her lips; after every few mouthfuls, she washed it down with a sip of weak tea.

God, I'd like to tell them where to shove their bloody cake, Jo thought. She would, too, one day.

Maureen couldn't. She had a houseful of kids and no husband. But still she struggled on and thanked no one for their pity. Her kids went to school well shod though she herself wore the same pair of plimsolls winter and summer. She was respected, respected but avoided. Luck like hers might be catching.

Maureen chewed her cake. Jo became aware that she had been staring at her too long, and looked away. Everybody she met today she seemed to be seeing for the first time. Perhaps it was because her own life was about to change so radically: every older woman became an image of the future, a reason for hope or fear.

Now, looking at Maureen Sullivan and thinking what her

life had been, Jo felt a sense of oppression. And then there was Lisa Goddard, whom she often saw in the supermarket, weighed down with kids and shopping, pushing her belly in front of her like another self. To Joanne, she looked ready to pop: she couldn't imagine a belly bigger than that. But Iris King said, No, she was still a good way off.

Jo turned towards the window. Autumn sunlight filtered down, hazy with smoke and soot. The grime on the glass almost defeated it, but enough got through to gild her face and hair. She gave herself up to it completely, lying back in her chair, her eyes screwed up against the brilliance of the light.

'It's been a long time.'

'It has that.'

'Well let's not waste any more of it then.'

He pushed her back on to the coat, and kissed her, pressing the whole length of his body against her own. The tree they were lying under moved a little in the wind, casting its net of branches at the stars which swam through unharmed in bright and glimmering shoals. It made her feel dizzy to look at them.

He pressed his weight down and instantly she felt something sticking into her back. She twisted round and found first one conker and then another, — green, unopened cases.

'Some kid must've dropped them,' Ken said. 'It isn't even a conker tree.'

She lay back. His mouth moved all over her face, blindly, like some weird, sucking creature of the sea-bed that lives by touch alone; hovered, and burrowed down to stifle the lonely cry that welled up from her throat.

He left her at once and began zipping up his trousers.

'You know what you were saying earlier? About those women fighting? I hope you don't join in with that sort of thing, because there's nothing worse than to see two women fight, nothing more common. It's real low-life, is that.' His mouth puckered with distaste, as he hurried his shrivelled flesh out of sight.

91

'Sometimes you've no choice.'

'There's always a choice. Decent women don't fight.'

Jo thought of Iris King, and wondered.

Meanwhile he had finished fastening his trousers.

It was always like this: after it was over she wanted to cuddle, to talk, to feel close. But he wanted to be on the move at once. There were times when she suspected that he wanted to get away from her, from what they had done together. Their lovemaking never brought them closer. In fact, sometimes, things she'd said earlier in the evening, things that had made him laugh, then, were brought up and held against her.

She lay looking up at the tree. At first its branches hardly stirred, but then a gust of wind shook them, loosening more leaves.

The tree had been green the first time they lay down beneath it. Now almost all its leaves were gone.

And in the wintertime? What would they do then? Where would they go?

'Aren't you cold?' Ken asked. The words were torn out of him. It shocked him that she should just lie there like that, not even trying to cover herself up. Lying there with her legs apart, she challenged his hatred of what his body had made him do. He resented her, even despised her a little. But since he was basically a kind-hearted man, a man who wanted more from a woman than he knew how to take, he was unhappy despising her. He could not do it without despising himself. And so he wanted to escape, from the situation, from her, most of all from himself. 'You must be cold,' he went on. 'I'm freezing.'

Jo lay and looked up at him, not speaking.

'Come on,' he said. 'We'll have a walk round the Vane Arms, shall we? They'll have a fire on there.'

She could not speak. Fear had sharpened her perceptions. She saw every gesture, registered every inflection of his voice that told of his anxiety to be gone.

The silence tightened.

'You all right?'

'No.'

'What's wrong? I mean, it was all right for you, wasn't it? You seemed . . .'

'It was fine.'

'. . . to be enjoying it.'

'It was fine.'

'Well, then.'

Silence.

'Well, then. What's wrong?'

She felt that he already knew. Or guessed.

'I'm pregnant.'

But she was wrong. She watched him take the full force of the blow. Disbelief, fear, anger, disbelief, fear chased each other across his face.

'Don't be daft. You can't be. I haven't been near you . . .'

'For six weeks? I've missed twice.'

She watched hope die.

'Well. Well, then. . . . You must've known before I left.'

'I was a few days late. That's all. I didn't see the point of two people worrying themselves sick. And anyway, I've been that late before.'

'You should've told me.'

'There was no point.'

He stared around him helplessly. Looked down at the shape their bodies had left in the grass and said violently, 'Come on, let's get away from here.'

'We've got to talk about it, Ken.'

'We can talk in the pub.'

'It's all very well for you. You haven't had the weeks and weeks of worry that I've had.

'Well, it's not my fault I haven't, is it? You rang me up. Why the bloody hell didn't you mention it then?'

'Oh, have a heart, man. How could I? On the *phone*?'

She was struggling to her feet. He put out a hand: — too late to help.

'I suppose you *are* sure? I mean if you've been late before?'

'I've never been this late. And anyway, I've started being sick in the mornings as well now.'

'Oh, my God.'

93

There were little pinpricks of sweat just below his hairline. He was sweating with fear, fear of having to marry her. She saw all that. But there was a certain detachment in her bitterness. She was not going to nag him into it. She would wait and see what he did.

'Did you try anything?'

'I don't know! Pills.'

'Where from? You might know where to get things like that — I don't. And if you're thinking of hot baths and gin, well, for a kickoff it doesn't work. If it did I wouldn't be here for one. And in the second place, we haven't *got* a bath, you daft bugger. If I started boiling meself to death in front of the fire don't you think me Mam'ld notice? Don't you think she'd want to know why?'

'You haven't told her then?'

There was so much relief in his voice she could have throttled him.

'No, I haven't told her. Because I didn't have to. The way we live she knows I'm late before I do.'

'What did she say?'

'Oh, what do you think she said?'

For a moment he almost got the full story, Joss included. But she stopped herself in time.

They began walking towards the park gate. By the lake they stopped. Geese and swans immediately took to the water and began sailing towards them in search of food.

She said, 'Ken, I'm frightened.'

'You've no need to be. We're in it together.'

'Are we?'

'Oh, yes.' She heard him catch and hold his breath to stop it becoming a sigh. 'Only you'll have to give me a bit of time. I mean, back home . . . they don't even know your name . . .'

Because you never thought it important enough to mention. Until now.

Suddenly he was laughing: an ugly sound. 'Do you know, my sister and her husband've been trying for a bairn for three year. Three bloody year.'

He cut the laugh off quickly.

'What do you think your Mam'll say?'

94

'A barrowful.'

They stood in silence under the trees. A dead leaf rattled along the path towards them. Jo thought, I'll remember this for the rest of my life: the relief. The despair.

She shivered. 'You're right. It is cold. Let's go for a drink.'

But even about this they couldn't agree. As they left the park he began walking very quickly with his head lowered and his hands thrust deep into his pockets, leaving Jo to follow as best she could. She was so preoccupied with her own thoughts and with the difficulty of keeping up with him that at first she did not realise where he was taking her. When she did it was already too late. They were outside the Bluebell.

'I can't go in there,' she said, panting for breath.

It was a steelworkers' pub. There was a strict men-only rule in the bar.

'There's a snug at the back,' he said, not looking at her. 'Women go in there.'

'Yes, and what women?'

'It's not to say you're one of them, is it?'

They stood together under the street lamp. Then the swing doors opened just behind them and Blonde Dinah came out.

'If it's all the same to you I think I'd rather go home.'

Evidently it *was* all the same to him, for he turned towards the railway tunnel without another word.

But in the darkness of the tunnel he hesitated. This was their last chance to talk. Heavily, almost reluctantly, he took her in his arms. She stood with her back against the whitewashed wall. She could not see his face. He loomed over her like a shadow.

'We've got to talk,' she said. But she had no faith in their ability to talk to each other. She thought of the girls she knew who had got married with a child on the way. She had thought it would never happen to her; her marriage would be different.

'I don't want to start raking it all over now. I can't take any more tonight.

He made it sound as if it were her fault. But at least he did not move away. He looked at her, and kissed her. And then — something he had never done before, though they had often stopped in this tunnel to say goodnight — he lifted her skirt, and began to thrust into her.

'Ken,' she said. In the distance, a goods train rumbled. It panted towards them, sounding at first rather out of breath and ineffectual. Then it was roaring and crashing above their heads. Flakes of plaster drifted down and landed in her hair.

Ken was panting, and thrusting into her as though he hated her, grinding and screwing and banging hard enough to hurt. She was afraid for the baby and immediately knew what he was trying to do: he was trying to screw it out of her. She went cold, pressing herself back against the wall, but he fastened on to her with a terrible, monotonous power.

There was something exciting in being used like this, in giving way to this impersonal, machine-like passion. For a moment she let herself relax, and his flesh bit into her like steel.

The goods train clanked and rumbled overhead, no longer roaring, but deadly and monotonous. She could see in her mind's eye the oiled pistons moving round. And round. Almost matching the thrusts of Ken's bum. With deadly corrosive hatred she began to move against him, imposing upon him the rhythm of the train, which was at first exciting, and then terrible and then, abruptly, ridiculous, so that he lost his erection and slid ignobly out of her.

She watched him shield himself and turn aside. There was nothing that either of them could say.

The silence sounded very loud after the train had finally pulled away.

'I'll be in touch before Sunday,' Ken said.

'All right.'

'And don't worry about it. She's not that bad.'

'I wasn't going to.'

Further along the tunnel they came across Blonde Dinah with the man who had followed her out of the pub. They passed with lowered eyes as the custom was: at this time of night you didn't notice other users of the tunnel. But out of the corner of her eye Jo glimpsed the white thighs and raised skirt of the other woman and a darkness rushed over her so that she stumbled and almost fell.

'What's wrong?' Ken asked. Then with sudden awkward concern, 'Are you feeling faint?'

'No. No. I don't know what's wrong.' She looked back and shuddered. 'A ghost walking over my grave.'

He put his arm around her, and together they walked on.

On the way home she bought fish and chips for herself and Joss, and put them in the oven to await his arrival. He would stop for a drink on his way back. In fact he had probably been in the Bluebell.

Another good reason for staying out of the snug.

She sat in the darkness and watched gangs of youths throwing stones on the streets of Belfast. Then turned the volume up for a story about petrol price increases. She wasn't interested, but Joss would be. His car was his god. Iris King, who knew him as well as anybody, used to say that was the real reason he'd never got married: he couldn't afford to run a wife and a car.

Joss came in as the news finished.

'You're back early. I thought you'd've gone for a drink.'

'Brought it back with me, didn't I?' He produced three bottles of Newcastle Brown and two of Guinness. 'The Guinness is for you,' he said. 'It's supposed to be good for the milk.'

'I haven't had it yet, man.'

'You need building up.'

'I'll be big enough without any building. There's fish and chips in the oven. Do you want them off a plate?'

'Paper'll do me.'

'They don't taste the same off a plate, do they? Have I to bring 'em through there?'

'Aye. And I'll build up the fire.' He looked at the telly.

'Petrol's up again.'

'I saw 'em queueing.' He turned off the set. They looked

97

PAT BARKER

at each other, exposed and vulnerable now that the other presence in the room was gone.

'Well, I'll get the fish and chips.'

Ten minutes later Jo was wiping her mouth on the back of her hand.

'My God, you didn't half knock that lot back.'

'I was hungry. That's the first I've had today.'

'Not my fault. It was offered.'

'Takes me stomach time to settle.'

The fire roared, clots and flakes of burning soot sparked up the chimney. 'I don't know what you're sat back there for,' said Jo. 'Come down here and get warm.'

'This is close enough. Over much like work, is that.'

'I suppose it is.' She had just remembered: he was a blast-furnace man. 'Bit like telling me to bake a cake.'

'How did it go tonight? With your boyfriend.'

'Oh, all right, I suppose. I'm going to meet his Mam and Dad next weekend. That is, if his Mam's willing.'

She pulled a face.

'And then?'

'Then we'll get married, I suppose.'

'You suppose?'

'I mean we will.'

Silence.

'Well, aren't you going to congratulate me? That's what people usually do, you know.'

'Sounds more like a funeral than a wedding.'

'You're dead right it does.' She piled the fish and chip papers on to the fire and held them down with the poker while they burned. More flakes of soot caught fire and leaped up the chimney. 'It's time you had this lot swept.' She scoured the back of the chimney with the poker, so that a cloud of soot billowed out into the room and for a minute the fire burned black and chill.

'Yes, well, there's no need for you to do it. You'll have the whole lot down.'

Jo stared into the deadened fire. 'The trouble is, I know he doesn't want to. Not really.'

'How old is he?'

98

'Eighteen. Same as me. Younger in fact. He's just turned eighteen.'

'Dear God.'

'He's not the only one who's trapped, you know. Though you'd think he was the way he carries on . . . I'm the one who's got to walk round with me belly swelling, being sick and all that. Then in the end get the poor little bugger out of me. I'm trapped ! Worse than he'll ever be. But I'm supposed to be grateful because he's doing the right thing, not leaving me to carry the can by meself . . . He started it! I didn't do it single-handed!'

'You must love him.'

'Must I? Why?'

'Well, you know you must.'

'Because I get on me back for him, you mean?'

'There's no need for that.'

'It wasn't love . . . I suppose I must've thought it was. And I'll tell you summat else: it was no bloody pleasure. A sparrow couldn't't've farted quicker.'

'It's no use going on like this. If you're going to marry him you've got to try and make a go of it.'

'What do you know about it? You've never been married, have you?'

'No.'

'Well? Do you think you're missing owt?'

'No.' He considered a minute. 'Sometimes I think I am. But not when I look round.'

'Some folks make a go of it.'

'Aye.'

'They're not all going at it hammer and tongs.'

'I never said they were.'

'Well, then . . .'

'Only there's not many you could say were really happy. You know, more than jogging along.'

Silence. Then, 'Oh, don't worry. I know what you mean.'

'Ted and Iris. You couldn't call them happy.'

'Happy! There's many a night we think they're coming through the wall. There's not much we don't hear, you know.'

99

'Same with these two next door to me . . .'

They both stared into the fire. Then Joss said slowly,

'Well, I hope he knows what he's getting, your young man.'

'Oh, what is he getting?' She was prepared to be aggressive.

'Why, best little lass for miles around.' He paused. 'Anyway, that's what I think.'

Their eyes met. Her heart was thumping. She could neither speak nor look away. She could do nothing to guard either of them from this sudden danger.

'But there, I expect he knows that better than me.' Joss looked down at his legs as if for once in his life he needed to be reminded of their length, and caught a sigh. 'Anyway.'

When he spoke again his voice had changed. 'You'll need to make it up with your Mam. You can't very well get married from here.'

But Jo was not thinking of the practicalities of a wedding.

'I never feel as if I can talk to him. I'm not his class. No, it's true . . .' She waved Joss's protests aside.

'Who's he when he's all at home?'

'Well, they've got a furniture shop and a nice house. I don't suppose they know where Union Street is. And he goes to the Poly.' She gestured, helplessly. 'You can see why he's afraid of telling his Mam, can't you? She's not going to be overjoyed.'

'It's him you're marrying, not her.'

'Oh, I don't know so much. I've a feeling it might be her.'

Silence. Then, 'Howay, lass. Get stuck in at your beer.'

Jo leant back against the sofa and closed her eyes. She saw Soppy Lil's face, grinning with terror. It was 'Soppy Jo' now. God, she needed her head looking at. The face faded, and was replaced by a long line of cakes. That was the worst of the job. You could be away from it for hours, you could think you'd forgotten it, but the minute you closed your eyes: there were the cakes. It was only after a good night's sleep that you got rid of them.

But she'd be leaving the bakery now. Three or four months and she'd be finished. Mebbe sooner. He mightn't let her work there after they were married. Wouldn't suit his ideas a bit. Nor his mother's.

Instead there'd be a house. Somewhere. Housework. And, eventually, a baby.

Well, that was what she wanted. Wasn't it?

She looked round the room. Firelight flickered over mirrors and furniture.

'I like it here. I wish I didn't have to go.'

Even the baby, which all day long she had 'felt' as a hard nodule of fear, seemed to melt away inside her, to float and merge with her into the peace and safety of this room.

She said, more wistfully now, 'I wish I didn't have to go.'

CHAPTER THREE
LISA GODDARD

It was late-night shopping at the supermarket. The shelves were piled high with tins, packets, fruit and vegetables ready for the weekend rush. And everywhere there was the cheerfulness of money to spend at last, after the scrimping of Wednesday and Thursday night. It was fish-and-chip night, too, for many of the families, so the women were able to shop without thinking of the meal they would have to cook when they got back.

Lisa Goddard walked down one of the aisles, wheeling a pushchair with a stout protesting little boy, about eighteen months old, strapped into it. He was fastened in too tightly. There was a shopping bag on his lap which tilted precariously whenever he struggled. Which was often. He was tired of the bright lights, and people's knees, and the sharp edges of shopping baskets banging him in the face. There was another, heavier shopping basket slung over the handle of his pushchair.

His mother walked behind, carrying a wire basket and hauling along a slightly older boy, who was pulling away from her and screaming. Most of the time she moved the pushchair along with little vicious jerks of her belly. Tiredness and desperation were written all over her face. And still the child hauled on her arm, trying to pull her back they way they had come.

'I wanta . . .'

He didn't say what he wanted, and probably no longer knew. He had reached the stage where he could not have given in even if he had wanted to. His rage possessed him completely. When his mother reached up to get a packet from the shelves, he seized the opportunity and wrenched himself out of her grasp. He didn't go far: the bond with her was too strong; but he backed away, and stood pressed against the deep-freeze counter, screaming now with fear of what his anger had made him do. For he had seen the expression on his mother's face.

She let go of the pushchair and swung round on him, her arm raised to strike. But the pushchair, top-heavy now because of the shopping basket on the back, began to topple over. She had to jump back, and succeeded in catching it only just in time. The baby screamed and struggled harder. The shopping basket on his knee overturned, and tins of peas and carrots rolled out on to the floor.

It was breaking point. Very deliberately, Lisa took off the heavy shopping basket, so that the pushchair would be stable, and went after the older child. He screamed with terror, but she was beyond hearing.

'I warned you, didn't I? I warned you . . .' She hit the child hard across his face. He gasped and then howled again, louder, but still he hung back. He was incapable of getting himself out of the situation. 'Come on!' his mother said, trying to drag him back to the pushchair and the squealing baby. He clung to the deep-freeze counter, and she hit him again and again, stinging, hard slaps, her face distorted by hatred as she looked at him. Yet, inside, another woman was watching, and that woman felt nothing but horror and shame.

'Oh, all right, have your sweets. Have them! And I hope you choke.'

The child clutched the packet of sweets, not even bothering to look at it. His little reddened face was raised hopelessly to his mother, mouth wide and screaming, upper lip smeared with snot.

'Oh, my God, and now look at you. ' She groped about her for a handkerchief, and couldn't find one. She could have sat down beside her son on the supermarket floor and cried as miserably as he was crying.

But there was still the shopping to be done. She took his hand and he allowed it to be taken, stumbling along after her blindly, sometimes tripping and being saved from falling only because she carried him along bodily for a few strides.

'Pick your feet up, can't you?' she said, bending down to whisper her threat. 'If you don't pull yourself together and start behaving yourself, I'll knock the living daylights out of you when I get you back.'

She raised her eyes and found a young girl staring at her. She was standing just by the tights counter and must have seen everything. Lisa walked more quickly, glaring at the girl as she walked past, daring her to say anything, to interfere. But she wouldn't, of course; people never did. Only looked. And despised what they saw.

The girl was familiar. Lisa looked back at her, taking in the dress, the shoes, the make-up. She looked down at herself, at the shapeless smock left over from her last pregnancy, and at the shapeless body beneath it — also left over from her last pregnancy. The baby's hands reached out towards the brightly coloured sweets that were placed so temptingly within reach. Lisa was too tired to stop him. Just let the assistant say anything, that was all. Just let her start . . .

Back at home, she dropped the shopping down and almost fell into the armchair. The house was empty, but she had expected that. She lay back in the chair, while Kevin stuffed himself with sweets and spoilt his appetite for supper, and the baby, still imprisoned in the pushchair, yelled to be let out.

Her ankles were swollen. Quite badly. They'd have something to say about that when she went to the clinic.

Are you getting enough rest, Mrs Goddard?

Her blood pressure was up. She had guessed that, though the nurse's face remained carefully expressionless as she wrote the figures down on the card.

Oh, yes, she said, eagerly. *I'm taking things very easy.*

She was afraid they would take her into hospital, as they

had threatened to do once before. Not that it mattered much now: she was due anyway. But then, it would have meant weeks away from the children and she did not know what would have happened to them. She looked at them now, and softened.

'Howay, Kevin, come and give your Mam a cuddle. Then we'll get his lordship sorted out, and see what there is for tea. Hey, shall we?' He came into her arms, his face still stained with tears, chocolate mixed in with the snot around his mouth. She had hit him too hard. And not for the first time. When he cuddled in close to her she could hear the tremor in his breath, the shudder where the sobs had been.

God forgive me, she thought. She held him close and rocked him. It wasn't that she didn't love him. It was only that she got so desperate. She loved him all right: this rocking gave her as much peace as it gave him.

Only there was still the baby. There was still Darren to be seen to.

'Howay, let's see if we've got something nice. What would you like?' She mentioned fish fingers, beefburgers, chips, trying to inject some enthusiasm into her voice, and was rewarded, at last, by a shaky smile. Why can't it be like this all the time? she thought. Why am I so bad-tempered with them? It isn't their fault.

She must try to be better. The resolution carried her through the last few hours of the day, until, having seen both children asleep in their cots, she came down to face the evening alone. Then, suddenly depressed, she sat down at the kitchen table. She was remembering the girl who had stared at her in the supermarket. She knew now who it was: Joanne Wilson. They'd gone to the same school, but never really known each other. Joanne had arrived the same year that Lisa left.

But she couldn't be much younger. Three years. Perhaps four. Lisa leaned forward, her arms folded on the table. Her breasts slumped forwards too, and rested on the bulge. She couldn't afford a proper maternity brassiere and the others no longer fitted. She remembered Joanne's dress, her shoes, her hair. She had looked at Lisa so contemptuously.

105

What right had she to look like that? What did she know about it? What did she know about anything?

As much as I knew at her age.

Lisa hid her face in her hands and wept.

After a little while she sat up and dried her eyes. She was alone in the house, but she was used to that. There were only the two children asleep upstairs.

She rinsed out the nappies that were waiting for her in a bucket under the sink, then built up the living room fire and put the clothes horse in front of it. She could never dry the clothes while Brian was in the house because he liked to sit huddled over the fire. The room was warm, fire-lit. She left the main light off and went to lie on the sofa. From behind the clothes horse came the roar of flames and the smell of wool drying.

The scene was peaceful enough. But inside her the baby boiled and heaved. It always seemed to be restless at this time of night, perhaps because she herself was so tense. Did it know pub throwing-out time already? Before it was born?

The baby kicked hard. Sometimes you could see a foot or a hand quite clearly, or even the whole sweep of an arm moving across beneath the surface of the skin. It had filled her with wonder in the weeks before Kevin was born.

Not any more.

She did not want this baby. They could not afford it: Brian had been out of work for the best part of a year. But even if there had been all the money in the world, she would not have wanted it. Brian was out drinking. As always. She did not want to have his child. The two she had already were as much as she could manage. More. There were times when she doubted whether Brian would ever work again. Oh, he said he was still looking. But she didn't believe him. He had given up.

And of course it wasn't his fault: the redundancy. It wasn't hers either. And yet so often she seemed to bear the brunt of his despair.

Been up to his tricks again, has he? Well, you know what your father said.

And what good would that do?

It might do him a power of good. It'd show him you've still got a family.

It's not often he hits me.

He shouldn't hit you at all! You should've left him when you only had the one. We'd've managed.

It's only when he's had a drink, Mam.

I'm glad he can afford to drink. Many a man in work can't afford to spend what he spends.

He has to have something. Ever since he lost that job . . . It seems to've knocked the stuffing out of him. Completely.

And has he any need to take it out on you?

'There's nobody else.'

She realised that she had said the words aloud, and was startled. You get taken away if you do things like that. It's supposed to be the first sign.

She stood up and moved the clothes horse away from the fire. Then she went into the kitchen and started getting his supper ready. He always wanted a hot meal whenever he came in: there was a row if he didn't get it.

Yet when he was in work he hadn't minded if she was a bit late. He would even sit and play with the bairns for a bit while she finished getting it ready.

She sighed, and went on scraping the carrots. She seemed to be so far away from her own childhood, from her youth. It seemed hardly possible that this heavy woman lumbering round the kitchen of a poky house should be the same person as that girl who had worked all day at the cake bakery and still found the energy to dance at night. Still less possible that she should be that child who had run shouting through the park.

It was almost closing time. God alone knew where he was finding the money from. Only last night he had complained of being broke. Perhaps he was sponging on his friends? But no, he wouldn't do that. She wasn't even sure that he had any friends. The ties formed at work were beginning to dissolve now.

The dinner was prepared and in the oven. Still he didn't come. She settled herself into an armchair and got out her knitting. If he didn't come soon she would go to bed. She was tired, and it was a mug's game waiting up for somebody who never seemed to notice whether you were there or not.

In spite of herself the fear grew. Where *was* he finding the money from? She went back into the kitchen, telling herself that she was only going to check that she had turned the gas on.

But after she had checked the oven she still stood there. The kitchen was very cold. It always smelled of cold fat in spite of all the time she spent cleaning it.

They had been going to have it all modernised. Until Brian lost his job.

She glanced at the pantry door. Perhaps she would just check. There was no harm in checking, was there?

For the last four or five months she had been saving up for the baby. Most of the things she'd got for Kevin were worn out now, and the maternity grant wouldn't cover replacements. At first she saved whatever was left in her purse at the end of the week. But that was usually just a few coppers. Then she made herself save all the 50p pieces. Sometimes when she saw a shopkeeper about to give her a 50p in her change she would pray for him to change his mind. She needed the money now.

But she made herself stick to her self-imposed rule. And was rewarded. The sum quickly mounted up. By now the jar was almost full.

She kept it right at the back of the pantry, behind everything else. Not that she distrusted Brian. More than once she had given him 50p and asked him to put it in the jar for her. She was horrified to find herself suspecting him now, so horrified that she almost closed the pantry door without checking on the jar.

But it was no use. She had come this far. She had to know. The jar was too light. She felt this, even before she saw that the money was gone.

She brought it out into the kitchen, convinced that there must be some mistake. Brian couldn't've done this to her. She even put her hand inside the jar and felt all round it, as though her eyes might be deceiving her and somehow, by some miracle, the money was still there.

She sat down at the kitchen table with the empty jar in her hand. Perhaps she had put the money somewhere else? It had crossed her mind to do that more than once. Yes, that must be it. She had moved the money to another place and then forgotten. She did forget things these days. He was always telling her about it.

She began to search. All the time she knew there was no hope, but the mere act of searching seemed to ward off the moment when she would have to accept what had happened.

At last, though, she was forced to return to the table and the jar. Of course, she told herself, she didn't *know* that it was Brian who had taken the money. Though he was the only one who knew where it was, and she always remembered to lock the door whenever she went out.

She looked at the clock. She would know as soon as he came in. He would not be able to hide it from her.

But she knew already. She had thought he would never be able to hurt her again, but it wasn't true. This hurt.

He was not back by eleven. Lisa sat in the armchair by the fire, with an old woollen dressing gown thrown across her shoulders more for comfort than warmth. She was so exhausted by now that she felt sick.

If only he would come, she thought. She wanted it to be over.

At last she heard his key in the lock. Immediately she became tense, tense almost to breaking point. But I won't say anything, she told herself. I'll wait to see what he does.

He continued to fumble with the lock. To her overstrained nerves he seemed to be making enough noise to wake the dead. If only he doesn't wake the children up, she thought. To have them downstairs and crying on top of everything else would be more than she could bear.

At last he was in the house. He paused outside the living-room door and for a moment she thought he was going upstairs. But no. There he was, swaying slightly, holding on to the edge of the door for support. But she knew him too well. He was not as drunk as he appeared to be. He was using drunkenness as a defence.

'Supper ready, is it?'

'Yes.'

He looked at the table in mock surprise.

'In the kitchen.'

'In the kitchen.'

'If you want it on the table you'd better let me know when you're coming home.'

He glowered at her as he went past. She no longer had any doubts. His guilt had made him hate her.

But still she said nothing, though she tensed again as he began banging and clattering in the kitchen. He was picking things up and crashing them down at random. It was a technique he had for making it seem as though the kitchen — neat and tidy as always — was a pigsty in which it was a miracle if you succeeded in finding anything. She stood it as long as she could, then went to stand at the kitchen door.

'Having trouble?'

She knew she sounded aggressive. Not just angry but coldly, bloody-mindedly aggressive. Normally when he came home in this state she humoured him. But not tonight. Tonight the words stuck in her throat.

'It's in the oven.'

He stood and glowered at her without saying a word. She stared back, and saw a flicker of fear in his eyes. He started to bluster. 'Well, aren't you going to get it then?'

'No. It's your supper. Get it yourself.'

'It's your job.'

'And it's your job to keep the family.'

'Oh, yes. I wondered how long it'd take you to throw that up.'

'I've never thrown it up. You can't say that.'

He bent down to the oven and, with a tea-towel wrapped round his hand, began pulling out the tray. It was stiff and he was jerking on it one-sidely, so that after a few minutes he had succeeded in jamming it completely. He kept his face down, but Lisa could tell by the set of his shoulders that he was painfully, irritably aware of her standing there, watching him. It seemed to drive him to a frenzy. He wrenched at the tray with his full strength. It flew out of the oven, sending the dish toppling over on to the floor. Brown stew splashed and splattered everywhere.

It was too much for Lisa. 'Dirty, filthy, drunken bastard. You clean that up yourself. I'm not doing it.'

He tried to scoop some of the stew back into the pot, and burnt his hand.

'I'm sick of you, coming in drunk like this. It's bad enough when it's your own money . . .'

He had to silence her somehow. So he stood up and hit her, not very hard, on the side of the head. But the blow liberated something in him, an enormous anger that had been chained up waiting for this moment. He hit her again. And again. It was easier now. She was driven back against the wall.

When it was over he stood and stared at what he had done.

She said, coldly, 'Would you pass me the flannel, please ?'

He stood and watched while she wiped her mouth. There was nothing much: one smear of blood where his ring had caught her. Regret for what he had done fought with the need to bluster, to keep up a front at any cost. She was too tired to wait for the outcome.

'I'm going to bed.'

He looked at the floor.

'Leave it.'

'But . . .'

'I said, Leave it.'

She lay on her back in bed. The ache that had been with her all day became briefly worse and then vanished completely. She moved her legs about, luxuriating in the space, dreading the moment when her husband must appear to fill it.

Meanwhile her mind played back almost automatically every detail of that scene. She went over every word, every action, until her anger went stale and bitterness took its place.

He had not admitted taking the money. He had hit her rather than face up to what he'd done. But it didn't matter. She knew.

When, finally, she felt him in the room with her, she lay with her eyes closed, pretending to sleep. She heard the soft thud and click of his clothes going off. Then the jingle of money in his trouser pockets.

'If you've got any left I think you might have the decency to put it back.'

No reply. She opened her eyes to find him with his trousers half down and an injured expression on his face.

'Put what back?'

'You know what.'

'I don't know what you're on about.' She turned her head away from him. 'It's me own money.'

'You know it's not.'

He started to bluster. It was intolerable, he wouldn't put up with it a minute longer, she did nothing but go on at him, didn't know what to pick at next . . .

'So you'd steal from your own child,' she said, quietly.

He tried to fight back. 'If that's what you think of me all I can say is I've been around too long. I've a bloody good mind to go.'

He waited for her to speak, his trousers halfway up his thighs.

'Well, what have I to do?'

She turned away from him again.

'Mind, if I go, that's it. I don't come back.' He waited. 'I mean it, mind.'

She sat up, leant across the bed and in one movement pulled his trousers up round his waist. 'Bloody go then!' she cried.

There was nothing left for him to do but to pick up his shirt and sweater and go. At the door he tried again, 'I'm not coming back, you know.'

'Go. Go.'

She listened to him go down the stairs. There was a pause, then the sound of the front door opening and closing. She sat on the edge of the bed, trembling slightly. Suppose he had really gone for good? The baby would be born in a few days. A week at most. How would she manage alone? Then she shrugged. She was managing alone already, wasn't she?

At the back of her mind was the knowledge that he would not go. He depended on her too much.

It was a relief to put the light out and lie in the darkness alone. She ought to sleep. It was midnight now and the baby would be awake before six. 'The baby' she called him, forgetting this other that was on the way. So near now. She closed her eyes and tried to sleep. It was useless. As soon as her eyes closed an automatic re-enactment of the row began. And always the resentment, the bitterness that grew and grew until it corroded everything.

That was the worst thing about these rows: each one seemed to arouse not only its own bitterness but the accumulated bitterness of so many previous rows. In between times she would sometimes think she had forgotten, but the next row brought it all to the surface again.

Worse than the row was the day after, when he would sit walled up in silence, trying to pretend that nothing had happened. He would not by any word or gesture acknowledge that he felt remorse. And so the remorse bit into him like acid. This was something that she could never get her mother to see. She couldn't find the right words to express it, though she knew exactly what was happening.

Once she had been sitting in the living room, sewing. It was the day after the worst of their rows, and, although she hadn't realised it, the light from the window was showing up the bruises on her face. Suddenly he had fallen on his knees and crawled towards her, burying his head wordlessly in her lap.

And she was sorry for him. She felt how like a child he had become. Underneath the drink and blustering and violence he was like this all the time.

Sometimes she thought that even if he found work now it would be too late.

And he wasn't looking.

In the mornings if he didn't have to go and sign on, he just sat in the armchair with his face in his hands. On a bad day there was no rousing him at all.

He hadn't always been like this. At first he'd been restless.

113

Up and down, up and down. He seemed as if he didn't know where he wanted to be. He'd even get up in the middle of the night, fancying something to eat.

Mrs Harrison had said George was just the same when he first retired. It had nearly driven her low, she said, the way he went on. And then, gradually, it started to wear off. It was the shift work, she said. He seemed as if he wouldn't get used to a normal day.

But with Brian it didn't wear off. If anything it got worse. At the finish he was walking round and round the sofa like somebody caged.

One day he'd begun to talk about his work. Slowly at first, then with increasing excitement. She'd never known much about his job. He'd never talked about it before. Now, through his eyes, she saw the blast-furnaces for the first time, bigger than the house they lived in. She heard the roar of flame; she felt the heat on her skin; she watched the molten metal poured out. The whole dark, cavernous building was full of the roar and crackle of heat. 'It doesn't matter how often you see it. It's a thing you never get tired of.'

She remembered the last talk. He'd laughed a bit, but not as if he thought something was funny. 'Them bloody seagulls, they're a real pest. They can't keep away — the heat draws them. There's hundreds of 'em. They always find a way in, specially if the weather's bad. You just look up and there they are. And they've tried everything to stop them. Even broadcast an alarm call — you know, the sound they make when they're frightened? But it was no use. Didn't seem to bother 'em. Drove us mad, but it didn't worry them! And ever so often . . .'

Lisa waited.

'They don't do any harm, you know. Only shit in your eye if you look up at the wrong moment.' He was staring into the fire. 'Ever so often one of 'em falls. Must be the fumes, I suppose. It can't be they just go to sleep because if they did they'd wake up when they felt themselves falling. And they don't. They fall like stones.'

She didn't know how to break the silence. 'What happens?' she asked.

'What do you mean, What happens?' He was grinning at her as if he hadn't a care in the world. 'They bloody burn, that's what happens.'

'They wouldn't feel nothing, though, would they?'

'Wouldn't feel a thing.'

He'd never talked about his job again. Or anything else. There were the morning silences. The evening drinking. Rows. Occasionally, violence. Nothing else.

Lisa was afraid. She didn't know how much there was left of the love she'd once felt for him. There were times when she hated him, times when she despised him. There were many, many times when she pitied him. But were there ever any times when she still loved him?

She lay awake for a long time, listening for the sound of his key in the door. But there was nothing, and at last she slept.

The dream woke her. She lay, still half-asleep, trying to recall the details. Something had been holding her too tight, squeezing her so hard that it hurt. But she couldn't remember what it had been. Nothing pleasant, anyway.

The empty bed didn't surprise her, and at first she thought Brian must have got up early, as he so often did. The early mornings were his worst time. He woke at four o'clock and could not get back to sleep. Then she remembered. Immediately, she pulled a sweater on over her nightdress and hurried downstairs.

He was asleep on the sofa. For a moment relief knocked the breath out of her. She could only stand and stare. A trickle of saliva had run out of the corner of his mouth and down on to the cushions. He looked like a sulky, disappointed boy. She went to pull the curtains back, but then stopped.

She could not bear the squalor of the ashy hearth. And she didn't want him to wake.

She didn't expect him to clear the kitchen up. She had told him to leave it. But she was still angry to find the mess untouched. There was another smell on top of the smells of

cold fat and stew: a thin, sour, acid smell. She went closer.
He had in fact tried to clear up the stew. Only the effort had
proved too much for his stomach. There was vomit there
now. On top of everything else.

Tea first. Definitely tea first.

She stood at the since to fill the kettle, and, as the ancient
plumbing groaned and shook, she felt a tightening of her
belly, the squeezing she remembered from her dream.

She knew it now for what it was. It was no more than
mildly painful yet she held on to the edge of the sink in
horror. It couldn't be. Not yet. Though why shouldn't it be?
She was already six days late. When it was over she put a
hand down between her legs and brought back a string of
translucent stuff rather like snot with a plug of dark red
blood at the end. Christ.

She felt the baby heave. She thought of Brian on the sofa
sleeping it off. She saw the mess of stew and vomit on the
floor. The situation was too horrific to be anything but
funny. She sat down at the kitchen table and laughed until
her chest ached. She wiped her eyes, made a cup of tea, and
carried it through into the living room.

'Hey up,' she said. 'I think I've started.'

She felt almost cheerful.

He woke with a start and stared wildly about him.

'I said, I think I've started.' He gaped at her. 'The baby —
Oh, here, have a cup of tea. I'll talk to you when you're
awake.'

Halfway up the stairs she yelled over the banister. 'And
clear that bloody mess up. I'm not doing it.'

Darren was cooing in his cot. He turned his head towards
her as she came into the room, and wriggled with delight.
Kevin was whimpering. Which meant he had wet the bed.

'Never mind, flower. You couldn't help it.'

As she picked him up another pain started. She buried
her face against the side of his neck until it was over, inhal-
ing his pissy-little-boy smell as eagerly as if it had been gas
and air.

They would have to go to their Grandma's while she was
in hospital. And, although they drove her to the edge of

desperation at times, she dreaded the separation from them.

If only she could have had the baby at home. One thing, she wasn't going to go rushing in. She would hang on at home as long as ever she could.

Iris King looked in that afternoon.

'I hear you've started.'

'Aye, and stopped again. Twice.'

'Aw, dear. It's awful when it's like that, isn't it?'

'You know, I feel now, if only it would get cracking . . .'

'You'll be having this'n in the new hospital?'

'Yeah.'

'Well, it's very nice up there. And one thing I will say, they don't leave you hanging about. If they don't think it's happening as quick as it should, they sharp shove dynamite up yer. I know. Our Lindsey had both hers in there.'

'I liked St Monica's.'

'Yes, well it was homely, wasn't it?'

'Oh, and they were good. Sister Richie was smashing. I tell you one thing, I'm not rushing in there.'

'No, don't you. Do you know, I had three kids in St Monica's and they never managed to shave me tash off once. There was never bloody time. I made sure of that. Sister Richie used to play war. She'd come to take the stitches out, you know. "What am I meant to do with this?" she says. "It's like hacking your way through the jungle." '

She shifted her considerable bulk around in the chair. 'Bairns gone to your Mam?'

'Yes. Brian took them. I didn't feel like going.'

'No. That's a nasty cut on your lip.'

Lisa flushed miserably. 'Yes, I walked into the coalhouse door. Last night, in the dark. Brian will leave it open.

'Sounds a bit like our Ted. He was forever leaving the coalhouse door open when we were first married. Till I fettled him.'

Lisa grinned in spite of herself. 'And how did you do that?'

'I took the meat chopper to him, love. Aye, you don't be-

117

lieve me, do you? But it's the truth.'

'Good afternoon, Mrs . . . ?'
   'Goddard.'
   'Goddard. Yes. Well, Mrs Goddard, Nurse tells me you've
been having a show?'
   'Yes. Since yesterday morning.'
   'Pains ?'
   'Off and on.'
   'Well, let me see.' He finished creaming the glove and
inserted two fingers into her vagina.
   'They were never really regular . . .' She stopped. His eyes
had a not-listening look. He was concentrating on whatever
his fingers were telling him. She tensed up a little as the
probing went on.
   'Try to relax. Bear down a little. Yes, yes.'
   He took off the glove. 'Well, Mrs Goddard. A week over
your date. Show. Pains, and I'm afraid . . .' He looked at her
card. 'I'm *afraid,* another little kick in your blood pressure.
I think we'd better have you inside.'
   She pulled a face.
   'Better to get it over with, isn't it?'
   'Yes. It's just . . . I've never really been in a hospital. I had
the first two in a nursing home.'
   'Yes. St Monica's. Well, I think you'll find you prefer the
new hospital.'
   She managed a smile. 'Yes. Like you say, it's better to get
it over.'

They had taken her name and address, her age, her religion and the date of her birth. They had written down details of her previous pregnancies. And of this pregnancy.
They had shaved her and poured pints, or what felt like
pints, of soapy fluid up her bum. They had draped her in
white and green cloths. They had raised her legs high
above her head, and fastened them into stirrups.
   Now she lay and looked at the doctor, whose head and
shoulders were framed by the deep V of her thighs. She
couldn't see his face, for he too was draped in white and

green, with a cap to cover his forehead, and a mask to cover his mouth. But she decided he looked kind. There were deep wrinkles at the corners of his eyes; they made him look kind.

Beside her, the nurse was getting the instruments ready. She heard the chink of steel. She felt the tightening of fear in her belly and looked up at the lights around the table: huge lights, like the one above the dentist's chair. She could see her reflection in the steel surround, but it was too far away and too distorted by the curve of metal to register anything so messily human as fear.

The doctor approached the table. 'Well, Mrs Goddard? And how are you today?'

'All right.'

'Let's see. This is the third . . . Third?'

'Yes.'

'Oh, well, then, you know what it's all about. I'm just going to break the waters. Shouldn't hurt at all. Might be a bit uncomfortable.'

He reached for a pad of cotton wool and began swabbing down the skin. Lisa winced and tried to pull away.

'Too hot? Sorry. Nurse!' He waited impatiently. 'It always amazes me, you know. In the bad old days when we used to stick a finger in the water to find out how hot it was, I never scalded anybody. Now I've got this marvellous little gadget for keeping the water at blood heat, I scald them all the time. Strange, isn't it? Nurse, wouldn't you say that was strange?'

The nurse obviously didn't know what to say.

'Pay no attention to me, my dear. I'm just an elderly Luddite. There, Mrs Goddard. Is that better?'

His eyes had acquired the familiar unseeing look as his fingers probed and delved.

'Bear down a little. Ah, yes. Not as . . .'

Lisa guessed from his tone that he was about to start. She closed her eyes. There was a fumbling at her skin, the coldness of metal, and then what felt like steel teeth began to nibble at the entrance to her womb.

'Just relax,' the nurse said. 'Breathe deeply.'

119

Finally the teeth got a hold, and bit. Instantly a warm, thick goo oozed out of her and down on to the bed.

'There.' He was already stripping off gloves and mask. 'There. Not too bad. Was it?'

'No.'

And it wasn't. It had hardly hurt at all.

The nurse gave her a sanitary towel and helped her off the table. One thing *hadn't* changed. You were still expected to keep the towel in position without benefit of pants or belt. She shuffled along the corridor to her room, like an old woman, hanging on to the wall for support.

'This is what I'm going to have when I have a baby,' the nurse said, sliding the needle into a vein and taping it down on to the skin. 'Speeds things up no end. You set them off at breakfast-time and the babies are here at tea-time. It's far and away better. You never get the cases of real exhaustion now like you used to get. Some poor girls, you know — they used to go days. You'd see them come up into the Consultant Unit and they'd be in a terrible state. You don't get any of that now. No.' She watched the clear golden fluid flow along the pipe. 'No. This is what I want. Either that or not come in till the head's there.'

The nurse waited with her for a few minutes to make sure that the drip was working, then left her alone. She lay and looked out of the window, waiting for the pain to start. But at first there was nothing. She had had no pains at all since she arrived at the hospital, though they had said that labour was about to start. She watched the drops of fluid flow along the plastic and into her arm. She was on the sixth floor. You could see nothing out of the window except clouds, clouds, and a solitary seagull riding the currents of air. The sunlight gleamed bonewhite on its breast and wings.

In the next room a woman who had gone into labour spontaneously the night before started to cry out as her labour advanced. There was an awful, familiar rhythm to her cries. Then came the trundle of wheels, a series of deep gasping breaths, and the 'singing' of the gas and air machine. With a preliminary tightening of the womb, Lisa's own labour began. The pains strengthened rapidly. From the beginning they were evenly spaced. This should have made them easier to deal with. But it didn't. They were harder to ride than those varied and unpredictable pains that come at the beginning of a normal labour. It was like trying to swim in a sea of corrugated iron. There was never any time when you could relax and allow the current to carry you.

The pains were stronger too. Very strong. There was something mechanical about their strength, their remorseless regularity. She felt them as extreme heat, as though she were being forced to stand too close to a furnace, to watch the door open, slowly, knowing that the heat would be strong enough to sear her eyeballs and burn her skin. Then as the contraction ebbed, as the door closed, came cold and ashen darkness.

This rhythm went on hour after hour for most of the day until her whole being was subdued to it. People appeared and stood by the bed, taking her temperature, her blood pressure, lifting her on to bedpans, listening to the baby's heart. At first she spoke to them, but as the day wore on speech became too much of an effort.

Dimly she realised that it was dark outside. There was a soft light on in the ceiling above her bed.

The doctor came. The sheets were pulled back. He waited for the current pain to die away, then delved deeply into her. The sister looked at him enquiringly and he answered with a barely perceptible shake of the head.

They changed the drip; the pains doubled and tripled in strength. The peaks were unbearable. Each one tore a cry from her lips.

Between pains, she said to the sister, 'I don't think I can stand this.'

'No, love. And I don't think you can either. I'll have a word with the doctor.'

Another needle; and, for a time, troughs of darkness between the glittering steel peaks.

Somebody pressed the mask down over her face. She tried to tell them she didn't want it, but it was too late. She heard a voice say, 'Come on. Make it *sing*. It won't work unless you make it *sing*.'

There was a moment of nausea as the room began to bend and shift around her. Then her head was free again.

'I don't really want it,' she said. 'I'm not in all that much pain.'

The worst of the pain was over now. The work had begun.

She lay with her legs in stirrups while they began the elaborate draping of cloths.

'I've got another pain coming,' she said.

'Well, push then! And again! Deep breath and hold. That's right. Shoulders back. Chin in.'

All the lights above the table were on. When she screwed up her face with the effort they exploded into little chips and splinters of light, so bright they hurt her eyes.

Rest.

Then another pain. She pushed and sweated and grunted, hearing the final shriek of exhaled breath dimly, as though some other woman was making these sounds.

When she opened her eyes again the doctor had arrived. She heard him say, 'All right, next time.' And saw the scissors. The next pain mounted to a swelling, gasping, bursting climax, in which her flesh was cut open, though she did not feel it.

'I'm going to give you a bit of help.'

She wanted to say, Oh no, but she couldn't. The next contraction had already begun. Now she sweated and laboured for delivery, bearing down as though the baby had to be forced through a solid wall of flesh. It was no good. She felt the head slide back.

Metal hands entered her, and, as the next pain swelled to a climax and she was told to stop pushing, guided the baby's head into the world. Water gushed out of her. Then a thin trickle of a cry, where only silence had been before.

The crying went on. A purple, howling dwarf appeared in the doctor's hands. Face grey-purple, blood-streaked.

Tiny hands clawing at the air.

A girl.

The nurse brought the baby for her to see, but briefly. It had to go to the Intensive Care unit. She craned her head to watch as it was taken away.

'Ten pounds,' somebody said. 'No wonder you had trouble.' The doctor sat between her legs, and sewed.

'How many stitches have I got?'

'Only five.'

In the next room somebody had started to groan. They all hurried away, leaving her alone.

Behind her head a clock ticked. She craned her head to see it. It was almost three a.m. The minute hand moved, not smoothly, but in a series of jerks. She lay and watched it until her neck was tired.

The lights were still on. They hurt her eyes. One of the drips in her arms had been taken down but the other remained. She found it difficult to move. Gradually, she realised that she wanted to be sick. There was a bowl beside her, but she couldn't reach it. There was a bell, too.

She couldn't reach that, either.

In the next room a woman screamed. There was a murmur of voices soothing her.

'Sister!'

She was afraid that if she vomited like this, lying flat on her back, she would choke.

After she had been shouting for what seemed like hours the Sister appeared. 'I'm sorry,' she said. 'There's nobody to wash you. You'll have to wait.'

'I think I'm going to be sick.'

The Sister came and moved the bowl closer.

'I'm sorry,' she said again. 'I'll send somebody in as soon as I can.' Her shoes squeaked out of the room.

Lisa lay with her eyes closed.

In the next room the unknown woman screamed again.

She was cold and shivery after she had vomited, and not all of it landed in the bowl. She wanted the lights to be switched off. She wanted somebody to come. Nobody did. She was alone with the whiteness of the walls.

At last a woman came. She was disgruntled because her 'dinner hour' had been interrupted. It was now four a.m.

'Where's your towel?'

'I'm sorry. I don't know.'

Her teeth were chattering. She could hardly speak.

The woman flounced out in search of it, every inch of an ample behind proclaiming that it wasn't *her* job to look for the patients' towels.

They took her not to the main ward, but to a single room. In spite of her exhaustion she could not sleep. Then, in the morning, they gave her some pills that kept her under for the rest of the day.

In the evening, her mother came. 'I've left Brian looking after the bairns. I asked him, Did he want to come, but he said no.'

'No, he wouldn't. He doesn't like hospitals.'

She could hardly keep awake. At last her mother said, 'I'm going now, Lisa. You have a little sleep.'

It was a relief to be alone.

Next day was Sunday. She lay with the *News of the World* unopened on her bed and watched the people going to Church. There were not many. After about an hour the doors opened again and they all streamed out. One woman wore a scarlet coat and hat, as bright as holly berries against the grey stone.

Lying there with the blood flowing out of her, she did not feel that she had given birth at all. It might as well have been an operation. There was no baby there. No babies anywhere, though sometimes in the distance she thought she heard one cry. Her room was a long way from the nursery. And the Intensive Care unit was on a different floor.

She had a clear picture of her own child, that howling dwarf who had clawed so desperately at the air, but it was encapsulated in her mind, unchanging, like the last glimpse of a person who has died.

One of the nurses went to see it. It had reddish-brown hair, she said. It looked as though it might be going to curl. Lisa listened dully. *Her* child had black hair, black and straight. She saw it again, wet and bloody from the womb.

124

No . . .

When she first learned she was pregnant she had asked for an abortion. Darren had been six months old. Kevin, two. The doctor had told her there were no grounds.

It might have died in labour. She knew they had been worried about it. Things had started to go wrong as soon as they strengthened the drip. The heartbeat had been too fast; the water had turned green. It could so easily have died.

Next morning at six the door was thrown open and a cot wheeled in. 'Here's your daughter!' the nurse said.

The baby was curled up asleep, mouth and cheek pressed out of shape by the mattress, bottom stuck up in the air. Lisa worked herself across to the side of the bed, grimacing as the stitches pulled, and stared at the child. Her hair *was* reddish, almost auburn, and, yes, it did look as though it might be going to curl. She saw blood pulsing across the opening in its skull. And drew back. There was nothing about this baby she recognised as hers. If she had been an animal she would have rejected it, would have sniffed at it and turned away, at once and finally.

Instead, she read the label on the cot. She read the label on the baby's wrist. Her mind told her that it was hers.

She found herself dreading the moment when it would wake up and demand to be fed.

There was nobody she could talk to. She listened as her mother and the nurses said what a beautiful baby it was. And prayed for the moment when she would be allowed home, when she would no longer have to lie in this little cell of a room, pretending.

When she was well enough, they transferred her to the main ward. Here at least there was the presence of other women to distract her, and by that time, too, she could move about more freely. She spent a lot of time in the dayroom, aimlessly flicking through old copies of *Woman* and *Woman's Own,* talking to the other women, waiting anxiously for the moment when she would have to go back along the corridor to feed the child.

They went together, a whole crowd of women in billowing, shapeless dressing gowns, smelling of milk and blood, walking with that curiously splay-legged, rolling gait that sailors and recently-delivered women share.

After the babies were fed, the women lay on their beds for an hour with curtains closed. There was supposed to be silence, but there never was.

As soon as the nurses had gone, Julie, married ten days and, at seventeen, the youngest woman there, sat up on her bed and looked out of the window. There was a building site immediately below.

'There's some smashing fellas down there.'

'You wait. One of these nights she'll be knotting the sheets together. We'll all wake up and find her gone.'

'I wouldn't mind. I'm sick of this.'

'Give us time to get me stitches out and I'll join you.'

This was Sonia, almost forty and the oldest by several years.

Lisa lay and listened. Normally she would have joined in, but the child, asleep in the cot beside her, dampened her spirits. Everything she saw or heard seemed to be taking place on the other side of a dirty window pane. So she lay and listened, passively.

'You've had your stitches out, haven't you, Maureen? What's it like?'

'Oh, just like plucking your eyebrows. It's nothing much.'

'You know that girl up the far end, her with the scar on her neck? They say she had it in the bath. Didn't know the head was there.'

'Gerraway.'

'Oh, I don't know . . . You talk to her.'

'My God, I bloody knew.'

'My husband's first wife only had a girl. You watch, when she finds out about him she'll be dead jealous.'

'Me Mam said if it was a girl I hadn't to bring it home. "Don't bring it round here if it's got a crack in it," she says. But I expect she'll come round.'

126

Brian came to see her twice in the first week.

'Well, how are the kids?' Her mother had told her, but she had to find something to say.

'Oh, they're fine. Darren's got a bit of a cough.'

'And you're looking after yourself all right?' He had refused to go either to her mother or to his own.

'Oh, yes. I'm all right.'

'You're getting your food, aren't you?'

'Yes.'

'Because you must, you know. You can't live on . . .' Beer she had been going to say.

'Your Mam always gives me something when I go over to see the bairns.'

He hardly looked at the child in the cot. She did not expect it. As this stage the children seemed hardly to exist for him at all.

She reminded him of what clothes she would need when he came to collect her. Then they sat in uneasy silence for a while, before both started to speak, simultaneously, on different subjects. She was restless all the time he was there and, although she did not know it, tense. Only after he had gone did she realise how talking to him had tired her.

She lay back in the bed — they always had to be in bed at visiting time — and closed her eyes. When she opened them again the baby was awake. It stared at her through the transparent side of its cot. Its eyes were still dark blue, birth-blue. It seemed to Lisa that somewhere in their depths was the beginning of pain, a bewilderment that mirrored her own. To the very depths of her soul she felt guilty. Yet she in no way neglected the child, was more than once told off for nursing it too long after a feed. She felt compelled to stare at it, to stare, and go on staring, as though the thin purple eyelids with their network of flickering veins was a code that she had to decipher or die. Afterwards she could not remember what she thought of at such times, though her mind was certainly not blank. There seemed to be a great pressure of painful feelings, aching like matter in a boil, too confused to be expressed.

She had not wanted this child. If she had had the courage

to express her deepest feelings, her gut reaction, she would have said to the nurses, 'Take it away. It isn't mine.' But of course they would have thought she was mad.

She did not for a second believe that there had been any actual mix-up in identities. It was simply that she could not believe the child was hers. There was no point in trying to talk to anybody about it: she knew she would not be able to convey the sheer force of her feelings without sounding either deluded or callous. She remembered her grandfather: he had had a stroke, a bad one, though he had lingered on for many months after it. He had not been able to accept that his left arm belonged to him. In the beginning, while he was still very confused, he had actually struggled with it, trying to force it out of the bed. Later, he had lain quietly, apparently accepting what his eyes and his reason told him must be true. But Lisa had seen him, sometimes, when he thought no one was looking, turn on that arm a glance of fear and distaste.

She felt like that now.

She heard the other women talk, counting the days and hours to their release. They were all, without exception, looking forward to going home. Lisa dreaded it. It took her all her time to cope with Kevin and Darren, whom she loved. How would she manage to care for this baby for whom she felt nothing? Its weakness terrified her.

She felt an enormous distance between them, and saw no way of crossing it.

Once and once only she felt a stab of recognition. One of the Sisters asked if she could borrow the baby to give a demonstration bath. Seeing it, red and howling, struggling in the nurse's hands, Lisa thought, Yes. And when it rose from the bath with dark and streaming hair the pain was so extreme that she had to turn aside; she could not bear to look.

The feeling vanished. But it had given her hope. The time she spent simply staring at the baby increased. And then one day, as she was changing its nappy, she found a smear of blood on the cloth. She parted the lips of the vagina and there was more blood. Her heart contracted with fear. She looked at the other women, each of them preoccupied with her own baby, and she could not tell any of them. She was afraid of what they might say. Nor could she put another nappy on the child and ignore the blood. In her heart she knew the baby had some terrible disease. She was to be punished.

At last a nurse came in. Dumbly, Lisa showed her the blood, and was startled when the nurse smiled.

'Oh, that. That's nothing to worry about. It's . . . well, in a way, it's her first period. All the female hormones in your blood get across to her, you see. Then when they stop, she starts to bleed. Just like a period. If she'd had a dirty nappy, you'd've been none the wiser.'

'You mean it's all right?' Lisa asked, still afraid to believe it.

'Oh, yes. It happens to every baby, every girl. Only normally, you don't see it. I don't see it all that often. And I change hundreds.'

'Then there's nothing to worry about?'

'Nothing at all.'

Lisa turned back to her child with a sense of relief, and wonder. She looked down at the baby and remembered that she had planned to call it Katherine if it was a girl.

Only somehow, she had never really believed it would be. She had not been ready for a girl.

Now that began to change. She felt a spurt of excitment, the feeling she had had for hours and hours after Kevin was born, so strong that it had kept her awake at night.

That little rounded stomach! The coil of dry and brittle cord! How strange that under that soft flesh there should already be muscles as strong as those which had thrust it into the world.

She picked the baby up, and felt it nuzzle and butt her neck as the automatic search for milk began.

'Greedy. You've just been fed.'

The child was warm against her skin, but she was back miles and miles away, back in her own childhood. She remembered how she and her brothers had gone bird nesting. She had always played with the boys, always been the tomboy of the family, in spite of the passion for dolls that had earned her childhood nickname: Doll.

They had climbed a stone wall up above Harrier's farm, right on the edge of the moors. They must have walked miles and miles that day. The boys had run on ahead but she had found a chrysalis clinging to the side of the wall and had stopped to examine it. Then, as she held it on the palm of her hand, it had begun to twist, curving into a crescent and rocking like a little boat. Some clear brown fluid had squirted out of it. Perhaps it was the warmth of her hand or perhaps she had picked it up just as the time came for it to split. She watched and felt it move. There was something wonderful about it; and terrible too. It squirted out more fluid and in a spasm of revulsion she threw it as far as she could across the heather.

Then she ran on to join the boys. Later that day in one of those meaningless orgies of destruction that children go in for, they smashed some of the carefully-gathered eggs, shouting and screaming, trampling on delicate chips of blue and white, smearing each other's faces and hair with yolk.

And she had shouted and screamed and smashed harder than any of them.

Now she held her daughter in her arms. And the thought that inside that tiny body was a womb like hers with eggs waiting to be released, caused the same fear, the same wonder. She walked across to the window holding the child in her arms.

The building site was deserted in the rain. There were puddles scattered over the gouged and rutted ground, looking like patches of trapped sky. Shadows of clouds and birds drifted across them.

My daughter.

CHAPTER FOUR
MURIEL SCAIFE

It had been raining heavily all day. The clocks had been put back only two days before and people were not yet used to the swift descent of twilight. They grumbled and looked pinched at the abrupt arrival of winter.

There were eight people huddled together in the porch of the doctor's surgery. It was difficult to move about without touching somebody else, a stranger, and so they looked down at their boots, or, vacantly, at the stripping trees.

One man poked his head out into the rain and said, 'I don't know. I can't see any sign of it.' But he was on the fringes of the group, able to move freely. Those at the centre, hemmed in by other people, felt a greater constraint and did not reply.

Muriel Scaife twisted her head round to look at her son. He was breathing on the doctor's brass plate and then rubbing the condensed breath away on his sleeve. Over the past year his nose and ears seemed to have grown out of proportion to his face, giving him a Mickey Mouse appearance that was both funny and pathetic. He didn't know what to do with his hands and feet and you could almost feel the spots pricking their way to the surface of his skin.

She said, 'Richard . . .'

Instantly he looked round at her and smiled. Then, aware of other people watching, blushed. It was an embarrassment to him, being seen to smile at his mother in a public place.

131

After a few minutes she felt him move closer.

'It won't be so bad,' he said.

'At least with Dad out of the way she'll only be able to go on about him behind his back.'

She looked at him gratefully. Richard seemed almost able to read her thoughts, to enter into the conflict of loyalties between her mother and her husband that was so painful to her. At times she wished he saw less. They were becoming too close. Too close for *his* good, at any rate. Once or twice recently she had caught herself thinking aloud in front of him, saying things that no twelve-year-old boy should be expected to understand.

'I'll be glad when it's over,' she said. 'Much as I love her.'

The bus arrived at last. Those getting on jostled those getting off and from the confusion an elderly woman emerged wearing a maroon-coloured raincoat and a professionally martyred expression.

After the greetings were over, after the usual comments on Richard's height had been offered and endured, they set off back to the house. Richard had reached the age when to walk with members of his own family, particularly his mother, was torture. He could not bring himself to walk beside her. Muriel, as she talked to her mother, felt her son tagging along behind, and her heart bled for him. But you couldn't say anything. He wouldn't thank you for it.

Richard, scuffing his feet in the gutter, was convinced that everybody who saw them was thinking, 'Oh, look, there's Richard Scaife. Funny you never see him with lads his own age. He's always trotting along behind his mother. Bit of a pouf, if you ask me. I mean it's not natural, is it?'

He found a stone and kicked it viciously across the street.

'. . . no worse than he usually is, Mam.'

'That's bad enough. Is he still smoking as much?'

'It's the only pleasure he gets. He says it eases the pain.'

'Does it hell! And it must be costing you a pretty penny. But then that's you all over. Too soft to make backsides of.'

Muriel lowered her head. Her mother's opinion of her intelligence had been made clear over many years.

'My stomach's bad 'n' all, you know. Some of us have to

carry on.'

'Well, Mam, if you get you can't manage there's a home for you with me. And it's not just me saying it, it's John as well.'

'Don't think I'm not grateful, but it wouldn't work and you know it wouldn't.'

'It's him, isn't it? You'd come to me like a shot if I didn't have him.' There was a long, dragging silence. Then Muriel said, 'Well, Mam, I can't bury me husband to please you.'

They turned into Union Street. It was full of women hurrying home from the shops to get the tea ready before the men came home. Muriel nodded or waved to the ones she knew.

'At least he minds the kids so I can work. I couldn't do the school cleaning if he wasn't there to keep an eye on them.'

'No sign of *him* going back to work, I suppose?'

'No.'

'Dear God.'

'He's bad, Mam. They wouldn't keep giving him the sick notes if he wasn't bad.'

'I blame meself. I should never've called you Muriel. It was always an unlucky name. God knows my mother never had any luck. And you couldn't say I did. And now you. Thank God you didn't lumber Sharon with it.'

'I wanted to. I wanted to call her Sharon Muriel. It was you put a stop to that.'

'She'll live to thank me for it.'

'It isn't names that does it, Mam.'

'Well, what does, then? Your father never worked. He doesn't work.'

'I don't know. Some people have it harder than others. That's all there is to it.'

'Well, I hope Sharon gets a husband what'll turn out.'

Richard listened to their talk but took no part in it. Everything seemed to be changing: nothing was safe or easy any more. Even his Gran. Once he'd looked forward to her visits. Now she seemed to have shrunk overnight into a silly, superstitious old woman, always going on about what she'd suffered.

Well, she had suffered.

Out of the corner of his eye he saw a gang of boys, two or three years older than he was, standing on the street corner. He cringed inside his coat, waiting for the jeers. They didn't come, because he was walking with his family.

Just as he had got himself safely past his mother turned round and said, 'Oh, look, Richard. There's Steve.'

'Yes,' he said. He hated her, then, because she couldn't see that for him the street was a dangerous place.

'You know, Mam, you forget one thing. John thinks the world of me. That makes up for a lot.'

'Gets the bairns here. Doesn't buy their shoes. If he give up smoking it might.'

'It's not all that much.'

'It's not what you buy him. It's what he sneaks out of you! I've seen him send the bairns out behind your back.'

'Not Richard.'

'Sharon. *And* she charges him for going. Only one in this family with any sense.'

They reached the house, took off their wet coats, and crowded into the back room together. The front room, with the three-piece suite John and Muriel had bought when they were first married, was never used.

'He's not here then?'

'No. He's gone to see their Betty.'

Silence.

'It's his sister, Mam.'

'Oh, I say nowt about that. She set on and brought them all up after their Mam died. He has a right to go and see her.'

So it went on. Tea was eaten and cleared away. Richard started on his homework. He couldn't avoid hearing most of the conversation, though he tried to shut it out.

'. . . and the bedsprings creaking. He's always on your bones, our Muriel, you know he is. You'd think when you have to get up and go to work at six o'clock he'd at least let you get your rest.'

'I am married to him, Mam.'

They'd forgotten he was there. Sometimes in the early morning, or late at night, Richard, too, heard the bedsprings creaking and it made him feel . . . excited, and ashamed at the same time. Sometimes he felt like playing with himself, but of course he couldn't. It would have been too much like joining in.

'That's the real reason you won't come to me, isn't it, Mam?'

'I couldn't stand it. I'd see you getting more and more worn out and I couldn't keep me trap shut. It wouldn't do.'

There was a long silence. Muriel stared into the fire wondering why John hadn't come home. He didn't like her mother, any more than her mother liked him, but he had promised to be back before she left.

Her Mam said, 'What's that you're studying, pet?'

Instantly, Muriel was on the alert to protect Richard, if he should need it. She saw him go tense. He seemed to dread questions about his school work almost as much as he dreaded comments on his changed appearance.

'Algebra.'

'And what might that be when it's all at home?'

Richard looked towards Muriel for help, but she didn't know the answer. He mumbled, 'Lettersinsteadofnumbers.'

'Oh. What's the point of that?'

'I don't know.'

'He has to do it, Mam.'

'I don't doubt it. I asked him what the point was that's all. I mean it's not like sums, is it? You can see the point of that. I mean, all this algebra and French and all that, but what's he going to do if he can't add up?'

'He can add up, Mam.'

'Not like your Dad, I'll bet. Your Dad could go down a column of figures like greased lightning. That's where he gets his brains from.'

'It's not from me.'

'You're right there. You stick in at your books, lad. *You'll* never have to work the way your Mam and me have had to work.' She lowered her voice. 'Pity Sharon's so slow. Still you've got it where you need it. He's the lad.'

Muriel listened, saying as little as possible. She was watching the clock, waiting for the moment when she could decently suggest a final cup of tea.

After she had seen her mother off from the bus station, Muriel walked back quickly through the misty October night, fully expecting to find her husband waiting for her when she got back. When he wasn't there, she felt a stab of misgiving, but pushed it to the back of her mind. It was no use worrying Richard, who was still wrestling with his whatever-it-was. She got the ironing board out and started work on a pile of sheets and pillowcases. From time to time as she worked she looked across at her son's bowed head. He ought to be in the street playing, as his sister was, but she had learned not to question him. He became irritable very quickly on the subject of homework and school.

They worked in silence. There was the roar of flames, the regular thump-thump of the iron on the board and an occasional sigh from Muriel as she bent down to pick up another sheet. When she sighed, Richard stirred and looked up. The iron was giving trouble again. She wetted her fingers on her tongue and tapped the base. The sizzle of spit reassured her.

'You can never tell whether this thing's hot or not.'

'It's clapped out. You want to get yourself another.'

'Oh, yes. I can see meself.'

As she ironed, her lips moved. The sight was a familiar one to Richard. It meant, usually, that she was at work on the endless sums of feeding and clothing four people on his father's sick pay. Her school-cleaning job didn't bring in much. The twitching of her mouth hurt him: it belonged to an older woman.

'He should be back by now,' she said, peering short-sightedly at the clock. 'Good God, is that the time?'

'He'll be all right.'

'Oh, he will, will he? He could hardly walk.'

'He's just making sure he stays out of Gran's way, that's all.' His mother went on standing there, blinking in her short-sighted, vulnerable way. It irritated him. 'You worry about him too much.'

Muriel opened her mouth to reply. Then shut it again, tightly. Only the heavier thumps of the iron on the board revealed her anger.

Richard went back to his Maths. It was his worst subject. He struggled with the meaningless squiggles on the page, trying to make sense of them. But his mother's uneasiness had communicated itself to him. There was a knot of anxiety in his stomach.

'He's mebbe stopped off for a drink,' he said at last, breaking a silence that had become intolerable.

His mother didn't reply at first. There was another silence, less strained now, and then she said, 'Oh I don't think so. He hasn't had a drink for months. He says he can't keep it down.'

'There's still plenty of time, Mam. He's been this late before.'

'You'll have to stop now, love. I need the table for supper.'

'I'll go upstairs.'

'Don't be daft, it's like a morgue up there. Surely you've done enough?' She looked at him, almost pleadingly. 'You seem to have been on with that for hours.'

'Yeah, O.K. It'll do.'

It wouldn't. But he could do the rest tomorrow morning in the cloakroom at school.

'You notice our Sharon's not back. She's staying out too late.'

Richard cleared away his books. Muriel started to lay the table.

'I wouldn't worry about him if he wasn't so yellow.'

'He's always been yellow.'

'No, he hasn't. You don't remember him when he was well.'

That was true. His father had been ill as long as Richard could remember. There had never been a time when he was not coughing, or holding his stomach, or complaining of this, that, or the other pain. Richard didn't take it very seriously. He had early adopted his grandmother's view of the matter: that there was nothing wrong with his father that hard work wouldn't cure.

The phlegm was the worst thing. Every morning his father brought it up, not in gobs and short, stringy bits as he did during the day, but in one long, sickening stream. Sometimes, when his mother had already left for work, Richard had to empty the bucket. He hated the job. He hated the blue stubble on his father's chin. He hated the foul smell of his breath.

Now, remembering those mornings, he looked down at

the fork he held in his hand. Like everything else in the house it dated from the time of his parents' marriage. There were bits of yellow showing through where the chrome had worn away. And suddenly he wanted to sweep it all aside — the little table, the knives and forks, the photos on top of the telly, the whole too-small, too-cosy room. It seemed to have shrunk around him, to fit too tightly, like a garment that might tear if he tried to move.

Half an hour later they were still waiting. Muriel no longer tried to convince herself that nothing was wrong. John should have been home hours ago.

'Well,' she said. 'It's no use just sitting here. I'll go and look for our Sharon.'

'I'll go.'

'No. You stop here.' She was already tying the scarf round her head. 'And she won't half get a piece of my mind when I find her. Worrying everybody like this.'

She paused on the doorstep of the house, catching her breath from the shock of wind and darkness. The Browns' house was opposite. They had still not had the window of the front bedroom repaired: she thought of the two girls sleeping in that cold room and her lips tightened. Neither of her two had anything like that to put up with, or ever would have, and she had less coming in than Mrs Brown.

As she looked, the door opened and Kelly Brown came out. What *does* she look like? Muriel thought, taking in the child's cropped hair and filthy clothes. 'Kelly,' she said.

The girl looked up. For a moment Muriel had the sense of a startled animal. Then Kelly hunched her shoulders and blinked. 'You haven't seen our Sharon, have you?'

'No.' She started to walk away. Then called over her shoulder, 'There's a whole gang of 'em on the corner of Alice Street. She could be there.'

Muriel hurried along the street, her anxiety quickened by the sight of Kelly and the memory of what had happened to her. But almost at once she heard the sound of children's voices and there was Sharon, playing with a group of other girls.

138

There was only one lamppost in Alice Street and the children gathered to play beneath it, while the great swoop of rain and darkness stretched away from them on every side. Muriel was about to call Sharon, but then she stopped, her imagination kindled by the group of figures in the circle of light. One girl was poised to enter the rope; the others chanted round her:

> There is a Maid lives on the Mountain.
> Who she is I do not know.
> All she wants is gold and silver.
> All she wants . . .

Their voices, as they sang the ancient words, were quick and passionate; their faces vivid under strands of rain-darkened hair.

When Sharon left the game, red-faced and protesting, Muriel could sympathise. The chanting took her back to her own childhood: the games, the fights, forged and broken friendships, love and betrayal and hate. As they walked home, she tried to take refuge in memories of that past.

But it was no use. She thought of Kelly leaving the house alone.

'I notice Kelly wasn't with you,' she said. 'Doesn't she play with you any more?'

'She doesn't play with anybody.'

Muriel looked down at her daughter's fair hair, still pulled back into childishly fat plaits, and wondered how much the other children knew.

'Your Dad isn't back yet.'

'Isn't he?'

She wasn't interested. She was still looking back over her shoulder at the little circle of light, dwindling away into the darkness. The singing had started again. Muriel sighed. Perhaps it was just as well Sharon didn't worry. It was bad enough to have herself and Richard twisted up — probably over nothing. He might be there when they got back. She walked more quickly.

But he wasn't. She swallowed her disappointment, and

hurried both children upstairs to bed.

After they had gone, she got together everything they would need for school the following day. She left the house by six o'clock, and John was in no state to deal with an outcry over a missing sock or tie. She picked up Richard's algebra book and put it in his satchel. It was better not to leave books lying round where John was: he hated them so much.

It had taken her a long time to realise why. When they were first married and letters came through the post John had always said to her, 'No, you see to it.' She hadn't thought anything about it: she took it for granted that she should settle the bills and write whatever had to be written. Then, for the first time, she'd tried to get something on the H. P. And that night she'd said to him, 'You'll have to have a look at this, John. I can't make head nor tail of it.' And she'd shown him the agreement.

To her surprise, he thrust it roughly away from him. 'You shouldn't get the stuff if you can't figure out what to do about it,' he said. 'I'm tired. A man doesn't want to come in from work and start puzzling his head over that rubbish.'

It was the first time she'd had anything from him but gentleness. She went very quiet.

After a long silence, he said, 'Well, lass. I suppose you had to know, didn't you? I can't read.'

'But . . .'

He looked at her. She went quiet again. He'd sat and read the paper, *seemed* to read it, many a time. She'd seen him stop and buy a paper on his way to work.

'I've never let on to anybody. I've always . . . Ever since we were married, I've dreaded the post.'

It dismayed her, that he should have been hiding this fear, when she'd thought they were happy. She said as much.

'But we *were* happy. And we still will be. If you can put up with a thick husband.'

''Tisn't to say you're thick 'cause you can't read. You can reckon up as good as anybody.'

'No, but it's always there. I live in dread of folks finding out.'

'Well, it doesn't matter to me.'

'That's easy said.'

'You don't want to let it bother you.'

Later that night, when she was standing at the sink washing up, he had come up behind her and cupped his hands round her breasts. 'I can't be all that thick can I?' he said. 'Or I'd never have married you.'

It had never mattered to her that he couldn't read. She read things to him, and they figured it out between them. If anything, it had brought them closer together.

After tidying round the room, she sat down by the fire to wait. The house was peaceful all around her, full of firelight and sleeping children. She was tired after her long day: the warmth and the roar of flames made her drowsy. Yet, beneath the surface of her mind, something that could not be so easily lulled roused itself to keep watch. She had never been able to take happiness for granted, perhaps because she had lost her father while she was still a child. She must always be aware of time passing, of the worm that hides in darkness and feeds upon innocence, beauty and grace. John's hands on her breasts, the children asleep upstairs: nothing was to be taken for granted. Love, security, order: these were achievements painfully wrested from a chaos that was always threatening to take them back. She remembered the children playing in the lamp-light. Life was like that. *Her* life was like that. A moment in the light. Then the lamp goes out, the circle is broken, the chanting voices are silenced forever.

She was being morbid. She was letting John's absence prey on her mind. In a moment, she told herself, she would get up and turn the telly on. The room would be full of flickering light, there would be no more pressure of darkness, no more sense that life is threatened, no more feeling that you must stay awake to guard it.

They brought him home shortly after eleven o'clock. Two of his mates had found him clinging to the railings outside the station. Until then everybody had walked past him, taking it for granted that he was drunk.

'It's lucky we happened by,' one of the men said. 'He

could easy been stuck there all night.'

They had a struggle to get him up the passage. His legs buckled underneath him or shot out at extraordinary angles.

'Hey up, Jack!' They lowered him into the armchair, their faces set from the strain, for he was a big man, though the illness had stripped flesh from his bones.

'I'd no idea he were as bad as this.'

They stood there, a little shy in the house they had never entered before. The younger man said, 'Have we to get the doctor for him, Missus?'

John started to gasp and struggle.

'No, thanks. If he needs the doctor I can easy send our Richard round.' Seeing them look doubtful, she said, 'I've seen him as bad as this before.'

After they had gone, she came back into the room and said, 'All the same, they're right. We've got to get the doctor in, John. You can't go on like this.'

'What can he tell me I don't know already?'

'It's not what he can tell you. It's what he can do for you.'

'Aye. Nowt.'

She was kneeling beside him, trying to smile. He mustn't know how much his appearance had shocked her. Perhaps it was only because he was so short of breath, or perhaps it was because she had been away from him all day and so saw him with fresh eyes, but to her he looked like death. His face was the colour of old newspaper. The bones of his skull jutted out. When he smiled, his lips stretched out like a band of fraying elastic. He looked as if he would never get his mouth shut again.

'I'm surprised your Betty letting you come home, the state you're in.'

'Nay, lass, don't blame our Betty, it was me. I knew you'd be worried. All I could think was, I must get home.'

'All the same.'

'I know what he'll say. I know before I go, so there's no point in going, is there? "Take it easy." "Drink plenty of milk."'

'I'll go with you.'

'Nay, lass, you've got enough to do. More than enough.'

They had a cup of tea together. His lips twisted with pain as he drank. Before the cup was finished he was asleep, his head slumped forward on to his chest.

Reluctantly, she shook him awake. 'Come on, John. Howay up to bed. You'll feel better once you're lying down.'

'You go on up. I won't be a minute.'

When she woke, hours later, the space beside her in the bed was still empty. She went downstairs, in darkness, because she was afraid of disturbing the children.

He had built the fire up and was sitting over it, half-asleep.

'John. What *are* you doing? Look at the *time*.' She went across to him. 'Come on up to bed.'

'No!'

He struck out at the arm she tried to put round him. She stepped back, shocked into silence. In all their married life he had never hit her.

'No,' he said again. 'You go back upstairs. Go on, now. I'm best off where I am.'

The following day she came hurrying in from work to find Betty sitting on the arm of his chair. Betty was a big, jolly woman, not unlike Iris King. As a child of twelve she'd been left to bring up a family of younger brothers and sisters. In return they all adored her.

There was a lot of laughter that tea-time. Even Richard, coming in from school with a pile of homework, joined in. Listening to that joyous, yelping laugh of his, Muriel realised how rare a sound it had become. But her eyes were mainly on John. Betty had the rest of them in stitches, taking off people they'd known.

Muriel put on her coat and scarf to see Betty to the bus stop. Normally the two women were suspicious of each other, each a little jealous of the other's relationship with John. But today they set all that aside.

'I had to come. Last night, well, I didn't think he'd get home to tell the truth. But he would go. There was no stopping him. He says two of his mates got him home.'

'Yes. He was lucky they happened by. It could've been a lot worse.' Muriel paused, looking down towards the High

Street. 'He didn't go to bed last night.'

'I wondered about that.' Betty's lips twitched. 'That's me Mam all over. She was like that. You couldn't even get her to sit down to begin with. No, she stood. Bolt upright. And all you could get out of her was, "I'm not going to bed. If I go to bed, I'll die." And when she lay down we knew that was it. That was the finish. All the Hodgkins go like that.'

'He's not going anywhere.'

'I never got it, you know. I was only twelve. Younger than your Richard. Oh, I know, I like a laugh, I don't give a bugger for anybody, but I've never got over it.'

'John's not going.'

Betty looked at her in silence. And in silence they waited till the bus came.

As she got on, Betty turned and looked back. 'You don't want to listen to what he says, you know. You get the doctor in.'

'Well, has he been?'

Richard threw his satchel down, and lowered his voice in response to a warning glance from Muriel. 'Well, has he been?'

'Yes. He come this morning.'

Richard waited for more. Muriel went on laying the table.

'What did he say?'

'Hospital.'

'Oh.' He took his time absorbing the information. 'When does he have to go?'

'He says he's not going.'

Her voice was flat, apparently indifferent. Looking closer, Richard saw that she was on the verge of tears.

'But if the doctor says he has to . . .'

'Well, he won't go. And that's that. I can't make him.

He didn't know what to say.

'Here, tek and give him this. I'm late enough as it is.'

'You're not going to work?'

'Of course I'm going to bloody work!' The futility of the question made her angry. 'We've got to live, haven't we?' She was already knotting the familiar scarf under under

144

her chin. 'And tell our Sharon not to go too hard at them mince pies. I don't know when I'll be able to bake again.'

Richard carried his father's tea through into the living room and put it on his lap. This was the time of day he dreaded most: his mother at work, Sharon out playing, himself and his father cooped up together, silent and ill at ease.

He got out his books and spread them over the table. He sat down, trying not to hear the steady chomp-chomp of his father's jaws, the disgusting way he swilled tea around an already-too-full mouth. He could feel the tension. He could feel how his father hated the books. He wasn't just indifferent to them, he wasn't neutral: he really hated them.

When he sat looking at the newspaper, as he sometimes did, his eyes did not move across the page. Richard had noticed this, but didn't know what it meant. Bills, letters, all that sort of thing, his father passed over to his mother. It was as though anything that involved reading or writing was woman's work.

So it was always like this in the late afternoons.

John Scaife hardly knew how it had come about. He knew only that he hated the books which were almost instruments of torture to him, so keenly did he remember the humiliations of his school days. Once and once only had he dared to show interest and that was because the book his son was reading seemed to be full of pictures.

'What's that you're looking at, son?'

'Nothing.'

'Well, it must be something.'

'It's nothing to do with school. It's from the library.' He stared at his father, defensively. 'It's about birds.'

'Birds!'

'Yes.' Briefly he showed a picture of some long-legged, white bird in flight.' That's a heron.'

'Not a lot of use that, round here.'

For there were no birds. Only sparrows and starlings. And seagulls of course.

'I like the pictures.'

'Ah, well.' John rustled his newspaper uneasily. 'Only birds I ever fancy are in here.' And he showed a picture of a woman with big breasts, smouldering on page three.

As soon as he had done it he was cursing himself. He saw Richard flinch and look away. He was at that awkward stage of early puberty: wincing, hypersensitive, fastidious. It was the last thing he should have said. Crude. Unnecessary. Not even true. What he wanted was to meet the boy on common ground: to share jokes and interests, to introduce him to the world of work, pub, football. But he couldn't do it. Of course the boy was too young, but that was the least of it. His feet were set on a different path.

Out of fear John did all the wrong things. He would hawk phlegm up whenever his son was in the room, or lift one buttock from the chair to fart, or wander round in his underwear with his scraggy chest showing, and the varicose veins in his legs. And when he saw the boy's involuntary recoil it was almost a relief.

Now he was ill and there was very little time left.

Richard heard his father clear his throat several times Then, almost humbly, John asked, 'What's that you're studying, lad?'

Richard looked up, uncertainly.

'Latin.'

'Oh. Latin.'

There was silence. Each of them searched for something to say. If only it had been something else. Arithmetic. Geography. Even French.

'It's quite easy.'

Now he sounded not just unfriendly but stuck-up as well.

There was no doubt about it, the lad had brains. At first, when he'd gone to the big school, John had tried to damp down Muriel's enthusiasm. She had poured her soul into the boy, and John was afraid she was going to be disappointed.

'Don't build on it,' he said. 'There'll be a lot of clever lads up there. You can't expect him to stand out there, the way he did in Ewbank Street.'

But, it seemed, Richard did stand out. He won prizes, he came first or second in nearly everything. But instead of making him relax, it only seemed to make him work harder, as if his whole life was geared to marks and percentages and prizes.

He was jealous. That was what they all thought, even Muriel. And perhaps he was, a little. Of the boy's chances, but also of the school, the part the school played in Richard's life.

'You know Dad, you'd be a lot more comfortable in bed. Why don't you go up? And I'll make you another cup of tea.'

'No. I'll stop where I am.' A pause. 'Thanks, lad.'

Over the next few days, John became worse. Sometimes, particularly if he had had something to eat, he would actually cry out in pain. Muriel tried to persuade him that the doctor was right, that he would be better off in hospital. He didn't argue with her, simply shook his head and waved her away. He needed all his concentration, all his strength, to cope with the pain. It was right what Betty said. He was like a sick animal that will not lie down, but sweats and strains to stay on its feet.

Muriel was worn out by it. After the first night she did not leave him at all, but slept on the sofa with a blanket thrown over her. She never got much sleep, though at six o'clock every morning she got up and went to work as usual.

One day, John, coming into the kitchen on his way to the toilet, found her crying.

'You go to bed tonight, lass. There's no need for you to stop up with me.'

'I'm not leaving you.'

She brushed the tears away, angry with him for finding her like this.

'I can manage on me own, you know.'

'Yes, I'm sure.'

John slept — if he slept at all — in the armchair, with Muriel's coat over him. She had offered him an eiderdown, which would have been warmer, but no, he wanted the coat. It smelled powerfully of fish and chips, more faintly of scent. The scent was Ashes of Violets. It was what she put on when she went up to Richard's school, that and a dash of lipstick, smeared carefully on to her lips and rubbed into her cheeks.

147

Muriel lay on the sofa. It was made of leather, cracked in some places, rubbed thin in others, and had not been new even when they bought it. They had made love on this sofa when they were a young married couple. Comfort hadn't mattered so much in them days. In fact she was pretty sure Sharon had been started on it. And she'd lain there in the early stages of labour, putting off the moment when she'd have to give in and go to hospital. It had seen so much of her married life. While she lay on it, nothing terrible could become real.

Though John's breathing rasped in the darkness, with unnervingly long pauses between one breath and the next.

Muriel could not sleep.

Once, John got up to use the bucket. It was too cold for him to make the journey across the yard at night, though he still insisted on doing it by day. Muriel screwed up her eyes against the light and turned to face the wall. The sight of her husband's wasted body frightened her. The light went out again. The night wore on. Muriel didn't think she had slept at all, because there seemed to be no time when she was not aware of the roaring of the fire and her husband's gasping breaths. But she must've done, because when she next looked at the clock hours had gone by.

She got up and tiptoed across to the mantelpiece to check on the time. While she was there, John gasped again, louder than before. Muriel turned to look at him. His face was just visible in the grey light that had begun to seep through the curtains. And for the first time she began to doubt what the doctors told him. Was it just ulcers? Was he going to get better? He looked like death. She waited for the next breath. It came with a shudder that shook every bone in his body. Then his eyelids flickered open, his lips curled back to reveal rows of white teeth, years younger than the surrounding skin. 'Not yet,' he said, smiling. 'Not yet.'

Muriel didn't know what to say. Should she go back to the sofa and pretend nothing had happened? Or should she try and respond in some way to what John had now so openly acknowledged? In the end, she did neither. She sat down in the other armchair and said nothing.

'See if you can stir the fire up a bit, lass. It's burning dead.'

Muriel poked and battered at the ridge of coal. When she looked round again she could see John's face quite clearly in the leaping flames.

He was trying to say something. It was an effort. There was a crust of some yellow sticky stuff at the corners of his mouth and his lips were so dry they looked cracked. He had to ferret about with his tongue to find a passage for the words.

'Thanks, love. There's nothing beats . . . a good fire.'

Muriel waited. John's eyes had closed again. After a while, they flickered open. 'You'll be all right you know, Muriel. There'll be a pension. And if ever you wanted owt you'd only have to ask our Betty.'

'It's not the money.'

She wanted to fold him in her arms and cover his face with kisses, but she forced herself to sit still. His eyes closed again. Even when they were open, there was a milky bloom over their darkness.

'He's a good lad. You always thought I didn't care as much about him as I do about our Sharon. Go on, be honest, didn't you?'

It was too late for anything but truth.

'Yes,' she said.

John smiled again. Struggled for speech. 'Nay, lass. I think every bit as much about him. Somehow you can't show it with a lad.'

His eyes closed again. Muriel sensed that he had no clear idea of how much time had passed between one flicker of his eyelids and the next. When she was sure he would talk no more, she went back to the sofa and lay down again. Surprisingly, she slept.

In the morning everything was normal again. The fire had burned low. The room was ashen in the early-morning light.

John was asleep at last. Muriel started getting ready for work. She was just putting her tights on when John woke up.

'Muriel?'

'Yes.'

149

'Are you off to work?'

'Yes. Unless you'd like me to stop at home?'

'No, love. You go.'

'Is there anything I can get you?'

'I think I'll come on to the sofa. I'll be better lying down.'

Muriel came back into the room with a cup of tea. John sat up, cradling the cup in his hands, while the steam rose into his face. He didn't look such a bad colour as he had the night before. He'll get better all right, she thought. She was ashamed of the morbid thoughts she'd had during the night. But you got like that at night. Everything looked worse than it was.

'Are you sure there's nowt else you fancy?'

Dimly, from the street outside, came the sound of men's boots tramping up the hill to work.

John smiled; 'Do y' know, lass, I think I could fancy a bit of bacon.

He looked surprised, and pleased. Indeed his whole mood seemed to have lightened. He patted his stomach, almost boastfully. 'It's a bit easier this morning.'

And so, Muriel thought, tilting the frying pan so that the fat ran evenly across it, it's going to be all right. She would have him on his feet again by Spring. There was a thick rind on the bacon, which he didn't like. She reached for the kitchen scissors, and as she did so became aware of a glugging sound, like water hiccuping from a too-narrow pipe. It went on and on. Suddenly, she was afraid. She ran back into the living-room and there was John, blood gargling from his mouth. Above the black hole his eyes rolled about, frenzied and unseeing. The flow of blood seemed to have stopped. It was like nothing she had ever seen before: so black, so foul-smelling, it didn't seem like blood at all.

She cried, 'John. Oh my God, John,' and bent over him. As she did so, a second eruption began, pumping out thick, black blood all over his chest and neck. His eyes rolled again. He was choking on the blood. She began pulling huge clots of it from his mouth. It seemed the only thing to do, and while she was doing it, she did not have to see those eyes. Her fingers found a thick rope of blood, twined round

150

it, and pulled. The clot slid out of his mouth, with the sound of a sink coming unblocked, and after it flowed a frothy, bright-red stream of blood, looking almost gay against the blackness of the other blood.

John's head fell back against the pillows. White on white. Muriel thought numbly, Shock, and tried to pull the eider-down up around his chest. She was distressed to the point of panic when she could not lift the limp arms to push them inside.

She put her hand over her mouth to stop the twitching of her lips. Then she went to the foot of the stairs and yelled, 'Richard!'

He came down, buttoning up his shirt, and grumbling, 'Aw, Mam . . .' He stopped when he saw his father. She watched his face go very blank and smooth. He said, 'I'll go for the doctor.'

'No. The ambulance. The fish-and-chip shop have a phone. Keep banging on the door till they answer. They won't mind.'

She fell on her knees by the sofa, and said, 'Don't leave me. I couldn't live without you.'

A sound came from the open, blood-smeared mouth. But no words.

The ambulance came. He groaned as he was carried along the passage. Then there was the redness of blankets and John's face, ashen, as the men sweated and strained.

A little crowd had gathered. There was Iris King, and Mrs Harrison, and a couple of girls who had been on their way up to the cake bakery.

Muriel hesitated on the pavement, torn between the de-sire to go with her husband and the need to stay with her children. Though she did not know it, she was whimpering, her fingers knotted against her teeth. Iris King came run-ning across the road and got hold of her.

'Howay, Missus, you hop up into the ambulance. I'll see to the bairns.'

'I've left the gas on!'

'Don't you worry, I'll see to it. Go on.'

She remembered nothing of the journey, except the

151

groans that came out of John's mouth whenever the ambulance jolted over a bump in the road. She stared and stared at the red blanket. It must be red so that you didn't notice the blood, she thought dazedly. And got hold of John's hand, reassured by the contact, though the fingers were limp and cold.

Only much later, in the waiting room at the hospital, did she look down at herself, and realise that she was covered with his blood. The front of her cardigan had dried and stiffened. You could bend it like cardboard.

They were bringing him home. Muriel sat in the armchair by the fire, her fingers knotted in her lap. Iris King, who had come across to help scrub out the front room, stood just behind her chair.

Very faintly came the sound of a car, drawing up outside the front door.

'That'll be them now,' Iris said.

Muriel looked up. 'Then you'd better go and let them in.' The words dropped from her mouth like stones. 'Richard, you go.'

She wasn't so calm now. Even as she spoke, the flesh of her cheeks twitched and puckered like porridge coming to the boil.

'Come on, love,' Iris said.

Muriel didn't even look at her, just jerked her head back like a horse avoiding the bit, and went on staring at the door. 'Let them in.'

Iris went to open the door. Muriel followed her into the passage and saw a man with a bald head and a dark, formal suit. Behind him other men struggled and strained, lifting something heavy out of the van. She could hear a muffled exclamation, a word of warning; then the measured tread of feet. The afternoon was dark. Only the men's hands and faces and the white fronts of their shirts were clearly visible. These patches of whiteness came towards Muriel until suddenly, blocking out the light, there was the coffin, swaying and lurching over the doorstep and into the house.

The coffin lurched, the men staggered, as they tried to

turn the corner from the narrow passage into the front room. Muriel's hand held her lips together as the men slowly manoeuvred the coffin round. They were bowed beneath the weight. There was a smell of fresh sweat mingling with the heavier smell of lilies.

She backed away. In the doorway behind her, Sharon whimpered and hid her face in her hands. But Muriel had eyes for nothing but the coffin. It tilted dangerously again and the man with the bald head called out, 'Mind!' Suddenly, Muriel cried out and started to run, her arms and legs jerking like a puppet. Iris followed, and they ran out of the house, across the yard, and into the back. It was wash day. Sheets and towels and pillowcases were draped and hung out all along the alley. Muriel ducked and dodged between them as she ran, though the wet sheets slapped against her face, and the arms and legs of wet clothes twined themselves around her neck. It was a nightmare. Then Iris caught her, and wrapped her broad arms round her.

'Where you going, love?' she said.

'I don't know.'

It was a wail. She would have liked to throw back her head and howl.

'Howay home.'

Iris tightened her grip on Muriel's shoulders, and they walked back up the alley together.

She made herself go into the front room to see him in the end. She and Iris had scrubbed and polished that room until it shone. Now she could see nothing in it but the coffin. It was so big. So big. The lid was off now and there was a white cloth over his face.

Betty stood at the head of the coffin and pulled the cloth back for her to look. She felt a great surge of relief, for it wasn't John lying there. It was somebody else. Nothing like John. She thought, They've sent the wrong body. She opened her mouth to tell them, but something stopped her, something that knew this was John.

'Doesn't he look peaceful?' Betty said. She bent over the sunken ivory face. 'You'd think he'd just this minute gone to sleep.'

Immediately, a mad hope flared in Muriel. Suppose he wasn't dead? Suppose he *was* just asleep? But the yellow cheek was cold and spongy to her touch. It didn't feel like skin at all.

She wouldn't accept what her eyes and hands told her. She said, in an irritated voice, 'Come on now, John, this has gone far enough.' Dimly she was aware of startled looks from the other people in the room. She neither knew nor cared who they were. She was beginning to get angry. 'Come on, now,' she said again. And she began pulling his head and shoulders, to make him get out of the coffin.

Hands pulled her away. And there was Betty, hissing and spitting, 'Get a grip on yourself, woman. At least think of the child.'

She saw Richard's face, stricken, as if he had seen her doing something obscene. She couldn't understand what was happening. She didn't know who all these people were. She turned and walked stiffly out of the room.

One by one the neighbours came in to see him. Muriel could not bring herself to go in with them. Always there was the flare of hope when she saw the face. It wasn't John. Or if it was John, he was only asleep. Hope wore her out, faster than grief.

It was Richard's job to take the neighbours in to see his father. He lifted the cloth back from the dead face, and his own face remained expressionless, though inwardly he was shaking with horror. He had not been afraid before, but he was afraid now.

People talked about sleep and death as if they resembled each other, but it wasn't true. This yellow doll, it didn't look like a man. It didn't look as if it ever had been a man. And, having seen it, he knew, not as some vague generality, but as absolute, inescapable fact that one day he too would die. His father's death left him exposed. There was nobody now to stand between him and that great void. Young though he was, he was the next in line.

His grandmother came to see his father. She stood looking at the old enemy for some time. Then, pursing her lips, said, 'Well, he looks lovely. I will say this: you can rely on the Co-op to do a good job. I had the Co-op when your Grandad died.'

Afterwards, he heard her talking to his mother.

'I don't know what you're thinking about, our Muriel, letting a child that age do that.'

His mother's voice said dully,'He's better with something to do.'

'He could've come to me till it was all over. Both of them could. You went to your Auntie May's when your father died.'

Later he said to his mother, 'I am going to the funeral, aren't I?'

She looked away from him. 'No, love, I think it's best you stop here. I need somebody to look after the house.'

He didn't argue. It was his grandmother's doing. He knew that.

For Muriel, the funeral passed like an unhappy dream. All the curtains in the street were drawn. Iris King and Mrs Harrison had gone from door to door collecting money for a wreath. And the church was full of her neighbours, standing a little towards the back, at a respectful distance from the family. Everybody seemed to have a cold. At every pause in the service the church was full of the sound of coughing.

The Vicar, too, had a cold. Once outside, he hurried through the remainder of the service, almost gabbling the words. There were specks of rain on the cellophane sheet he held over the page. The tip of his nose, which he rubbed repeatedly with his handkerchief, was as red, as raw-looking, as the clods of clay he threw into the grave. Muriel looked down at the coffin, and tried to imagine John's face as the earth thudded down on to the lid. And again she thought, He's alive. But the thought was dull and heavy inside her.

She went back to work the following day. The children went back to school. Nothing had changed. Everything had changed.

The numbness that had carried her through the funeral lasted several more days. Then one afternoon — John had been dead just over a week — there was a knock at the door. A young man stood there, a young man with ginger hair, and freckles on a dead-white skin. She stared at the freckles, she might almost have counted them, but it was an effort to concentrate on the words that were coming out of his mouth. He was saying that he had brought the things from the hospital. She remembered that she had promised to collect them: it had slipped her mind till now. She held out her hands for the parcel.

But when she had carried it back into the living room she did not want to open it. Instead she walked restlessly around the room, staring at the brown paper as if it concealed a bomb. At last she said, aloud, Oh, don't be silly, and, fetching the kitchen scissors, cut through the string and tore the paper off. There were his blue and white striped pyjamas, his battered leather shaving case, and his slippers. She pushed her face into the pyjamas and breathed in: there was the smell of his body, the smell of sickness, and the lingering, foreign smell of rubber sheets. The slippers. She had meant to buy him another pair this Christmas: these were a disgrace. The sole of one of them was actually hanging off. It lolled towards her like a tongue, and immediately she saw John's tongue, trying to clear a passage for the words to get out.

And then she burst. She told Betty about it afterwards. She said, 'I just burst. There was this horrible crying and I knew it was me and I couldn't do anything about it. I was telling him I loved him. Stuff like that. I was telling him to come back. And talking to him, and all the time I knew he was gone.' She ran down the yard to the lavatory and hung over the bowl to retch.

She was glad it hadn't happened when the kids were at home.

She tried to keep busy and, at work, succeeded. But at home she wandered from room to room, starting on a job only to abandon it half-finished. She seemed to be looking for something, but she didn't know what it was. And she listened all the time for John's voice. Even outside the house she went on searching. She had to look at the face of every man she passed in the street, though she knew that none of them could be John. And it was the same in the supermarket. Every time a man walked past she had to turn and stare after him. Once, she saw a man disappearing around the corner of the street and something in the set of his shoulders reminded her of John. Before she knew what she was doing she had started to run, and was pulling at his sleeve. Then there was the stranger's face, enquiring and concerned, a little embarrassed, perhaps. And she opened and shut her mouth, but no words would come. In the end she mumbled an apology, and turned away.

But that night, as she sat alone, her cheeks burned with shame. He must've thought she was mad.

She tormented herself going over the past. She shouldn't've sent him to hospital. He was dying anyway. He wanted to die at home. And she should never've left him. She had not been there when he died. She had gone to the waiting room to lie down for an hour, because she knew the end was close. And during that time he had died. She blamed herself. He might have recovered consciousness. He might have wanted to say something to her. She would never know.

Her mother came to see her every weekend, but they were often on the point of quarrelling. The old lady's conviction that her son-in-law had enjoyed excellent health, though a little shaken by his death, was by no means overcome. She tended to minimise her daughter's loss, to hurry Muriel along the road to recovery long before Muriel was ready. There was no open breach, but the relationship between them was more distant than it had ever been.

Muriel was left alone. People said, Well, at least you've got the children. But the children were no help. At times she felt the additional burden of *their* grief was more than she could bear. Sharon was easy enough. She simply retreated into babyishness, sucked her thumb and followed Muriel around like a young child. It was Richard.

He had caught a cold while his father was ill. It didn't get better but seemed to settle in his throat. He was permanently hoarse and although she took him to the doctor and got some pills, they didn't seem to do him any good. It was difficult to get him to take them. He, who had been so grown-up during his father's illness, such a help, really, was now withdrawn and uncooperative And he had developed a fascination with fire. On the night of his father's funeral, when she was exhausted and longing for bed, he had insisted on staying up to watch some film; and she had come downstairs to find a fire blazing halfway up the chimney and Richard crouched over it, throwing handfuls of salt into the flames.

She was afraid to leave him alone in the house. Yet twice every day he had to be left alone: in the early morning, and again the evening, when she was cleaning at the school.

Iris King rescued her from this dilemma by offering to have the children in her own house before and after school. But this could only be a temporary solution, because Iris, who would not accept payment, could not be allowed to go on doing it for nothing. Muriel wondered whether she should get a job cleaning in a pub, where the hours would be more convenient. But she dreaded making the change. It was better at the school where she knew all the other women and got on well with them. And there was another thing. John would not have wanted her to work in a pub.

She looked forward to the evenings when the children were in bed, though sometimes she was so tired that she went to bed almost immediately after them. They were all sleeping in the back bedroom: Muriel could not face the double bed alone. She lay and listened to the children's breathing. At least they could sleep. She could not sleep. Or if she did her sleep was disturbed by nightmares. She never dreamed directly of John's death, but always there was a sense of foreboding. And once she saw him in his coffin, and when she bent down his hand came up and stroked her face.

From these dreams she awoke with a cry and lay sweating in darkness, wondering whether she had woken either of the children. She lay and listened to their breathing. When she was sure they were still asleep, she turned over on to her side.

If only the night would pass. At night the line between reality and nightmare was blurred. She convinced herself that he had been alive when they put him into the earth. She saw him, in the darkness, begin to stir and open his eyes. She got up to face the day, most of her energy already spent in a battle with shadows.

Guilt was the hardest thing to bear. She should not have let him go into hospital, not when he was dying anyway. Though they had been able to give him injections. She couldn't've done that. He'd only said one thing to her after he went in. His eyes had opened and he'd said, Oh, Muriel, however are you going to manage? Oh, she'd said, don't you worry about that. Just you think about getting better.

His last thoughts, before he lost consciousness, had been of her.

She heard him moving about the house. Downstairs in the living room, poking the fire. At night, in the other bedroom, beating the pillows into shape. He had been such a restless sleeper. She lay and listened and heard him cough. The cough went on and on. Stop it, she said. Oh, please God, stop it.

It was no use. She had to go. In the door of the front bedroom, she stopped and called his name. Softly, so as not to wake the sleeping children. 'John? John?'

Darkness, then silence, answered her. She went into the room and drew back the curtains. Moonlight fell onto the counterpane and quickened the depths of the mirror. She sat on the bed and tried to think small, practical thoughts about changing her job, and Richard's tonsils, and whether she should take him back to the doctor. But gradually, as she continued to sit there, the moonlight peeled all such thoughts away, stripping her to the one.

She looked at the bed. Once, newly-married, the first shyness over, she had run her hands over his whole body, every inch of it, down to the spaces between his toes, and he had lain and looked up at her, half-delighted, half-afraid.

Where was he now? In your mind. In his children. Mechanically, her brain supplied the answers. They were not enough. Her mother believed in reincarnation. Her father hadn't believed in anything. He'd thought that when you were dead, that was it, you were finished. What did *she* believe? It was such a muddle inside her mind. She didn't know what she believed.

There was a footstep outside on the landing. She looked towards the door, hope flaring up again in defiance of reason. But it was only Richard.

'I heard somebody moving about,' he said. 'I didn't know who it was.'

She saw that he had been frightened. Poor Richard, with his enormous hands and feet, and his voice that squeaked whenever he was trying to sound particularly grown-up: this couldn't've come to him at a worse time. She had been about to answer him, impatiently, she often did now, though it was not what she wanted to do. Instead, she patted the bed beside her. He came and sat down and she put her arm around his shoulders. She could tell from the vibration of his chest that he was crying, though he made no sound.

'We ought to go back to bed, you know. Sharon'll be frightened if she wakes up. And you've got school in the morning.'

'Yes, I know.'

But they went on sitting side by side.

'By the way, I've got your blazer back from the cleaner's. Do you know what they charged me for it? 70p. They think they can get away with anything.'

'Well, it was a mess.'

'Even so.'

They sat in silence for a while. Then he said the last thing she expected him to say. 'I went to the cemetery on my way home from school.'

She waited. He looked at her accusingly. 'I couldn't find the grave.'

'Well, where were you looking?'

'The new bit.'

'He's not there. I had him put on top of his mother. Betty

wanted it. And I didn't mind.'

'Oh.'

He bent forward, his big hands clasped between his knees. She said, 'I should never've listened to me Mam. I should've took you with me. It was your place.'

He looked up at her. 'That's all right. It doesn't matter.' He squeezed his hands together. 'It's all over now, anyway.'

But it had mattered. She could see that.

'I was surprised how many people turned out,' she said. 'There was a lovely wreath from the street. Mrs King was saying, Everybody gave.' The thought made her throat tighten.

'There's no need to talk about it,' he said. 'Not if you don't want.'

He was offering her the means of escape. But even as he said it, he looked at her pleadingly. And she wanted to talk to him about his father.

She said, hesitatingly, 'You didn't miss much. The Vicar got through it that fast you'd've thought he was in a race.' Her voice was sharp with anger. 'Still, I suppose they must get tired of it. I mean, it's just another job to them. But it was what your father wanted. He always said, Don't have me cremated, Muriel.'

There was a long silence. Then Richard cleared his throat. He mumbled, 'Shouldn't think it matters much. I mean you're gone, aren't you?'

'Yes.'

Another long silence. 'All the same, I wish I'd been there.'

'I wish you had.' Her voice shook. There were tears running down her face, though for the boy's sake she would not sob aloud. She said, 'You know the night your Dad had the haemorrhage, he was talking about you.'

He looked up at her then.

'He said what a fine lad you were. That he wasn't as worried about me as he might've been because he knew I had a good son.'

Richard was looking down again, one hand clasping and unclasping the other.

'He said I thought he favoured Sharon, but he didn't. He

thought every bit as much about you, only it was harder to show it with a lad.' As she finished, her voice wobbled. And then she was sobbing openly. She couldn't've held it back any longer, not to save her life.

Richard looked at her almost with dread. He had never seen his mother cry. Even on that terrible day when they had brought his father home and she had tried to drag his body from the coffin, she had not cried. Then she held out her arms, and he started to cry too, pressing his wet cheek into her neck.

Richard was the first to stop. He put an arm round his mother's shoulders. And she started to dry her eyes.

'Well,' she said, on a shaky laugh. 'I think we both needed that.'

'We will be all right, won't we? I mean money and all that.'

'We'll manage. We always have done, haven't we?'

'I could get a Saturday job.'

'You're not old enough, love.'

'Well, a paper round then. I'm old enough for that.'

'We'll see. You go on back to bed, now, love. I'll just stop here another few minutes. No, go on, I'll be all right.'

After he'd gone, she went on sitting there for a while. The moonlight was stronger now, strong enough to cast shadows over the bed. She stroked the coverlet and said, very quietly, 'Oh, John, I loved you.'

Then she got up and wandered across to the mirror, but she did not look into it. It could show her only what she most feared to see: a woman, white-faced, sodden and alone. Instead she turned to the window and looked out on to the night. The moon was high and magnificent, ringed by haloes of frost. She was aware of it as another presence, a gaze she was compelled to meet.

And so she stood by the window, alone and not alone, until she heard Richard's voice calling to her from the next room. 'All right,' she said. 'I'm coming.' She took one last look, then, bracing her shoulders, went back to her children.

CHAPTER FIVE

IRIS KING

'What's this money on the mantelpiece then?'

Iris went to the kitchen door to see what her husband was on about.

'Oh, that. That's what we collected for John Scaife. There was a bit left over from the wreath. Mrs Sullivan and me, we thought we'd have a walk down the town tomorrow and see if we can't get a nice little vase or something to put on the grave.'

'Poor sod.' Ted put the money down abruptly.

Iris turned to Mrs Sullivan who was having a cup of tea with her in the kitchen. 'Ted used to work with him, you know.'

'Twenty year, nigh on. Up to a year gone March. I've seen him walking up that hill when he should have been at home in bed. And then folks turned round and said he was lazy. I'll tell you one thing, Missus. I wouldn't do it. No, by hell would I. I look at that place and I say to meself, Now then, Ted, don't strain yourself. It'll be there when you're gone.'

As he spoke he was putting on his coat to go out. After he'd gone Iris sat down and lit another cigarette. 'I had a hell of a job getting him to go to the funeral, you know. He's scared bloody stiff of owt like that. Says he wishes he didn't have to go to his own. And hospitals. He hasn't been up to see our Brenda once.'

'How is she?'

'Getting over it. She looked like death yesterday, mind. You know how you do. It upset me. I wished after I hadn't gone, because she wasn't conscious.'

'She's been an unlucky bairn. I mean, a girl of her age, having to go in for scrapes.'

'She's been in for a scrape — I think I'm right — six times.

'Poor bairn. What is she, fifteen?'

'Sixteen gone August. You know when he said it was her ovary I was pleased because I thought well, at least now they do know what's wrong. She's hardly had a normal period, that kid. She doesn't know what it's like. And pain! It was Ted spotted it, you know. She was bent double and Ted said you know this is happening every month. I said, gerraway. Well, you know she was only eleven. But after I thought about it and it dawned on me he was right.'

A groan from the living room interrupted her.

'That's our Laura back from me Dad's. I wondered why Ted was so keen to get out.'

Iris walked into the living room. Mrs Sullivan, following her, saw a tall, gaunt woman with hair cut like a child's and thick, brown stockings that drooped in folds around her ankles. She had staring eyes.

'Laura, this is Mrs Sullivan.'

Laura groaned again.

'They've only just let her out. She's supposed to be better but I'm buggered if I can see it.'

'It'll be her nerves, is it?' Mrs Sullivan approached timidly.

'No, it's schizophrenia.' Mrs Sullivan backed away. 'She's living in a different world. So *they* say. I have me doubts.' She bent down and peered into Laura's eyes, as if through the letter box of an empty house. 'Sometimes, I think they're right. Sometimes I thinks she's a lot more with it than she cracks on. Now and then you catch a very funny look in her eye.'

'It's a big responsibility, isn't it?'

'Oh, it is. No doubt about it. I don't like leaving her, you see. And Ted won't stop in with her. And there again when I go to work I can't take her with me. The old people don't like it.'

'Well, no . . .'

'Well, it's what she was in for, see. She was cleaning for this old man and one day she just took it into her head to set him on fire. One minute he was sat in his armchair, next he was up in flames. Or rather the chair was. He wasn't badly burned but I mean to say at that age the shock could've killed him. I said when I went to see her, I said, What d' y' want to do that for, Laura? She just turned round and said, Why not? He was no use. That was all you could get out of her: he was no use. I said to her, I said, Laura, that's not the point.'

'I'm surprised they let her out.'

'Well, to be honest, so am I. And the old people don't take to her, you know. They say she sits and stares at them. Which she does. She stares at me. For all I know she's making up her mind I'm no use.'

All this time Laura had stared straight ahead of her, her feet planted side by side on the floor, her back rigid.

'Laura, I'm going to see our Brenda now. Listen, Laura, do you want to come?' Silence. 'Talk to a chair leg, you'd get more sense. Laura . . .'

'I'll stop where I am.' Her voice boomed out, expressionless as a foghorn, seeming to come from several feet behind her head.

'You'll be all right, won't you? Not do anything silly?' Silence.

'It's the fire I'm frightened of,' Iris said in a whisper. 'I don't like the way she looks at it.'

'I think it's wonderful the way you manage. What with Brenda as well.'

And Ted, she might have said.

'Oh, I just carry on.'

In fact as she stood in front of the mirror to tie the scarf round her head you could see she wasn't well. She had the dull eyes and permanently grey skin of somebody who keeps going on cups of tea, cigarettes and adrenalin.

When she was ready they left the house together.

165

'Iris, what is she to you?'

'She's supposed to be me aunt. But if you believe that you'll believe anything.' Iris paused, deciding whether or not she should go on. 'Me Dad's stepmother had her fifteen months after the old man died. Now she always said it was me Grandad's bairn and she was late. Well. *I* think it belonged to me Dad. He was still living with her, see. But that doesn't matter to me. Whether she's me aunt or whether she's me sister she's still the only relation I've got after me father goes. I've got to see to her.'

'You've took a lot on, Iris.'

'When haven't I had a lot on? You tell me.'

They parted at the corner, Iris went up North Road towards the Hospital. She was thinking, as she walked, about Mrs Sullivan. Poor woman. Fell for a bairn whenever her husband looked at her. And what a husband. Ted was bad enough but Ernie Sullivan was a real blossom. At least *she'd* made sure there were no more bairns. Not after Brenda. Brenda. When she'd got over it a bit she'd take her away for a few days. Even if it was only as far as Scarborough. Or perhaps they could manage Blackpool: she'd always wanted to see the lights but every time she got saved up for it something happened and put the kibosh on it.

Well, if she could get the money raked together, this time she'd make bloody sure nothing happened.

'*Pregnant?*'

'Five months pregnant.' His voice was cold.

Iris stared at him, silhouetted against the window of his room. She heard the rattle of a trolley in the corridor outside, the gurgle of water in the radiator behind his desk. She licked her lips. 'She can't be,' she said at last.

'She is. And you must've known.'

'No.'

He smiled faintly.

'I didn't know.'

Silence. When he spoke again his tone had softened slightly. 'But *she* must've known.'

'Yes. No. I suppose so.'

166

'You suppose?'

'She's used to missing periods.'

'Five months, Mrs King. She must've been getting movement.'

'You know what it's like with your first. You don't know what's wind and what isn't.'

'She *knew*. I've spoken to her.'

Silence. After waiting, for her to speak he went on, 'I rather think she was hoping the operation might bring on a miscarriage without her having to tell anybody. Or perhaps she thought I'd do an abortion automatically when I found a baby there. If she did she was mistaken. And don't ask for one. It would be too dangerous.'

'You say you've talked to her?'

'Yesterday. As soon as she came round.'

'And she definitely said she knew?'

'Yes.'

The little cow. Iris felt the blood rush to her head. For a few seconds she was literally blind with rage.

When her sight cleared she managed to say, 'There's just one thing. I don't want you thinking you've been conned. Because you haven't. Not by me. When I brought that girl in here I honestly believed she was ill. I had no idea there was anything else.'

'Then I'm sorry to have given you bad news. How old is she?'

'Sixteen.'

'I can't do it.' He shifted uneasily in his chair. 'If she'd told somebody sooner . . .'

'I suppose there's no possibility . . .'

'No. It wouldn't be safe.'

'I see. Well, thanks for telling me.' Iris stood up. Her hands were trembling. She clasped them together and said, 'I'll just go and see her now if you don't mind.'

'You can always get in touch with the hospital social worker, you know. She'll know what to advise.'

Iris nodded. She was beyond taking in what was said. She walked along the shining corridor, her mind empty except for the single word *'pregnant'* which bounced from wall to wall and refused to make sense.

It began to make sense as soon as she saw her daughter. She was sitting on a chair beside her bed, flicking over the pages of a magazine. Her dark blonde hair hung like two curtains on either side of her face. But Iris was looking at her stomach. I've been a fool, she thought. It's obvious.

And immediately she wondered how many other people knew. Even Mrs Bell had said something about Brenda always looking tired. She'd thought nothing of it at the time. But now she felt that perhaps the neighbours all knew, that they were laughing, sniggering behind her back.

'Brenda.'

The girl looked up and went white when she saw her mother's expression.

'The doctor's just told me something about you.' She was gasping for breath, sucking in great lungfuls of air, but they weren't doing her any good. 'He says you're pregnant.'

Silence.

'Well, are you?'

Brenda mumbled something she couldn't catch.

'I asked you a question.'

'I must be if he says I am.'

'Oh, I suppose *you* didn't know? I suppose this is all news to you?'

'How was I supposed to know? I'm always missing, you know I am.'

'You knew what you'd done. You knew you'd been with a fella. Couldn't you've told me? Did you have to let me turn up here and . . . and get slapped in the face with it?'

'I didn't know.'

'Oh, pull the other one, it's got bells on.'

Brenda glanced miserably from side to side. 'I wish you'd shut up, Mam. Everybody's listening.'

'Let 'em listen. They'll have a proper lugful by the time I'm finished.' She raised her voice. 'Enjoying yourself, everybody?'

Instantly, all along the ward, heads darted into the cover of knitting patterns and magazines.

'*Mam!*'

'Now just you listen to me. There's things I've got a right to know. For a kickoff, who was it?'

Silence.

'Brenda . . .'

'I'm not telling you. You'd only go round shouting and screaming and showing us all up. You've done it as long as I can remember. You used to go round the pub and fight me Dad for his wages. I used to get that thrown up at me at school.'

'I did. I did fight your Dad for his wages. I'm not ashamed to say it. And think on, Brenda, there was many a week you'd've gone hungry to shit if I hadn't.'

'It's been the same all me life. Well, I'm not having it this time. Fighting and going on.'

'Oh I see. I suppose fucking and going on is all right? I suppose that doesn't show us up? Well, let me tell you when you're waddling down the street with a big belly you'll sharp find out it does. Soppy Lil. I never thought it'd be Soppy Brenda. I thought you had more off.'

'It's none of your business. I can take care of meself.'

'It looks like it.'

There was a pause. Mother and daughter each drew breath.

'Is he in a position to marry you?'

'Not exactly.'

'You mean he's married already?'

'I mean he's only fifteen.'

'Bloody hell.'

'Only just turned fifteen.'

'Why won't you tell me who it is?'

'I won't, that's all.'

'I know, you're ashamed to say who it is. But you weren't ashamed to get on your back for him. Him and God knows how many more.'

'You shut your face!'

'No! You shut yours.'

Iris's fist came up and hit the girl on the mouth. It was such a lovely relief that she did it again. 'Hey, steady on!' somebody shouted. Further down the ward another woman could be heard summoning the nurse.

By the time they arrived, Iris was dragging Brenda around the ward by her hair. The girl was white-lipped and moaning with fear. She had both hands pressed together over the wound in her belly.

'I'll give you shut your face, you little whore.'

'Mrs King!' The Sister's voice cracked across the ward. 'Stop that at once.'

'I'll murder the little bitch.'

'Not on my ward you won't.'

The two women stared at each other.

'Are you going? Or have I to send for the porter?'

'I'll fight you and the bloody porter.'

Though in fact the fight had gone out of her. Brenda was sobbing in the middle of the ward with a nurse's arm around her shoulders. Wherever Iris looked there were accusing faces. There was nothing to do but go.

At the door she turned and said, 'I wouldn't have you back now, our Brenda, not if you went on your bended knees.'

'I'll see you in hell first.'

So that was that.

When Iris reached home she stood for a few moments with her back against the door, helplessly staring along the passage. Then she called, 'Laura?' No reply. That meant nothing. Iris went to look for her, but no, she was out. Thank God she was out.

Iris crouched over the fire and began putting lumps of coal on to it, slowly, piece by piece. For a long time she couldn't control her thoughts at all. She stared at the fire, and the scenes she'd just lived through re-enacted themselves in her mind, certain words, certain looks burning themselves into her, until at last she was exhausted and could think about it no more.

Laura had most probably gone round to her father's. That wouldn't last long. She gave him the creeps, he said. He was almost as frightened of her as Ted was. An hour, two at the most, and she'd be back.

Iris got up stiffly and looked round the room. Flames flickered over china and cut glass and polished wood. Everything in the room shone. There wasn't a speck of dirt anywhere. It made her feel better to look at it. She was proud of her reputation as the cleanest woman in the street. Although she worked full-time as a home help, her own doorstep was scoured every day. Fresh curtains appeared at the windows once a week, sometimes twice. It was no hardship to her to do all this. She loved housework. This house of hers had been a right mess when she first moved into it, and gradually she'd got it put right. There was a bathroom, now, and an indoor lavatory. And it had all come out of her own money; there was no relying on Ted to do anything. If it'd been left to Ted they'd be living in a tent.

Her eyes roamed round the room. On the wall opposite were three plastic shields in a sort of reddy-brown colour that looked like bronze. She was proud of them: they were a recent acquisition. But the joy of her life was her china cabinet. Sometimes when she was upset she would touch the wood; it always made her feel better. If she ever left Ted, that would go with her. He could have all the rest, but she would take that.

She hadn't always lived in a nice house. She'd been born and brought up in Wharfe Street, near the river. As a young woman she'd battled her way out of it. But it was no use. She was no longer in Wharfe Street but Wharfe Street was still in her. She remembered it. Knew it. Knew every brick of it.

When she thought of Wharfe Street she remembered Mrs Biggs. She'd lived in the end house, the one nearest the river, and the wallpaper had peeled away and hung in strips. She'd kept herself to herself. She was a clean-living, even religious woman, respected, if not much liked. Then her son, who was a bit not-all-there, had molested and strangled a little boy and left his body on a rubbish tip. Then nothing that Mrs Biggs could say or do would save her. On the night before they hanged her son, somebody had gone and smeared dogshit all over her windows and all over her front door. And they'd gone on doing it, too. They never let up. She went loony in the end and had to be taken away.

And she remembered Blonde Dinah, traipsing about the room in a nightdress with bloodstains on the back.

There'd been men there, it hadn't been just women, but she hadn't cared.

Animals.

They were going to pull it down now. That was what they said. It was all coming down. Too late. Too late for her.

You could talk about it to people and they would say they understood. But they didn't, not really. Nobody who hadn't lived there could understand.

Her parents had split up a few weeks after her birth. When she was six weeks old her mother took her father to court to claim maintenance. Perhaps they didn't give her enough. At any rate when the case was over she'd picked Iris up and walked across the courtroom with her. 'Here,' she said. 'It's your bairn. You keep it.' And she'd dumped Iris in her father's arms.

That was the last Iris saw of her mother.

Now, whenever she felt bitter against her father, when she couldn't stop remembering some of the things that had happened, she thought, well, what else could he do? What could any man do, left to bring up a bairn on his own? He'd kept her, hadn't he? Many a man'ld've put her in a home.

They'd lived in a series of boarding houses and some of them weren't much better than brothels and some of them were brothels. Her father paid a long succession of women to look after her. Some of them did a good job, some didn't. Mainly they didn't. As soon as she could walk, she was shoved out on to the street with a slice of bread and dripping in her hand, lucky to get it too. And on the street she'd learned to survive.

Wednesdays and Saturdays were market days. By the time she was five she was stealing from the food stalls. 'Course she'd got copped. One day she was just reaching out for a banana when a hand came down on her bare arm. She looked up to see a man like a tower with a red face and eyes that bulged horribly. She'd been so frightened she'd pissed herself. Ever since, whenever she was worried about something, like going into the hospital for an operation, she pissed herself. Sometimes she woke up and the bed was swimming. She blamed it on that day in the market place.

Though in fact they were very kind to her. Somehow they'd realised she was hungry and not just doing it for devilment. God knows how, because she'd been too frightened to get the words out. And then they were always giving her food. They'd save some for her at the end of the day and cut off the bad bits with their penknives. And the men at the banana-packing place down by the river were just the same. Except the bananas there were still green. They all knew her. They'd even give her a carrier bag of stuff to take home. Not that she ever did. Even at five she'd had more off than that. No. She ate it all on the way, cramming it into her mouth till the juice ran down her chin. God, it was good. Nothing had ever tasted the same since. It had been part of her life. Bags of over-ripe fruit, Wednesdays and Saturdays. Thursdays and Sundays, the shits.

When she got to school things looked up a bit. The teachers rummaged round and found her some warmer clothes to wear, because in her first winter in school she'd only had a pair of plimsolls and a raggy cotton dress. Course, the other kids knew she was wearing their cast-offs. Quite often she was wearing a dress that had belonged to somebody else in the same class. They'd given her hell. Well, you couldn't blame them. It was only bairn-like. But fight! She'd had to fight all the way.

Probably it was the school that told the Cruelty Bobby about her. Anyway, there he was. Uncle Harry. When she saw him coming up the street she'd run to him like running home. Except if she had bruises. Then she'd steer clear. He knew it, too. He used to say, 'Howay, my bairn. Aren't you gunna give your Uncle Harry a kiss?' But she'd keep out of reach. She knew what he was looking for. And she had to protect her father. From a very early age she'd known that keeping Dad out of trouble was her responsibility.

As she got older, the beatings got worse. Her periods started. They were lodging with Blonde Dinah at the time.

173

She'd taken her out to buy her first sanitary towels and shown her how to fit them on the belt. Iris had had a soft spot for Dinah ever since, though there were those who'd cross the street when they saw her coming. But her father had been terrible when she was in her teens. 'Course, you could see it from his point of view. A young girl growing up in that area among a lot of old pros. He didn't know what to do about it and finished up beating the hell out of her every time she looked at a lad. At the finish she set her cheek up at him that bad he picked up a pan of boiling soup and poured it over her head. It'd been a hospital job that time, and when she come out she went to stay with her Auntie in Jarrow. And when she come back she got on with Ted, and married him. 'Course she had to, but by that time she'd've married anybody, just to get out. Irene had said, Don't do it. She'd offered to help her out. Even showed her the things she did it with. But no. No! The sight of the instruments made her shudder, and anyway she was in love with the idea of marriage. A home. She had never had a home.

She was married in white. She waltzed out of the Registry Office without a care in the world. She'd really thought all her troubles were over. Now, when she looked at her wedding photographs, she sometimes thought, You poor, silly little bitch. But it was somebody else. She couldn't feel any connection with that past self.

Three weeks after the wedding, he came in and found her still ironing his shirts when he thought the supper should've been ready. He belted her across the ear, hard enough to make her see stars, and slammed out to the pub.

After he'd gone, she sat down and took stock. Her first thought was to hurry through the ironing and get the dinner on. Then she thought, No, bugger it. 'Course she knew already about Ted's temper. He thought he had a right to hit you. His father had always belted hell out of his mother, so why not? It was just like God bless you to him. But he was making a big mistake. She wasn't his sodding mother.

When he came back she was waiting for him behind the door with the meat chopper in her hand. The blow glanced off him, though there was enough blood around to scare the pair of them stiff. It didn't stop him hitting her again, but it did free her from fear. She never lost her self-respect. The only times she was frightened of him were when she was pregnant or after she'd had the Big Operation. He was a bugger to her then, dragging her down on to the floor and kicking her in the wound. It was a miracle her stitches hadn't bust.

The first baby, a boy, was born dead. There'd been a mix-up over her dates all the way through. *She* reckoned she was overdue; they would have it she was only seven months, but when they saw the afterbirth they admitted she was right. The baby just hadn't grown properly. It lay on the doctor's hand, curled up and blue-black. 'Well, Iris,' he said. 'After all that time. Is this the best you can do?' He was rough, but it was only his way. She'd been in labour three days before they took her to the hospital.

Over the years her memory of the baby changed. Gradually it became more and more like Ted. Finally it was Ted himself lying in the doctor's hand, shrunken and dead.

It was Ted's father pulled her round from that. It was funny, he was a right bugger with his wife and bairns, knocked hell out of 'em, but speak as you find: he was goodness itself to her. He'd given her wormwood to drink to bring the clots of blood away and bound strips from a torn-up sheet tightly round her stomach, in defiance of the midwife. 'Never you mind her,' he'd said. 'You don't want a great big belly on yer, lass your age.'

She'd only been eighteen. And she'd crawled around for two years after that. More. Even the next pregnancy didn't lift the depression: she was too apathetic to care. Only when the pains started she thought, 'Dear God, have I got to go through all that again?'

The baby was a girl, very small but healthy. She was a crabby baby. More than once Iris threw up the window intending to toss the baby out; but gradually it became less fractious. She saw the results of her care. The baby gurgled and held out its arms. The layer of dirty cellophane that had shut Iris off from the world was ripped away. She had a purpose again. This child of hers would never be left, never be deserted as she had been. No matter how bad things got, and they were bad, very bad, she would never give in.

And it wasn't going to have plimsolls and cast-offs either. It was going to have the best. She called it Sheila.

Lindsey was born the following year. Then a gap of two years, and Brenda.

They'd got out of Wharfe Street by then, though only as far as Bute Street, which was six and two threes. But the house was kept fanatically clean. Iris looked out at her neighbours: the men in prison, the women spending the social security money at the prize Bingo, kids dragged up anyhow, an her lips tightened. It was the women she despised. On their backs for any bugger what fancied a poke, and the kids left to God and Providence.

It wouldn't happen to hers. She had to get out of Bute Street. By this time her Dad had a fancy woman a lot older than himself, but still, Iris enlisted her help and went out to work, first at the bakery, then on the Home Help. The work suited her. She loved charging around a messy house and setting it all to rights. And she loved the old people too. 'We've all got it to come to,' she often said. She would sit for hours listening to some old person's rambling memories of the past. And then there was the money. She sat and looked at her first pay packet and burst into tears. Money had been that short. If he was drinking heavily he could go through a big slice of it before he got in from work. And it was right what Brenda said, she had gone out and fought him for it. They'd had one bust-up outside the Station Hotel. The police were called that time. She'd thrown him over the bonnet of a car. She wasn't ashamed. She'd had to do it to survive. But that first pay packet, it was wonderful. They needn't starve, now. Whatever Ted did there would be some money in the house. 'You think on,' she'd said to her two older girls when they got married. 'It's nice to have a good husband but it's a hell of a lot nicer to have your own money. A fiver you've earned is worth ten of anybody else's. You can do what you want with it.'

Ted was very bad while the kids were little. Fifty times worse than he'd been since. She'd forgiven him a lot but there was one thing she couldn't forgive.

She was in bed trying to get to sleep. The pubs had closed but he still wasn't home which meant he had gone on somewhere, to one of the nightclubs perhaps. Which meant he had switched to drinking spirits. She wasn't as worried about the money now, but she hated the rows, the violence, the way the children went quiet whenever their father walked into a room. In a way, she still cared about him. She would defend him to other people. 'He hasn't a lazy bone in his body,' she would say. 'And he's never missed a day's work through drink.' Which was true. Then.

Suddenly, she heard voices. A muffled male giggle. The sound of a milk bottle rolling into the gutter. She tensed up, resolving to say nothing. But she was surprised. He had never brought anybody back with him before.

They were making a hell of a row. She got up and went to look over the banisters. She expected to see two of his mates but no, the men were strangers. She retreated to the bedroom. She only hoped he wasn't gambling, though the state he was in there couldn't be much left to lose.

Then she heard footsteps on the stairs. They were slow and uncertain but it couldn't be Ted, because whoever it was stopped on the landing, as if not sure of the room. She sat up in bed and switched the light on. As she did so the door opened, and a man stood there. He was obviously pissed. He was swaying on his feet. Worse than that, he was fumbling with his flies. He got it out. She stared at him, dumbfounded. He seemed to be in no doubt that he — and It — were welcome.

She grabbed her dressing gown. 'Hey, I think you're making a big mistake, aren't you?'

He gaped at her, too fuddled to take the situation in.

'Did he send you up here?' She saw him glance over his shoulder. 'Well, go on, did he?'

There was another step on the stairs. 'Hey up, Jock,' another man's voice called cheerfully. 'Don't take all night.'

There were two of them. He'd brought two complete strangers home and sent them up here. 'Get out,' she said. She advanced on the first man. He backed away until brought up hard against the banisters. There was time to notice the little bubbles of spit between his rather prominent front teeth. Then he was tipping slowly, slowly backwards. The blue eyes opened wide and he was gone. Then the silence that had surrounded her ended, the world rushed back. There was a crash, and a cry from Brenda's bedroom.

She thought afterward, she could have broken the man's back. At the time she wouldn't've cared if she had. He staggered to his feet. The other man grabbed him by the arm and they fell over each other to get out of the front door.

She went downstairs to find Ted. He was curled up on the floor like a foetus, retching. The final stages of his drunkenness were always like this. She bent over him and said, 'I ought to kill you. But I won't. You're not worth doing time for.'

When she went back upstairs she found Brenda on the landing in her nightgown. She was too frightened to cry. Iris swept her up in her arms and carried her to the big bed for a cuddle. She might as well sleep there. Ted wouldn't be making it that far tonight.

She never willingly had sex with him again. Perhaps once or twice a year when he got too bad, to shut him up; never more than that.

As for other men, well, the bairns came first. Had to. Even if she'd lost Ted, she didn't think she'd've married again. Live tally, her name on the rent book, yes. But marriage . . . no. She'd had enough.

When her children were very small she adored them. My little princesses, she said. As babies they had the biggest pram the street had seen, with all the trimmings: sunshade and broderie anglaise pillowslips. Later they took their first steps in Clarks' Start-rite shoes. No plimsolls for them. They were cherished, coddled, over-protected, overfed, overweight, forced to wear vests on even the warmest day.

As they grew older things changed. Iris would have given her teenage daughters anything, but they were separate people now. There was a conflict in her mind. Sometimes they were still her little girls who must have everything that

178

she had lacked. But increasingly, too, they appeared as rivals who might be resented for having more. Brenda's 'tash' started growing. At the same time grey hairs appeared in her mother's head. Iris, for the first time in many years, spent some money selfishly on herself. She went out and bought some bleach and dyed her hair blonde.

Iris, in these later years, was often depressed. A blackness would come over her, a blackness she linked in her mind with those early years in Wharfe Street. They were living in Union Street now, a big step up. And yet the past had never seemed so close. She would look around her at the home she had toiled and sweated to create and it meant nothing. She wanted to destroy something. Anything. Herself, if nothing else offered. She would go out and walk the streets for hours, aware only of the blood squeezing through the veins in her head.

The blackness lifted as suddenly as it came. But she knew as she got older that it would always return.

She was just coming out of one of these spells when Joss moved into the street. She hadn't seen him for years. He had lived opposite her in Wharfe Street, and had always been kind. His was one of the few faces from those days that she remembered with affection. They used to talk for hours when she was young. Perhaps he'd fancied her. He'd never said anything, perhaps his legs had held him back. And it hadn't really entered her head. She'd been too busy going out with every good-looking shit on the block. After a while, Joss came to her house like going home. At weekends she gave him his meals. And stuck up for him when anybody laughed at his legs, which they were inclined to do. She'd clocked one girl for doing that. Everybody thought he was her fancy man. But there was nothing like that. All that was over and done with for her. She was glad to see the back of it.

There were long spells when she was entirely well. Then she mothered half the street. Kelly Brown and the Scaife children, Lisa Goddard's little lads — they all knew and loved their Iris. Oh, my Iris, Kelly used to say when she was little. Oh, my Iris. And she sat with women in labour. Even laid out the dead, though there wasn't as much call for that now. They died in hospital and came back neatly packaged. Sometimes only as far as the front door, before setting off on the final journey. She thought that was disgusting; but it was the new way.

All this was meat and drink to her. She loved life. She loved to feel life bubbling and quickening all around her, and took it for granted that life included old age, suffering and death.

The girls grew up. The two older girls married, both very young but neither because she had to. Lindsey was settled away from home, but Sheila, after her marriage, was closer to her mother than before. They would sit and laugh about the old times. The time Iris had picked the carving knife up and threatened to kill the lot of them; the time she set the house on fire. When she was well these events seemed to have happened in another life. She could sit and have a laugh about them.

She valued her reputation in the street. She knew she was respected and her family was respected. Her reputation mattered more to her than anything else. It was the measure of her distance from Wharfe Street, the guarantee that the blackness that came from her past would never finally return.

It was this that Brenda threatened to destroy. Well, she wouldn't be allowed to. As Iris wandered round and round her living room, straightening ornaments and cushions that were straight already, she felt her anger grow. She would not have Brenda back in this house. Would not, would not, would not. She didn't care where she went. Her or the baby. She should've thought of all that before she got on her back. She'd learn. She'd grow up bloody fast. She'd sharp find out what having a bairn was like.

This resolve held firm to the end of the week. She did not go back to the hospital, but was kept informed of Brenda's progress by her eldest daughter, Sheila, who visited every day. This had come as a surprise. Iris expected unquestioning obedience even from her married daughters. She had not actually forbidden Sheila to visit, but she had assumed that she would not go. So it was something of a shock when every day Sheila came in with fresh news.

'She says she's made up her mind to keep it, Mam,' Sheila said, retrieving her own child from the coal scuttle in which he took a compulsive interest.

'She doesn't know what she's on about. It's bad enough when you've got a man bringing the money in.'

'She says everything's changed now.'

'Oh, aye. You mean, they've invented a bairn what wipes its own arse? I *have* missed out.'

'She says she'll get the Social Security.'

'She'll get a long way on that, the way she spends.'

'Oh, I know. She talks big, but underneath she's scared stiff. You can see she is.' Mixed in with Sheila's sympathy was a certain satisfaction. As a child she'd always got the blame when things went wrong. 'But she's bound to be scared, isn't she? I mean, she's only a kid herself.'

'If only she'd been honest about it. It could all have been over and done with months ago. He'd've done her if she'd gone to him straight away. And told the truth.'

'She was frightened.'

'What of?'

'Mam!'

'Well, I'm asking you. What of?'

'Of you leathering her. Which you would've done, so don't say you wouldn't.'

'I'd've took the skin off her back.'

'Well, then.'

'She didn't half want something to do. Five minutes pleasure and a lifetime of misery. How often have I said that to you?'

'I don't know, Mam. I've lost count.'

'But it's the truth, isn't it?'

'For her it will be.'

Iris was silent. There was a lot in Sheila's attitude that she didn't like.

'You see, Mam, mebbe with her not having proper periods and that she's been running away with the idea she couldn't get pregnant. And that was bound to make her . . .'

181

'She knew what she was doing was wrong. Didn't she?'

'Granted she did, yes.'

'She knew enough to keep her knees together. That's all you need to know.'

'Yes, Mam. But . . .' Sheila paused, wrestling with the child on her knee. 'Oh, go on, then, get mucky. You never got much pleasure out of it, did you, Mam?'

'I got none.'

'Well, it's not like that for everybody. You can't just . . . What I'm trying to say is, it's natural, isn't it?'

'I'm bloody sure it's not.'

The two women retreated into silence. Iris had always assumed that Sheila shared her attitude to sex. Now, suddenly, she was forced to see her daughter as a woman who apparently enjoyed 'it'. And wasn't afraid to look you in the face and say so! A thought struck her.

'Our Sheila, are you on the pill?'

'I've been on it a year.'

'You're as bad as she is. Rotting your guts out for a man.'

'The doctor said . . .'

'Doctors!'

'A lot of men wouldn't put up with what me Dad puts up with. Twice a year if he's lucky.'

'A lot of women wouldn't put up with your Dad. Keep it out, right?' She tapped the end of her nose. 'Anyway, she can't've got much pleasure out of him. If it's owt like the rest of him she'd need a winkle-picker to find it.'

Sheila looked guilty. 'We don't know who it is.'

'Don't we?'

'She's never said owt to me about it.'

'No. But you'll have seen that Sally Almond there, haven't you? Brenda was always round their house. And Billy Almond's fifteen.'

'I honestly don't know, Mam.'

'That's who it belongs to. And he goes to the daft school, and so does Sally, and so does the other brother. I used to know their Mam. She never had much on top. And what there was he belted out of her. He drinks, doesn't he? Loud-mouthed git. Well, I can tell you one thing, our

Sheila, if she was nine months gone with triplets I wouldn't
let her marry into that lot.'

'I can't see our Brenda going with somebody daft. She
was always the brainy one.'

'Aye. And she was always the one that wouldn't be told. I
used to say to her, you've got a head on you like a forty-
shilling piss-pot, my girl, but I'll see you brought low. And I
have.'

'Mam, if she wouldn't be told, whose fault was it?' Silence.
'Yours. She could do no wrong. She only had to ask and she
got.'

'I didn't just ruin her, I ruined the lot of you.'

'She got more than we ever got.'

'I had more! I was working then.'

'Anyway, it doesn't matter whose fault it was. She's the
one that's paying for it.'

'Aye, now she is. And later? Who do you think's going to
bring it up? She can't. She doesn't earn enough to keep
herself.'

'I thought you were having nowt to do with it.'

'Oh, that's likely, isn't it? Turn me back on me own flesh
and blood. If I could do that, I wouldn't be sat here. I'd've
left the whole sodding lot of yer, years ago.'

'They say she can go into a hostel.'

'She's going into no hostel. She's coming home.'

'She's frightened, Mam.'

'She has no need to be. I'll keep me hands off her. I don't
know how, mind, but I will.'

Sheila looked at her mother suspiciously. 'You've got
something up your sleeve.'

'Mebbe I have.'

'You're not going to go round their house?'

'No. Though I might be doing some other poor lass a
favour if I did. I'll tangle with that lot later.'

'So what are you going to do?'

'None of your business. I've got a lot more on my mind
than you think. Do you know what I'm really frightened
of?'

'No.'

Silently, Iris pointed towards Laura who was sitting in the far corner paying, apparently, no attention to what was going on. 'You see Brenda as she is now — you see Laura when she was young.'

It took a moment to sink in.

Sheila drew back. 'Oh, no, Mam, I don't think so.'

'Don't you?' Iris stared at Laura, expressionlessly. 'I do.'

'I don't mind stopping in with her, you know. If you were wanting to go out.'

Ted came and stood over her, waiting for a reply.

'She's all right,' Iris said, irritably. 'She doesn't need anybody stopping in with her. And anyway, I'm not going out.'

'It's your Bingo night.'

'I've told Joss I'm not going.'

Still he hesitated. Iris fumed with impatience, spooning hot fat over the eggs in the frying pan. She tried to look as if his going to the pub, or not, was a matter of complete indifference to her, and was glad when an egg broke because it gave her a chance to say, Sod it.

'You sure you'll be all right, now?'

'Of course I'll be all right.'

He looked back again before he opened the door. Then with an odd, ducking, evasive movement of his head he was gone.

That was something they could all do, every last one of 'em. She'd always tried to drill it into her girls: a man can put his cap on, you can't, you're stuck with it. And it isn't months, it's years. Sixteen years. They don't do as much as that for murder. She loved her bairns, she wouldn't have been without them. But she had no illusions left.

Ted knew the girl was pregnant. Oh, nobody had actually told him, but he knew all right. He'd heard them talking. But he never mentioned it. Worrying about that was her job.

She shovelled the other egg on to a plate, and called into the living room, 'Your tea's ready. Will you have it in there?'

'Yes, please.'

She carried the plate through. Brenda was lying on the

184

sofa, her bronze hair loose and falling almost to her waist. When she pushed it back from her face her eyes were so black you'd've thought somebody had belted her one.

Which they had not, thought Iris virtuously, amazed by her own restraint.

They ate in silence. Once Brenda looked up from her plate to say, 'Where's Auntie Laura?'

'Round me Dad's. I've got enough on.'

'Oh.' She was obviously not looking forward to a whole evening of her mother's company. Her face had dropped when her Dad went out.

'Did they feed you all right in there?'

'It wasn't bad.'

'You're not feeling sick?'

'Oh, no. That's wore off.'

So she had been sick. No periods, morning sickness, and she knew she'd been with that lad. And she still turned round and said she didn't know she was pregnant. You'd need to be a bloody imbecile to believe that.

When the meal was over — Iris had to force the fried bread down, it stuck in her mouth like concrete — Brenda switched the telly on.

'You can put that off. You and me have a lot to talk about.'

'I'll just put the plates in the sink.'

She was bent double when she walked.

'You should be standing straighter than that, our Brenda. When d' y' say you had the stitches out?'

'Yesterday morning.'

'You should straighten up after that.'

'Yes, well. I was smashing this morning. I think I'm a bit tired.'

She was grey with pain.

'Yeah, well, you're bound to be.' Iris was not going to show too much sympathy. To give Brenda her due she hadn't asked for any. She looked at her daughter, sourly acknowledging a stoicism equal to her own. She wasn't impressed. She'd rather the girl had shown some sense.

They sat in silence; the tension between them tightened.

'Well, Brenda?'

'It's no use going on at me. I've said I won't tell you and I won't.' The silence frightened her. 'I don't care what you do.'

'I'd only need to blow on you!' Silence again. 'I suppose you do know?'

'Of course I do. I don't get on me back for just anybody, you know.'

'No, Brenda, I don't know.'

'He's not old enough to do anything.'

'He was old enough to get you like it.' Iris forced herself to swallow the bitterness. 'Anyway,' she went on, 'I wasn't going to ask you who it was because I already know. There, that surprises you, doesn't it? I'll deal with that lot later. No, what I was going to ask you was, What are you going to do? That's more to the point, isn't it?'

'Have it.'

'That's true! And then what? What about when it starts yelling and you're up all night and you still have to turn out to work in the morning? Because don't think your father's going to keep it, my girl, he isn't. And don't run away with the idea I'm giving my job up to look after it because I'm bloody not. I've done my share.'

'I haven't thought.'

'Well, think then.'

'I can go in a hostel.'

'No, you can't. You're not showing me up.'

'I thought mebbe our Sheila . . .'

'Don't you think she's got enough on?'

'One more doesn't make much difference.'

'Oh, doesn't it!'

'I can get another job. They might have me back at the bakery.'

'They might. And who's going to look after it while you work?'

Brenda's tongue flicked across her lips. 'Auntie Laura's in all day.'

'You must be desperate! She'd fry the poor little sod.'

'Well, the only other thing I can think of is the Day Nursery.'

'Waiting list a mile long.'

Brenda said nothing. She had turned her face away.

'And don't think you'll be going out much in the evenings either. I'm not stopping in with it while you're off gallivanting. For all I know, falling for another. You can forget that. I stopped in years with you lot. And I'm not stopping in no more.'

'I'll manage.'

'You don't know what you're taking on. It's not like babysitting, you know. You can't hand this one back when it screams.'

'I'll manage.'

It had gone on too long; she was hardening again. Iris said quickly, 'I saw him the other day. He was stood outside the Chippy with his mates.' She watched her daughter's reactions closely. 'Laughing his bloody head off.'

Silence.

'Well, Brenda, was it worth it?'

'You know it wasn't, so why ask?'

'Because you mightn't have to go through with it, after all.' She saw Brenda flinch. After all this time hope was like a slap in the face. 'I was talking to a friend of mine the other day — I say friend, she's a woman I wouldn't piss on if I had the choice. I used to know her, oh, a long time ago. When I was young.' Her mouth folded bitterly around the words. 'She used to live opposite us. In Wharfe Street.'

Brenda waited for her to go on.

'Big Irene. That's what we used to call her. She hasn't half gone down. I wouldn't've known her.'

Brenda waited again, impatiently.

'She used to help girls out of a jam.'

'You mean get rid of it?'

'Yes.'

'Did you mention me?'

'Of course. I wasn't looking her up for old times' sake.'

Brenda would never know what it had cost her to go back to Wharfe Street, cap in hand to a woman like Irene. 'She said she'd look at you.'

'You mean . . .'

'I mean nothing. She said she'd look at you.'

187

Brenda sat and thought. Her hand went down to her stomach. 'The doctor said I was too far on.'

'It's a question of what *you* want, Brenda. Nobody else can make your mind up for you.'

'He said it was too dangerous.'

'He said that because he was mad. And who wouldn't've been? You took him for a trot, didn't you? Him and me.'

Brenda sat there, leaden.

'He'd've done yer, if you'd been open and above board. It was nowt to do with your ovary. It was the daft way you carried on.'

'Oh, Mam, do you really think so?'

'I'm positive.' She had told herself all this so often that in fact her voice did sound confident. Confident enough to take Brenda in.

There was a rush of colour to her face that drained away as quickly as it came, leaving her even whiter than before. She said in a trembling voice, 'Well, what are we sat here for?'

'You couldn't go like that.'

'Couldn't I? Mam, I could walk over hot coals.'

Iris breathed out, letting herself relax for the first time since they'd started to talk. 'Mind, it's your decision, Brenda. It's got to be. It's your bairn.'

'I just want it out of me.'

'Then you'd better get dressed.'

Brenda stood up and started to hobble towards the door. Halfway there, she laughed and said, 'This is no use.' She straightened up, biting her lip. 'I can't walk down the street like that.'

'You sure you're all right?'

'We can't wait, Mam.' At the door she turned. 'It's going to be bad, isn't it? The pain.'

'You're going to have pain no matter what you do.'

Brenda started to say something else, then shut her mouth tight.

'Leaving it there another four months won't make it any easier.

'No, Mam, it's all right, I know.'

Iris left her alone for a few minutes, then followed her upstairs to her room. Brenda was just pulling a dress over her head.

'I'm trying to think of what I've got that's loose,' she said. 'Anything tight rubs on the scar.'

Scar was the wrong word. It didn't look anywhere near healed. There was a red part near the bottom of the wound that looked as if it might have pus behind it.

'Didn't they say anything about this, Brenda?'

'No. He seemed to think it was all right.'

'Well, if he thinks so, it must be.'

But she was frightened. She tried to think back to her own operation. When they'd took everything away from her, had it looked like that? Perhaps it had. She could only remember what it looked like after Ted kicked it.

'I'm not building up me hopes, Mam,' Brenda said, after Iris had helped her do up the zip. 'She could easy take one look at that and chuck us out.'

'She might.'

If she wasn't so desperate to get her hands on the money.

'After all, it's not the end of the world, is it?'

Brenda's self-control was slipping away. She had got herself so tightly screwed up to face the worst. Now there was a chance of escape . . . She could hardly cope with it.

'You put a bit of make-up on, flower, I'll just go and get me coat.'

Iris went into her own room. Her hands were shaking. She thought, God forgive me if I'm doing wrong. She's only a bairn.

She opened the second drawer of her dressing-table and groped underneath a pile of clean underwear. Her fingers closed on a roll of notes. Nobody else knew about this money. She'd got it raked together in case Ted was made redundant, and she'd promised herself she wouldn't break into it for anything. Well, she was going to have to. She didn't know what Irene would charge. She'd been too flustered to go into all that. But she didn't expect it to be cheap.

As she withdrew the notes, her eye fell on a plastic crucifix she kept on top of her dressing-table. She wasn't what

189

you could call religious, in fact she couldn't remember the last time she'd been in a church. The crucifix had been bought on a trip to the seaside in the sort of shop that sells souvenirs. But it wasn't just an ornament. It stood for the things she believed in, for what she felt about life. Whenever the problems of her own life threatened to overwhelm her she would get down on her knees in front of it and pray. But now this had happened and she couldn't pray. She couldn't justify what she was doing. What was kicking in Brenda's belly was a human being and try as she might she couldn't pretend it was anything else.

But there was no other way.

With a last furtive glance at her reflection in the mirror, she shoved the roll of notes into her handbag, and fled.

They walked past the Bingo queue on their way down the High Street. Iris was cursing herself: if she'd left it a bit later they'd've missed all that.

'Aren't you coming tonight?' one woman shouted.

'No, I'm giving it a miss.'

Several of the other women waved.

After they had passed, Iris said, 'You're doing fine.' Brenda's reply was to squeeze her mother's arm. She was in too much pain to speak.

They turned into Wharfe Street. Iris lifted her face to the drizzling rain. She could smell the river.

'Here we are.'

They were quite big houses, some of them. Steps led up to them from the street.

'Doesn't look as if there's anybody in,' said Brenda. 'I hope she's not gone out.'

'Perhaps she's at the Bingo!'

'Yeah. We probably just walked past her.'

They giggled together like a pair of conspirators. Brenda, who was feeling light-headed with pain, sat down abruptly on the step. 'I'll have to stop here, Mam. I don't think I could walk back.'

'I'll see what's going on,' said Iris, and climbed the steps. There were ten milk bottles on the top step, unwashed and turning green. Inside, dingy lino, and a table with uncol-

190

lected mail: mainly postcards and circulars. It was a boarding house, sort of. Very sort of, if she knew Irene.

'What d' y' want?' a voice asked from the blackness at the top of the stairs.

Iris squinted into the darkness. 'I'm looking for Big Irene.'

'Who? Oh, Irene. She's on the top floor. Just go on up.

Big Irene had shrunk inside her skin, which was now as baggy as an old balloon. But she was still making an effort. There was blue irridescent eyeshadow on one wrinkled eyelid: she'd given up or got pissed before she reached the other. Her legs were bare and scaly, mottled with Granny's tartan. She'd always been one for sitting over the fire.

'Why didn't you ring, love? I'd've come down.'

'The woman said to come up.'

Brenda fell into the nearest chair.

'What's the matter with her?'

'You know what's the matter.'

'What else?'

'She's just come out of hospital. She's had her ovary out. At least I think they took it out.' Iris realised she didn't know whether they had found anything wrong with the ovary or not. Perhaps it had all been put on. She licked her lips nervously. 'Of course she's had the stitches out. They seemed to think at the hospital she was going on all right.'

Irene was bending over the chair to peer into Brenda's face. 'She's a funny colour,' she said, straightening up.

'Oh, she never has much colour.'

Irene pulled her thumb and forefinger together along her sunken jaw. Iris turned away so as not to see the struggle between fear and greed. And pity. Give the woman her due. It wasn't just the money.

When she could bear it no longer, she said, 'Will it make a difference, the ovary and all that?'

'Oh, I shouldn't think so,' said Irene. She didn't know what an ovary was but she wasn't going to admit ignorance. She'd always taken a pride in what she did. There wasn't a lot you could take a pride in these days. 'No, I shouldn't think so. But I'll have a look at her. Make sure she's no further on than she says she is.'

'Oh, I don't think . . .'

'One thing they all lie about, love, is that. It's bad enough if she's telling the truth.' She looked sharply at Iris. Then turned to Brenda. 'Howay, then, love, let's have a feel.' Her fingers poked and prodded the white mound. 'Yes. She's about as far on as she says. Well, love, it's not exactly a tiddler you've got in there, is it? You should've told yer Mam.'

'I know I should. I just kept on hoping and praying I'd come all right. And then when I started getting the pains I thought it was coming away.'

'How old are you?'

'Sixteen.'

'Sixteen gone August,' Iris said.

'Why won't they do her? I've known married women get them as easy as wink.'

Iris swallowed hard. 'He says he can't do her. But he's only saying that out of spite. She didn't tell him, you see. And of course he was livid.'

'He should've known. You can practically see looking at her.'

'Well, I can't say anything, 'cause I didn't know.'

Irene looked down at Brenda, who seemed almost too tired to care what decision was reached.

'Well, you'd better lie down,' Irene said at last. 'It's not getting any smaller while we're stood here gassing.'

'You're not going to do her [now?' Iris said, forgetting that this was what she had hoped for when she came.

'Better get it over with,' Irene said, in a loud, confident voice. Then whispered, 'She'll not sleep for thinking about it.'

'I'd rather get it over, Mam.'

Iris made as if to open her handbag.

'Give it us later, pet.'

There was a cup of tea on the table with cigarette butts floating on the dregs. She was a mucky cow. Iris twisted her hands together.

'You're not stopping, are you?'

'Oh, I couldn't leave her,' Iris said, though she knew she

would not be able to bear Brenda's pain.

'You go, Mam,' Brenda said. 'There's no sense us both suffering.'

'Well, if you're sure you'll be all right . . .'

Brenda grabbed hold of her hand and squeezed it hard. 'I'll be all right.'

'Course she will. That's a grand lass you've got there.'

'I could kill the bastard.'

'Aye, I know. It's an old saying, "The sins they do by two, by two, they pay for one by one." It's true, is that.'

She touched Iris tentatively on the arm for a moment; across the years that divided them, there was a flicker of friendship. 'Give us half an hour,' she said.

Brenda gave her mother one last, stricken look, then Iris staggered down the unlit staircase and out into the street.

It was still raining. She walked towards the river, past rows of houses boarded-up and waiting for demolition. She passed the place where in the last war a bomb had fallen and saw herself as a small child wandering across the blitzed ground. The tide was out, the river shrunken. She leant against the wall and gripped the iron spikes that ran along the top. They were wet and rusty: streaks of orange rain trickled on to her wrists.

Brenda might die. Iris wanted to run back, to stop it happening: the child would grow up as thousands before it had done. But she didn't. Instead she went on clinging to the spikes, pulling on them as if she was in pain.

Brenda got on to the bed. It sagged alarmingly under her weight. There was the sweetish smell of stale urine from the bucket underneath. It was full to overflowing: she couldn't've emptied it for days.

Irene was busy in the room behind her. She couldn't see what she was doing, though she heard the chink of metal in a bowl. It was a bit like the dentist. You just had to lie back and look up at the light and listen to the sound of things being got ready. Except at the dentist you knew it was all right really. Even if you were frightened, you still knew. The pain wouldn't be unbearable, nothing would go wrong, you certainly wouldn't die. Here there were no limits. Pain stretched ahead of her like a tunnel that she was afraid, and compelled, to enter. Any amount of pain.

She closed her eyes briefly, and opened them to find Irene's face between her and the light.

'I'll just have another look,' she said.

Her fingers prodded the white belly, digging in deep around the navel. She looked frightened. But she only said, 'You've got a good little figure on you.' Her eyes were all over, breasts as well as stomach. She was jealous to death. It was written all over her face.

If only she'd start.

'Right, then. Knees up. Let's be having you.'

Brenda spread her legs and shut her eyes, shuddering as the old woman's fingers opened the lips of her cunt and started to probe inside.

Iris waited outside the door, afraid of what she might see when she opened it. Then she drew a deep breath and went in.

Brenda was sitting up in a chair, drinking a mug of hot tea, laced with whisky. She looked white and sweaty but managed a wobbly smile.

'How are you, love?' Iris asked.

'Oh, I'm all right. It wasn't as bad as what I thought it was going to be.'

Iris turned to Irene, who was rinsing a bowl out at the sink. 'How much do I owe you?'

'Oh, just give us ten quid.'

It was cheaper than she had thought. Irene came towards her, drying her hands on a dirty tea towel. Iris handed the money over and as she did so Irene whispered, 'If she doesn't start within the twenty-four hours you bring her back.'

'But . . .' Iris looked at the girl and lowered her voice. 'What do you mean?'

'It's not over, you know. She's got it all to come.'

'I know that. But I thought you could more or less guarantee it starting?'

'No, I've known them come back nine, ten times before anything happened.'

'My God, don't tell her that.'

'She's like you, isn't she, Iris?'

'I don't think so.'

'I do. She puts me very much in mind of you as a girl.'

'Can I phone for a taxi?'

'I'd rather you didn't. I don't want her seen leaving.'

In case anything happened. 'All right. Brenda, have you finished your tea?'

Brenda stood up, and swayed. The two older women hurried across to support her. 'Howay, love,' said Irene. 'Your Mam'll soon have you home.'

They half dragged, half carried her to the door.

'Put a hot-water bottle in the bed, Iris. And get a bit of something in. Brandy.'

They passed an off-license on the way to the taxi rank in the middle of the High Street. Iris went in and came out with a full bottle of brandy. Brenda looked at it, but she didn't say anything.

Curtains twitched all along the street as the taxi drew up outside their house. You didn't see many taxis. It was like an ambulance, almost. Iris thought, Nosey buggers. Still, I suppose I'd do the same.

She put Brenda to bed, filled the hot-water bottle, and sat down to wait.

Ted was home before closing time — a rare event.

'How is she?' he asked nervously, poking his head around the door.

'Bit restless. I'm stopping up with her.'

'Is she all right?'

'Course she's all right. You go on to bed.'

He stood there in his stockinged feet, holding his shoes in his hand.

'Goodnight, flower.'

'Night, Dad.'

Then he padded across the landing and shut the door.

He seemed to have shrunk since she married him. It wasn't just her imagination: there was a photograph of them on their wedding day and she hardly came up to his shoulder. Whereas now . . . Perhaps it was with his chest, perhaps it was just he hunched himself up. And she'd put on weight. They'd ranted and raved at her up at the hospital to lose weight. But she couldn't. It wasn't that she couldn't stop stuffing herself; she ate very little. She seemed to need the weight. She wouldn't've known how to go on if she'd been thin.

Brenda moaned. Instantly, Iris was on her feet. 'Is it starting?' she asked.

'I don't know. I think it might be.' She looked up at her mother. 'It doesn't hurt much,' she said.

Not yet. Iris held on to her hand. She thought, It's funny — yesterday I could've killed her. Now if I could bear the pain for her I would.

By two a.m. Brenda's hair was stringy with sweat. She sat on the blue plastic bucket which sagged and pouched beneath her weight and tried to pee. Iris stood behind her, her hands on the girl's sides, and helped support her.

Brenda twisted round to look up at her mother. 'How much longer, Mam?'

'I don't know, love. I don't know.' She was almost sobbing herself.

'Can't even bloody well pee,' Brenda said. And laughed.

'Let's have you back on the bed. Piss on the sheets, for Christ's sake! I've got the mattress well padded.'

She heaved the girl back on to the bed. Brenda flopped back against the pillows, as white as they were, her face glistening with sweat. Iris offered her a swig of brandy, but she waved the bottle away.

'Is me Dad asleep?' She'd been moaning a bit earlier on, hadn't been able to stop herself.

'I think so, I don't know. Don't you worry about your Dad. Worry about getting that out of you.'

The baby was born, alive, shortly after dawn. It was a boy.

For the final minutes, Brenda gripped the head of the bed, mouth wide open, lips stretched to splitting, like the other lips between her legs. At the last moment she looked down and — 'Eyes!' Iris said, putting a hand over her daughter's face, as the bag of membranes bulged out and burst.

'I didn't see it, Mam,' Brenda said. 'I mean I just caught a glimpse . . .' She stopped. 'I didn't see it.'

'Didn't you, love?'

'No. No, I didn't see it.'

The baby clenched his fist feebly, lying on the floor of the lavatory with the *News of the World* spread over him.

Iris pulled back the sheets.

'It's all right, isn't it?' Brenda opened her eyes. She'd been drifting off to sleep.

'Oh, yes, it's all right.'

'I'm not getting blood on the sheets, am I? I seem to be losing quite a bit.'

'Oh, don't worry about the sheets. They'll wash.'

'I'm not losing too much, am I?'

'Why no! Don't worry about it. I've had four bairns. I ought to know.'

There had never been as much blood as this. Never.

Brenda's eyes closed. When she spoke again it was in a whisper. Iris had to bend down to hear what she said.

'It *was* dead, Mam, wasn't it?'

'It was never alive, flower. It's not a *baby*, you know.'

A few yards away, on the floor of the lavatory, the rustling of the newspaper ceased.

Brenda was asleep. Iris knotted a scarf round her head and went to find her shopping basket. The worst was still to come.

She took the child and wrapped him in newspaper and laid him in the basket. Then she slipped out of the house and down the street to the row of derelict houses at the end. The door of one of the houses was loose. She had seen children playing inside it the other day on her way home from work. At the back, where the yard had been, was a heap of rubble.

It was raining. Still, mercifully, dark. She took the roll of sodden newspaper and began digging a grave in the rubble. She hardly thought at all of what she was doing. Her mind was bound in by horror. Only her blood seemed to cry out against it. This was her own flesh and blood. She was burying her own flesh and blood.

When the last brick was heaped on top, when not a scrap of newspaper remained, she stood up and wiped away the dampness from her face, and never knew if it was tears or sweat or rain.

By the time she returned Ted had got himself up and off to work. She checked that Brenda was still asleep and that the flow of blood was no heavier. Then she went downstairs, slowly, like an old woman, and started to light the fire.

She thought of nothing; her whole being was preoccupied with the task of getting warm. As soon as the fire was lit she huddled over it, staring into the flames.

She felt rather than heard Laura come in. Rousing herself, she said, 'Hello, cock. How are you?'

Laura didn't reply. Perhaps she was sulking. She hadn't wanted to stay with Iris's father. Iris forced herself to try again. 'There's a cup of tea in the pot. Do you want one?'

Still no reply. Laura sat down in the far corner and fixed Iris with her stare.

Oh, God, keep me sane, thought Iris. This lot'ld drive any bugger mad.

She turned back to the fire, resolving to pay no more attention to Laura. If the bleeding didn't slow down soon she'd have to get the doctor in. Of course he'd be nasty, but after all, what could he do? They'd got it out of her. That was all that mattered.

She did not hear Laura get up. She did not see her go across to the sideboard and pick up the heavy, cut glass vase. She huddled over the fire and thought about her daughter while Laura, with the solemnity of an executioner, lifted the vase high in the air and brought it crashing down on to her skull.

'. . . and I wouldn't care, you know, but I still had me rollers in. I've been picking bits of plastic out of me head ever since. 'Iris laughed heartily, patting the bump on her head.

She was enjoying life again.

'She can't've known what she was doing, ' Joss said. He had come rushing round as soon as he knew what had happened.

'Gerraway. She knew. We went to see her, didn't we, Ted? And she was sat up in bed, cool as a bloody cucumber. Wasn't she, Ted?'

'Never blinked.'

'There you are. And she cracked on she didn't know who I was. Didn't she, Ted? But I could see it in her eyes. She knew. Mind you, what a carry-on. Two doctors come out to section her, you know. It's their fault for letting her out. She wasn't fit to be out. I said at the time, didn't I, Ted? I said, she's not fit to be out. Didn't I?'

'Aye.'

'The doctor said, mind, if I hadn't turned me head that would've been it. It's a heavy vase. Well, you can see it is.

They all turned to stare at the vase.

'Anyway, Ted says he's not having her back. Not without a very big improvement. I told them that. It was a lady doctor and she looked at me and I said it's no use, that's what he says, it's his house. It's his decision. I believe in a man being master in his own house. Told her that, didn't I, Ted?'

'Yes,' said Ted, not without irony.

Brenda came in, yawning. 'Is me tea ready?'

'It's in the oven.'

She trailed through in her dressing gown. The two men avoided looking at her. They were slightly shy with her still. There was a groan from the kitchen.

'Not liver again, Mam.'

'You'll eat liver till you look like it,' Iris said. 'I want to see the roses back in your cheeks.'

'Aw, Mam.'

'Never mind, "*Aw, Mam*". And when you've eat it you can get dressed and give your bloody mucky face a wipe.' She whispered to Joss. 'She's playing the old soldier a bit now.'

Ted stood up.

'Where you off to?'

'I thought I'd have a pint.'

'Aye, and the other seven. Don't come back here drunk. I've had enough.'

'A man isn't drunk till he's on the floor. You've never seen me drunk.'

'Bloody hell.' She turned her face away.

Ted nodded to Joss as he went out. Some people said Joss and Iris were having it off. He knew better. You'd need an ice pick.

'He's drinking heavy again,' said Iris. 'And he's picked a damn bad time. He wants to think on I don't have the bairns to see to now. If it gets too bad I can just up and off.'

'But you wouldn't do that, would you?' Joss was alarmed more for himself than Ted. He came here like coming home.

'Wouldn't I!'

There was silence. Joss stretched his legs out and said, 'I see Joanne Wilson's married.'

'Aye, I saw. Big wedding.'

'That was his Mam.'

'It's often the case, isn't it?'

'She was in two minds, you know. Right up till the end.'

'I know. I met her mother in the street. She said, Iris, we're doing all this, and do you know when it comes to the point I don't think she'll go.'

'Poor kid.'

'Oh, you don't want to worry about Joanne. She'll give as good as she gets.'

'Aye, but it's no life, is it?' He stood up. 'Will you be going to see your Laura?'

'Oh, yes.'

'Well, you know, if you want a lift . . .'

'It'd be a big help. I couldn't just leave her stuck in there. You look at some of them poor buggers and my God you wonder.'

Sheila came in with her husband and the baby and the conversation became general, light-hearted even. After they had all gone Iris carried the baby to the sofa and put the lights out. Then she crooned to him, softly, while the flames flickered over his face. He was flushed: the blood bloomed in him. Iris pressed her face into his little chest and his hands came up and tangled in her hair.

She thought of Sheila and Bobbie. She'd been scared stiff when they got married, Sheila had been so young. But they were happy: Sheila would never have to put up with what she'd had to put up with. And they'd got this boy. She slid her hand underneath him, feeling the curve of his bottom warm against her palm.

Unbidden came the memory of the other child, red as raw meat, gasping its life out on the lavatory floor.

She banished the image which always, in her rare moments of silence and solitude, returned to haunt her. She turned to the living child. Looking down at him, she saw his mother in the curve of his cheek and brow. It was almost like having Sheila a baby again. She nuzzled into his chest, hearing his heart beat, and the warmth consoled her. Her breath mingled with his breath.

CHAPTER SIX
BLONDE DINAH

George Harrison never hurried on the way home. He lingered by the river, leaning over the stone wall. He lit a pipe, the last of the day, and revelled in it. Beneath him the oily river slabbed against the wall, briefly irridescent where the light of a street lamp fell on it. He was alone, but he was not lonely. 'Lonely' was watching Crossroads because you couldn't think of anything to say. 'Lonely,' was the other body in the bed.

'What the bloody hell are you going to do?' One of the blokes had asked him that his last week at work.

'Me?' he'd asked, rather nettled by the question. 'Me? Nowt. After forty year I reckon I've done my stint.'

He couldn't remember now whether he meant what he said, for retirement had produced such a division in his life that everything on the other side of it seemed dim. They weighed on him now, those forty years. He spoke of them with bitterness, where once he spoke with pride.

They gave him a clock. Well, they gave everybody a clock. And for a few months he had sat and looked at it. There were afternoons when the time went so slowly that he was sure it had stopped. Time and time again he would get up and put it to his ear, but he could never hear it ticking: the blast-furnaces had seen to that. Only after a while he would notice that the minute hand had moved. So that was all right: he was still alive.

His wife hated having him in the house. She would bang and clatter the pots in the kitchen, and he found himself listening tensely to this, unable to read the paper. When she cleaned the living room, the vacuum cleaner was thrust aggressively between his legs. Well, you could understand that. She was used to having the place to herself. She was used to being able to get on with her jobs.

But even when the family came it wasn't much different. It was, 'Hello, Dad. How are you, Dad?' But it was their Mam they came to see. He didn't begrudge it her. She'd been a good mother, none better. But at times he envied her, she seemed so secure, with her children and grandchildren around her.

He spent as little time at home as he could. Though finding somewhere else to go was a problem. He tipped his pension up to Gladys and relied on her to give him what pocket money she thought he should have. Well, he couldn't do any other: there was little enough to keep them on as it was. Though he suspected the kids helped her out a bit, now and then. But his pocket money went nowhere. A couple of pints, a tin of tobacco, and that was it. Finish.

At first he'd tried to keep up with his mates from work. Not for long. It was too uncomfortable, sitting there trying to work out whether he could afford to stand his turn. Not that they expected it of him: they didn't. He expected it of himself.

And after a while the talk left him behind. The names, even some of the processes, were new. There was talk of new contracts, which didn't materialise, and of further redundancies, which did. None of it affected him. He gradually saw less and less of his mates. Eventually the meetings in the pub stopped altogether. He told himself bitterly that nobody wanted you when you were old, that everybody seemed to think you were after something — money, or a drink. But in fact they were not avoiding him. He was avoiding them.

Then there was only the park. In good weather. He sat on a bench at some distance from the other old men who tended to congregate together and sun themselves, wrinkled necks thrust out of knotted scarves, cautiously, like tortoises peering out of their shells.

In bad weather there was the reading room of the library. If the park had depressed him, the library terrified him. For there the real derelicts ended up, sitting at the benches muttering to themselves, pretending to read the *Freethinker*, or *Country Life*, or the *Christian Science Monitor*. They were dirty. They picked their noses and rolled the results between thumb and forefinger, making a pellet hard enough to be flicked away on to the floor. They made noises. They made smells. They were afraid. For the assistants in the library, lads and lasses in their late teens, had power over them and they knew it. They had the power of banning people from the library, of withholding warmth. So sandwiches were consumed furtively, a bit at a time. And those who were compelled to talk to themselves, thrashing out some unending internal feud, tried to do so quietly, though they did not always succeed.

One of the assistants had the habit of walking round the benches. He did so once when George was there and George was horrified to realise that the fear on everybody else's face was reflected in his own. He left at once and never went back.

He was not like that, he told himself. No, definitely not. Though it was hard to maintain any sense of dignity.

Then Gladys got herself a job: nothing much, just a part-time job in the canteen at the local school. But it was enough. He was up the labour exchange like a bolt from a gun.

Give me anything, he said. I don't care what it is. Just as long as it's work.

It was a job in a lavatory. He had to mop the floors and generally keep things clean. It didn't take long, and the rest of the time he just sat. Still, it was work. Money in his pocket. Independence.

Once he came back from work a bit early and heard Gladys and the two girls laughing. He stood outside the kitchen door and listened. The idea of him cleaning out a lavatory was a huge joke, it seemed. He never let on he'd heard, just went back to the front door and staged a second, noisier, entrance. But it hurt all right.

Though there was still the money in his pocket for a drink or a smoke. He jingled the coins now. Money in your pocket. It was everything. You never knew how important it was, till you hadn't got any.

He drifted along, thinking of nothing. Then he became aware of other steps shuffling along some distance behind, on the other side of the road. His stomach tightened. There were said to be people still living in the derelict houses by the river: down-and-outers, no goods, people what'ld cut your throat for a tanner and think nothing of it. He was an old man. The days when he could have tackled anybody were finished.

But a second later he was reassured. It was a woman's step. She staggered out into the light of a street lamp and he knew her at once by the brassy blonde halo of hair. Now there was somebody *ought* to think about retirement. In that job forty year was enough!

And she couldn't've been at it much less. For as long as he could remember she had been a legend. Blonde Dinah: sitting in the pubs all along the High Street, waiting for some man or other to walk into the trap. She never gave up. Sometimes for a few evenings she might be missing, and they thought perhaps she'd packed it in at last. But no. The next night, or the night after, she was back, perched on a bar stool, sweat breaking through the layers of make-up.

He turned back to the river, hardly sparing her a glance. Soon he would have to go home, get undressed in the kitchenette so as not to wake Gladys, and carry his shoes up the stairs to bed avoiding the second and the seventh step, which creaked.

He went on leaning against the wall. After a while he became aware that Dinah was staggering towards him. He was irritated. There was enough room surely to God, there was the whole width of the bloody road for her to get past. Unless . . .

'Least it's stopped raining,' she said.

He didn't reply.

'This afternoon I thought it was never going to stop.'

She waiting for him to speak. 'What's wrong with you, then? Cat got your tongue?'

'Not tonight,' he said, hearing the words rasp in his throat. He sounded as awkward as a boy. 'Thanks all the same.'

'What do you mean, "Thanks all the same"? Far as I know there's nowt been bloody offered. All I said was, it's stopped raining. It has stopped raining, hasn't it?'

'Yes!'

'Well, then.'

She muttered to herself for a few minutes. He heard, 'Dear God, if you can't say . . .'

He let her talk. She was hugging her grievance as if for warmth. He felt sorry for her. She must be sixty. At least. Same age as Gladys. No age to be hawking it round the pubs. He wondered what she charged now. Must be giving it away.

'I used to live round here, you know. Bit further down. Wharfe Street.' She stood with her back to the river, looking at the row of derelict houses opposite. 'Good houses, you know. Some of 'em.'

'Car parks.'

She glanced at him. 'Oh, so you can talk. Yes, car parks. Can't build flats because of the chemicals in the air. Not fit to breathe. My God, they took their time finding that out.'

She cleared her throat. The cough got out of hand. Soon she was bent double, clinging to the wall. When, finally, she straightened up there was a blue-black tear running down the side of her nose. She brushed it away carefully with the tip of one gloved finger. The gloves were made of pale grey suede: they added an incongruous note of gentility to her appearance. As though taking her cue from them, she went on in a distinctly refined tone, 'And whereabouts do you live?'

'Union Street.'

'Oh, yes. Behind the Bluebell.'

'That's right.'

'Is it coming down round there?'

'No. Not Union Street anyway. Just the bit at the end, and Ewbank Street. And the little streets near the railway line.'

'I think it's a crying shame. I don't like to see them come down.'

Well, she wouldn't, would she? Her old stalking grounds. But he listened to her talk. The cracked and seamed face lit up, her voice came out warm and spluttery between badly fitting teeth, and her hands, shaping the darkness, re-created a community, as she talked about the past, about the people she had known.

He found himself wondering about her, about what she was like, like . . . well, like. She must get sick of it surely, not to mention sore. Gladys . . . but then Gladys was different. He doubted if they did it twice a year. He left her alone as much as he could, and he believed she understood that and was grateful to him. So that when finally he had to go to her she didn't mind so much because she knew he'd been doing without. Women, decent women that was — well, anyway, Gladys, didn't go too much on that sort of thing.

But perhaps Dinah didn't either? Perhaps it was just a job, like cleaning out lavatories was just a job?

'Course there was no telly then or owt like that, was there?' she added, after a short pause. 'People had to make their own amusement.'

'Aye, and they were the better for it, 'n' all.'

'They were.'

'There's over much on tap these days. Nobody has to try for anything.'

There was silence again, a companionable silence this time. He sniffed the air: sometimes, standing by the river, you could smell the dawn, hours and hours before the light in the sky changed. It was a marvellous time: all the tension, all the bitterness dissolved away and you were left waiting, waiting for whatever life turned up.

'Do you fancy a walk round my place, then?'

The question ought to have jarred on him. It ought to have been answered at once by a brusque 'No'. But it wasn't. And by the time he opened his mouth to say 'No', he'd realised it wasn't what he wanted to say.

He turned and walked along the river path beside her.

'What do they call you?' she asked.

'George.'

'Oh, that's nice. George George is it, or George summat else?'

'Harrison,' he admitted. He was reluctant to let her know too much. He was wondering what he'd let himself in for. The clap, most like.

'I'm Dinah,' she said.

He wondered whether to say 'I know' and decided against it. She was drunk enough to think he was getting at her if he cracked on he knew who she was.

He was dragging his feet. He couldn't remember how this had happened. But he didn't have to go through with it. He could turn and walk away. A smell of beer and cheap scent decided him. He was off.

'Howay, then,' she said, tugging at his sleeve like a little girl.

'Look,' he said. 'I'm not as flush as I was.'

'A quid. Or whatever you can manage.'

A quid. It should have been disgusting. His mind supplied the word 'sordid'. Only it wasn't. The raw, cheap scent caught at his throat.

'Go on,' she said. 'Give yourself a treat. You never know, you might enjoy it.'

'No . . .'

But he had given in. They both knew it.

'It's not far. Just round the next turning, in fact.'

Though the houses on either side of them now were boarded-up and derelict. Their footsteps echoed along the empty street.

'More to life than money, isn't there?'

'You're drunk,' he said.

'Be thankful. Mightn't fancy you if I was sober.'

He was beginning to have visions of a dirty mattress on the floor of an uninhabited house. But no. They turned into another street, where the houses had glass in the windows and curtains up.

'This is it,' she announced. 'We're here.'

A strip of sooty grass. Steps leading down into the street. She fumbled for the key.

Then they were inside. Postcards lined up on a table, a

creeping smell of drains, and . . .

'Mind them milk bottles. Knock that lot over and we'll have the whole house awake.'

They staggered up the stairs together, she making exaggerated shushing sounds, he stumbling and leaning against her as though he was the one who was drunk. But it produced a sort of intimacy, a feeling of being conspirators. He was beginning to enjoy himself.

The light at the top of the stairs changed all that. The bed was grey, unmade. It seemed to fill the room. She kicked off her shoes. 'Thank God for that,' she said.

It was what Gladys always said at the end of the day. The tingling in his groin stopped. He sat down on a chair near the door and started to take off his shoes. Slowly.

There were photographs on the table beside the bed. Old ones. Yellow with age. An unshaded light bulb swung in the draught from the door. Not in a million years. He started to say something, but her hands were already on him.

'I don't seem . . .'

'Oh, it'll do all right, will this.' She pressed his cock into the valley between her wrinkled breasts. 'Why, man, it's like a steel rod!'

It wasn't. As a matter of fact it was nowt like. Her shammy-leather breasts enclosed him. He had never sat astride a woman like this before or even imagined it to be possible. Almost in spite of himself he started to thrust, but it was no good. Then her hand went down between her legs and came up again. She smeared cunt-juice all over his nose and mouth.

He was shocked. But then the smell started to get to him. People said fish, but it wasn't fish. It was wet seaweed, and rock pools and the sand shifting in-between your toes.

'Nowt wrong with that, is there?' She had rolled his foreskin back. When he didn't speak she laughed and said, 'Here, give us a lick.'

She took him into her mouth.

It was morning when he woke. He lay for a moment, dazed, looking at the clothes and shoes scattered on the floor, wondering how the bedroom came to be in such a mess. Then, remembering, he got up and started to hunt for his clothes. They had taken everything off. Both of them. He didn't know, now, whether he was shocked or pleased.

He looked down at her. She looked like Gladys lying there, her mouth open, a wisp of hair shaken with every breath. It disturbed him. She ought not to look like Gladys. He had always believed there were two sorts of women: the decent ones and the rest. He felt they should look different, for how could you tell them apart, how could you remember they were different, if every sag, every wrinkle of their used bodies proclaimed that they were one flesh? There was even a dark line down her belly, stretching from navel to groin. At some stage she must have borne a child. Though he had never heard of her having any family.

He looked down at his own body, at his limp cock, and gave the knob a friendly squeeze before he pulled up his pants.

He was in a hurry to be gone. He counted out some money, quietly, so that she should not wake. He put it down on the bedside table by the photographs. After a moment's reflection he took one two-bob bit back again: there was no need to go overboard. He thought, I could walk out without paying. But no, he didn't want to do that. And besides she might wake. Sleeping like that with her mouth open, thirst would wake her before long.

She was lying with her legs apart. The mound of hair was going thin on top, as though frequent shaving had made it lose heart. He had never actually seen it before. It was funny in a way. You spend your whole boyhood thinking about it, wondering what it's like; but when you finally get it you don't really *see* it. He had never seen Gladys naked. Not with everything off.

Almost against his will, he knelt down until it was on a level with his face. The lips gaped, still dribbling a little milky fluid. And there it was. A gash? A wound? Red fruit bitten to the core? It was impossible to say what it was like.

She stirred in her sleep, tightening her thighs as though aware of some need to protect herself. He took one last look and went. He almost ran down the stairs, unloading guilt behind him at every step.

The sun was shining. He stood on the steps and breathed deeply before setting off in the direction of the river. His step was jaunty. He was on the way to being his old self again: the self that would look back on this night's work with a mixture of pride, amusement, and shame.

Through the few remaining chinks in his perception, the morning struck at him. Seagulls screamed and dived in the air above the river. And one detached itself from the rest to fly under the steel bridge; wings, briefly shadowed, gleamed in the restored light.

The air made his lungs hurt. He remembered John Scaife who had died two months back, not much more than half his age. He was sorry for it but, remembering, stood taller. He thought of how much life there was still to live, of how much life there was inside him. You're not dead, no, not till they nail down the lid.

He did not think of Dinah, who stirred in her sleep and woke, aware of the empty bed.

A tom cat with tattered ears crossed his path. Though he did not normally care for cats, he exchanged a glance with this one: cynical and accepting. The cat stared back at him. Their paths converged, crossed, separated. He went on his way, whistling now. God knows what he would find to say when he got there, but he was glad to be going home.

CHAPTER SEVEN

ALICE BELL

It was January now. Alice Bell spent her days in bed: it was her solution to the price of coal. Whenever she moved newspapers stirred and rustled all around her. The bed was full of them. She had read somewhere that newspapers were as good as blankets, and the house was cold.

There wasn't a lot of fat on her to keep her warm. Her thighs were folds of creased skin, hanging from the bone. Yet beside her on the bed was a black handbag with £100 inside. She had saved it out of her social security money: the 'pancrack' as she contemptuously called it. What she got was barely adequate for heating and food. To save out of it, as she was determined to do, meant hunger and cold. Though she didn't usually feel hungry: she had been depriving herself of food too long for that.

She liked the feel of the notes, especially if she was lucky enough to get a new one, though the old, crumpled ones also had their charm. But she liked best to crisp the new ones through her fingers. When she was alone she would often take them out and count them. And yet she was not in the usual sense of the word a miser. This was no meaningless accumulation of money for its own sake. She was saving up for her funeral.

As a little girl, more than seventy years ago, she had witnessed the funerals of paupers. And she still remembered the old rhyme:

> Rattle his bones
> Over the stones.
> He's only a pauper
> Whom nobody owns.

Children followed the coffins, jeering sometimes, and throwing stones. Perhaps she'd been one of them, she didn't remember. But the horror of that final rejection had stayed with her all her life. The death grant would not bury her. Inflation had made her small insurance policy useless. And there had to be a proper funeral, paid for out of her own money. Her self-respect, her dignity as a human being, required it. And so she had to save. And starve.

Her other dread was the Workhouse. As a small child on her way to school she had walked past its gates, never without a shudder. It was still in use, though they called it something different now. But to her it would always be the Workhouse: the place paupers' funerals started from.

The 'pancrack' she had to submit to: there was no choice. She was entitled to nothing else. You could get what they called a seventy pension, but the man had explained to her that it was really the same thing. Her second husband had been self-employed and too mean to pay a stamp. Every six months she received a visit from the social security people, to find out if her circumstances had changed. The humiliation of these visits, the posh voices, the questions, the eyes everywhere, only strengthened her determination to preserve her independence at all costs. To hang on to her house, to save up for her funeral, and never, never to ask them for a penny more than she was forced. She wasn't going to lie in a pauper's coffin, and she would never, while she had breath in her body, let them talk her into the Workhouse.

'Them buggers have been here again,' she would say to Iris King.

'Well, and you shouldn't let them upset you.'

'Asking bloody questions. Begrudging you every penny

you get.'

"T'isn't coming out of their pockets.'

'You'd think it was, but.'

'Ah, well. You want to think: they'll be old themselves one day.'

And so Iris soothed her. And she let herself be soothed.

A stranger coming into the room would hardly have noticed, at first, that there was a body in the bed, for Alice's emaciated frame scarcely raised the covers, and her skin, over the years, had yellowed to the same shade as the pillowcases and the wall: smoke-cured. The room was always full of smoke because the chimney backs were broken and the smoke from her neighbour's fire poured into the house. When she was still well enough to leave the house, she had always carried with her the smell of smoke. The smoke formed layers of soot on all the furniture. You could dust it one minute, and it would be there again the next.

Still she loved the house. Over the years it had become a refuge. Finally, almost an extension of her own body.

It hadn't always been so. For Iris King, Union Street was a move up. For Mrs Bell, it was down. At first she hated it. The house was dark and drab, and it needed so many repairs. The kitchen tap shook and juddered whenever you turned it on, producing a thin trickle of brown water and a shower of plaster from the walls.

Iris King had tried to decorate the kitchen for her, but she'd had to give up in the end.

'I'm sorry, Mrs Bell,' she'd said. 'I just daren't mess on with this paper. It's holding up the wall.'

And they'd both had a good laugh because incredibly the old music-hall joke was true.

But afterwards Mrs Bell had felt a bit depressed. She was used to better. Her last house had had a bathroom and an indoor lavatory, with a little strip of green out the back. She'd had a bay window in the front room, too.

You take these things for granted till you haven't got them. The descent to Union Street was bitter.

More than anything else she hated the steam hammer. At first she hadn't known what it was. She thought the neighbours were banging. When it went on and on, she even began to think they might be doing it deliberately to persecute her.

Her nerves were very bad that first winter in the street. She'd just had an operation on her eyes and it'd gone wrong. She came out of hospital so low that for the first time in her life she thought about suicide. The depression went on and on. Sometimes, driven to desperation by the rhythmic banging, she would switch on the vacuum cleaner and leave it running for hours. Anything to get her own back.

Then she became afraid. Nobody else seemed to hear the banging. Perhaps it was inside her head? She didn't trust herself, not since the operation. And it was the first winter alone after her husband's death. Anything seemed possible. Gradually, by trying to trace the sound from street to street, she realised it was coming from the engineering works on the other side of the railway line. The fear loosened its grip. The other women in the street didn't hear it because they had lived with it so long. Only when it stopped there was an odd, uneasy, waking expression on their faces. They were short-tempered, and at odds with everything until it started again.

She avoided the other women as much as she could. She would even go to the shops along the back alley, 'arch' they called it round here, to avoid meeting them. She was ashamed of her poverty, and of the changes that sickness and pain had wrought in her appearance. She hardly knew her own reflection in the glass. And to meet other people, to present to them this transformed, deformed self, was more than she could bear.

Gradually over the years her health got worse, until she was confined to the house and almost bedridden. Immediately the neighbours she had ignored began coming to the door to offer help, tentatively at first, alert for the least sign of a rebuff; then as a matter of course. They shopped, made tea, lit the fire.

'You rely on them too much, Mam,' her son said, whenever he came to see her. She was a worry to him. He was horrified by the confinement of her life, which seemed to him an almost vegetable form of existence. And he foresaw a time when she would not be able to manage in her own home, even with the neighbours' help.

'I've got good neighbours,' was all she would say.

'But there's limits to what you can expect neighbours to do.'

At the back of his mind was the fear that he might one day have to offer her a home. And it would be the end between him and his wife.

'They've no need to do anything.'

'Oh, don't talk so daft.'

The situation improved when Iris King became her home help, for Iris came in far oftener than she was officially supposed to do, even calling in late at night to make sure that all was well. And, through Iris, Alice was bonded into the street in a way she had never been before.

There would be silence until Iris got the fire going, then she would start on her news. 'Well, we had a bit of luck last night. Ted did, rather. You know how he never goes to the Bingo? Says he'd rather have a drink? Well, last night his stomach was a bit upset so he said he'd have a walk down with us. Bugger me if he didn't shout on the last house. Didn't even know he was sweating. Hundred and twenty quid. And I wouldn't care but he only gets one book. He can't manage any more. And there's me sat there, four books and not even a line. Anyway he give Joss and me a fiver and then off he went round the Buffs. It had cured his stomach, see. Well, I thought he'd come back in a right state, but no, give him his due, he didn't. Then just as he was getting into bed, no warning, out it comes. He's gunna buy a horse.'

Mrs Bell thought bitterly that they had won more at Bingo in one night than she had saved from years of starvation. She said, 'Where's he going to keep it?'

'Well, that's just it. First off he said he was going to rent one of them garages up at the end. I said, Ted, you can't keep a horse in a garage, it's cruel, and besides who's going to muck it out?' She paused, whisking a sheet of newspaper away from the fire in a cloud of smoke. 'So now he's on about tethering it up on the Moor. I said to him I said, What about winter? You can't leave it stuck out there all year.'

There were times when, much as Mrs Bell loved Iris, she found herself counting the minutes until she left. Her life seemed to be lived at too fast a pace and on too large a scale. Even vicariously, it was exhausting.

'He's always wanted a horse. That's what he says. First I knew of it. But there you are, you see. You think you know people, you think you've got them summed up, but you haven't. There's always summat. There's always summat they come out with and you say, My God.'

'I don't know how she stays sane,' said Mrs Harrison, who lived directly opposite.

'She gets very low.'

'She's always seemed cheerful whenever I've had owt to do with her.'

'She puts a good face on it. What else can you do?'

Mrs Harrison had her own problems, and they'd got worse since her husband retired. 'It's no use, I can't be doing with him stuck under me feet all day. I'm used to being able to get on and get done. And he's not cheerful company. There's hardly a word out of him and when he does speak it's nothing pleasant. I wish he'd die or go and stay with their Freda. Give me a rest.'

The long marital battle was over. There was nothing much left, now, whether of love or hate. Only a weak vindictiveness remained. She remembered all the nights in the first years of their marriage when he'd turned her out of doors in her nightdress, sometimes with a baby in her arms. 'And I was stuck in the coal hole all night, because I was too ashamed to go and knock the neighbours up and it was too far to walk to me Mam's. Oh, I know he's changed, he can be as nice as pie when it suits him. But I don't forget.'

Dimly, through the years of bitterness and struggle, glowed memories of a happier time. 'You'll think me stuck up for saying this, but I was a lovely lass. The lads used to fight over who was going to walk me home from Chapel. I was, I was beautiful.' She sat with her head bowed, contemplating a past so distant that no vanity could be involved. 'When I think: I could've had me pick. They were all after me, you know. Not that they got anywhere. Not an inch above the knee. Well, it was like that then, wasn't it? We just didn't think of anything like that.'

Mrs Bell, who had, to her cost, remained silent.

'And then I had to go and get stuck with him.'

'Now then, he must've been the one you wanted.'

'He was the one I got stuck with.' Her face softened slightly. 'He was a handsome fella. What me Mam would've called a good-looking nowt.'

'She gives me the creeps does that old bugger,' said Iris. 'Always praying and singing hymns and telling everybody what a clean-living woman she is. Bad-minded old cow.'

Mrs Bell did her best to keep the peace. She relied on her neighbours, it was true. But she gave back more than her son ever understood. To the younger women, particularly Iris, she was almost a mother. And to the older women, like Mrs Harrison, she was a friend they could rely upon not to gossip behind their backs. But there was a certain amount of jealousy.

'It's her hats that get me,' said Iris. 'Where on earth does she find them?'

'Jumble sales.'

'There's no need for that. Well, is there?'

'Don't ask me. I don't know how much she has coming in.'

Iris had to be content with that. 'Have I to light the fire?' she asked. There were rumours of a miners' strike and Mrs Bell was trying to economise on coal.

'Yes, you'd better.'

'I was raking through the kitchen drawer the other night. I've got some candles left over from the last lot, I know I have, but I'm blowed if I can put me hands on them.'

'Do you remember how short they got?'

'Do I? I swore I'd never be caught like that again.'

'He'll go to the country this time. He'll have to. He's got himself into such a bloody hole.'

218

'I wouldn't care if he was the only one in it.'

There was a cold spell towards the end of January. The women of Union Street had to cope with the problem of keeping themselves and their families warm. There were continued reports that the miners were about to go on strike.

Mrs Bell had a final look at the deaths, muttering the names under her breath as her magnifying glass moved down the page. The list was longer now. After making sure there were no familiar names she pushed the blankets back and added the newspaper to those already in the bed.

She tried to do without a fire in the afternoon, so that she could have heat at night when the temperature dropped. Though she had a lot of faith in the newspaper, too. Tramps covered themselves with it, didn't they, and they should know.

Iris had discovered some coal in one of the corner shops and was carrying it home on her back. At the corner of the street she paused to get her breath. Further along, bending down, was the large black-clad arse of Mrs Harrison. Out gathering again. George Harrison'ld drop dead if he ever found out.

As Iris drew level Mrs Harrison straightened up.

'Now then.'

'Now then!'

Iris watched as Mrs Harrison picked up another french letter and transferred it to the Co-op carrier bag she always carried on these expeditions. Iris was outraged, but said nothing. She was in a hurry to get to one of her old men.

Later they met in Mrs Bell's house, where Iris had gone to light the fire.

'Well, Missis, did you get a good haul?'

'Only eight.'

'Only, she says. That's eight cold bums clagged against somebody's back yard wall. Buggered if I know what they see in it this weather.'

'I could never see what they saw in it any weather,' Mrs Bell said.

'Aye, but last night! Freeze anything off. You want to watch yourself, Missis. One of these days you'll pick one up and It'll still be inside!'

Mrs Harrison didn't like Iris King, who was loud-mouthed, vulgar and irreligious. She turned away slightly and stared at the empty grate.

'I wonder how long it'll be before they settle this lot.'

'As long as it takes,' said Mrs Bell.

'There's a lot of greed in it if you ask me. What is it they're asking? Eighty quid?'

'No more than a face-worker's worth. They risk their lives.'

'Aye, and there'll be a few lives risked if they go on strike. Old people.'

'They'll see the old people don't suffer.'

'Oh, aye? Seems to me the more people suffer the better they're pleased. That's what it's about isn't it? Blackmail.'

'Shut your face, woman. You don't know what you're on about.'

'I know what I get to keep him and me on. And it's a bloody sight short of eighty quid.' Mrs Harrison had carried her own extra coal home earlier in the day and her mouth was still blue from the strain. She looked as if she'd grown a moustache. 'Once this is over the price of coal'll rocket. And you know what that means.' She lowered her head stubbornly: her political opinions were no less passionately held than Mrs Bell's. They linked her with her country childhood. She'd had a pig's bladder hanging up in her back kitchen for years after she married George. And bunches of herbs.

But Mrs Bell was struggling to sit up. Socialism was more than politics to her. It was almost a religion, a way of life.

Iris hurried in with a change of subject.

'I see it says in the paper Alice Street's to come down. And Walker Street. All along there.'

'Bloody good houses, some of them,' Mrs Bell said. 'That's your Tory government.'

'You mean, that's your Labour Council. Government has nowt to do with it.'

No topic brought peace. Shortly afterwards they parted, and for once they did not part friends.

'Lock the door as you go out,' Mrs Bell shouted to Iris. She lay in the darkness, trying to get her breath and her temper back.

She remembered her youth: the meetings, the speeches, heckling, canvassing, marching. There wasn't much she'd learned in the Depression that still made sense in the seventies. And yet. She was poorer now than she'd been then. And worse housed. Then, she'd had a lovely little Council house in Briar Road, with a garden and a window at either end of the living room. It had been a lovely house. When she looked back that was what she regretted most: leaving Briar Road. She didn't regret the meetings, or the marches. She'd've done all that again.

Oh, but it was cold. She pulled her aching feet up the bed and tried to tuck her nightdress round them. And then she realised. No fire. They'd gone out without lighting it. Bugger it. Well, she couldn't go knocking on people's doors this hour, even if she could get that far. She'd just have to fend for herself. And she'd have to do something. The living room was like an ice-box.

She sat up. There was no coal in the bucket, or not much. Not enough anyway. That meant a trip across the yard. Probably several trips: she couldn't carry much at a time. So much for bloody politics. No, it was no use — she couldn't go. She only had a nightie on and a dressing gown, and the air outside was freezing. She would just have to make the best of it.

Half an hour later a hand rattled her doorknob. It might be Iris. She shouted as loudly as she could, but it was no use. She heard the footsteps go away. Even if it was Iris she could easily think somebody else had come in to light the fire. That was the trouble. It wasn't anybody's job. She had to rely on people doing it out of kindness.

The sound of her voice crying out in the night told her how frightened she was. They were always on at you to keep warm. You couldn't open the paper without somebody going on about hyper-whatever-it-was. There was nothing else for it: she would have to go and get the coal.

She put the light on. The floor near the hearth was covered with silverfish, millions of them, all scurrying for cover. They only came out in the dark. It was better than blackclocks though. They'd had them at home when she was a bairn. But even the silverfish . . . You didn't fancy walking over them in your bare feet. She waited till they were all gone before hobbling across to find her slippers.

She stood on the back-kitchen doorstep, bucket in one hand, stick in the other, nerving herself to face the trip across the yard. The air was so cold it seared her lungs. She pulled the scarf up round her mouth and set off.

Frost glittered on the surface of the yard. An emaciated moon looked down. She began slithering and clanking her way across to the coal house. The rubber tip of her stick slipped on the ice and her heart bulged into her throat with fear. Halfway across she stopped to get her breath. There was a waterfall of icicles near the drainpipe where the gutter had overflowed. She'd have to see about getting that fixed.

Then on again.

Snow had blown in through the open door of the coalhouse. She raked about looking for the smaller pieces that might burn more easily. She was very tired. She had to stop when the bucket was only half-full: she could not carry more than that, not with the stick to manage as well.

She set off back. But haste and growing exhaustion led her to take the nearest way, across the centre of the yard, forgetting that the drain as well as the gutter overflowed. There was a sheet of black ice and no time to feel fear before she was falling, falling, the world tilting above her head. Then there were stars like pinpoints of frost and the black wires of a telegraph pole cutting into the sky.

She felt no pain, though the fall had knocked the breath out of her. After a while she thought she ought to move her legs, and that was all right, they did move.

The coal had fallen out of her bucket. It lay scattered across the ice.

There was still an orange glow in one of the windows

next door. But they had the telly on too loud. Bursts of music and laughter came out and fractured themselves on the ice. She would never be able to make them hear. Even if she could manage to shout. She wasn't sure she could. Her tongue seemed to be very big inside her mouth. She tried to shout, but only a whisper came out. It was no use. Anyway, she needed all her breath to get back on her feet.

She tried to push herself up, but her fingers slid across the ice enclosing a mess of coal dust and frozen snow. The shock had worn off. She was afraid now, and in pain. Her back hurt. But fear was the worst thing. She couldn't get up and if she went on lying there she would die.

Then she thought of using her stick. Not to lean on: the rubber tip got even less purchase on the ice than her hands had done. No, but if she could manage to hook it round the drainpipe she might be able to pull herself towards the wall where there was no ice, like an angler landing a fish. But the handle wouldn't hook round the pipe. And her outstretched hand trembled so much that she dropped the stick and had to start all over again. Finally, she managed to hook the handle round the pipe, but now there was a new terror because the pipe creaked and shifted when she started to pull. It was eaten away with rust, fastened to the wall with a single screw that might give at any moment.

But it held. Slowly, she dragged herself towards the wall, her heels scrabbling on the ice, until she reached a place where the ground was clear and she could stand upright again.

Sobbing, muttering under her breath, she limped back into the living room and rattled the poker at the back of the grate, hoping the neighbours might hear. But nobody came. She was shaking all over from cold and shock. After a few minutes she climbed on to the bed and pulled the blankets up over her wet dressing gown.

Her mind was clear and cold as ice. She went back over what had happened, reliving the moment when the world had turned. She listened for the sound of footsteps in the street outside. Somehow, when the sound of men's boots signalled the first shift of the day, she must get up and go to the door.

Then, after she did not know how long, confusion darkness, pain. And suddenly there were people too many people pressing round her bed and a bright light that hurt her eyes and she wanted to say Get back and they all pressed in around her and their faces loomed up towards her with the fish-eyed distorted look of faces in curved glass and she tried to say again Get back but the words glugged out of her mouth like water.

Sheets. Tight and cool. The bed narrow. Too narrow for home, and high up. She forced her eyes open. Ice-green light splintered on a water jug. She moved her head: the light was green because of curtains round her bed.

There was a vase of flowers. Red. Familiar. But she could not find the name.

The curtains split around a head.

'Returned to the land of the living, have we?' And so, it seemed, she had.

When the sounds that glugged out of her mouth bore some resemblance to speech, when she could shuffle more than a few feet along the wall, they said she could go home.

At first she had thought they would never let her go. Who would look after her? they asked.

'I can look after myself.'

But this would not do. They did not even answer.

'I've got good neighbours.'

But you can't rely on the neighbours for everything. They told her so.

They were kind, but they didn't understand. They suggested a convalescent home. She refused, fearing that if she once agreed to enter a Home of any kind they would find some way of keeping her there, or else transfer her to another Home.

They were kind, but she didn't trust them. The need to get back to her own house was very strong now, like a physical pain.

In the end they gave in, though she could tell they disap-

proved. Old ladies are many, hospital beds are few. They
needed the bed.

Her son came to collect her in his car.

'My son's coming to collect me in his car,' she told the
nurses proudly.

They smiled, though they hadn't understood a word she
said. She was excited. When she was excited her speech
went altogether.

She sat perched nervously on the edge of the front seat.
She didn't like cars, though she liked her son having one.
And she looked out of the window at all the changes that
had taken place. She hadn't been into the town for many
years.

There were whole streets of derelict houses, rows and
rows of them, waiting to be pulled down. She pointed at
them.

'Yes,' her son said. 'Worse than the Blitz, isn't it? Council's
done more in one year than Hitler did in five.'

She tried to answer, but abandoned the attempt when she
heard the sounds that came out. The words clotted on the
end of her tongue. Sometimes in her excitement and frustration she felt herself start to slobber. She did not want her
son to see that.

He was saying, 'You know, Mam, you could've come to us
if it wasn't for Doreen being at work all day. Only it
wouldn't be much fun for you, would it? Stuck in the house
on your own.'

She might have pointed out that she was stuck in the
house all day on her own anyway, but she didn't. She didn't
want to hear him making excuses. She didn't want to see
him humiliate himself. She didn't blame him. It was
Doreen. And he couldn't go against her after all. He had
her to live with.

'Oh, don't you worry . . .' she began. But 'worry' came
out as 'worrah', and she couldn't go on. She wanted to cry
with frustration. She did cry often now, couldn't seem to
stop herself, and the tears dripped down her cheek on to
her chest.

Getting out of the car was a right performance. She felt

people watching her and that made her worse. Half her body was useless, dragged along by the rest. She had to cradle her dead hand in her living hand, and then how the hell could you manage a stick?

But she got herself out in the end and shuffled the few steps across the pavement and into her house. Her eyes lingered lovingly on every detail of dingy wallpaper and falling plaster. The passage was full of smoke. That meant they'd lit a fire for her in the living room. And so they had. There it was, banked up and blazing in celebration of her return, and the bedclothes aired and turned back. Iris. That's who that would be.

'I'll put the kettle on,' her son said.

She lay on the bed and looked at the fire. The wireless, the table, the armchair: everything. She would never be able to look her fill.

They drank the tea. Her son lingered, fussing over the fire, and getting her biscuits and a slice of cake to keep in a tin by the bed. She loved him but she wanted him to go. He wearied her.

'Now are you sure you'll be all right?'

'Yes.' Yes, yes, yes!

At last he was gone and she was alone. A few minutes' peace. The neighbours would be in later. All of them.

But now she was alone. She burrowed down into her house, savouring its various textures and smells, an old fox that had reached its earth at last.

She had hoped that everything would be the same. But it never was, quite.

Her doctor came to see her, a dry Scot with a badly repaired harelip, carrying his professional kindness from house to house like a charm against mortality. There was nothing he could do. Her speech would improve with time, he said. As indeed would all the after-effects of her stroke.

Meanwhile, they were hard to bear. Her right side was weak, almost paralysed. But not numb. There was a constant prickling sensation all over, like pins and needles. It exhausted her. Other people obviously believed that what was devoid of use must also be devoid of feeling. They handled the paralysed limbs quite roughly at times. But looking down at the dead-white, useless leg Mrs Bell could not blame them. It looked like some root vegetable, a turnip or a parsnip, that had never seen the light of day. And yet with such a rain of electric sparks it amazed her that other people could touch it and not draw back.

She turned the right side of her body away from people so that all her movements became crab-like. She could not wash and dress herself. She could not get around very well.

Words still clotted on her tongue whenever she became confused, though after the first few weeks her speech was generally easier to understand. Only she still had difficulty with the endings of words. They tended to get left off or to turn up attached to other words. Still more disconcertingly, she found herself thinking one thing and saying another, not realising, until she heard herself, that she was talking nonsense. People, seeing that she found speech difficult, behaved as if she was deaf. Since, in fact, her hearing had become abnormally acute, their braying voices exploded inside her head, sending splinters of pain to every part.

But she did not give in. No, would not, not if she was brought down to the gutter.

Only she withdrew into herself. She had to search through the wreckage of her mind, to find out what she had left worth saving.

And other people withdrew from her. They were sorry for her, but she made them uncomfortable. It was difficult for them to believe that this slobbering, glugging thing that could not make its wants known was a human being. They took care of her, but they left her alone.

She didn't mind much. She didn't want their pity anyway. When she cried it was not from misery, but from the frustration she was too weak to express in any other way.

Only Iris King still had the patience to sit and listen. And after a while Mrs Bell began to talk.

Something was happening to her, something strange. As her life drew to its end — and she knew that it was ending — she returned in spirit to her first beginnings. To her first home. Above all, as life ebbed, she returned to her mother.

Sometimes Iris was there to listen. Sometimes she was almost sure she was alone. Then there was only the sound of her own voice, threading the maze of the past.

'She used to send me for the meat in the morning before I went to school. It was really only the men got meat in them days. You just got the gravy. But me Dad used to give me a bite of meat from his plate. I was his favourite, see. Perhaps that's why she never liked me. Oh and if it was tough she used to leather me. I used to say to the butcher, Give it a good bashing, will you, Mister? She'll murder me if it's tough. And she did! She was hard. After our May was born she never walked properly again. She had what they called the white leg. And she had a crutch. She used to drop it on the floor and when you went to pick it up she hit you with it. My God. Still. Looking back on it now I can see she had a rotten life. She lost three out of the first four kids in an epidemic. And I think after that she must've gone a bit low because she used to hide our Annie in the blanket box with all the blankets on top of her. Well, she could've suffocated, you know. Me Dad used to come home from work and hear her crying and he used to say to her, What do you want to do that for? And she'd say summat about, They're coming to get her. Her mind had gone, see. But she got over it. Well, you had to. There was always another bairn on the way. At the finish her womb was fallen that bad she had to wear a big ring and when it slipped out she used to have to lie on the floor and wait till the doctor come to put it in again. You could see her womb, sticking out between her legs. And he used to say Oh, poor Mrs Stott. And I'm sure sometimes there were tears in his eyes he felt that sorry for her. That was later, after the twins. They both died. And then our little Eddie died. I think I felt that more than she did. He used to bite on her breast and she'd yell and slap him. So I used to have him in my bed. I can still see him sat on his potty. Our Galla, he used to say. Doesn't sound much like Alice, does it? He was only two when he died. I was fourteen. It was like I'd lost me own bairn.

But you were never told anything. When me periods

started I didn't know what it was. I ran in shouting and screaming, Mam, Mam, I've busted. And she had a man with her. I think it must've been the Curate. And she fetched me such a swipe across the face I went from one end of the kitchen to the other. And she said, Don't be so daft, you haven't busted. That was it. That was as much as you got. When our Winnie started I did me best to tell her what it was. But I didn't know. I was married. I still didn't know! And she was just the same when I was pregnant. Not so much as a bloody word. You won't believe this. I was walking down Jubilee Road five months pregnant. I still didn't know where it had to come out. I thought they got it out of your belly button. And I met a girl I'd been at work with and she was a bit more fly than the rest of us. She says, Why, it comes out the same place it went in. And she says, there's no need to be frightened, you know. It's just like having a good shit. Well, it wasn't! But still, it was good of her. I always remembered her for that. And after, when I didn't see me periods, I weaned him on to the bottle and when I went to see me mother she said, Well you daft little bugger you don't see when you're feeding. But how was I to know? You were never told.

Me Dad was the only one made anything of me. He used to take me out with him on a Sunday and carry me on his shoulders and show me off to his mates. He had this gold sovereign on a chain and he'd hold it up against me hair. It was the same shade of gold.

But me Mam. I judged her too harshly. Now I look back I see things more her way. She was a hard woman but she had enough to make her hard. Eighteen kids. And we never went without shoes and there was always enough to eat. It might only be broth but there was plenty of it. She was a strong woman. She lived to be eighty and do you know when she died there wasn't a grey hair in her head.'

She slept more during the day now. Day and night were running into each other. And she had extraordinary dreams. Once she stood by an open coffin and there was her first husband inside only in the dream she knew it

229

wasn't her first husband it was God and his hand came up and stroked her right side. And she woke up and lay in the darkness knowing that she had been stroked by God.

Physically she deteriorated. The worst thing was that she sometimes lost control of her bowels. The first time it happened she told herself it was just an accident. It could've happened to anybody at any age. But then it happened again. And again.

Half the time she was constipated. Egg bound. She practically lived on raw eggs beaten up in milk. Then suddenly without warning she would overflow into the bed. And she had to lie in it until her son arrived to change the sheets. Because obviously this was something that couldn't be left to the neighbours. It shouldn't really have fallen to her son. She had to grit her teeth to face it, lying there in her own stench. But she had to accept his help. There was nobody else. Once, Doreen came with him. She had taken on the job of washing the sheets.

Her face would've curdled milk.

By now it was obvious that the situation could not continue. Obvious even to Mrs Bell herself, though she would not admit it. Instead she lay in stubborn silence, waiting for somebody else to speak.

Then she had flu, badly. The doctor was called in. And that was it.

'He says he can put me in a Home whether I want to go or not. Some section or other. If you can't take care of yourself.'

Iris hesitated for a long time before replying. Then she said gently, 'Well, you know, it's all different nowadays. It's not like it used to be. I mean, the Workhouse. That was the end, wasn't it? It's not like that now.'

'St Anne's.'

'Doesn't have to be there. Could be one of the new ones. They're lovely. And even St Anne's. They've done it up, you know. It's all different inside.'

They all thought she was cracked. She'd been to St Anne's to see Jim's wife. Great big rooms. Thirty to forty beds. And the windows frosted so you couldn't see out. And some of 'em lying in bed with the sides up like a cot.

Rubber pants and nappies on and their minds gone. It'd need more than a coat of paint to change that.

None of this could she get out. Her tongue knotted up. She slobbered a bit, and lapsed into silence.

'Anyway, what did you say to him?' Iris asked, after another pause.

'I said I'd see the fella. What else could I say?'

She brooded about it bitterly. Whichever way you looked at it, it was the end. Defeat. As the time for the visit got nearer she started to get confused. Not by day. By day the issue was clear, if bleak. By night. The darkness, once barren, spawned unspeakable forms of life. Voices whispered in the corners. And although she could never hear a word that was said, she knew they were talking about her. There were heads on the walls, high up, looking down. And they talked in distorted voices, like speech under water.

One night she woke up and there was her husband by the fire. She asked him to put on some more coal and he wouldn't although the fire had burned right down.

Oh, the mean old man, she thought. The mean the mean the mean old man.

And found she had said the words aloud. It was morning.

'Who's a mean old man?' Iris wanted to know.

'Bill. Me husband.'

'Your second this is?'

'Yes.'

They had both been called Bill. Come to think of it, they'd both been mean.

'I used to get him his beer in a jug. And I'd allus crack on it cost a penny more than it did. And I'd buy meself a pound of apples and eat them on the way home. Well, we didn't have much. And I was carrying our Tom.'

'This is your first husband.'

'Yes. I wasn't having our Tom to me second, was I?'

'Go on, I'm with you now.'

'Do you know, I've never tasted anything as good as them apples. I used to worry at them. Like a dog at a bone. And they were only cookers. He never found out.'

231

She was already drifting off to sleep. The boundaries between sleep and waking were blurred now. She would fall asleep sometimes in the middle of a sentence. Slipping into silence.

If only they would let her be! But they wouldn't. They were too kind.

And besides she made them uncomfortable, lying there under layers of newspaper, emaciated and dirty. They wanted her clean, tidy, bound in white sheets.

On the morning of the visit she asked Iris to wash and set her hair. Then, when she was alone again, she hobbled across to the mirror and looked hopefully into it. My God.

The stroke was there for all to see. One side of her mouth was drawn down in a permanent leer. Of course she knew that. But something — some remaining shred of vanity perhaps — had prevented her realising how bad it was. She looked to herself like a madwoman. The kind of person who gets put away.

Her hands came up. She hid herself from the mirror. For years she had avoided looking into it: the hag it showed bore no relation to the person she thought she was. Inside herself, she was still sixteen. She had all the passion, all the silliness. Still there behind the grey hair and wrinkled skin. Now the dislocation between what the mirror showed and what she knew herself to be, was absolute. She would have liked to break the glass.

Instead she lay down on the bed and began to work on the down-drawn mouth, trying to mould it into some semblance of normality. She was afraid of her speech going. If she got upset she would mouth and slobber. Better keep quiet altogether than open her mouth and confirm their worst suspicions.

Doreen and Tom turned up an hour before the man was due. They *were* keen.

'I don't know,' Doreen grumbled as she tidied the room, 'that home help of yours doesn't seem to have done much.'

'I asked her to do me hair. Anyway, what can you do in an hour?'

232

'More than this.'

When she'd finished they all sat down. It was like a dentist's waiting room. Everybody nervous and stuck for something to say.

At last a knock on the door. And a small man came into the room, his scalp showing pink through sandy hair. His name, he said, was Wilks.

'So this is the old lady?' He looked at Mrs Bell but addressed himself to the younger woman. 'Well, we'll soon have things sorted out.'

His eyes took in the layers of newspaper in the bed.

'She's how old? Seventy-six?'

Tom cleared his throat. 'Yes, about that.'

'Ah, yes.' He was sitting close to her now though still looking the other way. The backs of his hands had red hair on them. She wondered if all his hair was that colour. 'And she has no income apart from the social security?' Pity his poor bloody wife. 'I'm sorry to have to ask you all these personal questions. It is necessary.'

The apology was not addressed to her.

Tom said, 'As far as I know that's all she gets.'

'I'll need to see the book.' He raised his voice in the direction of the bed, though he was sitting almost on top of her. *I'll need to see the book.*'

He took a form from the file and began filling it in, taking evident pride in his speed and efficiency. She watched the pen fly over the page.

'You see,' Tom was saying, 'we can't offer to take her ourselves. I mean Doreen goes out to work now and . . .'

The pen never paused.

'There's really nobody to see to her.'

'No. Quite.'

He wasn't listening. He'd heard it all before.

They all three watched mesmerised as his pen skimmed over the page.

'We'll find her a place all right. It's just a question of where. I suppose she can manage the toilet all right?' He looked at Mrs Bell for the first time and yelled, 'How are your waterworks, dear?'

Doreen spared her the need to answer. 'Oh, we don't have that problem. It's more a matter of . . .' She lowered her eyes modestly, 'the other.'

He pursed his lips. 'Often?'

'Well. More than once.'

He ticked a box on the form.

'Now then, Mother,' he said. 'The doctor says you've been seeing things. Is that right?' He peered at a scribbled note. 'Men's heads. Just the heads? Dear me, that's a bit rough.' He looked at the daughter-in-law and winked. She wasn't bad if you overlooked the teeth. 'How often does that happen?'

If he had been looking at her he might have seen her flinch.

'Do you know how often it happens?'

'No. She's only mentioned it once or twice. And that was to me husband.'

He turned back to her. 'Well, I don't know about that. Can't have gentlemen friends in the Home, you know. Matron'll have a fit.' He enjoyed his little joke. 'Now can I have a look at your pension book?'

She got it out of the bag herself, though it took time. Her dead hand seemed to be deader than ever. He glanced at the weekly amount, jotted down the number of the book, and handed it back.

'There. They won't take it all off her, you know. She'll still get pocket money. And if she gets she can't manage the Matron'll take care of it for her, buy her any little thing she wants.'

He turned back to the bed.

'Now then, Mother, all you've got to do is sign.'

Her glasses, which had broken two years before and had been stuck together with elastoplast, kept slipping off the end of her nose.

'Just make your mark,' Mr Wilks suggested.

Then she spoke for the first time. She said, very clearly, 'No. I can write.' And slowly she wrote her name on the form: Alice Bell.

'Where are you going to put me?' Now that she had spoken once it was easier to do so again.

'St Anne's.'

'But I don't want to go there.'

'Oh, you'll soon settle in.' In a more normal voice, he said, 'It's the toilet, you know. And she's virtually bedridden. She needs nursing. You can't get that in the smaller Homes.'

'The Workhouse.'

'It's not the Workhouse now. In your day it was. But it's all changed now.'

He had actually spoken to her in a normal voice. Evidently the experiment frightened him, because he didn't repeat it. 'The food's lovely. For your dinner you get your meat and two veg, and there's always a choice of pudding.

He was getting his things together as he spoke.

Tom said, 'How long is it likely to be?'

'Oh, very quick. Coupla days.' He snapped his briefcase shut. 'They'll send an ambulance of course.'

'No. I think I'd rather take her in meself. If you don't mind.'

After he'd gone Tom and Doreen sat on. And on. They seemed afraid to leave her. As if they thought she might put her head in the gas oven like poor old Mrs Bailes had done.

Well, they needn't worry about that. She hated the smell of gas. Always had done.

She made herself talk. It was the only way to get rid of them. She said she was coming round to the idea, that she could see it was for the best. She would soon make friends, she said. And anyway in a place that size there'd probably be people she already knew. And they'd come to see her. And the neighbours'ld come to see her. In fact it would be no different really, except she'd be better looked after.

By the time they were ready to go she had smiled so much that her mouth felt like a fraying elastic band. Her cheeks sagged with the weight of the lies she had told.

She heard them in the passage congratulating each other on the way she had taken it. Then, at last, she was alone.

For a long time she lay still, her eyes closed, her mind — not blank, worse than blank. Soon the night would come;

with whispering and laughter and talking heads staring at her from the walls.

But not yet. It wasn't dark yet. She could. Could something. No. Only wait for death.

And yet why should death appear so promptly? She had had long enough to wait for birth. Standing at the upstairs window in Walker Street listening to men's boots going up the hill and back again, while the midwife came and went, and the pain dragged on all that day and half the following night. Oh but it was worth it, to lie with the child in your arms and know that you had brought life into the world. There was nothing to equal that.

Even the memory of it strengthened her. She was able to sit up and look about the room. Because it had recently contained a stranger, she was able to see it through a stranger's eyes. Even to see herself, sitting up in bed, through a stranger's eyes. No wonder they wanted her put away. She could almost agree with them, especially when saliva dribbled from her loosened mouth and had to be wiped away on the back of ker hand. Rubbish. Ready for the tip.

Iris had promised to look in. And the others would soon be round. She did not want to see them. Their sympathy would sap her energy, divert her from what had to be done. She hobbled along the passage and locked the front door. Then she sat down in her armchair and stared into the fire.

She was finished and she made no bones about it. Her body: she squinted at it down the neck of her nightdress. Black dugs, belly silver-streaked from the child-bearing of half a century ago. Gone. And her mind. Her mind crumbled by the hour. She searched among the wreckage for some fragment of hope, but there was none. Her life would not renew.

She understood now the full indignity of rape. That man, the expression in his eyes when he looked at her. The not-seeing. And she could see no way out, except to submit, to accept herself at his evaluation. To give in.

She sat in silence and waited, all hope gone.

And then something stirred. In the ruins of her mind,

something so new and unused that it could only be spirit was struggling to stand up. Oh, but it was hard. She could not sustain the effort. She fell back, she dwindled, became again a heap of old garbage waiting for the pit. She preferred it like that. She turned to darkness and away from light.

And yet the growth once started was not so easily stopped. It made her restless. She began to wander about the house, opening and shutting drawers, caressing each battered object that had accompanied her through life. Everything was steeped in memory. The smell of mothballs from the drawers where she stored her bedlinen. The crack in the fireplace where she had dropped the iron. Gradually she came to herself. That new thing that had started to grow in her pulled itself up on tables and chairs as naturally as a toddler starting to walk.

Her home. They were taking it away from her. The dirt and disorder, the signs of malnutrition and neglect which to them were reasons for putting her away were, to her, independence. She had fought to keep for herself the conditions of a human life.

She was calm again. What she wanted was simple. She wanted to die with dignity. She wanted to die in her own home. And if that was no longer possible, she would go away. She would not be here waiting for them when they came.

She knelt down beside the chest of drawers and began pulling out clothes. Then she slipped off her nightdress and was naked, shivering and goose-pimply in spite of the fire. Normally she would have hurried over such a moment, not liking to see this body that had been fastened to her by time. But today she let herself look. Silver branches spread out across her belly, springing from the sparsely-rooted hair. A tree in winter.

She remembered her mother's body washed and laid out for the grave. How remote it had been, how shocking in its nakedness. Her body was like that now.

At the end her mother called for her and said, 'Alice. Alice.' Forty years ago. 'You always thought I didn't care as

much about you as I did the rest. But, you know, I did.'
Forty years. And it could still bring tears to her eyes.

Getting her stockings on was a struggle. It was hard to
bend and still harder to straighten up again. This body that
seemed to have less and less to do with her, demanded
more attention now than ever it had done in youth, when
the spirit suffused it so vigorously that there had seemed to
be no possibility of division.

At last, though, the stockings were on, the garters
snapped into place around the wasted thighs. At intervals
questions bubbled to the surface of her mind. What am I
doing? Where am I going? But more faintly now as the unnamed and unadmitted purpose gathered strength.

Finally, before she left, she got her black handbag from
under the pillows and set it squarely in the middle of the
bed. There was no need to hide it now. She stroked it.
There would be enough.

And so she accepted what she was about to do.

She hobbled across the icy yard, remembering her fall
but remembering it as something that had happened a long
time ago in another life. From the yard door she looked
back at the house. Everything known and loved, everything
trusted and relied upon, had to be abandoned now. She was
committing herself to an act of faith which, if it was ever
known at all, would appear to others as folly or madness or
mere senile confusion.

She was almost too weak to walk. Her mouth, her skin,
even her veins seemed to have dried up, to be cracked and
parched as the bed of an ancient river. She wanted. Wanted.
The chaos of cold and emptiness was reflected in the darkness of her eyes.

She did not know how she could walk, but walk she did.
The weak side dragged, but she had her sticks. She moved
slowly, pushing one foot out in front of the other. Then a
pause while she brought the stick on the other side into
line. Then the other foot, the weak one, could be dragged
level.

From the outside it must have looked like a triumph of
the will. She alone knew that it was nothing of the kind.

Willpower could not have moved her crumbling body from the bed, let alone have driven it out into this cold. She who had lived all her life by willpower alone had ended by setting it aside, to wait passively, to wait in darkness, for deliverance or for grace.

There was washing hung out across the alley, white sheets, frozen and stiff. She had no hand free to lift them aside, and so had to walk through, head lowered, while the hard cotton scraped against her face. And a bubble broke in her mind, releasing the memory of another day. A younger woman, running, running away. And the wet sheets stinging and slapping her face.

Then she was leaving the alley and entering the railway tunnel. Other memories rose to the surface, tugging at the corners of her mind like the mouths of tiny fish. There were more footsteps running, a child's this time, and the child stopped and looked behind her as if afraid of being pursued. And a young girl stood just inside the entrance to the tunnel, with a young man's arms around her. Flakes of plaster drifted down and landed in her hair.

She stopped in confusion as the memories threatened to overwhelm her. These fragments. Were they the debris of her own or other lives? She had been so many women in her time.

She passed the Bluebell. She moved from familiar to unfamiliar streets. Now there were park railings on the left. A steep hill led up to the gates. So steep that after the first few steps she doubted if she would ever make it to the top. But she hooked her sticks around her wrists and began hauling her needled flesh from railing to railing. It was darker now, though not yet dark. And all around her was a web of voices.

At first she thought the ordeal of her nights had spilled over into the day. But no, this was not the sterile torment of the talking heads. This was something different. This was something else again. At first the voices were soft but they grew louder and clearer as she toiled up the hill: a child shouting, a young girl laughing, a woman crooning over her child. She carried the web of voices with her up the hill.

And at last she reached the gates. There was the sky, and pools of clear water, and silence. And her own mind again, simple and clean as a rinsed plate.

Oh but it was cold. And the body stupid. It did not seem to understand that this cold, for so long an enemy, was now a friend, but must be rubbing its hands and turning up the collar of its coat and looking for a sheltered bench.

The pools of water reflected light into the sky and the light did not disperse but gathered to a radiance that beat down again upon the earth. The light was bewildering because it seemed to come as much from the earth as the sky. She was confused. And the cold seemed to have got into her bones. The small bones of her face and ears vibrated like struck tuning forks, or like a bell after the sound has died away.

A bench. Dead horse chestnut leaves starred the ground. She noticed that one had drifted down and lay on the bench beside her, brown, discoloured, the flesh wasting away between raised veins. She moved her hand and the leaf moved. It didn't surprise her. The membrane that had divided her from the world was permeable now, self and not-self no longer an absolute division.

The sky was a clear eggshell blue fading towards the horizon through turquoise, rose-pink and yellow to a sombre, glowing red.

At first there was total silence, except for the beating of her heart, quickened by the long walk up the hill. Then a murmuring began, as of the wind through the summer trees or waves unfurling on the shore, only darker and more secret: the sound of the sea in an underground cave or blood coursing through the hidden channels of the ear. Then, mixed in with the murmuring, a series of sharp, electric clicks as if a group of women were talking and brushing their hair at once. The noise became louder. And now when she looked at the skyline she saw that one tree stood out from the rest, its branches fanned out, black and delicate, against the red furnace of sky.

Nothing could now have moved her dying flesh from the bench where it had taken refuge, but she began in spirit to walk towards the tree. At first it seemed to be bare like all the others, though with a jaggedness of outline that suggested not winter but death. By now the murmur had become a shout, a fierce, ecstatic trilling; and when she looked more closely she saw that the tree was full of birds, clustering along its branches, as thick and bright as leaves. And all singing. But then, as she came closer still, as her white hair and skin took on the colours of blood and fire, she saw more clearly, and in a moment of vision cried. It isn't the birds, it's the tree. The tree is singing.

The light was unbearably bright, bubbling in every vein, shaking her heart. She could not bear it. She shrank, she fell back. The world dwindled to a park bench and a litter of dead leaves in the grass.

But there was a child there, now, a girl, who, standing with the sun behind her, seemed almost to be a gift of the light. At first she was afraid, the child had come so suddenly. Then — not afraid. They sat beside each other; they talked. The girl held out her hand. The withered hand and the strong young hand met and joined. There was silence. Then it was time for them both to go.

So that in the end there were only the birds, soaring, swooping, gliding, moving in a never-ending spiral about the withered and unwithering tree.

BLOW YOUR HOUSE DOWN

For David, with love

PART ONE

Whoever fights monsters should see to it that in the process he does not become a monster. And when you look long into an abyss the abyss also looks into you.

NIETZSCHE, *Beyond Good and Evil*

CHAPTER ONE

There were two beds and a wardrobe in the room. To get
between them you had to stand sideways and shuffle your
way along.

Brenda was in a hurry to get out and grumbled as she
bent down to tuck a blanket in. 'I don't know, when I was
your age I was making me own bed.'

Her daughters, getting ready for bed in the corner,
turned and looked at her. Lindsey, the elder by two years,
said, 'I don't see why I have to go to bed the same time as
our Sharon.'

'Because if I let you stop down you'd only have a carry-
on and wake everybugger up. Besides, you'd start picking
on your Uncle Norman, you know you would.'

'It's him picks on me.'

Brenda pulled back the sheets on the other bed and a
powerful smell of urine filled the room. 'Sharon, I wish
you'd tell me when you're wet. I could've had this changed
this morning if you'd told me.'

'God, what a stink,' said Lindsey.

Brenda rounded on her, 'Shut your face, you. You want
to think on, she's been ill.'

'I couldn't help it, Mam.'

'No, love, I know you can't. But you've got to tell me.'

Brenda bundled the wet sheets together and thrust them
out onto the landing. There wouldn't be time to put them

247

into soak even, and if Norman saw them he'd start playing his mouth.

In the bedroom behind her the girls had already started to quarrel.

'Well, it does stink.'

'It isn't my fault.'

'I don't know who else's fault it is. It's your piss.'

'The doctor says it isn't my fault.'

'He doesn't have to sleep in it.'

Brenda swept back into the room. 'And since when have you had to sleep in it? The only muck you sleep in's your own.'

'I don't wet the bed.'

'No.' Brenda pulled Lindsey towards her and scooped up a handful of hair. 'And you don't wash your bloody mucky neck either, do you? You could plant a row of taties in that. Go and wash it.'

'Aw, Mam.'

'Never mind Aw Mam. Do as you're told. And take your bra off. You're not meant to sleep in it.'

'Kerry says if you don't keep it on in bed you start sagging.'

'Sagging!'

'She's got nowt there to sag,' said Sharon.

'I heard that!'

Sharon raised her voice, 'Pair of fried eggs!'

'I don't know what you're in such a hurry for,' said Brenda. 'It'll happen soon enough.'

Lindsey came back into the room, drying her neck. 'Did you have much bust at my age, Mam?'

'I didn't know what a bust was at your age. Anyway, it's all rubbish, sagging. They don't sag till you've had bairns. Then every bloody thing sags.'

'Aw! But you wouldn't be without us, would you, Mam?' Lindsey butted her mother, half-jeeringly, half-longingly, in the breast.

'Oh, wouldn't I?' But she stroked Lindsey's hair before she let her go. 'Now come on, Sharon. This'll get done quicker if you help.'

248

The sheet ballooned out over the bed. As Sharon bent to tuck it in Brenda noticed how thin her arms and shoulders were. 'I wish you'd eat more.'

'I'm alright.'

'Well, you don't look it.'

They finished the bed in silence. When both girls were tucked in Brenda said, 'Your Uncle Norman's stopping in tonight, so you'll be alright.'

They looked at each other.

'We don't need anybody to stop in,' said Lindsey. 'We can take care of ourselves.'

'It's not you I'm worried about. It's our Kevin.'

'Well, so what?' Lindsey said. 'Kevin cries, he comes in here. Norman doesn't bother with him.'

'*Uncle* Norman.'

'It's bloody stupid. We can look after Kevin.'

Brenda decided not to argue. 'Anyway, he's staying in tonight. Now I don't want to hear any talking. If I hear a squeak out of either of you I'll be back up them stairs and I won't half salt your tails. I've had just about enough.'

She kissed them goodnight. Sharon clung onto her until Brenda untwined her arms. 'I won't be late,' she said. 'Now you go to sleep like a good girl.'

'Can I have the landing light on, Mam?'

'It gets in my eyes,' said Lindsey.

'Then look the other way. Goodnight.'

Before going downstairs Brenda went in her own bedroom to check on Kevin. He was fast asleep, and scowling. She pushed his fists under the blanket, but he only took them out again. The size of them. He'd always had ruddy great mitts on him, right from him being born. 'My God, I think this'n's gunna be a boxer,' the midwife said. And it was true. Other babies you looked at their hands and you thought *Aw*! Not Kevin. If ever a bairn come into the world with its fists up it was him.

She smiled as she bent and kissed him goodnight.

There wasn't a sound from the girls' room. Not even Lindsey and she was never quiet. Must be the shock of a clean neck. Brenda raised her eyebrows, listened again,

249

and tip-toed downstairs.

No Norman, of course, and he'd promised he'd be in by nine. She hesitated, wondering whether she dare go out and leave the kids in on their own. Lindsey was old enough. Dear God, plenty of bairns younger than her got left in on their own. But she'd never done that with hers. She'd always thought, well, suppose something did happen — how would I feel?

No. Definitely not. If he didn't turn up soon she'd pop round Audrey's and tell her it was off. Apart from anything else it wasn't fair on her leaving her stuck in waiting.

Just as she was on the point of giving him up, he arrived. She looked him up and down. He was swaying on his feet, pretending to be drunker than he was because he knew it would rile her. He wasn't that far gone: he was at the nasty-nice stage when most of their rows took place. She was going to have to watch her tongue.

'Dinner ready?'

'In the oven.'

'In the oven.'

'Yes, that's right, in the oven. I could've left it on the table but if I had've done it'd be stone cold by now.'

He turned from her without a word and went into the kitchen. She could hear him banging and clattering about, grumbling because there were a few dishes in the sink. When she could stand it no longer she followed him in.

'There's no need to wash up. There's plenty more in the cupboard.'

'Do we have to use every plate in the house before you'll get off your arse and wash up? Anyway why can't Lindsey do it? She's big enough.'

'If I want Lindsey to do owt, I'll tell her. Anyway, you don't need a plate, it's on a plate already.'

She got it out of the oven and slapped it down in front of him.

'Well?' she asked after a while. 'Is it hot enough?'

'Luke.' Spoken grudgingly with his mouth full.

'It was hot enough when it was got ready.' Brenda tried

to stop herself and failed. 'I thought you said you'd mind the bairns?'

'I am minding them, aren't I?' He looked away. 'I got on talking.'

'You mean you got on drinking.'

'No. *Talking*. If you must know I ran into Bill. Me Mam's bad again.'

'She always is when she wants owt doing. What is it this time?'

'She's bad. I've said I'll have a look round. *In the morning*. It's alright.'

Silence.

'You can still go out.'

'Don't worry, I'm going. It'll be a run round the block at this rate.'

'I just hope Sharon doesn't wet the bed again.'

'Nobody's asking you to see to it.'

'You want to rattle her chops a bit. That'd sharp cure her.'

'Now just you listen.' Brenda leaned across the table and tapped the end of his nose. 'Keep it out. Right? Them bairns are nowt to do with you.'

'They're nowt to do with me, but I'm expected to stop in and look after them.'

'I don't see you at the back of the queue when the money's spent.'

He pushed the plate away from him. 'Now that's one thing you can't say.'

'Aw, gerraway, man. Do you think I'm keeping you on what you give me? Doesn't keep you in cigarettes.'

'It isn't my fault I can't get a job.'

'Oh, come off it, man, you'd run a mile.' She was going the right way for a clip round the ear, but she couldn't stop. 'You make me sick, you and your bloody mother. Least little thing goes wrong you're running round there for a bit of titty. And your Bill's no better. She's never let you either of you grow up.'

'You need talk. What about Kevin? You're making a right little pouf out of him.'

251

She stared at him. 'He's *four*.'

There was silence while she put on her coat.

'How long are you stopping with her?' Brenda asked.

'Oh, I thought I'd just look in. See how she was.'

'Aye and we've heard that before.'

She touched his shoulder as she went past. 'Anyway, don't stop up.'

'And you watch what you're doing, mind.'

'Oh, don't worry about me.' She pulled a face. 'I was born lucky.'

Audrey was peering into the mirror above her mantelpiece, stroking mascara on to her upper lashes. 'I'd just about given you up,' she said.

'I was stuck in waiting of Norman. His mam's playing up again. He's off round there tomorrow.'

Audrey shifted the direction of her gaze. 'You got your period?'

'No.' Brenda laughed. 'Why, do I look as if I have?'

'You look tired.'

'Well, I am tired. I'm tired of bloody Norman.'

'Now you know you don't mean it.'

'I do. If he goes back home this time he can stop.'

'Well, tell him. If that's how you feel.' Audrey was putting her lipstick on. She paused, and grunted through stretched lips. 'You'd miss him.'

'I'd miss a pain in the arse, but it's not to say I want one.' She caught Audrey looking at her. 'Oh, he is. He's always on at the bairns. Pick, pick, pick — he doesn't know what to pick at next. And he hates Lindsey, 'cos of course she won't take it. He gets it back.' She picked at her nail varnish. 'He puts me very much in mind of my husband. He was always running round to his mam, I used to tell him he should've married her. Oh and she used to give him anything he asked for. He only had to say and her hand was in her purse. "There you are, my son." And of course it all went on booze. I never got sight nor sound of it. Or the bairns. But she did, she ruined him.' She grinned. 'I tell you one thing; if he goes, it'll be a long time before there's another.'

'You're young to say that.'

'I don't see you bothering.'

'Never have done. Oh, I don't say I don't like a night out now and then. And I like men as friends. But as soon as I see that little gleam in their eye, I think, *No.*'

'It's a good job it doesn't take everybody the same way. I mean, look at Elaine.'

'Yeah. Look at Elaine.'

'Yes, well, I know he's a sod. But you try telling her that. She wouldn't thank you for it. Sun shines out of his arse as far as she's concerned.'

'And he treats her like muck. I walked back from the hospital with her yesterday. And mind, she did open up a bit then.'

'Is she alright?'

'It's still in there. You believe me it'd be a blessing in disguise if she lost it. She just keeps on bleeding, you know. She's no idea of her dates or anything. She says three month, but I'm blowed if I can see it. I think it's a small baby and she's a hell of a lot further on than she thinks she is.'

Audrey was on her knees by the sideboard, searching among the jumble underneath it for a pair of shoes.

Brenda said, 'Last time I saw her she was gunna pack it in.'

'I'll believe that when I see it. You mark my words she'll be walking down that street when she's like a house-end. I can't see him letting her stop.'

'No. Nor me. I think she'll be like Kath. You know what happened to Kath, don't you? She was actually with somebody when her waters broke.'

'I'd like to've seen his face.'

'And his wife's. Well, he'd go home drenched. "A funny thing happened on my way home from the pub. . ." '

They laughed, and Audrey said, 'No, I can't see her giving it up.'

'And let's face it, if you do go on, you're raking it in. It's the one time you really do make money.'

'I know. Do you know, when I was expecting our

Stephen, I used to stand in front of the mirror and his dad had just gone and I was feeling really down. And I used to look at meself and I used to think, My God, who'd fancy that? I should've gone and stood on a corner, I'd've sharp found out who fancied it.'

'Poor Kath.'

Audrey paused in the act of putting on her coat. 'You were fond of her, weren't you?'

'I still am. What there is left.'

'Yeah, well, she's let the drink get a hold. Speaking of which . . .'

They looked at each other and laughed.

'No, seriously,' Audrey went on, 'Do you think we've got time?'

'Why, aye. I don't fancy going out cold, especially a night like this.'

'It's not still raining, is it?'

'Pissing.'

'Aw,' Audrey looked in the mirror again. 'I dunno why I bother. Least little bit of damp it frizzes.'

'Put a rain hat on.'

'I can't.'

'Well, I would. Get yourself stuck under one of the arches, whip it off.'

Audrey got out a polythene hat stamped with pink umbrellas and put it on. 'Look at that. Fry's Turkish Delight.'

'I hope not. They only cost 14p.'

'Cheeky bugger!'

CHAPTER TWO

Brenda and Audrey ran the last hundred yards down Northgate and arrived at the Palmerston flushed, wet and out of breath.

'I'll have to go for a pee,' said Audrey, hopping from leg to leg.

'You've only just been.'

'It's the rain,' said Audrey, and ran.

'What'll you have?' Brenda shouted after her.

'Anything. Lager-and-lime.'

That wouldn't help much when she was stood out in the rain again.

Brenda went into the back room and stood at the bar waiting her turn to be served. After a while a group of women in the far corner spotted her standing there and waved.

The place was crowded, as it always was by this time of night. Other pubs were livelier, with music and skin shows, and more comfortable too. The Palmerston's dingy lino and balding plush seats had been there as long as anybody could remember. But to the women who used its back room the Palmerston was special. They drank in all the pubs, moving in a nightly gavotte up and down Northgate, along Church Row, down Melbourne Terrace, under the viaduct, and back into Northgate again. But the Palmerston was different, and that was because of its owner, Beattie Miller.

Last Christmas one of the girls had suggested holding a raffle with a bottle of gin for whoever came closest to guessing Beattie's age. Too hard, everybody said, and it was too. Her hair was red, there was make-up on her face an inch thick, cracked and flaking into the wrinkles round her mouth and eyes and when she went round collecting up the dirty glasses she moved with extreme caution on her stick-insect legs, like a very old woman venturing out onto ice. In spite of all this Brenda wouldn't've put her much past fifty. You never saw her outside the Palmerston. Only the other night Brenda had said to her, 'Beattie, one of these days you and me are gunna have a day out. Because I want to know what you look like when you're not sat behind that bloody bar!'

No time for nattering tonight: she was rushed off her feet.

'You look drowned, love,' Beattie said, as she took the money. 'Is it still as bad?'

'Pissing down. And there's a nasty wind as well.'

'Oh well. Good for trade. You want to get your coat off, dear. You won't feel the benefit.'

Good for trade, Brenda thought, as she carried the drinks across the room. Good for *hers*. Wasn't doing anybody else any good.

The group in the corner parted to make room for her. Elaine was back.

'How you feeling, cock?' Brenda asked.

'Oh, I'm smashing now, thanks.'

She didn't look it. She had more shadows round her eyes than a panda. If they were shadows. Brenda looked more closely, and intercepted a warning glance from Jean.

'Oh, hello!' said Audrey, coming up behind Brenda, 'I thought you were packing it in.'

'Oh, I decided I'd give it a bit longer.' Elaine brought her upper lip down over her slightly prominent front teeth in a way that was both rabbit-like and touching. 'Seems a pity to pack it in while I'm still feeling alright.'

'Well, there is that,' said Brenda. 'And just you wait till you start showing. You'll be raking it in.'

256

'There'll be no business left for the rest of us,' said Jean.

'Oh well, if I'm gunna be doing you all out of a job I'd better buy the next round.' Elaine smiled with that vulnerable quivering lip of hers, and went across to the bar.

Audrey said, 'Is that mine?' She picked up a pint of lager and turned to Brenda, 'I meant a half. Cheers, love.' As she put the glass down her eyes fell on a pair of sunglasses in Elaine's place. She shook the raindrops off her coat, miming amazement. 'Costa del Sol, was it?'

'No,' said Jean, crisply. 'Costa del thump-in-the-eye.'

Audrey looked across to the bar and pulled a face.

'She's just got to toughen up,' said Jean. 'Nobody else can do it for her.'

You couldn't help wondering what experiences had toughened Jean up. There was a scar at the bottom of her neck, the worst Brenda had ever seen. Oh she wrapped scarves round her neck to try and hide it, but she had a habit of sticking her chin out when she'd finished saying something, almost as if she was daring you to clock her one, and then the scar showed. She couldn't be more than twenty-two or -three but she made herself respected alright, and with none of the effing and blinding that a lot of them went in for. With Jean it was the blow first. She'd cuss you afterwards if she had time.

'You heard from Carol?' Brenda asked.

'Not a sausage,' said Jean. 'I can't understand it. I mean I know she was getting nervous about this bloke. She was always on at me to pack it in and go down London with her. But I can't see Carol just going off and not telling me. In fact I know she wouldn't.'

'No point moving to London,' said Maureen. 'If you're gunna meet one you'll meet one anywhere.'

'That's right.'

There was a general murmur of agreement.

'Stick to your regulars,' said Audrey. 'That's your best bet.'

'That's what I told her. She said he was somebody's regular.'

'It's no use, Audrey,' said Brenda. 'They're determined

257

to cheer us up.'

'But it's true, isn't it? You can go with somebody ten, twenty times and he'll be alright, and then something'll happen and he'll flip.'

Elaine came back with the drinks.

'Anyway,' said Brenda, taking hers, 'Look on the bright side. There hasn't been a squeak out of him. For all we know he's buggered off.'

'I wish I had a fiver for every time I've heard that,' said Maureen.

The others stared at her.

'I was in Bradford, you know.' She watched it sink in. 'Oh there was a lot moved out, but there was a lot more stayed. And they were always on: "Oh he's given it up." "He's gone away." "He's topped himself." Like bloody hell. And there were all sorts of ideas flying round. "Always get out of the car." "Never get out of the car." "Take the numbers." "Work in pairs." "Don't bend down." "Don't turn your back." "Don't suck them off." Load of rubbish. I never did any of it. I did start carrying a knife and then I thought well, you dozy cow, you're just handing him the weapon. So after that I didn't bother.'

'Did you ever get anybody you thought was him?'

Maureen smiled slightly, 'Every night.'

'I couldn't've stuck it,' said Audrey. 'I'd've had to get out.'

'It's not that easy, you know. I had the bairns with me then. And I'd just got a council flat. I was on the waiting list three year to get that.'

'You must've been frantic.'

'No. Not really. Oh I suppose there was once or twice. I know one night I was stood on a street corner and there was an alley just behind me and this bloke jumped out. "I'm the Ripper," he says. Only of course he didn't say it like that.' Maureen stuck two fingers in the sides of her mouth and pulled her lips apart. ' "I'm the Ripper." I don't know what he thought I was gunna do. I just looked at him and I says, "Oh aye?" '

'What did he do?'

'What do you mean, "What did he do?" What they all do.'

'You never went with him?'

'Of course I bloody did. You had to. If you listened to them every stupid little prick with a few pints inside him was the Ripper. They used to get me. I don't care what they say, a man that'll go around attacking women, well, he must have something wrong with him. But *them*. They just used to scare the shit out of you, just for the fun of it, and then they'd stand back and have a bloody good laugh.'

This was the most Maureen had said since she first showed up in the Palmerston a few weeks before. Generally she seemed a rather dour, phlegmatic girl, unwilling to talk about anything much, though she had once showed them a photograph of two children on a beach somewhere.

Elaine had said nothing while all this was going on. She just sat and used a little pool of spilled beer to make patterns on the table. But she looked sick. Brenda tried to think of a way of changing the subject.

Suddenly Jean leant forward and said, 'Hey, you see him sat over there? In the corner. No, don't let him see you looking.'

Brenda directed a carefully casual glance around the room. 'Him on his own? Yeah, I've got him.'

'He's the one . . .' Jean's voice wobbled so that she had to stop and try again. 'He's the one pays her forty quid a week to piss on him.'

'It isn't every week,' said Maureen. 'I've known him go as far as a month.'

'It's the *rent*,' said Brenda. 'Bloody near.' She turned to Audrey. 'Where do they find these men?'

'I don't know,' said Audrey. 'It's never been my luck.'

'And look at her,' said Jean. 'She has the nerve to sit there supping gin.'

'And what am I meant to sup?'

'Beer. *Beer!* Give the poor little sod a run for his money.'

'She's mebbe afraid of drowning him,' said Brenda. 'Forty quid a time, I know I would be.'

'You think that's a joke,' said Maureen. 'But it worries me. He could easy choke.'

'Oh, my God,' said Audrey. 'It's not in his mouth.'

'Well, you daft bugger,' said Brenda. 'Where did you think it was?'

'Lower down.'

'He's very nice, you know,' said Maureen. 'He doesn't say "piss".' With a glance at Jean. 'He says "wee-wee".'

Jean, who had just taken a mouthful of gin, released it in a fine spray all over the table. 'My God.'

Maureen stared at her. 'Now what have I said?'

The door opened and Kath Robson walked in. She nodded to Beattie Miller, crossed over to the bar, and hoisted herself with some difficulty onto one of the stools. Then, out of breath from the slight effort, she turned and looked round the room.

There was a moment of complete silence, one of those inexplicable, simultaneous pauses in conversation that come over groups of people in a crowded room. Outside the wind howled and the rain spattered against the glass. Then a woman laughed, and instantly the noise rose up higher than before as if some communal, unconscious decision had been taken to forget whatever lay outside.

Brenda stood up. 'I'm gunna go and buy Kath a drink.'

'Aright,' said Audrey, 'But go easy. She's tanked up to the gills already.'

Brenda pushed and jostled her way to the bar.

'Now then, Kath,' she said.

Kath turned, a drunk's turn, keeping the head steady and swivelling from the hips. 'Now then.'

Kath was pleased to see her, no doubt about that, though her face was so puffy it didn't show emotion easily.

'What'll you have?'

'I'll stick to cider.' Her voice was a throaty whisper, hoarser and more slurred than Brenda remembered it.

'Well,' said Brenda, while they waited, 'I haven't seen you around much.'

'I've been bad with me chest.' Her eyes were on the bottle of cider that Beattie had taken down from the shelf. 'You keeping alright then? And the bairns?'

'I'm alright. Sharon's not been too . . .'

Brenda stopped. Kath wasn't interested. Couldn't be.

Yet.

The drinks arrived. Kath drank deeply, only coming up for breath when the pint was half gone. She wiped the line of moisture shakily from her upper lip. 'Sorry, Brenda, what were you saying?'

'I was just saying our Sharon isn't so good.'

'Aw dear, what's the matter with her?'

'Cystitis.'

'Never. At her age? Why how old is she?'

'Eleven.'

Kath looked shaken by the passing of so much time. 'It's still no age to be getting that. Bad enough when you're a woman. There was once over you know I had a real run of it. Couldn't shift it. Oh and it doesn't half pull you down. Anyway the doctor at the hospital said it was that that'd done me kidneys. You know it'd all spread up me tubes.'

'That's what they're frightened of with her. I had to take her up the hospital and get her X-rayed.'

'Poor little soul. You want to make sure she drinks plenty. That'll shift it quicker than anything.' Kath, as if to demonstrate her faith in this advice, downed the second half of the pint.

Brenda was a bit startled by the rate of consumption, but immediately said, 'Have another.'

The hesitation was only momentary. 'Thanks, love. I'd offer to buy you one, only I'm a bit . . .'

'That's alright.'

'But it's no good, I'll have to go and make room for it. Here, save me place.'

Beattie Miller, refilling Kath's glass, raised her eyebrows expressively. She didn't need to say anything. She and Brenda were probably the only two people in the room who could remember Kath as she'd once been. She used to be pretty, Brenda thought, and looked around for somebody else who might remember. There was nobody.

Kath came back. Her eyes crossed as she neared the bar because she was focusing so hard on the waiting drink. This time Brenda waited till she'd had the first few gulps before she asked, 'And what about your bairns? Are they alright?'

'Smashing. Well, the two boys are. They're in that home in Whitley Bay now. You know they send them there when they get into their teens.' Her voice was so hoarse Brenda could hardly follow what she said. 'David's doing very well. They're on about getting him a job on the golf course when he leaves school. I says to him, I says, "Is that what you'd like, son?" And he says, "Oh, yes, Mam." You know what I mean, Brenda, I've no worries about the lads. It's our Julie. I used to go and see her in the foster home and just because I got meself a little bit upset once or twice they said I hadn't to go no more. Like, I could still see her but it had to be at the social services and there had to be somebody there all the time. Well, it was awful. You know, we had to sit on these chairs and the bairn couldn't think of anything to say and neither could I and there was this stuck-up bitch staring at you all the time. They do, you know, they look at you as if you're muck. Anyway at the finish I give her a right mouthful, I says, "What do you know about bringing up bairns? You've never fucking had one." And do you know when they tried to pull her away from me she clung on, she didn't want to go.'

Kath lapsed into silence. Brenda went on sitting beside her not even trying to console her. What could you say? She'd lost too much. There was no way of reaching out to her now, when the world had shrunk to an inch of liquid in the bottom of the glass. It was like sitting by the bedside of a very old woman, so old that memory and mental faculties have all decayed and the person you knew is gone, and yet you go on sitting there for the sake of what they were and what they've meant to you. And yet Kath wasn't old. What would she be? Thirty-three? Thirty-four?

Brenda saw Audrey stand up. She touched Kath on the arm.

'I'll have to love and leave you, pet. Here.' She pushed a pound note into Kath's hand. 'Buy yourself another.'

'Oh, are you going, love?' She looked down at the note and up again. 'Thanks.'

'Take care of yourself, now.'

In the hallway Audrey watched Brenda in silence for a

few seconds. Then, 'She's upset you, hasn't she?'

'No.'

'I don't know what you want to go and buy her more for. She'd had more than enough.'

'It's all she's got.' Brenda didn't want to talk about Kath. 'Anyway, she wasn't the only one knocking it back. Did you see Jean?'

'Yeah, well, she can afford to, can't she? She's raking it in. She'd been on the go since six.'

'Oh, I know,' said Brenda, 'And doesn't it make you sick? I've seen bigger tits on a fella.'

'Ah, but she's got what it takes.'

'I know she's got it. I just wish I knew what it was.'

'Well, don't ask me. If I knew I'd be charging double.' She waited for Brenda to finish fastening her coat. 'I'll tell you one thing though, she's worried about Carol. She puts a very good face on it, but underneath she's worried sick.'

'In case anything's happened to her? Gerraway, woman, she's in London. Probably making a bomb.'

'She wouldn't be.'

'Well, no, I know she wouldn't. Whatever Jean's got, Carol didn't have it. But that was part of the trouble. Carol was jealous and Jean couldn't see it. You mark my words, that's where she is.'

Audrey opened the door and immediately the wind blew in, almost knocking her back against the wall. 'My God, they'll have to be keen tonight.'

'You mean, we'll have to be keen. It's not them stood out in it. Come on.'

'Do you know,' said Audrey, 'I've seen the time I'd've gone out in that with nothing on me chest. You know, "Show 'em what they're getting!"' She threw her arms wide, and let them drop. 'These days it's as much as I can do to wash the Vick off.'

It was a struggle to pull the door to behind them, but they managed it at last. Then, heads and shoulders bent into the wind, they began to walk towards the viaduct.

CHAPTER THREE

Audrey clicked first. Brenda made a great show of taking the number, then withdrew into the shadow of the chicken factory as the car pulled away. The arrangement between them was that whichever one of them got left behind should wait for the other's return. It didn't always work like that because of course you had your regulars and you couldn't very well tell them to go away and come back later. But that was the idea.

The chicken factory stank. Brenda was used to the smell because as a young woman she'd worked there for a time. In fact she'd still been working there — officially, anyway — when she met Kath.

God, what a winter that had been. Brian had just buggered off and left her with the two bairns. Well, that was no surprise, she'd seen that coming. What did come as a surprise was the bills. Brian wasn't like other men, he didn't give you money to keep the house on, he just give you money for food. Anything else, it was, 'Oh, I'll see to that.' He'd seen to it alright, all the way to the pub. After he'd gone she found bills stuffed away all over the place, pushed down the sides of the sofa, under the carpet. Everywhere. Then, just as she thought she'd found the lot, there were more. The telly broke down, the man came to mend it, lifted it up and there they were.

She took them to his mother. Fat lot of good that did her!

If Brenda had got into a muddle with money that was her look-out, she said. And no, she didn't know where her son was living. She didn't even bother to make it sound as if she was telling the truth.

That shouldn't've come as a surprise either because she'd never liked Brenda. Brenda was sixteen when she married Brian — pregnant, of course — and his mother made no secret of the fact that she thought her lad had been trapped into marrying a common little cow. All his family was against her, and there was a lot of it: his mother, his granny, his three married sisters, their husbands, their kids. They all lived within a few streets of each other.

To begin with she tried very hard to fit in with them. She didn't have any family of her own, just one foster mother she still kept in touch with, so she wanted them to be hers. 'Have I to call you Mam?' she asked her mother-in-law when she was first married. 'No. I think you'd better call me Edith,' her mother-in-law replied.

Edith was turned sixty: she'd had Brian in the change, when she thought she couldn't have any more — perhaps that was why she made such a little tin god of him. Her hair was dyed dead black and her skin was yellow from the smoke of cigarettes and the fire. She sat over it all day while her daughters took it in turns to clean the house, and often there was no sound except the roar of flames and the slight click of her hand as she rubbed it up and down her stocking when her granny's tartan tingled.

One job she still did herself: she dusted her husband. Well, that was what it looked like. When he was ready to go out and he always wore a buttonhole — she'd get this little stool and stand on it and brush him all over with a little clothes brush she had. And he just stood there and let her. He didn't even turn round; when she'd done one side she carried the stool round and started on the other. At first Brenda couldn't see why she did it, because, let's face it, she hated the old bastard and not without reason either. Then one day she realized it was just like scrubbing the front door step. It didn't matter what you thought about the bloke, it was just something you had to do.

Sometimes he'd look over his wife's shoulder at Brenda, and wink. It used to worry her a bit because she never knew what it meant. He was all the time going on as if he and Brenda knew something the others didn't. 'That lot,' he'd say, meaning his wife and daughters. 'That lot — as long as they've got a scrubbing brush in their hands and a fag stuck in their mouths and everybody saying, "*Eeee, by, isn't she a clean woman?*" they're happy. Their minds don't reach beyond it.'

What tickled Brenda, he'd say this with the old woman sat there, and she didn't say anything. She'd have this little butt end stuck on a pin and she'd be sucking away at it for dear life, and she'd just look at him. Never a word.

Now, when Brenda remembered the old man getting ready to go out, she knew damn well he wasn't just going to the pub. She'd think, *Aye-aye, lad, I know what you're up to*. You couldn't blame him, mind. If he'd got it out at home she'd only have dusted it.

The old man was very polite, so much so that it sounded a bit sarcastic until you knew him better. He'd never let a woman open a door for herself or carry anything heavier than a handbag. And yet at the same time he'd been a right bugger to his wife. All the kids remembered how one night he'd pushed her over the banister and swung her to-and-fro by the hair. You'd've thought with all that behind her she'd've had a bit of sympathy for Brenda when Brian belted her, but she hadn't. If you wanted the God-honest truth she was over the moon.

The only one of the women in the family who was kind to Brenda was Edith's mam, and she was only nice because she'd do anything to rile Edith. She was a tall, bony, straightbacked woman, well into her eighties, very religious — and a champion shit stirrer. Every Christmas she'd go from one to the other, stirring like mad, and then, when she'd got them all at each others' throats and there were rows going on in every room of the house, she'd clutch at her heart, raise her eyes to the ceiling and pray: 'Peace till I come!' And You want to make the most of it, thought Brenda, because You'll have none when she gets there.

'My one wish,' she used to say, looking round at her assembled children, 'is to see them all safely buried. I shan't rest easy if I don't know where they are.'

'Your family are mad,' Brenda told Brian. It was hopeless. She couldn't even make friends in the street. One woman went and told Brian's mam every single thing Brenda'd confided in her. Since this included what she thought of Brian's performance in bed it was a bit of a disaster.

Things got very bad between her and Brian, really right from Lindsey being born and that was only five months after they were married. Even before they were married he'd thought nothing of belting her if she didn't have his shirts ironed. But she was pregnant and his nerves were bad and she thought, Oh, well, it'll be different when we're married. It was. He hit her harder.

Most of the quarrels were about money. She had no idea, she'd never had to lay money out, and he was no better because his mam was always *give, give* behind his dad's back. 'Why do I have to give you all this?' he asked her once. 'Keith only gives his mam ten quid.' There was no answering that. He kept most of the money back, and he'd never crack on what he earned, but afterwards when she found all the bills, she thought, Well, I mightn't've done any better than you, Brian, but I couldn't've done worse. He hadn't paid the electric or anything.

He got at the finish as soon as he had a few pints inside him he was moaning on to anybody who'd listen: 'My life ended when I was nineteen.'

'You're bloody lucky,' she used to say. 'I was only sixteen when mine ended.'

They both meant it too. So it was no surprise at all when he went. The only surprise was where he found the guts.

Brenda had thought that nothing Edith did to her now could hurt, but she was wrong. The way Edith just ignored the two bairns — that hurt. She wouldn't even mind them while Brenda went to have a tooth out.

It was no use going on living in the same street as her, so as soon as she could, Brenda moved further in, to

267

Melbourne Terrace. She was safe enough there: none of her stuck-up in-laws would've been seen dead walking down a street like that. She didn't like it all that much either, but she couldn't afford anything better.

Her first evening she got a shock: she nipped round the corner shop for a pint of milk and there was this car coming up the road very slowly as if the driver wasn't sure where he was. Oh, he's lost, she thought and when he pulled into the kerb and beckoned to her she went across to see if she could help.

'Do you suck?' he said.

Well, her jaw dropped. She just stood and looked at him. He made a little impatient, clicking noise with his tongue as if it was her fault! — and drove off.

She laughed about it afterwards, but at the time she was quite upset.

CHAPTER FOUR

A car drew up a few yards away from her and a face peered out. She looked around for Audrey, but there was still no sign of her. It was no use, she'd have to go: she couldn't risk losing George.

'Been getting a new car, then?'

'No. I just got a lend of this'n. The other's in dry-dock.'

'Oh dear, what's the matter with it?'

'Brakes and gear-lever. God knows how much it'll cost.'

He sounded down. Brenda sighed: down meant down in every sense, and she wasn't in the mood for one of George's marathons.

'Walker's yard alright for you?'

It seemed a long way to go, but he'd already turned the car in that direction so she didn't bother to argue. 'Yeah, that's alright. Long as you don't mind dropping me back.'

He didn't answer. He was in a funny mood tonight, she'd never known him so quiet — though all he ever talked about was how many coloured people there were in his street and how much noise they made and how if it wasn't for them his wife'd still be alive.

Generally they went and parked by the river, in one of the boarded-up streets. Probably he wanted to go to Walker's yard so they could get out of the car. God help her, there'd be no finding it this weather. She could feel him looking at her out of the corner of his eye. She turned and gave him a quick, stiff little smile, but he only looked away.

The silence was starting to get on her nerves.

'Had a bad week, have you?'

'Yes.'

She twisted round to look at him again. But there was only the faint orange light of the street-lamps and that was enough to make anybody look peculiar.

'Yes. They were having a party till three o'clock. They'd not do that if they had to turn out to work in the morning. But of course they don't have to. It's only mugs like me work.'

It was on the tip of Brenda's tongue to point out that anybody with a job should count themselves lucky, but she checked herself. She didn't know what he did: probably it was a bloody awful job. Almost as bad as this'n.

'Well, there's nowt worse than noisy neighbours,' she said. It paid to agree with them.

They were slowing down ready to turn into the alley that led to Walker's yard. George took the corner slowly and carefully — and hit the kerb anyway. Good old George.

There was a big pool of rain covering the middle of the yard.

'Oh, I'd forgotten it gets like this.'

'There's a dry bit over the far corner if you want to get out.'

'No. No, we'll stop in the car.'

He did want to get out, she could feel it off him, but she was blowed if she was gunna argue with him this weather. She'd only just got thawed out.

She opened her handbag with a click. He took the hint at once and handed over. You never had any trouble with George. The only trouble with him was trying to bring the poor sod off.

'I'm afraid he's not quite ready,' he said, straightening his thighs.

An understatement. Brenda got to work on his cock, but it was no use. After a while she looked up.

'What's the matter, love?'

'Nothing.' He pushed her head down again, harder than

270

he would normally have done. 'Don't stop.'

She tried everything she knew: stroked, rolled, pulled, licked, nibbled, nuzzled, guzzled, flicked, swirled, kissed, sucked, hoovered, popped... Finally, he had the beginnings of an erection.

Then, 'It's no good,' he said. 'I can't come with me knees bent.'

Brenda stifled a sigh.

'We could get in the back of the car,' he said.

He'd never suggested that before.

'There's more room in the back.'

She turned round to look. There was more room. There were also childproof locks on the doors.

'No,' she said. 'You still couldn't get your legs stretched out. Let's go over there.'

She got out of the car and waited for him. By now she had begun to feel uneasy. He seemed to be so tense, and she responded to it by becoming tense herself. She watched him get out of the car.

He took his time, looking all round the yard and up at the windows on the far side. Factory windows. Blank.

'You seem a bit jumpy tonight,' she said, keeping her voice steady.

'Oh, it's nothing. I just don't fancy being watched.'

'You won't be.' She picked her way between the puddles to a patch of dry ground by the far wall. 'Look, it's dry here,' she said. 'And we can't be seen if anybody walks past.'

He followed her into the shadows.

'I'm afraid he's not quite ready,' he said. His voice and hands were shaking.

'Don't worry about it, it'll be alright.' Brenda knelt and re-applied herself to the task. All George ever really wanted was sucking. She knew, though he'd never come right out and say so, that he actually disliked cunt.

She unzipped his trousers, which he'd done up again for the short trip across the yard, and a cloud of talcum powder shot up her nose. Complete waste of time putting a rubber on George: you'd more like get silicosis than VD.

Progress? Could be. She went on sucking but then his

271

hands came down, gripping the top of her head and forcing her mouth so far down onto his cock that she gagged. She was afraid, but she went on sucking. There were voices in her head: Audrey's voice, Jean's voice. Carol's voice.

- *Stick to your regulars. That's your best bet.*
- *That's what I told her. She said, He is somebody's regular.*

The skin at the nape of her neck crawled. Suddenly it was too much, she fought to get her head free.

'I'm sorry I'm taking so long.'

And it was only George, blinking down at her.

'I think we're making progress,' Brenda said, and got back on the job fast before any of it could be lost.

A minute or two later George came, a weak trickle that hardly seemed to justify the groans coming from his open mouth. Brenda got up, brushed the gravel from her knees and thought, *Christ*, what a way to earn a living.

They walked back to the car together. As she was getting into it, she remembered the man who'd stopped her on her first day in Melbourne Terrace and asked, '*Do you suck?*'

She sat back in the seat and closed her eyes.

Oh, yes, mister, I suck. I suck till my jaws ache.

CHAPTER FIVE

As soon as she was sure that Brian had left her, she'd gone round to the Social Security offices to put in a claim. She wouldn't ask Edith to mind the bairns because she knew if she did there'd only be a row.

It was the first time she'd been there. There was a long row of chairs stretching in two lines down the centre of the room, and a circle of chairs further out near the walls. At the far side of the room was a grille with two officials behind it. The chairs in front of the grille were riveted to the ground.

Brenda, carrying the baby, Sharon, in her arms stood just inside the door and waited for a chair to become vacant. Whenever people at the head of the queue went across to be interviewed, everybody stood up and moved to the next chair, the wave of movement beginning at the front and spreading to the back like the humping of a caterpillar.

The morning dragged on. The baby whinged, Lindsey ran about shouting and a woman came out of the office to shush her. Brenda gave her a bar of chocolate to try to keep her quiet and it melted all over her face and hands. Then, "Wee wee," she said, and set up a wail. She hated being wet.

A woman a few seats away said she would mind Sharon. Brenda queued for the key to the toilet. There were only three people wanting to go so it didn't take long. Then, as she came out, she got told off for giving the key to the next person in the queue. You were meant to give it back to them so that *they* could hand it out.

When finally she reached the grille she was told to go home: they would send somebody round to see her. There was no question of money being handed out there and then. She knew now why the chairs were riveted to the ground. It was in case you picked one up and hit them with it.

But they were as good as their word: they sent somebody round the same afternoon. There was a middle-aged dumpy woman with glasses and another younger woman who didn't say anything and was obviously there to learn the trade.

'It's just till I can get a job,' Brenda said. It made no difference: they still wanted to know the far-end of a fart and which way the wind blew. 'I've got an interview at the chicken factory next week.'

'Now your husband left you on the . . .'

Brenda went through it all. The pen scribbled, then remained poised.

'You *are* married?'

'Course I'm bloody married. How d' y' think I got that lot?' Brenda pointed to her children.

Sharon, hearing her mother's voice raised, whimpered in her sleep. Lindsey stared at the strange women.

'We have to check.' Her face softened a little as she looked at the children. 'But since you are married your husband should be paying.'

'I don't know where he is.'

'We'll find him.'

'His mam might know. Number 15 Beaconsfield Road. But I warn you: you'll need a tin-opener to get owt out of her.'

Their eyes were everywhere. The dumpy one even forgot which door to go out of. She ended up in the clothes cupboard having a bloody good look at the coats.

'That belongs to me husband,' said Brenda. 'He left it behind.' She looked the woman straight in the eye. 'I know what you're looking for and you needn't bother. The last thing on my mind is another fella.'

After they'd gone Brenda sat down and pressed her hands together to stop them shaking. What got her was the hypocrisy of it all. They went on about being married, but when you got right down to it, past the white weddings and the romance and all that, what they *really* thought was: if you're getting on your back for a fella, he ought to pay. *That* was what they really thought. And where did that leave you? You might just as well be standing on a street corner in bloody Northgate — at least it'd be honest.

CHAPTER SIX

As soon as she got out of the car Audrey came running across the street to meet her.

'You've had me worried sick,' she said. 'I thought you were gunna stop here?'

'Oh, it was *George*. I had to go.' She hoped Audrey wouldn't go on about it. The last thing she fancied was a post-mortem on George: she was still picking bits of gravel out of her knees. 'Anyway, you were gone long enough. If I'd stood around any longer I'd've took root.'

'Black tights,' said Audrey.

'Oh.'

They walked across the road and into the shadow of the viaduct together.

'You know he worries me,' Audrey said when they were settled. 'There's something about him I just don't like.'

'Rough?'

'No! Far from it. He just . . . I don't know . . . He's always sort of drawing attention to us, you know what I mean?' She looked at Brenda. 'He's . . . Well, like if there was a police car there he'd go and park beside it.'

'Oh, charming!'

'And I think meself that's the way he gets his rocks off. It isn't the tights, it's the thought of you getting lifted.'

'Audrey. Steer clear.'

Audrey was picking at her fingernails. She looked up.

'Pays well.'

'Well, let's hope he pays the fucking fine.'

'And it's mebbe just me thinking it. I get very jumpy, Brenda.'

'You're not the only one. I worked meself up into a complete panic with George just now, and he'd done nowt.'

'I wish to God they'd catch the bugger.'

'Too busy catching us.'

They separated and began patrolling opposite sides of the street, Audrey under the arches of the viaduct, Brenda up and down the chicken factory wall. After a few minutes a car drew up by Audrey and she bent down to speak to the driver. Brenda walked across to look at the number.

'I think you're the flavour of the month, aren't you?'

'Well, if I am it's not before time. I won't be long.'

'Hey, mind yourself,' Brenda said, pointing at the car.

'Oh, he's alright. I been with him before.'

'Not him. The dog.'

Audrey grinned. 'That's alright, it's a bitch. I made sure of that before I got in the car.'

She looked back and waved as the car drove off. Brenda, as the agreement was, withdrew into the shadow of the chicken factory gate, burrowing down into the familiar smell.

CHAPTER SEVEN

The smell had hit her as soon as she'd got to the gate. A greasy smell. You could feel it sticking to your clothes.

She was frightened, she needed the job so badly. In her anxiety to get the interview over, she blundered in at the wrong entrance and saw a line of live chickens fastened to a conveyor belt by their legs. They jerked past. At the end of the line a man hit them with something to stun them and another man chopped off their heads.

The tiles were spattered with blood. They must've been able to smell it, but there was no struggling, no panic after the first frantic clapping of wings.

They didn't even squawk.

'Who you looking for, love?'

Brenda jerked her eyes away from the chickens. 'I've come about a job.'

'Oh, you want to be in at the other side. Howay, love, I'll show you.'

She was a bit shaken. She must've looked it, too, because the manager offered her a cup of tea.

Most of the questions they asked were about the child-minder, how reliable she was and whether she'd take the children if they were a bit off-colour. Well, you could understand that: they didn't want you taking time off for every little sniffle. But they were funny. It wasn't enough to say you needed the job and you'd work hard and all that. You had to go on as if you'd wanted to gut chickens all your life, as if you couldn't imagine a better way of spending your time. She wasn't very good at that. God knows how she got took on: perhaps she was so quiet they thought she wouldn't waste time chattering.

The supervisor took her down to the main room.

'I went in there,' she said, pointing to the other door.

He seemed quite shocked. 'Oh, you don't go in there,' he said. 'Killing's for the men.'

He opened the right door. 'There you are,' he said.

The noise hit you just as earlier on the smell had done, six or seven different hums and whines and creaks bouncing off the white-tiled walls. A line of headless chickens, naked, with plump thighs, jerked around the room above the women's heads. At intervals they were taken down to be gutted, cleaned, chilled, trussed and frozen.

'I won't take you in,' he said. 'You're supposed to wear boots.'

You'd need to. The floor was slick with blood and guts.

None of the women looked up, though some of them must've seen the door open. Their lips moved. After a while Brenda realized they were singing.

On her first day they kitted her out with the uniform. You had to wear overalls with a long plastic apron over them, and scrape all your hair back under a plastic cap. You were supposed to get into trouble if your hair showed, but she soon noticed that a lot of the women didn't bother. She pulled the wellies on and flapped and crackled down to the main hall.

'I've put you on with Mrs Braithwaite, dear,' the supervisor said.

Brenda looked at the older woman standing beside her at the bench.

'Annie,' the woman said.

There wasn't time for more. The noise started up and a procession of headless chickens advanced into the room. At the gutting table the green-clad women took the birds down, wiped blood from their necks and, pushing their hands into the vent as far as the wrist, pulled out piles of

279

steaming guts.

'Messy job that,' Annie screamed above the noise. 'This is better.'

'This' was basically shoving chickens' legs up their arses, only it wasn't as easy as that because the chickens were chilled, sometimes near-frozen, and you had to really force the legs inside. The other women worked at an incredible speed. Brenda couldn't keep pace with it at all, and the chickens piled up on the bench in front of her. Sometimes she even missed taking one down and then she had to chase along the belt and get it back. By the time the first tea-break came her hands were frozen, but the rest of her, inside the nylon and plastic uniform, streamed with sweat.

The belt was switched off. The song that a few of the women had been singing faltered into silence, and there was a general laugh. The gutting women took off their goggles and threw them down onto the bench.

They all trooped upstairs for tea. Annie touched Brenda's arm. 'Well, what do you think to it?' she asked.

'I can't keep up,' Brenda said. She was near to tears.

'You'll get the hang of it. First week I was here I spent that much time chasing the buggers you'd've thought they were still alive.'

They queued for the tea which was grey and dotted with globules of fat. Brenda looked at the clock and tried to imagine what Lindsey and Sharon were doing. It was the first time she'd ever left them and she felt like her arm'd been cut off.

'Don't worry,' one of the women said. 'It might never happen.'

'This is me friend Renee,' Annie said.

Brenda forced herself to smile.

Renee worked on the gutting table. With her goggles off she looked permanently surprised, the skin around her eyes seemed so white. Brenda looked down to avoid seeing a particularly succulent bit of something-or-other that was clinging to her chin.

'You don't want to worry, love,' Annie said. 'It's surprising how soon you get the knack.'

'Why aye,' said Renee. 'You get you whistle through 'em in no time.'

'It's not that,' said Brenda. 'I'm missing me bairns.'

The older women looked at each other. 'Is this the first time you've left them?' Annie asked.

'Yeah.'

'Oh, you don't want to worry,' said Renee. 'A lot of the women here have bairns. Her over there, she's got six and her husband's disabled.'

'With a bad back,' said Annie.

'Hey, you want to watch her,' said Renee, jerking her thumb in Annie's direction. 'She's got an awful mind.'

'I don't mind the ones that've got to work,' said Annie. 'But you see that lot over there, you want to hear them on. "Oh, I'm only doing it till I've paid for me fitted carpet." And then when they've got their fitted carpet paid for it's the holiday in Spain or the new car or something. And I wouldn't care but it's all luxuries. You wouldn't catch me pouring my life down the sewer for a fitted carpet.'

Brenda was beginning to feel got at. 'Well, I'm on me own with two bairns,' she said. 'It isn't luxuries for me. It's the *rent*.'

At the end of the day Brenda crawled up Northgate. She wanted to run because she was going to get her children, but she hadn't the energy. Her wrists hurt so much she could've cried from the pain.

'Did they settle alright?' she asked the woman.

'No bother.'

They seemed a bit subdued.

On the way back a big Alsatian jumped up at her and the owner dragged it away. He looked a bit embarrassed — perhaps he thought she had her period or something. But of course it wasn't that. She couldn't go into a shop or anything: she just stank.

She was OK till she got the kids into bed. Then she sat and looked at the empty kitchen and the nappy bucket waiting under the sink, and started to cry. It wouldn't've been so bad if she could've seen an end to it, but she couldn't. It was going to be like this till the kids grew up and

281

by that time she'd be old and useless and nobody'd want her anyway. She cried till her chest ached.

The first month was terrible, but then gradually the job didn't seem so hard. She wasn't always chasing chickens down the line, and the other women were nice. If you'd asked her what she thought of it at the end of two months she'd probably've said. 'Oh, it's alright. You get a laugh.'

She settled; the children didn't. She knew Lindsey hated the child-minder, but she never protested about being left there. Only there was always some reason why she couldn't go. She felt sick, or the minder was sick, or she'd broken her leg and couldn't look after them any more. But Lindsey never cried, she was stoical beyond her years, and wasted no time on pleading.

Sharon cried. Her screams followed Brenda down the street. 'Oh, she's having you on,' the minder said. 'She's as good as gold as soon as you turn that corner.' Perhaps it was alright. Sharon was never crying when Brenda came to fetch them. They were both sitting on the sofa, with Lindsey's legs sticking out over the edge. No toys. No mess. Never a hair out of place. 'I like to get them cleaned up before you come. You don't want to be stuck around here waiting after you've worked all day.'

Sharon always started to cry on the way home, a quiet, hopeless grizzle. She didn't sound as if she expected anybody to come. Lindsey held onto the handle of Brenda's shopping bag and stared straight ahead.

'I know there's something wrong,' Brenda burst out one day during the afternoon tea-break.

'Look, love,' Annie leant over the table towards her. 'If you think there's something wrong, it's no use just bottling it up. You'll mek yourself bad. You want to get yourself up there when she least expects it and *walk in on her*. Don't knock or anything.'

'How the hell can I do that? I daren't take time off.'

'You could be taken bad during the day and have to go home early. There's always ways.'

That night Brenda dragged herself up Northgate to the child-minder's and then back home. The children whined and pulled at her. She put her hand on their foreheads and decided they were hot. My God. The last thing she needed. They clung to her: she could hardly move for them. She'd seen a bitch once trying to wean a litter of pups and every time she stood up there'd been pups hanging on her tits.

Don't sit down, she told herself. If she'd sat down she'd never've got up.

Usually she cooked a proper meal for them, but tonight she just couldn't. Baked beans'd have to do. 'Howay, love,' she said, swinging Sharon up and onto the draining board, intending to wash her while the beans warmed through.

Her legs were covered in tiny bruises. Brenda had noticed these many times before, but Sharon was just starting to pull herself up on the furniture. 'They're always knocking themselves at this stage,' the child-minder said. Which was true: Lindsey had been covered in bruises when she first started to walk. But Brenda had been there then, she'd known what was going on. Now she just had the woman's word for what happened.

It was funny how they all came in twos. Every single bruise had another similar bruise beside it. Brenda stopped soaping one tiny, stick-like leg and bent forward for a closer look. Tentatively, she tried fitting her thumb and fore-finger over each pair of bruises. Every time, a perfect fit.

The funny thing was she didn't feel angry, or not what she would have called angry. She finished washing the children, gave them the baked beans and put them to bed. She sat on the top step until she was sure they were both asleep. Lindsey cried out once or twice before she finally settled.

Then Brenda went downstairs and out into the street. There were Pakistani families on either side of her: you saw the men come and go, but not the women. There was nobody in this street she could ask to sit with the children. She'd just have to go and ask Annie.

Annie peered round the chain on her front door, and relaxed when she saw Brenda's face.

'I've got to go out,' Brenda said. 'I wondered if you'd mind keeping an eye on the bairns?'

Her voice sounded peculiar, but Annie didn't seem to notice. She just said, 'Hang on, I'll get me coat.'

Brenda saw her settled over the gasfire with a pot of tea and then set off for the child-minder's. While she was talking to Annie she had forced herself to appear normal, but there was no need for that now. Her feet ate the ground.

There was rubbish scattered all over the basement steps where the dustbins had overflowed. Her own flat was spotless, but she wouldn't clear this up. 'It's them up there,' she said, pointing towards the West Indian family on the first floor. 'Mucky sods.' Brenda had nearly put the kids with a West Indian minder. Great big woman she was, tits on her like footballs, and the floor crawling with bairns. They were, they were crawling over each other. Brenda had taken one look and thought, My God, no. But many a time afterwards she wondered whether that woman wouldn't've been the better choice. At least she liked bairns, you only had to see her with them to know that.

The child-minder answered the door cautiously, as women did round here. Her eyes widened when she saw Brenda. Aye, thought Brenda, you know. 'I've come to pay you,' she said. 'I'm not feeling so good and I can't see meself getting in tomorrow.'

At the mention of money the door opened. They stood together in the neat hallway, while Brenda got her purse out and counted notes into the woman's hands. 'There,' she said. 'That's for the three days this week. That's right, isn't it?'

The woman nodded, made nervous by something in Brenda's tone, but unable to identify it. She had a long, sallow, perpetually damp-looking nose. Brenda's fingers itched. 'Well, then,' she said. 'That's what I owe you. And this is what it feels like.'

She pinched the woman's nose between her thumb and forefinger and started to twist. The woman made no sound until Brenda forced her to her knees and then she suddenly let out a scream. 'There,' said Brenda. 'Perhaps you'll pick on somebody your own size next time.' The money had fallen onto the floor. Contemptuously Brenda kicked one of the notes towards the woman. 'Here, buy yourself a handkerchief,' she said and walked out, wiping her fingers on the side of her jeans.

Upstairs a window which had been opened when the woman screamed closed again quietly.

Brenda walked home slowly, trying to calm herself down. The girls were out in force. She lowered her eyes as she passed them, because if they got the idea you were staring at them they could turn very nasty. Not that you could blame them for that. The way some people went on you'd've thought it was a zoo.

At the corner of Melbourne Terrace she stopped and looked back. Any one of those girls must take home in a night more than she had left at the end of a week. She put her head down, and started to walk more quickly, but the thought wouldn't be shaken off.

Annie was asleep when she got back. Brenda tip-toed past her and put the kettle on for another pot of tea. When she came back into the living room Annie was awake. 'That's the worst of being old,' she said. 'You drop off during the day and then at night you can't sleep.'

'You're not old.'

'I don't know what else it is.' Annie looked more closely at Brenda. 'I hope you're not thinking of going into work tomorrow? You're not fit.'

'I can't go in. I haven't got anybody to mind the bairns.' She told Annie what had happened.

'What the hell d'y' want to pay her for? Twist her nose OK. Break the bugger. But don't pay her.'

Brenda pulled a face. 'I was born honest.'

'You were born soft.'

Brenda sat on the rug and sipped her tea. 'They'll keep the job open for me, won't they? I'll have to take time off to find another minder and get them settled in.'

Annie didn't reply.

Brenda burst out, 'It's a fucking awful job, who'd want it?'

'Plenty.'

Brenda clasped her hands round the mug and rocked herself. 'Oh, Annie,' she said. 'What am I gunna do?'

CHAPTER EIGHT

Make your mind up, Brenda thought. He'd been stood in the shadow of the viaduct for ages now, peering out at her whenever he thought she wasn't looking his way. One thing she couldn't stand: bloody window shoppers getting a free wank. Put your money where your thoughts are, lad.

Must've read her mind, he was coming across.

He was tall, broad-shouldered, with a long swinging stride. Brenda's heart sank. If there was one thing she hated more than window shoppers it was off-duty policemen turning up to claim their free fuck. But no, he couldn't be police. A policeman would've come right up to her, he wouldn't't've hung around like that. The way some of 'em shoved their vice-squad cards up your nose you'd've thought it was American Express.

'How much is it?' he asked.

That sorted that out! But he was very young, too young.

'Fiver. Straight sex with a rubber.'

She did her best to sound discouraging. She didn't like doing it with young men, especially if they were good-looking, and this one was. They made her feel shy.

'I don't like them. Rubbers,' he said.

The way he said it she knew at once he'd never had it, with or without. Why not, she thought. Shy? Kinky? There had to be a reason, unless all the girls up his way were blind.

'Well, sod your luck, son,' she said. 'You're not getting it without.' She turned and started to walk away.

'Alright. Only I haven't got one.'

'Oh, that's alright, dear. You don't have to bring your own.' She smiled at him. 'You're not in a car, are you? Alright, let's just go over there.'

She hated walking ahead of him into the shadows, hearing him stumble after. She hated being under the viaduct because that was where you ended up when you got too old for the car trade. Fucking dirty men and worrying about crabs. *Ugh, never.*

'You know, you don't need me,' she said to him. 'What do you need me for?'

He grinned nervously at her.

He couldn't be much older than Audrey's lad: probably been to the same school. *Aw, shurrup, woman, get on with the job.*

'Howay, in here,' she said, and led him under one of the smaller arches. It was very dark and smelled powerfully of piss. Used rubbers lay here and there on the ground. 'Well, come on then,' she said.

He gave her the money and she braced herself against the wall. It'd have to be a knee-wobbler: she was damned if she was gunna lie down in all that muck.

He came twice, more rapidly than she'd've believed possible, and was obviously looking forward to another.

'Hey,' she said, pushing him off her. 'There's limits to what you get for a fiver.'

He laughed, perhaps with relief as much as anything. 'That was smashing,' he said.

'Glad you enjoyed it,' she said, not bothering to keep the dryness out of her voice.

'When can I see you again, darling?'

It was just like he'd slapped her face. 'Don't call me that,' she said.

'Why not?'

'Because I don't like it, that's why not.'

'Sorry.' He paused, then, 'You called me *son*,' he said, sounding outraged and every day of twelve.

'Did I?' It was impossible not to soften slightly. 'Well, I'm sorry too.'

They looked at each other and laughed.

'I am a bit older than you, you know.'

'I like older women.'

'You get yourself a girlfriend, lad.'

'Can't I see you again?'

'Look, I'm stuck out here five or six nights a week, all weathers. If you want me, you'll find me. And now piss off, you've had long enough.'

You'll get rich quick that way, lass, she thought as she watched him go. But she couldn't help it, she didn't want him to come back. There was no winning at this game: if they were nasty you hated them; if they were nice you hated yourself. She'd rather hate them. And the young ones were awful, because you started doing sums. Simple sums, like how old would he be when I first started? She'd just done that one and it added up to another drink.

Where the bloody hell was Audrey? She need talk about me, Brenda thought, as she settled back into the chicken factory gate. You didn't see her rushing back.

CHAPTER NINE

The chicken factory had sacked her. Well, you couldn't
blame them: she hadn't even bothered to get in touch
and tell them what was wrong. She wasn't even looking
for another child-minder, though she told herself she was.
It was just like a spring inside her had gone bust. She
looked after the children, she did the bare minimum on the
house. When the kids were in bed she didn't even bother
switching the telly on. She just sat. She was behind with all
her payments and she didn't care.

Then one week there was no money for the rent. She got
allowed for it, but she'd spent that on the electric, she was
using that much, now they were in all day. That did it. No
tent meant no house. No house meant no kids. She went to
meet Annie coming home from work.

'I've got meself a job in a pub, Annie,' she said. 'Five
nights a week. Will you mind the bairns for me? Just till I
can find somebody.'

Annie agreed straight away. She was glad of the chance to
get out at nights, or that was what she said.

'I'll pay you.'

'You will not. Don't worry, love. I know what it's like
when you're in a hole. I've had some.'

So there she'd been: stuck on a street corner in
Northgate. Butterflies with jackboots on trampling all over
her stomach. For God's sake, she said to herself, they're

289

only men. You're not going off with a bloody werewolf. The pep-talk didn't help much. Every time a car showed signs of stopping she shrank back into the doorway. Come on, now, she told herself — *next time*.

But the next person who walked up to her was a woman. Afterwards she wondered how she could ever've been so daft: just going out like that and plonking herself in the middle of somebody else's pitch. But she knew nothing, not a bloody thing. Many a woman'd've clocked her one and asked questions afterwards, but Kath didn't. She was really nice and somehow it all came flooding out, Brian and the kids and the chicken factory and the rent. What would I have done without her? Brenda used to think. Because Kath carried her through the first few weeks, she did, she absolutely carried her.

She was unlucky with the first. He realized she was new and Oh God didn't he have a field day. He'd've done it in her lugs if they'd been the right shape. She fell out of the car, two hours later, too shocked to cry, even smiling slightly because she didn't know what else to do. If Kath had said something nice to her then, that'd've been it: she'd've burst into tears and gone home. But Kath didn't. She came sweeping across the pavement like a bloody tornado.

'What do you think this is?' she said. 'Your bleeding honeymoon?'

Brenda stared at her.

'Look, love, you want to run your cunt as a soup kitchen, that's entirely up to you. But you don't do it from here.'

The next one got half an hour.

'Right,' said Kath. 'Knock ten minutes off that and you might start making money.'

She was incredibly hard. 'The maximum for the minimum,' she used to say. 'They want more they pay more. They want you to smile while you're doing it . . .' She clicked her fingers together under Brenda's nose. Her only warm feelings seemed to be for her two boys. She once said to Brenda, 'Always remember your mouth's your own. When he's shot his muck you've got to go back and kiss them bairns.'

290

Brenda told Annie the bar job was working out fine. Annie just nodded: she'd gone very quiet. Brenda closed her mind to that. She was enjoying her kids for the first time since Sharon was born. Sharon was walking now, quick little bursts from one piece of furniture to the next and when she made it her face split open in a gurgle of delight. At least I'm here to see it, Brenda thought.

She needed to cling to the consolations because it was still very hard. There were evenings when just the sheer smell of them, their weight on top of her, made her want to scream. And their cocks! Long, short, thick, thin, spindly, straight, skewed, curved, sticking out of flat bellies, or sunk in rolls of fat, the hairy, the hairless, the washed, the un-washed . . . And the things they wanted to do. Some of them were really weird.

'He never wants to do anything to me. All he wants is for me to watch him wank.'

'You should worry. It's money for old rope, that. You can pass him on to me if you don't want him.' Kath paused and looked at her intently. 'Trouble is, Brenda, you haven't learned to switch off. You're still there, aren't you?'

Gradually, Brenda learned to switch off. She never managed to do it completely, there were always times when she came back and found herself lying under some sweating hulk, and then she wanted to cry out in horror, *No, it isn't me.*

But these times became less and less frequent. If anything, she started to have the opposite problem. She couldn't switch herself on again during the day. Everything seemed to be happening on the other side of a dirty glass. But it was worth it: a skin had formed over her mind, and she was free inside it.

Make-up helped. She'd never worn much before, but now she plastered it on, aware of Annie and the kids watching her, hardening herself against their stares.

'How's the job?' Annie would say.

'Oh, it's fine.'

'You don't get a rough crowd in there, then?'

'No. It's pretty quiet.'

One day as Brenda was walking home from the shops a woman she knew crossed the street to avoid speaking to her. At first Brenda told herself that she'd imagined it, but she knew she hadn't. From that moment on Brenda began to be afraid: not the fear she felt every night. *Is he alright? What will he do?* No, this was a deeper fear. She felt as if she was exposed on a high ledge, with lights shining on her, and crowds of people underneath all looking up and staring. Because if that woman knew, everybody knew. The shops she went in. The neighbours. Everybody.

Annie? No, she'd've said.

She started spending, because spending money made the fear stop. There was no controlling it, the money seemed to want to be spent. She could still deny herself things, but anything she saw for the kids, she just went in and bought, it didn't matter what it cost. If she saw a little dress in a window she went in and got it, and their shoes were the best. She bought Lindsey a bride doll for her third birthday that was as big as she was. The spending worried her sometimes because the whole point of doing this was to get clear of debt as fast as she could; but she wasn't paying the bills off any faster than she'd done at the chicken factory. She tried, but she couldn't. She had to buy things.

She lived in dread of Annie finding out, because there was no doubt in her mind that if Annie did find out she wouldn't mind the kids again, and they loved her. But it was more than that: she couldn't face Annie's contempt.

It happened. She'd just got out of one car and was looking around for Kath when another car drew up. Generally, they didn't stop, or not completely, not till you went towards them. But this one did, and the man got out. Something inside her said, Police. She couldn't move, she just stood and waited. The man — he was quite tall, and well-built — walked up to her, and, smiling pleasantly, asked, 'How's business?' Then he punched her in the face, went back to his car, and drove off.

Kath found her staggering round.

'What did he want to do that for?' Brenda asked when she could speak.

Kath didn't bother to answer: she was too busy mopping up the blood.

'I wasn't doing anything to him.'

'Howay, love. I'll walk you home.'

Too late, just as they turned into Melbourne Terrace, Brenda remembered that she couldn't go home, not like this.

'I can't go in,' she said. 'What am I gunna say?'

They stopped under a street lamp.

'I'm supposed to be working in a pub.'

Kath looked at her. 'Bloody rough bar you're in, love.' She started to laugh, a deep, wheezing, choking laugh, and after a while Brenda joined in. They clung to each other under the lamp and laughed till their eyes streamed.

'All the same, you've gotta go in,' Kath said. 'Tell her you had a nose-bleed and they sent you home.'

Brenda walked into the passage, praying for the kids to be in bed. They were. Annie looked up as she came into the room and Brenda thought, She knows. She's known all along.

It staggered her. All she could do was sit there while Annie washed the blood off her face.

'I daren't go too near your nose. It'll stop it clotting.' She stood back to have a look. 'There. You'll do.'

Brenda pressed delicately all round her nose and mouth.

'You know you should've told me. When you first start you make things hard for yourself. You don't realize you're doing it, but you are. There's many a little thing I could've helped you with.'

Brenda stared at her.

'Why, aye.'

A week later another car stopped, another tall, well-built man got out. Brenda braced herself for a blow and found herself looking at a card instead. This time it was the police.

It was terrible, it was really humiliating, and it changed you completely. You felt as if you'd had the words 'common prostitute' stamped right through you, like 'Blackpool' through a stick of rock. It was the 'common' that hurt. 'Prostitute', well, you couldn't very well deny it; but she wasn't common. They had no right to say that.

It hardened her, though. She thought, Right, if that's what I am, OK, I'll bloody well be it. It wasn't all bad, not by any means. There was a lot of things you could enjoy. Oh, not the sex, not that side of it, but there was the company, the excitement, the chance of a drink whenever you fancied it, going out and looking in the shops and not having to think all the time, Eee, can I afford it? And she had the best-dressed kids in the street. That made up for a lot.

Most nights started in a pub, usually in the back room of the Palmerston, where Beattie Miller had just taken over. You needed a couple of drinks to soften the edges a bit. Kath was knocking it back, though not more than most. Her laugh could always be heard, ringing out across the bar, a rich, wheezy, bubbling sound. You felt she'd got her teeth into life.

One night they were stood on the corner snatching a few minutes' chat before they resumed their separate pacing up and down when a woman walked past and turned to give a long, lingering stare. You couldn't really say she looked down her nose, but it stung as much as if she had.

'Stuck up cow,' Kath said, and jabbed two fingers in the air at the woman's retreating back. 'That's what I can't stand,' she went on. 'Them looking at you as if you were muck.'

She didn't sound frightened, but Brenda had lived with that particular fear too long now to be deceived.

Kath lived for her two boys. They lived with her mother, but she went to see them three or four times a week, and she was always buying for them. She didn't seem to bother with men. In fact she was quite hostile. 'Men?' she used to say. '*Men?* I've shat 'em!' Of course like everybody else she had her regulars, and some of them she quite liked, but that was different. Away from work she never bothered.

So it was a bit of a shock when she got herself a fella.

'You know, Brenda,' she said. 'He's really nice. And it's a chance to get away from all this. He's nothing to do with it, you see, he's got a job, it's completely foreign to him, and he's always on at me to pack it in. He says he'd help me and if I went with him I could have me bairns back.'

'So what's stopping you?'

'Oh, I don't know. Well, yes, I do. I'm afraid he'll throw it up at me. He says he won't, but you know what it's like, Brenda. When you start rowing everything comes out. And you're bound to have rows, aren't you?' She looked straight at Brenda and gave a little laugh. 'I don't think I could stand that. You know, I'd rather it was over now than for it to end like that.'

She was gone four years, four years in which Brenda's own determination to get out of it waxed and waned, but never quite saw her clear. It was hard to say really why you stuck with it. Money, friends, habit — and of course it was easy, if you were ever short, if you ever needed anything, it was always there.

'You don't give it up, love,' said Annie. 'It gives you up.'

But she didn't want to believe that.

Kath, you could see at first glance, had gone right down the drain. She was either fat or pregnant, you couldn't tell which until you saw her sideways on and then it was obvious.

'Hello, Brenda,' she said. Her voice had changed: it was slurred now and very soft. She seemed to have had all the fight knocked out of her.

Her kidneys were bad, she said. She stretched out her legs to show her swollen ankles.

'Why, they shouldn't be like that. How far on are you?'

'They think about five month. I think it's more like six, but I can't be sure 'cos I keep seeing.'

They went back to working together, though now it was Brenda who took the lead. Kath seemed content to drift along, she hadn't the energy for anything else. There were nights when she had to drag herself out of the pub and onto the street. She'd been told to stop drinking, but of course she couldn't.

As the time came closer, Brenda expected Kath to give it up, but she didn't. The men flocked, the money rolled in, she needed every penny of it. Her mother was dead now and she was paying a woman to look after the boys. She didn't dare miss the payments, because she knew the social services were looking for a chance to get the kids into care.

She took chances, the sort of chances the old Kath would never've taken and of course she got clobbered. One night in particular she let a man take her back to his house and when she got there there were three of them. It was four hours before they let her go. 'Bloody animals,' said Brenda. 'They could see how you are.' Kath didn't waste any breath on complaining.

When she went into labour it was Brenda who got her to the hospital. The man she'd been with just tipped her out onto the pavement and drove off. Brenda took one look at the water dripping down Kath's legs and yelled, 'You mean bastard, you could've given us a lift.' She turned to Kath. 'Howay, love. I'll take you home.'

But Kath's jaw was sagging with fear. 'There isn't time,' she said.

The baby was born two hours after they got to the hospital, a tiny, black-haired, bright orange scrap. Kath looked up from the pillow and smiled. 'Isn't she lovely?' she said. 'I wanted a girl.'

It wasn't for long. She was lifted, went to court expecting a fine, and got prison instead. She hadn't made arrangements for the bairns so they were taken into care. Of course she tried to get them back, but she never managed it.

From then on it was all down. She got so you couldn't rely on her, she just didn't care. It was a relief to Brenda when Kath disappeared again, because she could never've said, Look, Kath, I won't work with you. As it was Kath came and went, Brenda teamed up with Audrey, and there was never an actual break. And every time Kath showed up again, she was fatter, pufffier, more out of breath: there was no doubt about it, she was drinking herself to death.

You looked at Kath now and it was difficult to remember the woman she'd been. 'I don't know why you bother,' Audrey said. *Because she bothered with me when she needn't've done.* There was nobody else who meant the same. Audrey, Elaine, Jean: they were a good crowd, you wouldn't find many better, but there wasn't one of them whose arms she would've cried in the way she'd cried in Kath's. That whole part of her life was gone.

'How you doing?'

Brenda looked up, surprised to see Audrey because she hadn't heard the car return. 'I'm not sure,' she said. 'But I think I've taken root. How was Speedy Gonzales then?'

'Slow.'

Teach her to complain when Brenda was late back after George. Still there was no point arguing about it. 'Where have all the quickies gone? Must be some of 'em left.'

'Third time lucky?'

'Aye. Perhaps.'

CHAPTER TEN

Kath didn't leave the Palmerston till closing time. She paused in the doorway, taking time to realize that it had stopped raining, or rather to remember that it ever had been. Then she stepped out onto the pavement.

She stayed close to the wall where it was more sheltered. There wasn't so much breath left that she could afford to share it with the wind. She peered up and down the road, trying to make her eyes focus, but it was no use: the lights of the street lamps melted and flowed down into pools of liquid gold.

She felt very peaceful, not drunk at all, though she was glad of the wall's support when it veered towards her. The cider had carried her back to her childhood, to the orphanage of the Holy Rood. She could see the candles, she breathed in the mingled scent of incense and lilies.

> The Church's one foundation
> Is Jesus Christ her Lord.
> She is his own creation
> By water and the word . . .

She'd had a lovely voice once: good enough to sing solo in the choir. And it still did well enough. She loved singing hymns. The two boys used to go on at her about it. 'Aw, Mam,' they used to say. 'Change the record.'

From heaven he came and sought her
To be his holy bride
With his own blood he bought her
And for her life he died.

As she got to the crest of the hill a car slowed down and
seemed about to stop, but he changed his mind, sod him.
Turning up the collar of her jacket, she wandered further
down to where the arches of the great railway viaduct
soared overhead and trains rattled and flashed across the
sky. There her voice, sounding thinner and more tremulous now, lost itself among the dark vaults and dripping
walls.

'I'd stand well back off the pavement if I were you, Audrey.
You might get knocked over in the rush.'
   'Where are they all?'
   'I don't know. It's mebbe Cup Final night and nobody's
told us.'
   Audrey peered into the darkness. 'Isn't that Kath up
there?'
   'Could be. Yes, it is.'
   'Well, I shouldn't think she'll have much luck.'
   'I don't like to say this, Audrey, but I think she just did.'
   Audrey turned round and together they watched as Kath
crossed the road and disappeared under the arches with a
man.
   'Well, all I can say is, he must be fucking desperate.'
   'Now then.'

Ten minutes later Kath was back on the pavement with a
fiver in her pocket. The man walked off. She called
'Goodnight' after him, but he didn't bother to reply.
   She was starting to sober up, getting that awful dryness at
the back of her throat. The pubs were shut, but that didn't
matter. She knew other places where drink could be had at
virtually any hour of the night. With any luck she might get
picked up and given a lift in the right direction.
   She started walking up and down again. The viaduct had

become a second home. It was nice: you could shelter from the rain and the wind and then if he didn't have a car you could always take him under one of the arches. There were lots of places you could go, if you didn't mind the thunder and rattle of the trains and the steady drip-drip of water from the walls.

There was even a mattress, though it was on top of a rubbish tip and soaked right through. People dumped all kinds of things there.

She watched a man come out of the public lavatory opposite. He turned his collar up, crossed the street, and disappeared into the shadows. A moment later another man came out and followed the first. Ah well. Be a lot of girls go hungry to shit if that caught on.

She decided she was wasting time. She'd do better to start walking home and pick up a lift on the way.

As soon as she moved she squelched — awkward bugger, wanting it without. If it ever got round she was doing that the other girls'd be down on her like a ton of bricks. But somehow these days, especially since she'd had the big operation, there didn't seem to be much left that was worth arguing about. Except her mouth. That was still her own, the only bit she had left.

There was a tune nibbling away at her memory: it had been there on and off all night. To take her mind off the need for a drink she started to sing, though she had to ferret around inside her mouth, wetting the sides, before she could get the words out.

> 'Midst trials and tribulations,
> 'Midst tumult of the war,
> She waits the consummation
> Of peace forever more.
> Till with the vision glorious
> Her longing eyes are blest . . .

She was under the viaduct now. Her voice boomed out, lonely and hollow-sounding, becoming lighter and more tremulous again on the other side.

Now that she was closer to the river she could smell the dawn. She stopped singing and breathed deeply, though the effort hurt her lungs. Down here by the river you could smell the dawn hours and hours before there was any light in the sky. Her mood lightened again. She sang cheerfully:

> Till with the vision glorious
> Her longing eyes are blest,
> And the great Church victorious . . .

'Shall be the Church at rest.'

He surprised himself by saying the words aloud. Earlier on tonight he'd heard a woman singing, and he was almost certain it was the same hymn. So perhaps it was meant? He let the thought form and rise to the surface of his mind, gently, like a tiny bead of air. He'd been waiting a long time, waiting for the moment when it *felt right*. However much you planned and calculated and prepared it was important at this stage not to be too active, to wait, to let the decision take itself.

He started the car and began tracking her down the street. She must be making for the river. He could see her quite clearly. He could even see the knotted veins on the calves of her legs, sticking up like wormcasts on a beach. He remembered how such protuberances looked close to: the raised veins, bluey-purple, the dead-white of the surrounding skin.

The car headlights threw her shadow far out across the road. You could see her legs apparently marching up a wall and her head and shoulders flattened against the side of the building beyond. *This one?*

There was a moment of complete peace.

— *Yes. This one.*

Kath was irritated by the car that neither drew up nor went past. Why the hell couldn't he make up his mind? Look, mister, she said to herself, you either want it or you don't. If you don't, piss off and leave us alone.

He was pulling into the kerb. It was probably worth it, if only for the lift. She walked towards the car.

'Looking for business?' she asked.

'How much?'

Faint memories of the past floated through Kath's mind, when the answer would have depended on his clothes, his car, his urgency. Then it was back to the present with a bump. She knew how much she fetched. 'Fiver?'

'Right. Hop in.'

He leant across to open the door.

'Got any idea where you want to go?' she asked.

'I don't mind,' he said. 'As long as it's quiet.'

He liked to let them choose.

'Right then. Just go on up this road and take . . . Wait a minute.' She wasn't used to giving this particular set of directions. 'Yes, that's right. Third left, then second right.'

He followed her directions, keeping his eyes fixed on the road. He wasn't what you might call cheerful company — she liked the ones what chatted on a bit, if it was only about their bloody wives. It generally was about their wives.

'Married, are you?'

'No.'

'Oh. I just wondered.'

The car was freezing, just when she'd been hoping to get warm. She thought about asking him to turn the heater on, but then decided that she wouldn't, after all. She felt . . . well. Tired. Shivery. Depressed. She started thinking about her kids. The two boys — she had to look up to them now! And the baby, her little Julie, and what that bloody woman was doing to her. No wonder the bairn was upset, she'd been knocked from pillar to post. They had no more idea of bringing bairns up than the man in the moon. Every one you met was a Miss. She could still see Julie with her hair fluffed up after the midwife had bathed her, such long dark hair. She'd never seen hair that length on a baby before; they were generally like little boiled eggs. The two boys were anyway. There wasn't a day went by she didn't ache for Julie. She hadn't minded so much when they took the boys off her, because to be honest they were getting to be too much for her, they were a real handful. But they could've left the baby with her. Instead of that they'd pulled it out of her arms.

'Round here?'

She jumped — she'd forgotten all about him! 'Yes. Then second left.'

They were driving down a street of boarded-up houses. Once or twice he swerved to avoid a hole in the road.

'Just park anywhere,' she said. 'That's if you want to stop in the car.'

He thought about it. 'Is there anywhere else we can go?'

'There's a house we can get into. I don't live there.' (Never crack on where you live.) 'But I do know we can get in.'

'Will there be anybody else there?'

'No.' She leered at him. 'Just you and me. You can park the car up that alley if you're worried about being seen.'

She *was* being helpful.

'There. Do y' see?' She was pointing to an alley that led off the crossroads ahead. 'Don't drive too far in, though, because there's a wall down further up and you'll only have to back out.'

He switched the engine off. She got out of the car straight away, shivering as the wind lifted her thin skirt. She was bare-legged too: that was why the veins had shown up so clearly. He slipped a sweet into his mouth and sucked it. His breath smelled bad because all his life he'd been afraid of dentists, and he always carried with him little purple, violet-scented sweets to slip into his mouth if he was going to be close to anyone. Then he got out of the car. All the preparations had been finished hours before. He took a deep breath and looked up at the sky. He sometimes liked to imagine that he was on another planet, a dead planet: miles and miles of ice cold rock, no, colder than ice, much colder, and the sun a feeble, twinkling speck in the sky.

'Been stood empty for ages, these houses,' she said.

It was an effort to talk to her. He forced his voice down the funnel in his head. 'I wonder why they don't pull them down?'

'Costs money, I suppose. All the same, it's mad, isn't it, clearing folks out? They're good houses, some of them.'

He didn't reply, but she rambled on anyway.

'I wouldn't say no to one of them.'

'You've got one.'

'Oh, yeah! No light, no water, and the roof falling in. I mean a proper one.'

'Are you sleeping rough, then?'

She wrapped the thin jacket, and her dignity, more tightly round her. 'For the time being.' Then, in a sudden rush of confidence, she added, 'I got threw out where I was before.'

They walked up the alley together. The attempt at dignity and reserve had vanished, she was pulling on his sleeve like a little girl, telling him about the unfairness of it, how she should never've got threw out like that. He didn't listen. The touch of her hand on his sleeve drove him mad. He edged away from her, but she followed, jostling against him at every step. He realized she was trying to be seductive, and the thought made him go cold. Thank God she was on his left. If she'd felt what he had in his right pocket she'd've got a shock.

Somewhere in the distance he could hear a train, slowing down as it approached the viaduct. A lonely sound. As a child in bed at night he'd lain awake and listened to the trains.

A man came out of one of the backyards and staggered towards them. The skin around his eyes sagged: the lower lids drooped so much that two red crescents showed, as raw as if they'd been put there with a knife. 'The buggers,' he kept on saying. 'The buggers.'

He peered at them, attempted to say something else, and then lurched off. Kath, glancing sideways, caught the flicker of contempt.

'He's alright,' she said. 'He's had a lot of trouble in his life.'

'I'm sure.'

He turned and watched the drunk out of sight. There was nothing to worry about there, he'd've forgotten all about them before he got to the end of the street. All the same, he didn't like it. How many of the other houses

304

contained unofficial tenants? He wiped his hands down the sides of his jacket.

They went further into the alley. Piles of rubbish lay around, the unwanted possessions of those who had moved out. He picked his way delicately between the heaps as if one slip might land him among the human debris forever.

They must be getting nearer now. She was giggling about something and that irritated him. He couldn't stand women laughing, even if they weren't laughing at him. She kept bumping into him, he thought deliberately, and she seemed to think this required some response, but he didn't know what to do or say.

She stopped outside one of the doors and leant against it. For a moment he thought she was going to hoist her skirts up then and there, but no — she was only getting her breath back. After a moment she pushed the door open and he followed her inside.

'Mind how you go,' she said. 'There's all sorts here. Mind you don't trip.'

The yard was full of rubbish. In spite of her warning he caught his trouser leg on an old wringer that stood, half eaten away with rust, outside the back-kitchen door.

'I've got a torch.' he whispered.

'Not yet. Wait till we get inside.'

He followed her into the house. Kitchen. Boiler. Sink. Then round a sharp bend and into what had been the living-room. The window was boarded up. Three or four thin lines of moonlight lay across the floor. There was a smell of candle grease, and something else. Dried urine?

'You can switch it on now.'

He flashed the torch round the room. A living carpet of blackclocks scuttled for cover. He waited until the last one vanished before examining the rest of the room.

Mattress. A packing case pulled up and used as a table. There was even a chair. She was lying when she said she didn't live here. Somebody had scraped all this together. And you could tell by the way she looked at them that the things were hers.

He shone the torch full in her face.

305

'Hey!' she said, and raised a hand to shield her eyes.

He cupped his hand round the glass, but continued to point the torch straight at her.

'Do you bring many men here?' he asked.

'A few.'

She stared at his hand. The bones showed through as shadows in the red, translucent flesh. Then a floorboard creaked and he swung the torch round.

'There's nobody there,' she said. 'You always get noises in an old house.'

But he didn't believe her. There could always be some old tramp or other hanging round. He went to the living-room door and peered out into the darkness of the passage and up the stairs. There was a smell of damp everywhere, of rotten floorboards. Wallpaper hung in great strips off the wall, like lolling tongues.

Kath watched him. He seemed to be very nervous, but that didn't worry her: she'd coped with a lot of nervous men.

She said, in a deliberately cosy voice, 'Well, now, my motto is business before pleasure. So if you could just . . .'

He handed the fiver over. At the last moment, when his fingers should've loosened their grip, he tightened them instead. She had to tug at the note to get it away from him, and she never liked doing that. But some men were like that. It wasn't so much they objected to paying you, it was wanting to make the moment of paying last.

She lay down on the mattress and spread her legs apart. The business with the money had left a bad taste. She wasn't stripping off for this'n — she'd see him in hell first.

He put the torch down on the packing case and lay beside her on the mattress. After a while he got his cock out and it nestled against her thigh, as moist and confiding as a puppy's nose, and about as much bloody use.

'Don't worry about it, love,' she said. 'It'll come.'

The choice of word made her want to giggle, but she stifled the urge. If he once got the idea she was laughing at him they'd be there all night. You'd need scaffolding to get the bugger up.

He whispered something, but she couldn't hear what it was and had to ask him to repeat it. He hissed, 'I said, I think it would be better if you turned over.'

'Anything to oblige.'

As she turned he heard the booze slosh from one side of her stomach to the other.

'There,' she said. 'Is that better?'

It was: he didn't have to look at her face. He began kneading her buttocks, squeezing them together so that the cleft deepened, pulling them apart so that he could see the fuzz of hair around the dark brown hole. He put a hand under her belly, pulling his fingers down across the soft, creased flesh and into the spongy dampness underneath. God, what a swamp.

At first he thought it was going to be alright. He could dampen down the nausea if he really tried, he would *make* himself come. Then some feathers escaping from the mattress tickled the end of his nose and made him sneeze. She giggled and, briefly, farted. She was too drunk to fuck.

He felt himself begin to slide ignominiously out of her and his eyes misted over with rage.

She tried to say something, but he pushed her face down into the mattress, hard, deriving some satisfaction from the squeal of pain. There was hair in his mouth or it could've been feathers from the mattress. Whatever it was he spat it out. He lifted himself off her and started to smear cunt-juice over her arsehole. She tried to wriggle away from him and he hit her with his clenched fist.

At first he could make no progress, forcing himself against the tight ring of flesh. He stopped, shaking with excitement, and tried again. This time a crack opened, a way into her darkness. He thrust deeper. She groaned, and tried to get away from him. He hit her again, not very hard, just enough to make her keep still.

He was ready for the other now. He pulled himself out of her and tried to plunge in again, but missed. The failure maddened him. He hit her again and again until he found his way back inside. She'd arched her back to make it easier for him and he thought in exultation: you *filthy cow*. She was moaning and crying all the time now, but he didn't care. His fist, pummelling the back of her head, kept time with the rhythm of his thrusts. Once his hand strayed off the mattress and clutched at a heap of rubble in an unconscious attempt to add weight to the blows.

Kath, terrified and in pain, risked one look round and saw the whites of his eyes turned up. There was a heavy smell of violets and decay and it seemed to be coming from his open mouth. Oh God. She'd landed herself a real nutter this time. Give *him what he wants*. She arched her back still further, opening herself up to the thrusts.

Only the pounding of his fist kept him going now. Her arsehole had gone slack, it was looser than her cunt. *Useless*. But still he groaned and sweated and drove into her, the shadow of his head and shoulders jerking to and fro across the wall.

He could feel himself dying. In his mind's eye he could see his buttocks, labouring in and out. Ridiculous. It was no good. He fell forward: sweat dripped off his forehead and ran into the creases of her neck.

After a while he opened his eyes and looked around him. There were feathers everywhere. Pounding the mattress seemed to have released them, along with the smell of piss. She must just lie there and piss herself. *Christ*. There was a moment when all he wanted to do was to get away from her as fast as he could. Then she started to struggle. Instinctively he tightened his grip, forcing her face back down.

His cock felt small and worm-like inside her stretched arse. He pulled it out and examined it carefully. At first it looked much the same as usual, purple and glistening in the torchlight. But then a drop of gingery fluid gathered on the knob and dripped down onto her bum. He smelled the thin, sour smell of shit. And looked. Her cleft was full of it. He lashed out at her then, but she wriggled away from him and tried to stand up. She got as far as her knees.

'There's no need for that,' she said. 'Look, you can have your money back.'

Those were the last words she spoke. He hit her again, full on the jaw, and she crumpled up on the floor and lay still. He dragged her back onto the mattress. Then reached into his pocket for the knife.

It was almost soundless. There were only slight grunts of effort and the shadow of an upraised arm coming and going on the wall.

At some point, unnoticed by him, Kath died.

After a few minutes he was able to stop and look down. It wasn't enough that she was dead, he needed more. He gathered handfuls of feathers together and started shoving them inside her cunt. It wasn't easy: as fast as he pushed them inside they turned red. He had to practically stuff her with them, like stuffing a chicken, before he could get the effect he wanted: a ridiculous little white frill between her legs.

Satisfied at last, he stood up. He looked around for her pants, found them, and used them to wipe the blood off the front of his shoes.

When he straightened up again her eyes were open. It shook him a bit because he was pretty certain they'd been closed. He bent over her, but there was no sign of life.

Deliberately then he turned away and started searching the floor for anything he might've left behind. This was an important stage: it couldn't be hurried over or skimped in any way. Though the shaking that followed a death had already begun.

He could feel her staring at him, though he kept his back turned. He kept thinking, *Why don't her eyes close?* But he didn't let it make him careless. He went on searching until he was sure he'd covered every inch of the floor.

Then, with a final look at the mattress and what it held, he went out into the yard, switched on the torch and removed the single thread of cloth that had stuck to the leg of the old wringer when he'd stumbled against it going in.

The shaking wasn't so bad now. He hesitated, wondering whether he should close the yard door or not. He didn't want her found too quickly, but on the other hand he did want her found. They still hadn't got the last one and it infuriated him when the newspapers got his total wrong.

In the end he decided to leave the yard door open.

Sooner or later some old drunk in search of a bed for the night would stumble in and find her.

The sleeping and the dead. Any resemblance between them is a contrivance of undertakers: they do not look alike. Kath's body seems to have shrunk inside its clothes. If you approached the mattress casually you would see nothing but a heap of old rags. You would tread on her before you realized a woman's body lay there.

The window is boarded up, the room dark, except for five thin lines of moonlight that lie across the mattress like bars. One of them has just reached her eyes. They look so alive you wonder she can bear the light shining directly into them. Any moment now, you feel, her eyes will close.

CHAPTER ELEVEN

Hello. sunshine!' said Audrey opening the front door. There was Kevin with a bright yellow tractor clutched in his hands. 'Where's your mam? She's never let you walk round on your own?'

She picked Kevin up and carried him out onto the pavement. Brenda and Sharon were just turning the corner.

'He ran on ahead,' said Brenda. 'He was that keen to get here.'

'Well he's my little flower-pot, isn't he?' said Audrey, kissing Kevin on the cheek.

'I've brought me shopping bag in case you want any doing.' Brenda followed Audrey through into the living-room. 'Oh, I see you got your covers back on.'

'Yeah, and what a job I had. You know it says in the catalogue they're shrink-resistant.' Audrey tapped the arm of a chair. 'Look.'

'It'll mebbe wear loose.'

'Aye, mebbe.' Kevin struggled to be put down. Instantly all Audrey's attention was on him. 'Howay, my son. I've got a bit of pastry you can play with. Make me a man, eh, like you did last time?'

Sharon hung back, aware of not being the favourite.

'Howay, love. You too.'

Sharon looked at her mother.

'Yeah, go on. There's no rush.'

'Have you time for a cup of tea, Brenda?'

'Aye, go on, I'll have one with you. I don't know, I was gunna break eggs with a stick this morning and look at me.'

'What did the doctor say about Sharon?'

'Oh, she's clear. I have to take her back again in a fortnight.'

'That's a relief. It's an awful thing for a child to have. Bad enough when you're a woman.'

'And how's your Steven?'

Audrey started to reply, but then had to go into the kitchen to admire Kevin's man. 'Oh, alright, I suppose,' she said when she came back. 'Growing up.'

Brenda waited. When Audrey just stood there saying nothing she asked, 'How old is he now?'

'Thirteen. Oh, but it's not just his age Brenda. When I was mucking his room out I found this letter from the school. You know, asking you to go down and talk to the teachers. And he never said nothing. He just shoved it under his bed.'

'Oh you don't want to let that worry you. They're all the same. Our Lindsey's just like that. The school burned down I'd be no wiser.'

'But you know what I mean, Brenda. It's not as if I've gone down there showing him up. I've always gone dressed nice.'

There was a howl of rage from the kitchen. The two women rushed in to find Kevin dancing up and down red-faced with temper because Sharon had eaten one of the currants he needed for his man's eyes.

'Howay, pet,' sait Audrey. 'Shush, I'll get you some more.'

Peace was restored.

When the pastry men were in the oven, Brenda said, 'Do you mind if I leave them with you while I have a walk round the shops?'

'No, you go ahead.'

'Is there anything I can get you?'

'Packet of them oven-fried chips. The small size. He's got he won't have chips from the pan.'

'Oh, I know, doesn't it make you sick? Our Lindsey's got

me at me wit's end. She's dieting. *Dieting*. She stands side-ways you can't see her.'

'Can I come with you, Mam?' asked Sharon.

Brenda, who'd been looking forward to half an hour's peace, hesitated, but only for a second. She brushed back a strand of her daughter's hair. 'Aye,' she said.

'Take your time, Brenda,' said Audrey. 'There's no rush.'

'I didn't steal his currant, Mam,' said Sharon as they walked down the street. 'He dropped it on the floor.'

'No, I know you didn't, love,' said Brenda automatically. But then she looked down and saw that the slight injustice had darkened the little girl's day. 'No, I know you didn't,' she said. 'I tell you what, when we've got the shopping done we'll go to the Wimpey and have an ice-cream. Right?'

Sharon nodded, ecstatically.

And all the time Brenda was thinking, Stay like this. Don't get like Steven. Don't change. *Don't find out*.

That night Brenda was back under the viaduct again. She'd been there some time before the first car stopped. She walked across. Youngish, bright, nervous eyes. A gingery, nibbled moustache. Bit of a joker perhaps. She got in.

'You know what, kidder?' he said. 'You're a stroke of luck for me. I've been driving up and down for the best part of an hour, and you're the first girl I've seen. Where is every-body? I've never seen it so quiet.'

'It's Monday.'

'Even for a Monday it's quiet. I went in a pub just now and the bar was empty.'

She could feel him looking at her, but she stared straight ahead. There was an excitement in his voice that she distrusted.

'River bank alright for you, pet?'

'Yes.' She managed to stop herself adding, 'And don't call me pet.'

'You know I don't really do this all that often. In fact you probably won't believe me but this is the first time in oh, I don't know. Must be a year.'

He was right. She didn't believe him.

'I'm only here now because I had a bit of a shindig with the wife. Last night, but she keeps it up, my God she does. I walked in tonight and you could've cut the atmosphere with a knife and I thought, Aw to hell. I wouldn't care but she's a lovely girl and we get on really well together, except for one thing. And it's not that I'm unreasonable, I don't think I'm unreasonable. I mean I know she gets tired with the kids and the house and then she works full-time and I'm not saying the money doesn't come in handy because it does. But you know what I mean, kidder, it's always, *Oh, do we have to?* I can honestly say if my wife wanted me to dress up as a frog and sit in a bath full of cold custard I'd do it. No sweat. You know what I mean? If that was what got her going I'd do it. There wouldn't be any of this, *Oh do we have to? Why do we have to do it like this?* I'd do it gladly. But her. Oh she used to. I mean not dress up as a frog exactly. But she used to . . . You know. Now. I've only got to mention it and she groans and even when she does it's *trudge, trudge*, over to the wardrobe and then it's *trudge, trudge* back again. Half the time I feel like saying Oh, look, love, don't bother. I mean to say, where's the pleasure in that? Well, I mean to say, where is it? And all I want her to do is put on a little bit of plastic. Needn't even be a mack. *Dustbin liner.* Anything. But no. It's always, *Why do we have to do it like this?*'

Why indeed? Brenda looked onto the back seat to locate the dustbin liner. It was there alright. Oh God.

After it was over he went very quiet.

As he was zipping himself up, Brenda saw the evening paper lying on the back seat and turned it over to see what the headlines were. Kath Robson's face stared up at her. She didn't need to read the headline or the story underneath. There was only one reason for Kath to be in the paper.

The print blurred. She pushed the paper away.

'I see he's got another.' There was no mistaking the satisfaction in his voice. 'He doesn't half pick 'em. Look at that. Right old sperm-bucket, that'n.'

Brenda didn't reply.

'I mean I don't want to be crude or anything like that, but

my God, you'd think she'd just climbed out of a tree.'

Brenda opened the car door. 'There's no need for you to give me a lift back,' she said. 'I'm fussy about the company I keep. And next time you're fancying a bit just shove it up your arsehole and make a jug handle of it, right?'

She walked along Northgate, head well down, not bothering to brush away the tears from her face. The cars swished past, sending up silver plumes of rain. As she paused on the kerb waiting to cross the street, one of them pulled up.

'Fuck off!' she yelled at the top of her voice. 'Just fuck off.'

She was aware of people staring at her, and then looking quickly away. *Drunken prostitute shouting in the street. Better pretend we haven't seen her.*

She wiped her tears away in streaks of black mascara on the back of her hand. Then crossed the street and walked the few yards further down the hill to the Palmerston.

A mile away in the police mortuary Kath Robson lies on a marble slab. She has been stared at, poked, prodded, measured, photographed, the contents of her stomach analysed, the secrets of every orifice laid bare. Now, gutted, filleted and parcelled up again, she is left alone.

Life has withdrawn still further from her. The face under the white cloth looks less than ever like sleep.

Her eyes are open. If you were to pull the cloth back from her face they might even shine, momentarily, catching the slight gleam of moonlight from the frosted glass above her head. She looks . . . not alive. Certainly not alive. *Present,* perhaps? Whatever it is, the effect is disturbing. Even those who work here do not readily pull back the cloth.

In life Kath Robson hated being stared at. Not in death. In death she looks ready to outstare anybody.

PART TWO

CHAPTER TWELVE

'Irene Waddell. She was the first one he killed. Look, I've got a snap of her somewhere.'

Beattie got up and tottered across to the sideboard. They were all gathered together in her flat above the Palmerston.

'That was took just after she come out of hospital with her appendix. She'd gone down a bit there. But you can see . . .' Beattie made ballooning movements around her own flat breasts. 'She was a big woman.'

The photograph went all round the little circle, except Brenda who waved it away.

'Wad*dell*, she used to call herself. There was all hell let loose if you forgot and called her Waddle, because she did, you know. Duck's disease, especially as she got older. Ee, and she was a scream.' Beattie took the photo back and looked at it. 'I've seen her go up to a car and her motto was: Show 'em what they're getting. Alright, in moderation, but she used to hoist her tits through the window at them. And you could see this bloke . . .' Beattie made wanking movements in her lap. 'But it never seemed to register with her. She'd just go on, doing her spiel. He'd come and gone by the time she'd finished. Rita Bush was stood just opposite one night and she come across. "Hey, Beattie," she says. "You're on a quick route to the workhouse here." "I know," I says, "But what can you do? She won't listen." Penny never dropped.

319

I remember her saying, "Beattie, there's money in this." '
Beattie laughed. 'Ee, poor lass, she never saw none of it.'
'There didn't seem to be much fuss made at the time.'
'I don't even remember it being in the paper.'
'No, there wasn't much. And it was a long time before
they linked her up with the others, because she wasn't bat-
tered, you see. She was strangled.'
'So how do they know it was him?' asked Jean.
'I don't know,' said Beattie. 'It must be something he does.'
The women were silent as their minds ranged over the
possibilities.
'I put a verse in the paper for her,' said Beattie. 'And the
bloke I was living with at the time, he says, "You daft cow,
what do you want to do that for? Wasting your money." I
says, "It's my money. I'll do what I like with it." '
'I'm gunna put one in for Kath,' said Brenda. 'I went
round the *Gazette* office today and they aren't half a price.'
'Well, let us know, Brenda,' said Audrey. 'We'll all chip in.'
'No. I don't begrudge it.'
'I don't suppose her bairns'll put one in,' said Beattie.
'They'll be too young.'
'No,' said Brenda, 'And her mam's gone. She used to de-
pend a lot on her mam.'
There was silence. Beattie sat on a straight-backed chair
with the light from the window hlling directly on her. One
eye was perfectly made up, in mauve and silver; the other
was as naked as a fried egg. What does she look like?
thought Brenda.
'I wonder who'll tell the bairns?' asked Audrey.
'Social worker,' said Beattie. 'Whoever it is, I don't envy
them.'
'It's not so much the boys, is it?' asked Brenda. 'It's Julie.
I mean what do you say to a seven year-old? And they've
got to say something, because Kath went to see her every
Thursday. She mightn't always've been sober, but she went.'
'It's Thursday today,' Elaine said.

Julie Robson plays in the street outside her foster-mother's
house. From a distance it looks like hopscotch. Only as you

get closer can you see there are no chalk marks on the pavement. She is simply . . . avoiding the cracks.

They have told her that her mother is dead, that she will not come to see her again, today, or any day. They watch her all the time to see how she reacts, how she is 'taking it'. Julie goes out into the street to play.

She didn't always look forward to her mother's visits. Sometimes she dreaded them, because her mother talked funny and cried a lot and clung on when it was time to go. Now she will never come again.

Julie hops across the pavement, carefully. *Step on a crack, break your grandmother's back. Step on a crack, break your* . . .

Step on a crack.

The Palmerston was so quiet these days it came as a shock, like walking into a roomful of people and finding them miming instead of talking. You could hear the click of Elaine's heels as she walked across to the bar.

'Keeping alright, are you? That's right, you take the weight off.' Beattie looked over the edge of the bar. 'Haven't they said anything about them shoes?'

'You mean at the clinic? Aw, they're always on.'

'You looked washed out.'

'I'm alright. Just a bit tired. Nothing this won't put right.' She took a swig from her glass before putting it with the others on the tray. 'Right, how much do I owe you?'

As she was giving the change, Beattie nodded to the group in the far corner. 'Bet I know what they're on about.'

'Well, there's no prizes for that.'

Elaine carried the tray across the room and slid it carefully onto the table. Sure enough: *Yap, yap, yap.* Brenda didn't even pause long enough to say 'Cheers'.

'You can say what you like, you've no more chance of bumping into him than you have of . . . of being run over by a bus. You're not gunna stop crossing the road, are you?'

'I'm not going to stop doing anything,' said Maureen. 'I'm just going to start doing it indoors.' She leaned forward and rapped on the table with one forefinger. 'He's never killed indoors.'

'Then that's his obvious next move, isn't it?' said Jean. 'He's got to vary the routine a bit.'

Elaine said, 'I've heard he goes round dressed as a woman.'

The others stared at her.

'Well, that's what they say. They say that's how he gets them. They don't run.'

'Oh, bollocks,' said Jean. 'If you believed everything you hear . . . one minute he's a taxi-driver, the next minute he's a cop. For all we know he's a bloody vicar.'

'I've known some funny cops.'

'I used to know a funny vicar.'

'It doesn't give you much heart, does it?' said Brenda. 'I mean, think of all them women going home in taxis 'cos they think it's safer, and then somebody comes along, "Oo, he's a taxi-driver." '

'Better pack it in,' said Jean.

Silence.

'A lot are,' said Audrey.

Brenda pulled a face. 'Aye, the pocket-money brigade.'

'What about you, Elaine?' asked Jean. 'What are you gunna do?'

Elaine flushed. 'I haven't really thought about it. I suppose I'll just go on as usual.'

Obviously she didn't want to be questioned. In fact she finished her drink so quickly that some of it dribbled down her chin. She wiped it off on the back of her hand, and smiled.

'Can I get you another?' asked Jean.

'No, I'd better be going, I think. Thanks all the same.'

They watched her leave. Made clumsy by so many critical eyes, she stumbled as she got to the door and almost fell.

'Have you seen the shoes she's got on?' asked Audrey. 'It's a wonder she doesn't break her leg.'

'Wouldn't be her luck,' said Jean. 'Do you know she's been out every night since Kath died?'

'I think that's awful,' said Maureen. 'In her condition.'

'Oh, come off it,' said Brenda, 'If there was a bloke out there with a big enough prick to poke that out of her he'd be doing her a favour.'

There was a shocked silence.

'Well, it's the truth, isn't it?' She stared round at them. 'Without that bairn she's still got a chance. With it, she's finished.'

'That's right,' said Jean. Nobody else answered.

Maureen said, to change the subject, 'Must get on Beattie's nerves, this.' She nodded towards a silent group at the next table.

'Won't bother her,' said Brenda. 'They mightn't be talking, but they're all drinking.'

Brenda certainly was. Audrey picked up her empty glass and said, 'My shout.'

'I'll just go and make room for it,' Brenda said.

Left alone, Maureen and Jean eyed each other warily.

'We haven't heard from you, Jean. What are you gunna do?'

'Oh, I'm like Elaine. I'll just go on as usual.'

But she smiled as she said it, so you had no idea what she meant.

'There's nothing stopping you working at home, is there? They've all got family.' Maureen nodded across to the bar.

'No, but I can't say I fancy it.' She paused. 'You need somewhere that's your own. Least I do.'

'So what *are* you gunna do?'

'I've told you.' She grinned. 'Can't even say I'm gunna be careful. I'm always careful.' She threw her head back, as if daring Maureen to comment on the scar.

Instead, Maureen reached down and picked up Jean's bag, which was lying on the floor between them. She seemed to be weighing it.

'I carry a lot of change round with me, Maureen. Can't seem to get rid of it.'

'You're a fool, Jean. He'd have that off you like taking candy off a bairn.'

'I doubt that.'

Brenda came back. She'd put a bit of make-up on, and run the comb through her hair. Not before time, Jean thought. She looked a wreck.

Maureen said, 'Did you see where it said in the paper that if a woman was found with pepper or anything like that on her she could face a charge? Possessing an offensive weapon.'

'No,' said Brenda. 'But they'd never do it. There'd be too much of an outcry.'

'If it was one of us they'd do it. There'd be no outcry then.'

'Well, it's a bugger if you can't defend yourself.'

'Yes,' said Jean, looking at Maureen. 'It is.'

There was no sound except for the click-click of Elaine's heels on the pavement. Everybody kept telling her she was daft for wearing shoes like that: if she slipped over on a heel she'd know about it. But the men liked them. And Dave liked them. It was Dave liking them that mattered.

She turned at the furthest limit of her beat and began to walk back. As she did so she glimpsed, some way ahead, a man's head and shoulders quickly withdrawn into the shadow of a door. There was no need to be afraid, she told herself, it was probably just an ordinary man trying to make his mind up. But her hand slid into her coat and cradled the bulge.

She was almost level with him when a voice called out behind her: 'Elaine!'

It was Jean. Elaine turned, and waited for her to come up.

'I'm afraid I just lost you a customer,' she said, pointing towards the man who was now walking rapidly away.

'Doubt it,' said Elaine. 'I think he was only window shopping.'

'Oh, I know. Doesn't it make you sick?'

They walked along together.

'You know, I've been thinking,' said Jean. 'It might be a good idea if you and me started working together.'

Elaine was surprised, and a bit flustered. She'd never seen much of Jean alone; they'd only ever met as part of the group in the Palmerston, and she was a little in awe of her.

There was her temper, and the scar on her neck, and her reputation among the other girls, and the fact that she never told you anything about herself. Why me? was Elaine's first reaction. But she knew better than to ask. If she was Jean's partner her stock would rise. She wasn't doing any too well on her own, as Dave had more than once pointed out.

'Alright,' she said, trying not to sound too keen. 'You work further down that way, don't you?'

'Yeah, but I fancy a change. I'd thought I'd have a go at the viaduct. See if there's owt doing there.'

There was a short silence. Then Elaine said, 'Kath worked there.'

'Yes, I know. But it isn't to say he picked her up there — she was all over the shop. And even if he did — that's the last place he'll come back.'

Elaine nodded, unconvinced. 'What happens if Carol comes back?' she said. 'Wouldn't you want to work with her?'

'Oh, I wouldn't worry about that.' Jean looked down the hill towards the viaduct and seemed to shiver. 'I don't think she'll be coming back.'

CHAPTER THIRTEEN

'Hello, Elaine!' Brenda stepped back to let the girl in. She did her best to seem welcoming, but in fact she was anything but pleased: the living-room was a tip.

'I was on me way back from the clinic. I just thought I'd pop in.'

'Here, sit yourself down. If you can find anywhere.' Brenda swept a heap of old magazines off a chair onto the floor. 'Would you like a cup of tea?'

'Oh, yes, I'd love one. I've been sat there hours. And I says to the girl next to me, "What time's your appointment?" She says, "Eleven o'clock." I says, "Well that's the same time as mine." '

'That's what they do. They give everybody the same time.'

'It's not so bad for me. But there was one woman there with three little kids. And you know they were all screaming.'

'Just a second, Elaine. I'll get the kettle on.' Brenda wandered into the kitchen, looked at the dishes in the sink and groped at the back of a cupboard for the remaining clean cups. When the kettle was on she went back in. 'Is Sister Walker still there?' she asked.

'Oh, I don't know,' said Elaine. 'I don't know their names.'

'It was Sister Walker delivered Kevin, and do you know the doctor said all along it was a small baby, and as soon as she felt me stomach she says, "Gerraway, it's got a back on it like Mohammed Ali." I says, "My God, I hope it's a boy." '

'That's what I want.'

'Me mother-in-law always used to say, "*Boys everytime!*" Like, she was only saying it to get at me because I had the two girls. Still, she was right. She used to say, "A boy'll shit on somebody else's doorstep. A girl brings her trouble home." And it's true. I worry meself sick about our Lindsey. Do you know the other day I was stood outside the Comp and I watched a bloke pick a girl up. Now, if he'd been had up he'd've said, "Oh, I thought she was older." Nothing of the sort. He'd sat and watched her come out of school.'

'There's a lot of that going on now. Girls of fourteen, fifteen.'

'Lindsey says there's a few girls in the fourth year doing it, but you know you can never tell with Lindsey. Sometimes I think she's just having me on. You know, to see what I'll say.'

'Does she know?'

'Oh, I think so. There's nothing been said, but she's not daft. Audrey kids herself her lad doesn't know, but he does. Stands out a mile.'

'I'm going to get out of it while mine's still little. I wouldn't like to think it was going to be thrown up at him.'

'It's not that easy getting out. I used to think it was, I used to think you could just move away and that'd be it, Finish. But it's not like that. I mean you'll hear women going on, "Oh, I don't know where to turn." "I don't know where the money's coming from." And you're listening to them, but it's like they're on another planet. Because you *know* where to turn, you *know* where it's coming from. And if you're ever really hard up, you'll go back to it, because you know it's there. Oh, mebbe you'll just do one or two, but you'll do them. And you'll think nothing of it.'

'It's not going to be like that with me.' Elaine stopped picking at her nail varnish and looked directly at Brenda. 'I'm packing it in before the baby's a year old, and I'm not going back.'

Brenda was a little taken aback, Elaine sounded so determined, so unlike her usual self. 'Well, I hope you make it,' she said, finally.

While she was making the tea, Elaine called into the kitchen, 'Anyway, we'll have the money for a house by then. Dave's putting it in a building society every week.'

It was on the tip of Brenda's tongue to ask if she'd ever seen the book, but of course she didn't. Instead she said, 'How is Dave?'

'Oh, he's fine.'

'He'll be looking forward to the baby, is he?'

'Yes.' Elaine paused. 'Well, you know what men are, he doesn't say much.'

'No, but he'll be pleased.'

'Oh, yes.' She looked round for an ash-tray. As she stubbed out her cigarette she said, 'You know, sometimes I think people run away with the idea that Dave's forcing us to go out, but he's not. It isn't to say 'cos he hits me it's always about that. He's very jealous. You know, he's only got to see me with another man and that's it. So he must think a bit about me, mustn't he?'

Brenda didn't know what to say.

'It's just I've got Jean going on at me, "Oh, he's no right to hit you, he's no right to make you go out," but the way I look at it, if you're living with a bloke he's gunna hit you about something. If it's not that it'll be something else.'

'How is Jean?' Anything to change the subject.

'Oh, she's fine. Got "Made in Sheffield" stamped on her bum.'

'That's what I could do with.'

'Aye, and me.'

Silence. The murders which were talked about endlessly in every pub were never mentioned at home.

'Have they asked you if you're going to feed it yourself?'

'Yes. I said I hadn't thought about it, but I can't see meself. I just don't fancy it.'

'No, well, all mine were bottle fed. I can't see where it did them any harm. But they do go on at you about it. There was a girl next to me and the doctor told her she should be ashamed of herself, all the milk she had, and he wouldn't give her anything to dry it up. She used to wake up, and the bed was flooded, she'd leaked all over the place. But she couldn't breastfeed. She shared a bedroom with her two brothers. Well, can you imagine? Teenage lads.'

'I just said I'd think about it. I don't think it's worth arguing. You can always put it on the bottle after you get home. I just wish it was over, that's all.'

'Oh, you don't want to let it worry you. I tell you, out of my three the first 'un was the easiest, and it's supposed to be the hardest. You can't go by what people say.'

'Was it really the easiest?'

'Oh, yes. No bother. That's why I had the next 'un so quick. But you notice I didn't rush into it again after Sharon. My God.'

Elaine handed Brenda her empty cup and started struggling to get up. She seemed to've got a lot bigger in the last two weeks.

'You look after yourself,' Brenda said. 'You've got two to think about now.'

'Thanks for the tea, Brenda. I was ready for that.'

'Will we be seeing you tonight?'

'Oh, yes, I expect so. It's only if Jean decides she wants to go straight out.' Elaine pulled a face. 'I don't like that. I like a drink.'

'I'm surprised at Jean. I've seen her drink every bugger under the table and then go out.'

'I've heard a lot of stories about Jean.'

'And most of them are true.' Brenda hesitated. 'What's it like working with her?'

'Alright.' Elaine pulled her upper lip down to cover the slightly prominent front teeth. 'It's fine.'

CHAPTER FOURTEEN

Audrey peered in the mirror, pulling one eyelid slightly to the side as she smeared eye-shadow on. 'Have you seen these?' she asked. 'Duo-mates?'

Brenda leaned forward to look. 'Yeah, our Lindsey's got one. Only hers is brown and gold. I can't wear brown these days, I look awful.'

'You look a lot better than you did.'

'Oh, I'm gradually getting meself pulled together. I don't know why it knocked me end in the way it did. It isn't as if we were all that close. Once over, yes. But not in the last couple of years. I mean, I hardly saw her.' Brenda lapsed into silence; then straightened herself up. 'Anyway.'

Audrey turned back to the mirror.

'You'll never guess who I saw the other day,' Brenda said. 'Norman.'

'And what did he have to say?'

'Not a lot. I was just coming out of the bakery and there he was and I thought, Have I to walk past? and then I thought, No, why the hell should I? So I stopped. He says, "Oh, hello." He didn't know where to look, because he hasn't been round, you know. He even sent their George's wife round for his clothes. So I thought, Right, you bugger. I says, "Do you fancy a drink?" you know, just to see what he would say, and he says, "Oh, OK then." But he was alright, once we'd got on talking, and of course at the finish it

330

all come out. It was nothing to do with his mam, it was this girl in the pub, she'd called him a pimp, and of course that was it. I says, "Well, you should've come out with it. Not just go off like that." But it was the one thing he could never stomach.'

'Well, you can understand that.'

'Oh, yes. I wouldn't care, Audrey, but in all the time we were living together he never once said, "Look, love, we're a bit short. Are you going out tonight?" He never once tried . . . And yet just 'cos he was living with me he was a pimp. Bloody stupid. I was doing it long before I met him.'

'You should've packed it in when he moved in with you, Brenda. It's the only way.'

'Aye, and live on fresh air. It's not as if he was working, and even if he was, what man's going to set on and keep another man's bairns? It's stupid.'

'So how did you leave it?'

'We're going to go for a drink this Friday.'

'Oh.'

'There's no "Oh", about it. We're just going for a drink.' She paused. 'I don't think I'd want him living with me again, anyway. I mean, I missed him, I missed having a man about the place, but after a bit . . .'

'Oh, I know. I don't think I could live with anybody, not now. I've got used to doing as I like. There's no, "Oh, I've got to do such-and-such . . ." You can please yourself. Kids don't bother.'

There was a blast of music from upstairs. Brenda nodded towards the ceiling, 'How is he?'

'Bloody awful, and that's swearing. He's been up there hours.'

'By hisself?'

'Far as I know. He never brings anybody home. And I wouldn't care, Brenda, but . . . Do you know, when I first started I never thought of it in terms of money. I used always to have a definite *thing* in me mind, like a bike, or a colour telly, and I used to tell meself I was working for that, and nine times out of ten it was something for him, it was never *me*. That . . .' She jabbed her finger towards the stairs.

'*Music centre*. It wasn't fucking Father Christmas that got him that, it was me. And damned hard graft.' She turned back to the mirror and finished putting her make-up on in silence.

'I think you could do with a drink,' Brenda said.

'You're right there.' Audrey picked her coat up from the chair and called upstairs. 'Steve?'

No reply.

'Steve? I'm just off out for a bit. You'll be alright?'

The volume was turned up.

Audrey pulled a face as she turned towards Brenda. ' "Yes, Mam." "That's OK, Mam." "I'll be alright, Mam." God, doesn't it make you sick?'

'He'll be alright.'

Audrey opened the front door. They paused on the top step, as each of them, separately, prepared herself for the night.

'Hey, lasses, listen to this.' Ginny, a tall West Indian girl, about seventeen years old, came rushing across to the group in the corner. 'You know what you were saying, Jean, about the police turning a blind eye and all that? Well, listen to this.'

Her sister came up behind her.

'We were in Lawson Street and there was this car just in front of us with a couple of cops, you know a man and a woman, in the front seat, pretending they were having it off.'

'Perhaps were,' said Audrey.

'Not that'n,' said Teresa. 'Her pants are welded on.'

'Anyway they could see what we were doing, but they never said nowt, and then this old woman comes out of the house opposite and taps on the window. *Their* window. "Hey," she says, "There's somebody trying to get in me back." Well, you should've seen his face. "You'll have to tell the police, honey," he says. "What do y' mean?" she says. "You are the police." She was peeing herself laughing.' Ginny jerked her thumb at Teresa.

'Still, it's nice to think you're being watched over, isn't it?'

'Oh, definitely.'

'You bloody daft sods,' said Jean. 'Honestly, none of you

need worry about getting your brains bashed out. He'd need to find 'em first.'

'What do you mean?' asked Ginny.

'They're not there to stop it happening. They're just taking the car numbers so when it does happen they'll know who was in the area.' She looked round the table. 'Don't you see? That's why they're leaving us alone. They're waiting for one of us to be killed.'

'Somebody's watching me.' Elaine had said this every night for weeks. She hated the viaduct. The darkness. The dripping walls. She hated the smell of the chicken factory. It was Jean who insisted they work here. Most of all she hated the shadows under the arches that shifted and took shape and dissolved again.

'Somebody's watching me.'

'There's nobody there.' There was an edge to Jean's voice, but she made herself be patient. 'Look, I'll go and check.'

And she did, running lightly across the road and in under the arches of the viaduct, with a courage that took Elaine's breath away.

She came back, breathless. 'I looked everywhere,' she said. 'There's nobody.'

'There was somebody.'

But you couldn't argue with Jean.

They didn't stand together for long. 'It puts them off,' Jean said. 'You go back over the road. They're more likely to stop if they think you're on your own.'

Jean went back across the road. Left alone, Elaine closed her eyes, because she didn't want to see the shadow that was already taking shape again among the other shadows. But even with her eyes closed there was no escape. The sense of a presence close by her grew and grew until she almost expected to feel its breath on her neck.

She opened her eyes. Jean was bending down, talking to the driver of a car. Too late, Elaine came out onto the road to take the number. The car had already driven away.

Jean would be furious when she came back. She was always so careful to take the number of any car Elaine got into. Worried, Elaine withdrew into the chicken factory gateway, and settled down to wait.

Jean got out of the car.

'Are you sure you wouldn't rather stay inside in the warm?' she asked.

'No,' he said. 'I want to lie down.'

'Well, you sure as hell can't do that here.'

They were on a strip of waste land backing onto a street of boarded-up houses.

'Look, there's quite a few of them open,' said Jean. 'Let's try over there.'

She started to pick her way across the bumpy ground. As she came round the corner of the terrace the full force of the wind hit her so that she staggered and almost fell. Instantly his hand was on her elbow steadying her and for a moment they might have been any man and any woman. Then Jean lowered her head and walked on, moving, though unobtrusively, out of his grasp.

'Here?' he asked.

'Yes. Here.'

There were some old sacks piled up in one corner of the room. At least he didn't expect her to strip. She lay down on the sacks and waited.

After a while he raised his head and looked at her. The room was in darkness, but a thin strip of moonlight had found its way through the boards at the window and lay across her face. The whites of her eyes gleamed.

'You might put something into it,' he said. 'It isn't natural just lying there.'

'Look, mate, this is my living. You're lucky if I like you.'

Baffled and angry, he lowered his head, while Jean stared into the darkness beyond his shoulder and waited for it to be over.

Outside the yard door was blown off its catch and started to bang in the wind.

'This is bloody awful, this is,' Brenda said, struggling to

keep her skirt down as they climbed the hill.

'Well, we don't have to stop out,' said Audrey. 'Why don't we pop in there and see what's doing?' She nodded towards the Marimba on the other side of the street. 'There's generally a bit of life there.'

Once inside Brenda felt a pleasant tingling as the sudden warmth opened the pores in her skin. Oh, yes, she thought, looking round, this is miles better.

Audrey came back with their drinks. 'Well, anything doing?' she asked.

Brenda pointed at a line of women sitting over by the wall. 'All bloody worms and no fish. Still at least we're out of the wind.'

All over the city people are hurrying to get out of the wind. A few take shelter in doorways, but most make a dash for home. Soon the streets are empty. The sign above the Palmerston's door rattles loose from its chains.

Those lucky enough to be indoors draw their curtains more closely and switch their televisions on. Every window is shut fast, every door locked, and yet the wind gets in, finding here a gap between floorboards and door, there a space between window and frame. It fingers the material of the curtains, tests the pile on the carpet, as if it were asking: How strong is this? Will it last? How long before it gives?

In the silence between one commercial and the next it howls and moans around the house and the people inside look up and say, 'Listen to the wind.' And turn the television up so that there will be no need.

On the waste land behind the houses there is nothing to resist it. The bonfire that the children have spent weeks building is destroyed. A hundred yards further on, the rubbish tip is scattered. Right at the top of the heap a polythene sheet that for many months has hidden the ruin of a sofa breaks loose and flaps in the wind.

A black rain begins to fall, drumming insistently on polythene and plastic and cardboard, on roof tops and on window panes, so that people turn in their sleep and mutter, sensing the approach of dawn.

Silence. On a broken fence a line of raindrops glitters in the sun.

Towards noon the children come to inspect the ruin of their bonfire and to search among the scattered rubbish for material to build another. One boy, bigger than the rest, climbs up to look at the sofa which alone among the sodden debris seems to offer hope. The younger children watch as he tries to lift it. It won't move. He gropes underneath to see what's holding it and his fingers encounter something that has the consistency of soft cheese. He kneels to look underneath, peering into the darkness behind the rusty springs.

The younger children watch as, stiff-legged, he walks towards them off the tip and, kneeling, vomits into the grass.

'Apparently it was bairns found her,' said Brenda. Her voice was completely flat. 'They were out gathering for their bonfire.'

Nobody replied. They were all sitting in the back room, in a big circle, with the evening paper on a table in the middle.

'I suppose they're sure it's Carol?' asked Beattie. 'I mean she must've been down there a good while.'

'Yes, they're sure,' said Elaine. 'She had her handbag with her with everything in. That's how they got her address.'

'Well,' said Audrey. 'Jean always said she hadn't gone to London.'

'Yes, that's right,' said Elaine. 'She did.'

'Have you seen Jean?' Brenda asked her.

Elaine shook her head.

Brenda looked round the circle. 'Has anybody seen Jean?'

PART THREE

CHAPTER FIFTEEN

You do a lot of walking in this job. More than you might think. In fact, when I get to the end of a busy Saturday night, it's me feet that ache. There, that surprised you, didn't it?

I work on me own now. Nobody else fancies this place, because they've all got it worked out that he must've picked Kath up from here. I've got the whole viaduct to meself some nights. Except for Kath, who's still here in a way, stuck up there on her billboard. Hiya, Kath.

I watched them putting that up and it was very strange if you knew Kath, because it was too big to go up all at once. I watched them pasting across first one eye and then the other and I thought, My God. Because her eyes, they follow you. They do, they follow you everywhere. I can be walking along with me back to her and I still feel them. And they've got such a funny look. You'd just think they'd taken that photo after she was dead — that's the effect it has on you. Which is mad, because you can see she's alive, and anyway dead people's eyes close.

I was in the Palmerston when she come in that last night. There was this funny silence just as she come through the door and of course everybody said afterwards that they'd known. Stupid cows. I bought her a couple of drinks after Brenda left because I couldn't stand the way she was sat there like something from another planet, and mebbe I

341

shouldn't've done because she was blind drunk when she left. But he'd've got her anyway. He got Carol, and she was sober.

Underneath the photo there's an appeal for information and I think if I could laugh about anything I'd have a good belly laugh over that. I mean, who reads it? The women from the chicken factory I suppose, but it's not likely they'll know anything. Apart from them, there's the dossers underneath that little arch at the end, there's the men hanging around the toilet over there, there's the punters, and there's girls like me. A few. As I say, these days not many. Which of that lot is gunna go running to the police? You see what I mean? It's ridiculous. Not worth the paper it's printed on. Even I wouldn't go to the police unless it was forced work, and I want to catch the bastard more than most.

All the same I'm quite glad the poster's there. It's company on nights like this when there's nobody else around. I've even been known to talk to it, and when I catch meself doing that I say, *Hey up, Jean, you get put away for doing that,* and then I think, *Aw, what the hell?* Time enough to worry when it starts talking back.

It's surprising how few people actually look at it. I watch them and I see them duck their heads and hurry past. There's not many'll look her in the face.

I used to work with Elaine. She got at the finish she was like a house-end. Her ankles were all swelled up and could you get her to stop wearing them shoes? Could you hell. She looked like she was tottering round on a couple of steak-and-kidney puddings. Anyway at the finish the doctor says, 'There's something wrong with your urine,' and he told her she had to go to the hospital for a test. Well. That was what she thought he said. She was terrified poor kid and she said, would I go with her? Well, we turned up on the ward and the Sister looked at her as if she'd gone barmy. 'Oh, no,' she says. 'Not a *test*. A *rest*.' And they made her stop in, wouldn't even let her go back home and get a nightie, which was crafty of 'em, because if they had've done they'd

never've seen her again. I had to go round the flat and collect all her things and break the sad news to Dave that his
meal-ticket was out of action. It gave me a lot of pleasure,
did that. Normally I'd be the last person to say anything
because people've got to sort themselves out, but Dave did
one thing that absolutely finished me. He made her go out
and work on the night of Kath's funeral, and none of us
worked that night. Of course, when I got back to the hospital, she wanted to know everything he'd said, and I didn't
know what to say for the best. 'Oh,' I says, 'you could tell he
was upset.' And he was. In his way.

I'd been working with her a good few month then. I remember the night we started — it wasn't all that long after
Kath died. We were sat in the Palmerston and for once —
and this is a miracle — we weren't talking about *him*. Because Elaine had been to the clinic and they'd let her listen
to the baby's heart, and of course she was thrilled to bits.
She actually had a bit of colour for once. And then the talk
turned to what she wanted, you know, was it a boy or a girl?
Beattie went upstairs and come back with a needle and
thread. She dangled it over Elaine's belly, and by this time
she had quite a little pot, and apparently if it's a boy the
needle swings backwards and forwards and if it's a girl it
goes round and round. Well, it went backwards and forwards and Elaine was over the moon because Dave wants a
boy. (God knows why, a girl'd be a better investment.) I was
just sat there and for once I was quite happy, joining in, you
know, and then all of a sudden it swept over me, and I saw
her the way *he* would see her: drained face, swollen belly,
and I knew, not thought, mind you, *knew*, I knew he would
want to know what sex the baby was, and he'd have his own
methods of finding out. I sat and watched the needle swing
to and fro, knife, needle, needle, knife, and I couldn't
move.

Because for a long time, oh, about six months I suppose,
before Kath died, I'd been trying to get inside his mind. It's
the only way of finding him: you've got to see what he sees,
you've got to know what he would do, and all that time I'd
been trying, pushing against the doors of his mind. And

then just as I relaxed, just when for once I wasn't thinking about him, the doors swung open, *but from the other side.*

Later that night I followed Elaine down Northgate and offered to work with her. She jumped at the idea, as I knew she would. There aren't many girls round here who wouldn't. But even though she was so keen she still said, 'But what about Carol?' A lot of people wouldn't't've bothered to say that.

Elaine's like an aching tooth with me, I can twist and turn, and poke and prod, but the pain never goes away. I shouldn't have a conscience I suppose. After all, you can live without one — *he* certainly does. And I remind meself that she wasn't working to support *me*, it wasn't *me* blacked her eye when she didn't bring enough in. It wasn't *me* shoved a dirty great heap of rubbers in her mitt and told her to get through them. Oh, no.

And then you've got to look at the alternatives, haven't you? The alternatives for Elaine were either to work alone, in which case she'd've stuck out like a baby thrush, or to work with one of the others. Let me tell you something. I was in the Palmerston one night and the talk turned to lucky charms, and they all had one. Audrey had a pencil with a little red plastic man on the top that her lad'd given her when he was a bairn, Brenda had a golliwog, Elaine had a little imp she'd seen advertised in the *News of the World* and sent away for, Ginny had a crucifix. Which I suppose is OK if you can believe in that kind of thing. Kath did, so it can't be foolproof. And they'd got all these things out and there they were in a circle on the table, I'm not kidding you, it was exactly like bloody Bingo. It only needed Beattie to come in and say, Eyes down. I don't think Elaine was in any more danger with me than she would've been with one of them.

You're lying again, Jean.

We took car numbers. Right? I think the majority of women do take car numbers now, but there's very few actually sit down and work out why they're taking them. There's two reasons. One, you scare the bloke, because he's knows your mate's got his number so he's less likely to try his little tricks. Two, if he does, the number means you can trace the car. The first way he's got to see the number being taken, the second way it's better if he doesn't, because in fact you're not trying to stop him doing anything, you're just making bloody sure you can trace him afterwards. In other words you're using the girl as bait.

I always took the number of any car Elaine got into, but I didn't always let the driver see me doing it.

There.

I was glad when she went into hospital, because I knew she was frightened and I thought in there she'll be safe, away from him, and away from me. She knew what I was doing. There was no way Elaine could ever've put that into words, but she knew alright. I'd catch her looking at me sometimes and I'm bloody sure by the end she was more frightened of me than she was of him.

I expect you're saying My God, how awful, but I wouldn't be in too much of a hurry to say that. I'm not the only one round here who goes fishing with live bait. You can walk up Northgate any night of the week and the girls'll all be there. There hasn't one of them been lifted in months. Why? Because they're too bloody useful where they are, that's why. He can go up there and take his pick, and the police'll watch and wait and take down his number and watch him drive away, but whatever happens they don't interfere. Only the other week there was a girl got badly beaten up, the other girls went to help her, but the police didn't. Because they couldn't. They're not supposed to be there. Just think: a whole row of juicy maggots, waiting for one fish to bite.

At least when I go fishing I put my own life on the hook.

Don't forget Elaine was only in the car half the time. The rest of the time I was in the car and *she* was taking the number, except she wasn't, because Elaine is as blind as a bat. Half the time when she was scribbling away in her little notebook I knew she was hard put to it to see the car, never mind the number. Dave doesn't make passes at girls who wear glasses.

Even now I'll get a girl come up to me and say, 'Eee, I

don't know how you can work on your own.' I don't even
bother to answer them. I always was on me own.

There's not a lot doing as early as this. Normally I'd not be
out for another few hours because you find the majority of
men need a couple of pints inside them before they'll come
up to you and ask, even though they are paying. And of
course earlier on you get a lot of ordinary women just going
out for the evening and I hate that, because they look at you
as if you were a lump of shit, some of 'em, and I always
think, What right do they have to do that? If we weren't
stuck here, some of the men we get might be after them, or
their kids, because there's more men fancy *that* than you
might think.

It's dead boring when it's as quiet as this. I'd go up and
talk to Ginny and Teresa if I thought they'd be there, but
they're probably still in the Palmerston. And I certainly
can't face that. It's been like this ever since they found
Carol. I go in there and the girls don't know what to say to
me, and I don't know what to say to them. I suppose you
could say I'm bottling it all up, but then what else can I do?
I never talked about Carol while she was alive so it's not
likely I'll start now she's dead. And I don't think they would
want me to.

I feel very cut off from them now.

The only reason I'm stuck out here this early is I can't
stand the flat. I know that sounds as if I can't stand to be
anywhere. Nowhere's right. Yeah. It's exactly like that. I
can't rest, I can't eat, I can't sleep, I can't sit still and I'm no
sooner settled in one place than I want to be somewhere
else. One of the reasons I like this is the walking, because
I'm prowling up and down all the time everywhere, but at
least when I do it here it looks normal. I don't feel such a
freak. Because I do find it very difficult to behave normal. I
find meself doing absolutely insane things like chasing a
girl through the streets because she had hair the same colour as Carol, and of course when the girl turned round she
was nothing like her. Try talking yourself out of that! And
the flat's full of noises. I don't mean just the usual crackling

and rustling you get in any empty place. I mean footsteps. I hear her moving about in the next room. Always the next room. Never the room I'm in. And I smell her too, I smell her scent, not the stale smell you get on clothes, a sharp, fresh scent as if she'd just walked into the room behind me. I even went to the doctor because I thought, Hell, I'm going mad, and he just said, 'Don't worry. It's normal.' He gave us some pills, but I didn't take them. If it's normal, I'll bear it. I don't believe in pills.

Do you know, I once had a cat — she was called 'Socks', because she was all black except she had four white feet — and she had kittens. Well, me stepfather drowned them, only he kept putting it off and putting it off and by the time he finally got round to it they were quite big. That cat yowled for a week. She kept going from room to room, searching, she even looked in the cupboards and the drawers and all the time the milk was dribbling onto the floor. I've got I'm just like that cat. I know Carol's gone, I saw her, I actually went and identified her, and yet I'm still looking for her. And I can't stop. I've actually scrabbled about in her wardrobe like some kind of maniac, because I'm that bloody desperate for the smell of her. The smell fades, you see. And not just the smell, either. I had moments to begin with when I really panicked because I couldn't remember what she looked like. All I could see was what I saw when the police pulled back the cloth. And that was a terrible time, when I couldn't remember her, because then I seemed to've lost her twice.

Sometimes I think the only thing that keeps me alive now is hating him.

It's better out here, under the viaduct, than it is in the flat. I suppose part of the time I let myself imagine she's still alive and that she'll be waiting for me when I get back. Not very often. I like the place, I've got to know it, I can see why Brenda was so fond of it, though I used to think she was mad working right down here. Her and Audrey are at the top of Northgate now. Along with everybody else.

I like to have a little rest here with me back to the railings and the chicken factory behind me, which isn't exactly the most sweet-smelling spot in God's universe but never mind. Elaine used to stand in here, but well back, so she didn't have to look at Kath. She hated that poster.

I never let anybody pick me up on my way here. Even if I'm just round the corner, I'll still say no. I need to be *here*, where everything's familiar, before I start tangling with that lot.

Speaking of whom. That car went past slowly — I rather think he might be back. I'll just walk along to the end and be there to meet him if he is. Yes. Here he comes. But still a bit uncertain, he slows down and has a bloody good look before he stops. *Oh, be my guest. Welcome to your friendly neighbourhood supermarket.* I go across the road and make his mind up for him. Question. Answer. In. Off. And he's driving me down to the streets by the river which is fine by me as long as he'll bring me back. Nice warm car. And the front seats go right back. One of his kids's drawn a little smiley face on the roof in blue biro. Bet he doesn't know that. But he's no bother. The money's safe in me bag, I put in a couple of groans at the crucial moment and that's it.

Back on the pavement with a tenner in me pocket and already I'm looking for the next car. I can't stop you see, I can't even go home and get washed, I'm that afraid of missing him. He might drive past and I wouldn't be here. Of course a lot of people might think this is the last place he'll show up, because he must have picked Kath up somewhere near here. I told Elaine that. But it isn't true. He'll come back, and he'll come back here, because it's impossible to police. Too many corners, factory yards, alleys leading off each other, streets with the windows boarded up, bricked up houses, and then under the arches, the timber yard, the place where the old iron foundry used to be, and the waste land beyond that. I don't suppose there's much more than a square mile if you looked at it on a map, but you'd get lost five times if you tried to walk across it. No, it's a good place from his point of view, especially if you compare it with Northgate and one or two other areas I could mention, where it's packed deep with girls — I'm not exaggerating, it's bloody ridiculous — and there's a vice-squad car in every alley. We know the cars. I bet he does too. And when you think that he's not doing this as a hobby, I mean he must *need* to kill, then the viaduct area becomes very attractive. I mean, I admit there's nights I think it's useless, I'm just looking for a needle in a haystack, but I have thought it through, and I think I stand a better chance here than anywhere. And there's other nights when I *know* he's coming back. I couldn't explain how I know, but I do.

Meanwhile life goes on. I turn under Kath's poster and start walking back down the hill and I can feel her eyes boring into my spine every step of the way. You know when people say, 'Life goes on,' they always say it as if it's this great marvellous discovery they've just made and you're supposed to be pleased. I'm not bloody pleased. What is more, I don't accept that this is life. 'Life' is what I had with Carol, and it didn't go on — it stopped.

CHAPTER SIXTEEN

'I'd seen Carol around the place for a good few weeks before we actually met. Quite often she was drinking in the
same pub. Once I saw her stood just across the street with a
girl I knew, once I saw her coming out of the bakery with
one of them long loaves under her arm. Of course I noticed
her, but I doubt if we'd ever've got together just like that,
because I couldn't stand the crowd she was hanging around
with and I don't think most of them had much room for
me. I don't know what you'd call them really. I know what
I'd call them. They were all drop-outs, of a sort, dead tough
kids, till they hit a rough patch and then they'd go back to
Dad for a cheque. And of course smoking themselves silly. I
don't know how Carol got in with them — she said it was a
girl she knew, but something tells me it was a man. You
could never rely on anything Carol said. At the same time
she'd already started, in a way. Oh, nothing regular, but the
penny had dropped, she knew where to get a few quid if
she was short. Typical of Carol to be hanging round with
that lot, she was always hankering after something she
couldn't have, and of course, although they all hung round
together and she might've thought she was in with them, I
doubt if she was.

Anyway, there was no way I was going to get to know her
while she was with that lot, and it mightn't've done me
much good even if I had. I probably wouldn't've been able

to speak to her, because I'm like that. I get very shy with beautiful girls, nobody else, I can talk to anybody, but a girl like Carol, no. I even notice it with men. The only time I feel bad about what I do is if a bloke's young and reasonably good-looking and then I'd just as soon not do him.

I suppose I was a bit turned in on meself generally then, because I'd just got back from London, out of hospital, and the scar was very bad. I mean it's no bloody ornament *now*, but at least it's gone white. It was purple then and it really stood out. I wore scarves to hide it, but I was so aware of it meself that I just thought everybody was looking at it. I never mentioned it, and of course nobody else did, so I had no way of knowing what people were thinking.

The scar was a big factor in my life at that time. Feeling I looked awful. Feeling weak, and on the defensive. Which I would've been anyway with working a new area, because although there's always familiar faces anywhere you go, they aren't always the right ones, and anyway you've still got to get yourself established in a place, not tread on any toes, but at the same time make it bloody clear that you're not going to be messed around with. And of course that goes double if you're trying to work on your own. And I was. I didn't want any of the local Daves getting ideas about *me*. It's no picnic. Your fists are up more often than they're down, and you've no friends because until you've got it all sorted out you can't afford to have friends.

I was in no state then to demand respect, or anyway I didn't feel as if I could. I was still weak, I used to run out of steam without any warning at all, one minute I'd be walking along right as rain and the next I'd feel that tired I had to go home and lie down. It was just like somebody pulling the plug out. *That* made me more snappy and jumpy than I need've been, and it was all rubbish because when I got meself together a bit I realized the scar was having the opposite effect on people from the one I thought. People were frightened of it. They still are, which if you stop to think about it is mad, because one sure thing: I didn't win *that* fight!

Anyway. I was getting out of a car in Northgate one

evening when I suddenly had one of these . . . well, very near blackouts. All I could do was stagger over to the wall and hang on for dear life. The next thing I knew there was this fair-haired girl running across the road to me and shouting, 'Are you alright?' She told me afterwards she thought I'd been attacked, and I could see at the time that was what she thought, but I couldn't get the words out to tell her I hadn't. I just clung onto the wall and saw stars. After a bit it started to go off, and her voice stopped sounding as if it was booming towards me down a long tunnel.

'Are you alright?' she asked again.

'Yeah, I'm fine.'

I could just about stand up. On the other side of the road there was a girl called Rita. I noticed she hadn't stirred her pins. I tried to start walking, but my legs were all over the shop.

Carol grabbed hold of me. 'Come on,' she says. 'We're going for a drink.'

We started to walk up Northgate, and I was thinking we might go to the Palmerston, when suddenly I got a whiff of fried chicken through the open door of a restaurant. I wasn't aware of showing anything, and yet she says, '*I* know what's wrong with you. You've had nowt to eat.'

It was true, I hadn't, not because I couldn't afford it or anything like that, but because I'd got used to making do with a cup of tea and a cigarette. You get like that when you live on your own. 'Howay,' she says. 'We're going in here.'

She had a kind of confidence that I'd lost and that she lost later. She'd walk into anywhere and sit down as if she owned the place. You can't do that, you know, especially not the area you work in, because, fair enough, your money's the same as everybody else's, but *you're* not and people've got ways of making that clear. You get you don't take things back, even if they're rubbish, you don't complain, you pay through the nose and you take what's on offer. Even me, unless I've had a few, and then I'm too much the other way.

But there was Carol sat at a table near the window, looking all round her. Quite happy. Because she wasn't a pro, you see. Not in her own mind, she wasn't. She hadn't even had a caution then.

The meal arrived and I stuck into it — I didn't realize how hungry I was till it was there in front of me. I don't remember what we talked about, though I remember she did most of it. I didn't surface till the meal was over and we were waiting for the coffee. Even then I didn't say much, I was content just to look at her. She wore a lot of bangles, not the kind that cost a lot, but not cheap either, you could tell she'd put a lot of effort into choosing them, and she had a way of bunching them all up together round her wrist and then letting them cascade down her arm. Her arm was brown and so thin you could see the division between the two bones. Too thin, I suppose, but it didn't seem like that then, I was so taken up with watching the bangles fall across the brown skin, and the dusting of golden hairs. Of course she was very beautiful, but there was always something more than that. She had a way of closing her eyes when she was talking to you with a little fluttering of the lids as though the eyes were trying to roll up, and this was incredibly sexual — not sexy. Deeper than that. A bit frightening. You felt there was a capacity for *letting go* in her that you mightn't be able to match.

I wasn't *just* gawking, though it might sound as if I was, I was listening to her as well. She actually managed to get me laughing, and that was something I hadn't done a lot of, recently.

So it came as all the more of a shock when she lit a cigarette and said, 'So how did it happen? That.'

I was staggered. I mean, you just don't ask. I got ready to freeze her off, I think I actually had me mouth open, and then suddenly I heard meself starting to talk. I told her things that evening that I'd never told anybody, not the doctors, not the police.

The way it happened, I was working in an area I didn't know, something I never do now, I won't even do a man that pulls me up on me way to the viaduct, I tell him to piss off, I want to be *there* before I start. But there I was walking down the street and there was this bloke coming towards me and he says, 'Are you doing business, love?' Well, I wasn't, but as soon as he said that I thought, Oh well, I'll just do him and then I can go round the off licence and get meself a packet of fags, because I was right out. That's the thing about London, you make the money but by Christ it goes. I never seemed to have anything, no matter how many I did. Anyway, I says, 'Alright, but I've got nowhere to take you. It'll have to be up one of them alleys.' 'Oh,' he says, 'That's alright. I know somewhere.' First warning sign. Nowadays I always ask them where they want to go, just so I know where we're *not* going. *Keep your own ground.* If I was talking to somebody just starting out, I'd think that's the first thing I'd say to her: Keep your own ground. But I went with him. I needed me head looking at, I can't even say I was young and daft, I wasn't. So anyway he took me up this alley and into this factory gate where the shadows were pretty deep and I got the rubber on him, and oh dear me, could I hell do anything with him. I says, 'For Christ's sake, come on. I haven't got all night.' That was it, he flipped. All of a sudden I felt this thing pressing into me neck. I didn't know what it was, it could've been a key or anything. But he says, 'I've got a knife, you get in there.' And he pushed me back against the gate and it was one of these gates that has a door in it and the door was open. I tripped over the step and went sprawling head first in the dark. I'd twisted me shoulder or something, in fact at first I thought I'd broken it, and it was pitch black. He pushed me up against the wall and then he says, 'Get your things off.' Well, I twisted me head round as far as it would go and I still couldn't see anything and then he dug it in a bit deeper and I knew it was no key. 'Now,' he says, 'Get your clothes off,' and I thought, Oh, he just wants me to strip, I'll play along with him. But I think it was a mistake because it was freezing cold and you go numb and not only that but with your clothes off you feel cowed, you feel there's no point sticking up for yourself, and I think mebbe he was reckoning on that. 'Lie down,' he says. 'Now look,' I says, but he dragged me down. He started biting me, I was black and blue and all the time he was saying, 'You're gunna pay me for this. How much are you gunna pay?' He got me bag open and took what bit of money I had, which was only the notes he'd given me, plus a few odd coppers, and he screwed it all up into a ball and he started pushing the coins against me teeth, and all the time he was saying, 'You're gunna pay *me.*' He wasn't having much trouble at the other end now, the thought of me paying *him* was a real turn-on. 'Move,' he says, 'Don't just lie there. Fucking well move.' All I could think was, He won't kill me till after he's come, and I tried to think of a way of getting the knife off him, I actually tried prising his fingers open, but there was no shifting him. In fact all I got was a poke in the eye. After he'd come he looked at me like a sick dog, I don't think he knew *what* he wanted, then he says, 'You *cunt*', and he slashed me with the knife. I don't think he intended killing me, I think his idea was to slash me across the breasts, but I reared back and it hit me on the throat. It didn't feel like a knife, I mean not like you'd expect a knife to feel, more like being slapped, or hit with something flat. There wasn't much pain, in fact for a minute I thought he'd missed me altogether, but then I felt something warm running down me neck, and he took one look at me and, my God, did he scarper. He just says, 'You go to the police and me and me mate'll come looking for you.' Then he picked his jacket up and he was off. I waited a minute to make sure he'd gone then I wrapped me coat round me and staggered out of the yard. I still wasn't *feeling* anything much, I think I was a bit light-headed, me throat felt the way your stomach feels when you've just undone a zip, and I was walking along quite happy, I'm sure anybody watching me'd've thought I was drunk. Except I knew I had to get a move on in case he decided to finish the job, because I could see that'd be the safest thing for him to do. You see I wasn't confused or anything, I could still think. I collapsed outside a phone box, just as I was opening the door. Next thing I knew I was in hospital and there was this policewoman sitting by the bed. I thought, My God, what have I done? Anyway they started. Who was he? What did he look like? All that. I says, 'Look, I'm telling you, I don't remember.' It was an inspector doing most of the talking. Anyway, at the finish this police-

355

woman turns round and she says, 'You're covering up for somebody,' she says. 'Well look, *dearie,* we want him behind bars even if you don't. The next girl he attacks might be somebody decent.' 'Oh,' I says, 'Pardon me for breathing.' Most of the time I didn't even bother answering them, all I could think about was getting out of the hospital and back home. 'Home' was here, which is surprising when you think about it because I was taken into care very young. I've never really felt I had roots anywhere, and yet as soon as that happened to me, I knew I had. I knew I had to come back here. In the end I discharged meself. They'd done all they could for me anyway, and I was fed up of lying there being grilled, so I just put me clothes on and walked out. Oh, and the smell of King's Cross when I went to get the train, it was smashing. *And* I'd got me nerve back, I knew that because I'd had to do a few to get the money for the ticket. You might think I come back seething with hatred. Well, you'd be wrong. You expect a certain amount of violence in this job, you expect to get slapped around. Admittedly you don't expect a knife being pulled, but it happens. I just got unlucky, that's all.

Anyway I told Carol all this and after it was finished I felt worn out, it was just like living through it again; and I also felt a bit threatened, because I don't let many people into my life. I suppose I've always prided myself on not showing weakness, since . . . oh, I don't know — some ripe old age. Three? But there it was, I'd told her and I was already looking at her pretty sharp, because I wanted some kind of hold on *her,* in return. She talked about herself as easy as ninepence and it was only later that you realized how little of it was true. Oh, she was a terrible liar. Terrible in both senses. Most of the time she didn't even *try* to make it sound convincing. She'd sort of hand it to you with a little smile as if she was asking, 'There. How did you like that one?' I got I could tell when she was telling the truth. Like she had fifty stories about how and why she left home, how and why she got on the game, and she'd tailor them to what she thought you wanted to hear. I can't remember the one she told me that night and it doesn't matter, but I do remember the odd

356

bit of truth. She once said to me, 'Jean, I was pig-sick of having nowt.' *That* was true. And another time she opened her mouth and made me look inside and she says, 'Look, you've never seen a mouth like that, have yer?' And I hadn't. To be quite honest me first thought was her teeth were false because there wasn't a filling, there wasn't a mark on any of them. She says, 'That's what comes of eating your vegetables raw.' She says, 'We used to cook with electric and the bugger was never on.' I think her mother had been a right blossom. Carol never went back to see her family though it was only . . . what, ten miles? She used to say she'd turned her back on all that. Poor Carol, she'd brought it with her, it popped out every time she opened her mouth, but she never ever faced up to that.

Looking back I can see that the beginnings of a lot of our rows were already there at that table. Even that first night I made it bloody clear there was no way I was going to London again, and London was Carol's Mecca. She had this vision of herself smoking a cigarette in a posh hotel, looking all the blokes up and down — but dead-cool, none of your street corner hassle. Oh yes, she wanted that. I remember one night we were sat in a bar and a girl come in wearing a white suit, she wasn't even pretty, but everybody looked at her, and Carol . . . her tongue was hanging out. There was such a look of hunger on her face, I've never forgot it. The girl only stopped just long enough to realize it wasn't her kind of place and then she said something to the man behind her and off they went. I waited for a white suit to appear in Carol's wardrobe, but, give her her due, it didn't. What did appear was a pair of boots. Would you believe ninety quid? I didn't, but it was always a mystery to me what Carol would spend her money on. She'd've lived in a pig sty as long as she had money for clothes.

That night living together anywhere was a long way off. In fact if anybody had told me it was going to happen I wouldn't've believed them. Quite honestly, what was next on my list was bed, and we did walk home together, but I think I already knew it wasn't going to happen.

It went on not happening. We saw each other every day,

we even worked together, but there was nothing doing. She didn't even have to say anything, I knew. I don't quite know why. Except I think Carol had been very badly hurt, she was in no hurry to rush into anything. It was odd really, because there we were jumping in and out of cars, pants up, pants down, sex in ten minutes flat, and yet all the time there was this long, slow, gentle unfolding going on between us. I think it was a good thing. It meant I had to pull meself together, and I did. I stopped jumping down people's throats, I stopped going round looking for trouble, I was even *nice*. Which was a remarkable change when you think only a few weeks earlier I'd been banned from four pubs.

I've got some very happy memories of that time. The early evening when I went to call for her, and the starlings were coming in. The sky was black with them, and I used to walk through the streets and listen to the cries, all the whistles and chatters and clicks, and it was like walking through a shower of electric sparks.

As I say, it took us a long time to become lovers, even longer to decide to live together, because of course two girls living together is a brothel. Which is hilarious, when you think there was never a man in the place. Right from the very beginning we decided that. The flat was *our* place, we didn't want any of them in it. Nevertheless, there was always this nagging feeling in the back of our minds, we could get done for living together — to the point where I sometimes felt it would've been worthwhile me keeping my flat on, just to be able to say, 'Look, I don't live here. This is my address.' But I don't think it would've helped, and, anyway, it never came to that.

It wasn't all plain sailing, not by any means. We rowed about all the usual things, whose turn it was to muck the place out. Needless to say, it was always mine. Money. Like I say, Carol's money went on her back. If the flat needed anything doing to it, I paid. Not that I was an angel. Some people drink when they're depressed, and it just makes them go deeper. I drink when I'm high and it sends me right over the top. So in an odd sort of way the mere fact that I'd got Carol and I was so happy with her made me do dreadful things, and I do mean dreadful. I did things in that first six months that I don't like to think about even now. She was always having to pick up the pieces. I don't know how she put up with me.

A lot of these things got sorted out. One thing we never managed to sort out was the different ways we looked at the job. I like this life. I'm not in it because I'm a poor, deprived, inadequate, half-witted woman, whatever some people might like to think, I'm in it because it suits *me*. I like the company. I like the excitement. I like the feeling of stepping out onto the street, not knowing what's going to happen or who I'm going to meet. I like the freedom. I like being able to decide when I'm going to work. I like being able to take the day off without being answerable to anybody. The money . . . well, I'm not pretending I don't like it, but I'm not one of the greedy ones. I get out, I earn me twenty quid, and that's it, I'm happy. I don't want to graft for every penny, thank you very much, and I certainly don't want to clock on and clock off, if I did I could go and work in the bloody chicken factory. But Carol was just the opposite. She wasn't cut out for it at all, in fact I think she hated it, but she liked the money. And she was always wanting more. Of course, she could probably've got more round here if she'd gone and worked in a sauna, but she didn't fancy that. She wanted her little bit of glamour.

I think she'd've got into it deeper anyway, because, like I say, she wanted money and there's only one job a girl like Carol can make money in. But I have to keep telling meself that, because the *fact* is she got into it deeper through me, and look where it led.

Incidentally, whenever we had a row, Carol won. I think that might surprise a lot of people, people who knew both of us, because I suppose on the surface I was the toughest. But being tough isn't everything. I battled my way through life, Carol bobbed along, but I needed her more than she ever needed me. I don't know whether she knew that, but I always did. Until I met her my life was one long disaster. I don't even remember a lot of it, and when I say 'a lot' I don't mean the odd patch here and there, I mean years.

You get like that when you move around a lot, it's not so much you don't remember things, but they're all jumbled up together. You remember faces, but you don't know where they come from. There's one face I remember — woman in her forties, plump, bright blue eyes, red veins on her cheeks — I've no idea who she was, but she must've been kind to me because that's a good picture. There's nothing really clear till the approved school, and that's a bit sickening really, the one bit you want to forget you can't. Though even there there's things I want to remember. One afternoon me and another girl were scrubbing a floor, I think it must've been a punishment, because I know I was feeling pretty sick, but it needn't've been, because you did a lot of scrubbing floors in that place, punishment or not. I mean it was mad, new lino, and you had to set on and scrub it. Any fool knows if you scrub lino you just scratch it and take all the oil out so it needs doing again quicker, only this time the dirt's sunk in and it's a harder job getting it out. Perhaps it wasn't mad, perhaps they knew what they were doing. Anyway, there we were, me and this other girl, wet little piece, but harmless, God knows what she was in for, when along comes Gloria. What a name, eh? Gloria was in for stripping an old woman naked and keeping her in a cold bath for hours. Every time the poor old bitch tried to get out Gloria plants her hoof between the old girl's tits and shoves her back in again. She'd done something of the same kind before, only that time she got off. This time her luck ran out, which was why we were enjoying the pleasure of her company. She was one of the only two wicked people I've ever known, and I've known some bruisers. She hated me from the moment she first clapped eyes on me, which I took as a compliment.

Anyway along comes Gloria and as she goes past, what does she do but she kicks over the bucket. Mess everywhere. No way we could finish by tea. More trouble. I gave Gloria one look and I started mopping it up. Mop, wring, mop, wring, mop, wring, and after a bit the water started to go pink. I looked at — do you know, I've forgotten her name — and there she was scrubbing away for dear life at her bare arm. She'd actually got blood dripping off her hand onto the floor. I said, 'You stupid cow,' but there was no getting through to her. I took her to Matron and then I come back and finished the floor. I felt as if I was on fire and partly it was wanting to have a go at Gloria, but it was a lot more than that. Something in me hardened out that day. I could see how all these years I'd been twisting and turning on the end of a hook, lashing out, yes, but more than half the time hitting meself. I thought, *No*. If there's somebody trying to destroy you the one thing you *don't* do is give them any help, and they *were* trying to destroy me, oh, they used words like 'help', 'reform' but I was on the receiving end, and I *knew*. I think that was one of the turning points in my life. I mean, it might sound obvious, *don't help other people to destroy you*, but it wasn't obvious. Not on that floor. I'm grateful to that approved school, I learnt a hell of a lot. Mebbe not what they wanted me to learn, but that's their bad luck, isn't it? The main thing is, I learnt.

One of the things I learnt was never to trust nobody, and I went on and on and on not trusting nobody until I met Carol. And why I chose her I don't know, because I can see in lots of ways she was a silly little thing. Doesn't make much difference now, does it? I used to be walking along sometimes and I'd think about her and I'd know that when I got home there'd be somebody there. That's something I'd never had before. I look back on all the faces, the faces I can't put a name to, and I know exactly what I've lost. More than a friend. More than a lover. She was the one fixed point.

We always used to look forward to Thursday nights because that was one of our regular nights off, our way of getting ourselves together to face the weekend. Generally we went out, but that Thursday we didn't because we were decorating the flat. We'd finished the bedroom and started on the living-room, in fact we'd been painting all day. So by the time we sat down in front of the gas-fire to eat our Chinese take-away the whole place stank of paint stripper and turpentine and God knows what else, and it was a bloody good

job we were hungry because otherwise we'd never've got
any of it down.

Carol had gone out to get it while I finished putting the
first coat on the ceiling. I hate ceilings. Talk about warm air
rising, I was sweating like a pig. And all the time at the back
of my mind I was thinking about Carol: nothing special,
just imagining her sitting in the take-away. Then walking
home, down Northgate, and round the corner into Melbourne Terrace where we live. Lived.

I heard her high heels clicking along the pavement and
then there she was in the doorway with the light shining
down onto her hair. I can still see her, but her face is in
shadow. I don't know why. Perhaps it was, or perhaps it's
because the memory of her living face has been overlaid by
that horror on the slab.

Now she's coming into the room. She's in a rotten temper
because they've kept her waiting and they've packed the
sauce all wrong so that some of it's leaked out and dribbled
down the leg of her jeans.

'You'd've had to wash them anyway,' I said. 'You've got
paint on the back.'

'Now she tells me!' She plonked the parcel down onto the
table. 'It's no good,' she says, 'I can't sit in these. I'll have to
change.'

Which seemed mad to me, because all we were going to
do was sit and have our suppers and then go to bed. But she
was like that.

She came back wearing her pale yellow jeans with a black
top and her hair fastened back with a black velvet ribbon.

She was very quiet. She'd been in a funny mood all day,
it wasn't just spilling the sauce on her jeans that'd done it.
She did have these moods when she got very tense and
depressed, but generally they blew over. Now of course I
can look back and see that the black patches were getting
worse and lasting longer, but somehow when you live with
somebody, when you see them every day, you don't notice
that they've changed. People who hardly know them at all
see the change in them before you do.

Or perhaps I'm kidding myself. Perhaps I didn't want to see.

Anyway, we sat on the floor with the gas-fire popping and spluttering away and a couple of bottles of Newcastle Brown that I'd got out of the fridge. The beer and the warmth from the fire were starting to make me feel drowsy — I'd been on the go all day.

Then Carol said, 'I bumped into April today.'

I could feel her looking at me.

'When I went shopping,' she said. 'She was stood outside the Crown.'

There wasn't a word of truth in any of this. I knew for a fact April was in Glasgow.

'She says she's going back to London.'

I didn't crack on I knew. 'Oh,' I said, 'I thought she was doing alright where she is?'

'She is. I mean she was. But she's met this bloke and he says he can get her into the hotels.'

'We've all met one of them.'

'It's a hundred quid a night, Jean.'

'It is if you don't get slung out.'

'Well, why should she get slung out? She doesn't go round looking like a slag, you know.'

'And she doesn't sound like one either, till she opens her bloody gob.'

We'd had all this out before. I could never get her to see that it wasn't enough to *look* the part. 'They're not after bloody elocution lessons,' she used to say. And I used to say, 'It's not *them*. It's the waiters, the doorman, the detective. *You've got to fit in*.' I never had the heart to come right out with it and tell her she wouldn't. It was always some other girl we were talking about.

Part of the trouble was, she didn't make a lot of money, and she always thought she could, if only she was somewhere else.

She wasn't right for round here. For one thing she was too beautiful — that puts a lot of men off, at least it does round here. They don't go for the slim-and-elegant look. Except for a kinky few, and *they* only want to muck it up. Oh, I'm not saying she did that badly, but she wasn't doing well. And of course there was me, with a face like the back of a truck, raking it in. That can't've helped.

'She asked me if I'd go with her.'

I went very quiet, because that was new. She'd never said anything like that before. I suppose I was frightened. Even though I knew it was all a pack of lies about April, I was still frightened.

'That's up to you,' I said.

Then, because she knew she'd hurt me, she had to justify herself by starting a row. I never row with anybody if I can help it. I can't afford to, because with me it's no sooner the word than the blow. But of course she managed to get me going in the end. If you love somebody you know how to needle them. It wasn't long before we were stood there glaring at each other like a couple of strange cats.

'You know I hate living here,' she said.

And that really hurt — I'd just taken every bit of skin off me hands painting the sodding place.

There was a long silence. Then she said, 'It's mad. We're just stuck out there waiting to be killed.'

So at last she'd come out with it. It's funny, but we'd never talked about it all that much, not when we were on our own, though I knew she was frightened. More than most, I mean. We were all frightened. I started going through the old routine. You know, if you're gunna meet one you'll meet one anywhere. And it's all true. There's many a girl been carved up in her own bedroom because she was too frightened to go out on the streets. 'You can take all the precautions you like,' I said. 'In the end it's luck.'

She just looked at me. Then she said, very quietly, 'I'm not lucky.'

That ought to've stopped me, but it didn't. 'You'd be no safer in London than you are here,' I said. 'My God, I ought to know.'

She looked at my face and then at my neck. And then she stubbed out her cigarette and walked out of the door. She didn't take her coat with her or anything. I was left looking at the paint brushes and the empty cartons and bottles and her cigarette ash lying like neat little turds on the hearth.

I was buggered if I was gunna clear the mess up. She could bloody well come back and find it. So I went to bed. Then after a while I got up again and put the paint-brushes in to soak, because it goes against my nature to leave tools lying around dirty after I've finished a job.

Then I tidied round, making every job last as long as I could, because I didn't want to admit even to myself that I'd really got up to wait for her. When I couldn't pretend any longer I went to the window and looked out. It was still raining, tipping down in fact. I could see the drops bouncing off the pavement. I thought, My God, she'll be drenched. And I went and put the kettle on so she could have a cup of hot tea as soon as she came in. Which sounds daft, I know, but you see I really did think she was just walking round the block, just giving herself time to cool down.

At two o'clock in the morning I finally admitted to myself that she wasn't coming back, not that night anyway. And then I started thinking, Well, mebbe I'm wrong. For all I knew April *had* come back from Glasgow, and Carol *had* met her and now perhaps Carol had gone over to April's to say, yes, she would go to London. The mood she was in when she left she'd've done that just to spite me.

All the time I was thinking this I knew it wasn't true. I knew perfectly well all that stuff about April was another of Carol's ploys to get me to go down to London with her. She was always on at me to do that.

I went back to bed and told meself to stop worrying, she'd be there in the morning, she'd probably knock me up. I told myself to go to sleep. Then I lay awake and listened to the wind.

It howled all that night and most of the following day. By late afternoon I'd talked to everybody Carol might've gone to, and I knew for certain that April was in Glasgow and had never left it, because I'd rung a mate of hers who'd been out with her the previous night. The only thing I could think was, she'd been so angry or, God help me, so terrified that she'd just set off for London on her own, hitch-hiking perhaps, because I knew she had no money on her, she'd had to borrow off me for the take-away. I even started thinking that perhaps the man who talked about the hotel trade was for real and she'd gone off with him.

But I never seriously considered that. Even at the worst times. I knew she wouldn't leave me, I knew the strength of what we had going between us.

Which left only one possibility.

I lay awake for the whole of another night and then I went to the police. I didn't dare go sooner, because if she *had've* turned up we'd both've been facing a charge. Or we could've been. I know it isn't likely. But you can't trust them.

They weren't all that bothered anyway. Girls like Carol go missing all the time. They turn up, a few weeks or a few months later, in another town. 'She'll turn up,' they said. 'She mebbe fancied a change.'

And I couldn't tell them why I knew it wasn't true.

So it was back to the flat and nothing to do but wait and think. Oh, I did a lot of thinking; and of course I asked round everybody I knew, trying to find somebody who might've seen her after she left the flat, but nobody had.

I started going back in my mind over everything she'd said. There was one thing stuck: whenever anybody talked about the murders, and of course they did, though there wasn't anything like the panic there is now, she used to say, 'He *is* somebody's regular.' Because of course that's the first thing everybody says, 'Stick to your regulars,' and for somebody like Brenda, who's got a good few regulars that she's built up over the years, it makes a lot of sense. Not for Carol, though. She didn't have enough regulars.

I thought and thought about it: He *is* somebody's regular. And the more I thought, the more certain I became that she had a particular man in mind and that I knew which one it was. As I say, she didn't have many. He told her his name was Steve. Which means absolutely bloody nothing, because they don't use their real names any more than we use ours. He took a long time to come, but he always paid up without any trouble, and he sometimes paid a bit extra. A bit over the odds. No violence. No threats. No bother. She just didn't like him. He used to keep a packet of little purple sweets in his pocket and slip one into his mouth, so that by the time he finally managed to get it up, his breath smelled of violets. I can see Carol now, wrinkling her nose. 'I'd rather have bad breath.'

That was it. You couldn't even say he was a regular, not really — she only had him three or four times. I never saw him. It seems incredible, looking back, but we still went out on our own. Even when we were together, one of us would get into a car without waiting for the other to come back.

It could've happened any night.

I've only got one photo of her, and that isn't a very good one. Sometimes I wish I had more, but then I think, No. The pictures in my mind are better than photographs. Because in my mind she moves about, she laughs, she looks in the mirror above the mantelpiece, and pulls a face because she doesn't like what she sees, she stands in the bedroom naked, rubbing the red mark that the waistband of her jeans has left, she comes running towards me across the road like she did on that first night, she lies on the bed on a wet day and paints her toe-nails and yawns.

It's odd, but the clearest picture of all is something I didn't see. Carol standing on a street corner, bare-headed in the rain. She stands there, rubbing her bare arms. She walks to the kerb and looks hopefully up the road. She won't come back, you see. She wants to show me I can't just ignore everything she says and so she's going to go the pub and let me sweat it out for a few hours. But for that she needs money, and she hasn't got any money. So, she thinks, one car, just one, and then I'll go for a drink.

I watch. The car appears over the brow of a hill, slows down. Stops. Carol runs across the road and bends down to talk to him and her hair is dark and stringy from the rain. She gets in and the windscreen mists up, it's so warm in the car, and she turns to him and laughs and says . . . I see it all so clearly. Except his face.

CHAPTER SEVENTEEN

Last Wednesday I went back to the Palmerston again. I got there just after opening time, because I wanted to make sure I was the first there. I didn't want to walk in and find them all sat in the corner together. Too much like old times. But I'd got things badly wrong, because as soon as you pushed the door of the back room open the noise hit you.

I stood there looking round, and no, there wasn't a sudden silence for me. Everybody went on chattering nineteen to the dozen, and when I say 'everybody', I'd never seen the place so packed.

Beattie was still behind the bar, but she was stuck on a big high stool at the far end and most of the serving was being done by a fat blonde-haired woman with her sleeves rolled up. Beattie saw me come in. I waved. I didn't expect her to do anything, but she got off the stool straight away and came tottering over like a hen on ice.

'Trade's brisk,' I said, because I was afraid she was going to say, 'Hello, stranger', or something like that.

'Oh, it's brisk alright,' she said, but she didn't sound happy about it. 'You've never seen such a going on,' she said. 'It's all . . .' And she waggled her fingers from side to side to show there was trouble brewing.

I could feel it, and if you can feel it at opening time, God help you.

'Who are they all?' I said.

'I'm buggered if I know,' she said. 'The word's got round you don't get nicked in Northgate. And there's a lot of trouble.' She lowered her voice as she said it.

'Well, you're no stranger to trouble, Beattie,' I said, and grinned at her, because there was one night she flung me out.

She didn't smile back. 'This is different,' she said.

I got me drink and went round talking to a few of the women I knew. Some had come in from other towns, but when you talked to them you could understand why: it wasn't just they knew they were safe from arrest here, it was because the number of arrests had gone up everywhere else. They were being herded into Northgate, like into a pen. And then watched.

I sat down in the corner, joggling the arm of a big dark girl who turned on me, and then thought better of it. Everybody was on edge. You couldn't tell at first, because of all the laughter and the shouting, but they were. It'd only need a drink to get knocked over.

I felt the old Palmerston was dead. And I felt sorry for Beattie, who I've always had a soft spot for, bloody old battle-axe that she is. The night they found Kath I'd stopped in the back room very late. At the finish there was only Beattie and me left, and when closing time come she put the bolts on the door and we just went on drinking.

I think we drank ourselves sober that night. Beattie looked like nothing on earth by the time we'd finished. Well, she didn't look any too marvellous to begin with, because she'd been making her face up and she must've just finished one eye when the paper come through the door. She never got to the other. Anybody else'd've looked ridiculous.

All you could get out of her was this Irene, the first'un he done, and apparently she'd been a mate of Beattie's. In fact they'd worked together, and this was a new departure for Beattie because she would never ever talk about the past. The most you ever got out of her was she'd once kept a boarding house in Blackpool. I believe Blackpool. Anyway, this Irene used to sit in the Palmerston a lot, after Beattie took it over — she can't've been a chicken, by this time — and her favourite spot was by the window. Well, as Beattie was telling me this, she kept glancing over to the window and I knew she could see her and I made meself keep looking straight ahead, because if I didn't I was afraid I'd start seeing her too. There was nothing spooky about this, nothing like you see on films, with shadows and doors creaking. No. Just the opposite, in fact. Everything got clearer, every stain on the beer mats, every fag-end, every scuff on the lino, every tear in the seats, and yet you looked round that empty bar and you knew bloody well it wasn't empty at all. And there was Beattie, stuck up on her high stool behind the bar, with the make-up cracking over her wrinkles and her one naked eye staring out like the eye of God.

Well, like I say, we'd had a few.

A few nights later the bar was crowded again, everybody drinking doubles for what they'd forced themselves to miss. But the atmosphere. I've known livelier graveyards. At the finish, Beattie bangs on the bar to get everybody's attention. 'Howay, girls,' she says. 'You see this bottle? I'm going to put it on the bar. Drop your odd coppers into it and we'll have a party the night they nail the bugger. Right?' Teresa got up and passed the bottle round and everybody tipped the loose change out of their purses. You could feel the place coming back to life. Somebody at the back of the room shouted, 'Hey, Beattie, no nicking off to France with it, mind.' But the money went in, my God it did. The bottle was half full by the time it got back to the bar.

It's still there. People still drop the odd copper into it, but nobody mentions the party any more.

Maureen was the first in and I was glad to see her because I'd been wondering how she'd got on since she started working at home. She was the only one changed completely after Kath. She won't touch the cars at all now and that's funny when you think she went through Bradford, but everybody has a breaking point.

'How's it going?' I said when she got sat down.

'Oh, all right,' she says. 'I had a cup of tea with Barbara

this afternoon.'

'Big lass, is he?'

She had to laugh. 'Pretty big, yes.'

'I always used to wonder why you never got a little'un. But you don't, do you? They're all strapping big fellas.'

'I'm sick,' she said, wiping the beer off her moustache. Oh, she's no oil-painting isn't Maureen. 'You never get a laugh,' she says. 'You daren't laugh, they think you're laughing at them.'

I've never noticed Maureen laughing much at all, in fact I've never thought of her as having that much sense of humour. Still you can always be wrong, I suppose.

'Well, that's what you miss, isn't it?' I said.

'This,' she said, looking round the bar. 'I've tried to keep coming in, but you can't always manage it, and when you're just stuck there you feel like a bloody battery hen.'

All this was leading up to something.

'I was hoping I'd bump into you,' she said.

This was it. I didn't give her any encouragement, I just sat and listened. She said she was thinking of working the boats, and of course I could see she was angling for me to go with her, but I didn't say anything. You need a special temperament for the boats, because once you're on a boat you're on your own except for the girl you're with and you've got to be able to rely on her not doing anything daft. And I don't know Maureen all that well, though if I had to pick somebody I think it'd be her. But then I'm not sure about meself at the moment. Normally, yes. I mean, to be honest, I'd love it. Because you really are stepping into the unknown and you come off with all kinds of things, watches, transistors, it isn't just money, and I like that. A lot of people can't stand it, but I like it. Only at the moment, as I say, I'm not sure. If I started feeling cornered, and you can, you know, I don't know how I'd react, I think I could flip or go berserk or anything. And another thing. He isn't a sailor. If he was they'd know, they'd only have to check what ships were in. And there's no sign of them watching the docks, they're all round here. For me, that's it. But I didn't come right out and say I wouldn't, you never know when you're going to want to take something like that up, so I just said I'd think about it.

We'd finished talking about that when in come Ginny and Teresa and of course they were bubbling over, they always are. 'Look at this,' Ginny says, waving her hand at the bar. 'Did you ever see anything so soft? One of these nights they'll be dragging some poor sod out of his car and splitting him down the middle. And we've got a couple of lasses opposite us. Fourteen years old. Two quid. No rubber. It's bringing everything in.'

'Well, haven't you told them to get lost?' I said.

'Try telling them anything. Couple of daft kids, *fourteen,* over the moon because they're *keeping a man.*'

'Well, you know, we've all been there,' said Maureen.

'Speak for yourself,' I said. 'It sounds to me as if you want to get a bit tougher. It only needs two like that and we can all go home.'

'We can all go home anyway,' said Ginny.

Brenda and Audrey came in. They were late because they'd been up to the hospital to see Elaine and the baby. Oh, yes, she's had it. And it's a boy, so all that business with the needle and thread did come right. She's going home tomorrow. Dave's still around, but according to Brenda only just.

'I think he's ready for off,' she said.

'You'd think the bairn'd keep him, with it being a boy,' Maureen said.

'Ah, but he's got another woman,' said Brenda. 'Apparently he got on with her while Elaine was in hospital. Or so he says. I think meself she's been around a bit longer than that. Elaine'd never've known, only they let her out for a weekend just before the baby was due, she walks into the flat and there's this girl stood in the kitchen frying chips. Daft little bitch hadn't told him she was coming because she wanted it to be a surprise.'

'Sounds as if it was,' I said.

'Of course he swore black was white there was nothing in it, it'd only happened the once and all that, but Elaine says the girl's things were all over the flat. And he's never been in to see her, you know. He's never clapped eyes on that bairn.'

'She's well rid of him,' said Ginny.

'It's a big flat, though, if she has to keep it on by herself,' said Audrey. 'And she can't come back yet. She's got to give it two months.'

'Oh, longer than that,' said Brenda.

'What did he do?' asked Teresa. 'When she come in and found him with his fancy bit.'

'Oh, he did get dressed and chase her out,' said Audrey. 'But Elaine said he was only funny with her all weekend, and the second evening he just put his coat on and went to the pub and she was just stuck there crying her eyes out. I said, "You daft bitch, you should've come round mine." But you can't talk to her, she's soft.'

'Not as soft as she was,' said Brenda. 'I mean she's talking about packing him in.'

'Sounds as if he's packed her in,' I said.

Brenda looked at me. 'She was asking after you,' she said. Oh, dear.

'Yeah, I know. I'll have to go and see her,' I said.

'We're going up on Saturday. Dinner time, when he's at the pub. Why don't you have a walk up with us?'

'Yeah, fine. I'll see you at your house.'

'Just on twelve.'

Brenda's bounced back a lot. There was one time, just after Kath, when you wouldn't've given tuppence for her.

By the time I got up to go the room was spinning a bit, not that I'd had a lot to drink, but I hadn't had any food. I've only been on one real bender since Carol, and that didn't work. After I come round, I just felt ashamed, I felt dirty. She was worth more than that.

Beattie come over just as I was leaving and put her arms round me. 'Don't make it as long next time,' she says.

'Oh, I'll be around,' I said. 'Always supposing I can get in.'

'I know, isn't it awful?'

'Oh, go on. Think of the money.'

'Think of the *work*.'

Ginny and Teresa were going the same way so we all walked down Northgate together. They're very happy and relaxed, those two, and it's not hard to see why. If anybody's safe round here they are, because they go in the cars together. It must be nice working with your sister, because it isn't only safety, if one of them's feeling a bit off or she's got her period the other'll take the weight of the work off her that night, but they still share the dibs out, same as usual. They're very close.

We'd just got to the corner of Church Row when Ginny nudged me.

'There. That's one of them,' she said.

I was so far away it took me a minute to realize what she meant, but then I looked across the road and there was this tarted-up kid, looking like I don't know what. 'You're going to have to sort her out,' I said.

'Don't worry,' said Teresa. 'We know.'

Seeing Ginny and Teresa go off together, I felt more on my own than ever. In fact, the first few minutes were bad, I felt quite peculiar. I kept getting this feeling of being watched, and for once it wasn't Kath.

I didn't want a car to come. I wanted to stand in the chicken factory entrance for a few minutes and get meself together, because it isn't like me to start imagining things. But then a car drew up, and it's no use refusing business. I went across.

He wound the car window down. I couldn't see his face, it was in shadow, but I heard him ask, 'How much?'

'Five quid,' I said. 'With a rubber.'

'Right,' he said. 'Hop in.'

I got in and no sooner was I in then I remembered I hadn't looked at his number plates. It isn't much of a safeguard, but still . . .

'Is there anywhere you want to go?' I asked.

'I don't know the area,' he said. 'You choose.'

'Alright. Under the viaduct and bear left.'

There was a little white dog trotting home all by itself, looking very busy. The car headlights caught it as we came up the hill and threw its shadow half-way up the side of a house.

He wasn't what you could call talkative. That doesn't bother me: to be quite honest it wouldn't bother me if they never spoke. I looked at his hands as he drove. Thin hands with a dusting of black hairs on the back and the knobs of knuckle and joints pushing up strongly underneath. I can remember staring at his hands.

I just sat there, not talking except to give directions. Then he decided he'd start. Nothing much, nothing personal, just the Royal Wedding and all that. He dried up after a bit, and I asked him about the car because I could see it was new. That was the right topic, he was well away. I don't think I got more than one word in ten.

It was warm in the car, too warm. There was his voice going on and on, and the steady swish-swish of the windscreen wipers and the patter of rain on the roof. What with that and the drink I was starting to feel drowsy and I wound the window down for a gulp of air. I gulped alright. There was a Panda car in the next lane.

'Don't worry,' he said. 'I've seen them. I'm not going to get picked up.'

Then he laughed.

Looking back, I think that was the moment when I first started to feel uneasy, because it wasn't a nice laugh. It was the kind of laugh people give when they've just told themselves a private joke, and you know they're not going to let you in on it.

'Down there,' I said, and pointed.

I'd left it a bit late, what with the police and everything, but he didn't have to brake hard. The car had already slowed down.

I didn't say anything, but after that I watched him, and I noticed that time and time again he had the brake covered before I told him to turn. He knew where we were going, which meant he *did* know the area. He must've been here before with other girls.

Still, that meant nothing. You always get the professional virgins, the born-again first-timers. Only doing it because they've just had this awful row with the wife.

I realized suddenly that I was tired, not just drowsy from the warmth, but real, deep-down, bone tired. It was a mistake trying to work tonight, I should've gone straight home. And because I was so tired I started to get jittery, which is a different thing from being careful — I'm always that.

'Left here,' I said.

This time he did brake a bit quick because he had no way of knowing which road I would choose. It wasn't much of a choice. All the houses round here are bricked up and waiting to come down, though it never seems to happen. They're all dead-ends: there's a brick wall built along the bottom to divide the houses from the railway embankment on the other side. It used to be railings, but the kids kept pulling them up and chucking them on the line.

It isn't a place I've ever used much, though a lot of the girls do use it. Carol used to bring them here.

I came back to the present with a jolt. He was driving too fast and too close to the kerb. For one awful moment I thought he hadn't seen the wall at the end. I wanted to say, *'Hey, watch out,'* but before I could say anything he'd driven the car hard up onto the left-hand pavement. We stopped just short of the wall.

He switched the engine off. As soon as he did that, the windows started to mist up, but even when I rubbed mine clean all I could see were planks, nailed across the door of the house. I was trapped. We were parked too close to the house for me to get my door open. The only way out was past him.

There was no need for him to've parked like that. He'd had the whole width of the street to choose from.

I turned to look at him. He was staring straight ahead, both hands still holding the wheel. He caught me looking at him, and turned. I saw the pale gleam of his eyes behind the glasses. It's funny how somebody's appearance can change. He'd looked quite normal when we started out. He didn't look normal now.

I think I was more reluctant to touch him than I've ever

been to touch anybody. But there was no point thinking like that. There was a job to be done. I did everything I could think of, but he never even looked like getting hard. There was a funny smell coming off him, and I couldn't think what it was, because he seemed so clean, and then I realized: it was the way sweat smells when you're afraid.

'Let's give it a rest, shall we?' I said. 'Have another go later.'

I'm not generally that patient. As far as I'm concerned you're not in it for pleasure, they get so long and if they don't come, that's it. But I was treating this one very gently.

He mumbled agreement and started tugging at his zip. Like most men, he didn't want it on show when it wasn't in a state he could be proud of. There was still this smell coming off him, and I couldn't understand why. I mean you get the odd one that's nervous, but nothing like this. I wanted to ask him what was wrong, but I didn't. I think I was afraid he might tell me.

Then he said, 'I'm frightened.'

He said it so softly I had to lean across to hear him, and even then I wasn't sure I'd got it right.

'You're frightened?' I said. 'But there's nothing to be frightened of.'

I had to force every word out because I was petrified. I thought I'd seen everything. I've been slashed, punched, kicked, slapped, raped, oh, yes, *raped,* it does happen to us too. But I've never been as frightened as I was then. You see, at that moment, I *knew.*

'I think I need a pee,' he said.

'Well, go on, then.'

He got out of the car and walked across the road.

I wriggled across into the driver's seat and sat with the door open and my feet on the pavement. I could've run away easily at that point: I had all the time in the world. But I'd come too far to turn back.

He was coming back to the car. As he bent down to get in I noticed the smell of violets on his breath. I didn't panic or anything. I think my mind was wiped clean. I scrambled back into the passenger seat and he crowded in after me.

377

I couldn't think. The one thing I knew was, he couldn't kill me in the car. I saw what he did to Carol, and there was no way he could've done that in a car. He'd've needed a week to wash it out.

He raised his head. His face looked heavy and pallid, his glasses had misted over, he looked blind. He said, 'You know I think we'd be better in the back. There's a lot more room.'

He was already getting out, taking consent for granted. But I saw meself bending over to get into the back seat with him behind me, and I didn't like that idea at all. 'No,' I said, 'We'll be alright where we are.'

He looked disappointed, but there was nothing he could do except get back in.

Peeing hadn't solved any of his problems. It was a bit better, but not much. He kept tugging at his tie, trying to loosen it or get it off, and all the time there was this smell, the smell of violets on his breath, and it seemed to get stronger and stronger. I had to keep telling myself, You're alright as long as you stop in the car. Then I watched him pulling at his tie to get it off and it was like a cold wave breaking over me: *Irene Waddell was strangled.* And I thought, Oh, Jean, you bloody fool. I slipped my hand down into the bag I always keep open beside me and clenched my fingers round the hilt of the knife. I thought about Carol, I saw her lying on the slab, I thought how he'd fucked her and stabbed her and left her on a rubbish tip, and just as he got his tie off I brought the knife up and stabbed him in the neck.

He didn't twist and turn or anything like that. He just stared at me. Then his mouth opened, it opened very wide, and he was gasping and gurgling and trying to speak and I held onto the knife and I watched his lips and I held onto the knife and finally it came, one single word, with a rush of blood like a baby splitting open a cunt, one single word: '*Why?*'

It was over. His eyes rolled up and he slumped to one side away from me.

I took my scarf off and used it to wipe all the surfaces I

could remember touching. Then I got down on my knees and checked and double-checked that I hadn't left anything behind. I searched him, too, groping underneath him because he was too heavy for me to move.

I don't think I missed an inch of that car.

Then I started walking towards the river with the knife wrapped up in my scarf. By the sharpness of the air I thought it was about two o'clock, but I couldn't be sure, my watch had stopped. I came out onto the quayside and stood for a while, checking that there was nobody about. Then I walked down the steps to the river, carefully, not holding onto the iron rail. The water was dark-brown, almost black, slapping against the bottom step. I looked all round again, then threw both knife and scarf far out into the river. There was not sound, not even a plop. The water just closed over them, as if they'd never existed.

I stood for a while flexing my fingers. The blood had dried on them. It felt tight and silky, like fish scales do when you've been gutting fish.

Then I went home. I let myself into the flat and stood just inside the door, listening to the silence. I'd've liked to go to bed, to huddle under the blankets and go to sleep, preferably forever, but I had to get washed.

It didn't take long for the water to run clear.

I got into bed, into clean white sheets, and pulled them up around me. My teeth were chattering and I couldn't understand why, because I didn't feel anything. Except cold. I was very cold.

I don't remember anything else.

There isn't much more to tell. I went to see Elaine's baby and oh, he's lovely. I held onto him that long at the finish Brenda says, 'Hey, mind what you're doing, Jean. It might be smittin.' I says, 'I wouldn't mind if it was.'

Elaine wasn't feeling too good, because she's still afraid Dave's going to leave her. Apparently he's been spending a lot of time with this other girl. *I* can't see him leaving her, though. I think it's more likely he'll stay away long enough to get her nicely softened up, then he'll show up again and run her *and* the other girl. By that time she'll be desperate enough to settle for anything.

But the baby really is lovely. I put a 50p piece in the palm of his hand and he didn't half hold onto it. You could actually see his little knuckles turning white. 'Eee, look at that,' says Audrey. 'He'll never want.'

I was alright that day, though I knew they'd found him. His picture was in all the papers, him and his wife and his big posh house and his garden and his kids. It never bothered me, all that. Well, the kids did a bit, because somehow I'd never thought of him having kids. But I brushed it aside, I just thought, *You bastard*.

But now I'm back under the viaduct and there's Kath staring at me from her billboard and there's cars going past, but none of them are stopping, and it isn't so easy not to think.

You see, that was only one way of telling it. I could tell you another story, a story about a fat, middle-aged man who went to see a prostitute and parked in the deep shadow next to the houses because he was afraid of being seen, and sweated a lot because he was nervous, and started to take off his tie, and . . . I don't like that story very much.

There was no knife. I scoured every inch of the car, and there was no knife. And there had to be a knife. He strangled Irene, he battered the others, but he stabbed them all. That's the one thing he *has* to do. So where was the knife?

It's true I didn't look in the boot of the car. To be honest, my nerve ran out. But the police'll've looked, and there's no hint in any of the papers that *they* think it's him. And I walked down Northgate tonight, and there's just as many vice-squad cars around as there ever was. But perhaps there would be. Perhaps they'd just go on as normal, waiting to see if there was another death. How else could they be sure?

How else can I be sure?

Oh, but you say, the smell. His breath smelled of violets. Yes, it did, and I killed him for it. Does that seem reasonable to you?

There was no violence. He didn't hit me, he didn't

380

threaten me. He didn't put a foot wrong.

I can't even be sure of the smell. Sometimes I smell Carol's scent in the flat, fresh scent, not the stale scent on clothes; but she isn't there.

I met a stranger. I had sex with him, and killed him. I did what he did. Or does.

Last night I dreamt about him, the man who killed Carol and Kath and the rest. He was standing under an arch of the railway, with his back turned. I went up to him and tapped him on the shoulder. He turned round . . . *and I was looking into my own face.*

Kath, it's bad tonight, talk to me. Please. But she won't talk, she's sulking about something. She just stares through me with those awful eyes.

I used to tell myself that if he died before I got to him, if he did himself in or anything like that, I'd know straight away because her face would change. It would change and soften and her eyes would close. Because they follow you, they follow you everywhere, and you feel yourself getting thinner and thinner, more and more transparent, until every nerve and bone and muscle is laid bare.

I'm alone with her now. I go up to her and stand on tiptoe. I can just reach the edge of her jacket, and I'm telling her, It's alright, he's dead, you can sleep now; and I look at her and I look at her and I wait for her eyes to close.

But she just stares past me, through all the wind and rain and darkness, down to the viaduct where she met her death. And her eyes don't close.

Why don't her eyes close?

PART FOUR

CHAPTER EIGHTEEN

"'C' birds!'

When Maggie had first heard that cry, ten years ago, her mind had filled with the cry of gulls and the buffeting of the wind on the cliffs at Boulby. You crawled on your belly to where the land fell away, sheer, and watched the sea splinter itself on the rocks below and draw back, foaming around them like lace; and then, in the middle air, the grey and white backs of the gulls.

Then, as now, the first of the 'C' birds had arrived. Grey-skinned. One wing missing. After it, a whole line of others. Maggie didn't think of the cliffs at Boulby now. Her mind was subdued by the whine and clatter and hum of the belt, and by the line of shadows that moved past along the high white walls. Headless chickens, dripping blood. Their necks swayed a little as they jerked along, like a dancer's tassels.

By this time of the day the floor was slick with blood. Maggie's boots shifted tackily from side to side as she moved around, trying to ease the ache of the varicose veins in her left leg. A few of the younger women had started to sing.

At last the break came. The women stared at each other, dazed by the silence. Then, gradually, a babble of voices arose, as they peeled off their rubber gloves, leaving them behind on the tables like heaps of sloughed-off skin.

Maggie waited for Renee to appear from the plucking

room where she worked.

'Not long now,' she said.

Renee started to reply, but was stopped by a fit of coughing. Maggie didn't like to say so, but the plucking room was doing her no good. The feathers seemed to get on her chest, but then she still had two more years to do, and she couldn't've stuck the gutting table any longer, her legs were worse than Maggie's, and that was saying a lot. Maggie walked slowly on the way upstairs, and did all the talking, because she didn't want to draw attention to Renee's breathless state. It meant you didn't get much time to drink the tea, but then the greasy muck they had the cheek to serve up . . . You were probably better off not drinking it.

On the first landing Renee stopped, drew a deep breath and said, 'Oh, sod it, I've left me flask.'

She'd given up on the tea altogether and brought her own.

'I'll get it,' said Maggie.

'No, don't bother. I've got me tabs.'

Her and her bloody tabs, they'd be the death of her. 'No bother.' Maggie was already on her way downstairs.

'It's the second window along,' Renee called down the stairs. 'In me . . .'

'I'll find it.'

The plucking room was hardly more than a shed, though a long one, and well heated. The windows had boards nailed across because they looked out onto the slaughter yard which for some reason the women were not supposed to see.

Maggie didn't bother to switch the lights on: there was enough light coming through cracks between the boards. She went straight to Renee's chair and bent down to get the flask from the carrier bag Renee always carried round with her, though you weren't supposed to, all personal belongings were supposed to be left in the cloakroom. As she bent down the feathers that were everywhere stirred. One brushed against the back of her bare hand. It was only a draught from the door of course, you knew that, but all the same it was a funny feeling. You felt you were not alone.

She went to the window and peered out through the crack between two boards, hoping to see some of the men who worked in the yard, but there was no-one, no person, only a line of chickens, upside down, moving past on their way to be stunned and killed. As she watched, one of them, only one, started to flap its wings.

She turned back to the room. Before her on the table was a half-plucked bird, its plump, naked, white thighs spread wide. Some of the surrounding feathers were still white, some blood-sodden from the severed neck. She stared at it, and as she stared the presence that she had sensed all round her grew stronger and stronger until it roared in her ears.

She had to get out, but it was a long way to the door, and the air was thick. You didn't walk through it, you waded or swam. But there, at last, was the corridor, the white walls, the thin, breathable air.

By the time she got to the tea-room she'd convinced herself that nothing very much had happened, just a dizzy spell. Hell, she was forty-seven, it was only what you could expect, but she wasn't going to mention it to Bill because he was always saying the job was too much for her and she ought to pack it in.

'I don't know about you, Renee,' she said as she sat down, 'but I'll be glad when today's over.'

'Are you coming round the pub, Maggie?' Sandra shouted from further up the table.

'You try stopping me,' she said. 'You want to come 'n' all, Renee. Do you good.'

'Oh, I don't know . . .'

'Howay . . .'

The supervisor appeared in the doorway. '*I* don't know,' said Renee, 'I'm bloody sure these breaks are getting shorter.'

'And later,' said Sandra, tapping her wrist. 'This'n was a full six minutes late.'

She said it loud enough for the supervisor to hear, too, but she only shrugged.

'Howay,' said Maggie, 'You're wasting your time. See you

in the cloakroom, Renee? Right?'

'She won't come,' said Sandra as they went downstairs. 'Too busy rushing back to that bloody cat of hers.'

But she did, and they had a good evening, a bit too good, perhaps, thought Maggie, as she staggered out of the Crown, well, not staggered exactly, but she'd had a few. Trouble was you got talking, and you needed a drink, you needed something to swill the blood and guts away, and make you fit to face the world. Which she was doing very nicely, thank you, though a bit brought back to earth by the thought of what to give Bill for his supper. It'd have to be fish and chips. Not that he'd grumble, he'd've ate them every day if she'd let him, him and his land and sea. And that time at their Moira's when he'd patted his belly and said, 'Folks think this is beer you know, but it's not, it's . . . "Twins,' she'd managed to get in. 'And by the looks of it, not long to go.' 'You cheeky bugger,' he said. Oh and Neil's mam sat there, she could've wrung his neck. 'Don't you go showing our Moira up,' she'd said afterwards. 'She's got enough on her plate without you.' 'What's so bloody special about them?' he wanted to know. 'They're very nice people,' she'd said. 'Aw, gerraway, Maggie, their shit stinks.' There was no doing anything with him in that mood, and anyway you knew he was right, it was just you didn't like to see Moira shown up. She had enough to put up with from that old cow, without *them* letting her down.

'*Change.*'

She must've been stood there staring at it, you could tell by his voice. She picked up the packet of fish and chips and left the shop, remembering too late that she should've asked about the baby. It must be a month old by now, because it had arrived the week before Ben. Eleven and a half pounds. No wonder she hadn't pulled herself round. Mrs Bulmer wouldn't have it. 'Eleven and a half pound,' she said. 'I don't believe it. My tumour weighed six and a half pounds and Mr Lamb said he'd seen nothing like it.' 'Well, you daft sod, that was a tumour. A baby's natural.' 'Not at eleven and a half pound it isn't.' But then somebody said, 'Oh, she's got sugar . . .' She ought to go home by the main road, the long way round, but it was late and the fish and chips'd get cold and anyway the buggers'd already dribbled grease and vinegar in a brown spot on her coat, and it was her good coat too, she always wore it on a Friday because of going to the pub after work. She dabbed at the stain with her hanky, but it was no good, it'd have to go into soak. And that decided her. She crossed the road, she'd cut down Blind Lane, it wasn't so badly lit now half the houses had been knocked down. She was just about to go into it when a man passed her on her left, she couldn't see him properly and anyway didn't look because if you started showing too much interest he might think you were one of them, and anyway he'd already said, 'Goodnight!' in a firm clear voice and strode ahead of her into the darkness. At least he had the sense to overtake, not like some, padding along behind you like the hound of the bleeding Baskervilles. She only hoped Bill was doing his bit and remembering the Newcastle Brown. That'd been just about the only treat they got when the kids were little and she couldn't go out to work, fish and chips on a Friday night with a couple of bottles of beer and a bit of how's your father on the rug in front of the fire. She couldn't let herself think when they'd last done it that way. You get older, you value your comfort more.

God, it was cold. She pushed the fish and chips inside her coat. There was plenty of room in there, she'd never had much in that department and what there was seemed to be migrating to her bum. Not that Bill'd complain about that either, you don't live with a man the best part of thirty years and not know what he fancies. *Legs,* he said. Aye. Pity she hadn't known when they were courting. The times she'd laid with her elbows clamped into her sides trying to make a valley when there weren't any mountains. Oh and that bloody song. He only had to sing that and she went mad. *'Oh Maggie, Maggie May, why have you gone away, and left your raggy knickers on the wa-all?'* 'Well, you daft bitch,' her mam'd said, 'You don't want to let him see it bothers you. If he knows he can get a rise out of you he'll do it all the — '

This was the moment the back of her head exploded, and she fell.

Drifted back to cobbles greasy underneath her cheek, and high-heeled shoes an inch away from her eyes.

'Are you alright?'

She opened her mouth to say 'Yes' but her top teeth had been broken in the fall and bulged out when she tried to speak. She tried to gobble them back in before anybody saw because now there were more people around her and others came running too many and all towered over her and pressed in. 'Mind her hand!' the woman with high-heeled shoes said.

'Better get an ambulance. There's a call-box just down there.'

'Has anybody got 10p?'

'You don't have to pay, you just dial. *Go on.*'

Somebody was pushing a something a rolled up coat under her head.

'You're sure she's not just drunk?'

'With all that blood?'

'She could've done that when she fell.'

She opened her mouth to tell the first speaker a thing or two, but her teeth bulged out again.

'You'd be better without them, honey,' high-heeled shoes said, and gently took them away. She wanted to protest but she didn't have the strength, and anyway the ground was dropping away beneath and she was going down, down . . .

Then a bright light and voices that knew what to do and she was being lifted and carried and slotted in and swung along and there were faces all pale faces staring and the doors clanged shut on a smell of antiseptic and red wool.

CHAPTER NINETEEN

Voices, and a bright light overhead.

'You're sure I'm not in your way?'

A chair scraped across her brain.

'No, honey, you stop where you are, I can get round.'

She felt, not saw, the face bend over.

'She's a lot better colour, you know. You want to keep saying little things to her. If they recognize your voice it seems to pull them round quicker.'

She got her eyes unglued at last.

'There you are, you see.'

Ivy leaned towards her. 'Maggie? Bill's just gone for a cup of tea, flower, he won't be long.' She turned to the other voice. 'Well, he's had no sleep. I says, Go and get a cup of tea. You'll not do her any good knocking yourself up. He did, he looked desperate. And it's not as if the daughter could come in, you see. She's got a baby three weeks old. Mind, she wanted to, she was getting her coat on, but her father says, No, you need your sleep. Sleep? she says, *Sleep?* I won't bloody sleep. But anyway her husband talked her out of it. It was him brought me over, he's a really nice lad.'

'She's your sister, isn't she?'

'Yeah, that's right.'

'You can't half tell.'

The curtains burst open round a gaggle of white. Ivy stood up. 'Have I to go?' she said.

'If you wouldn't mind. Just wait in the waiting room at the end.'

A trolley rattled up to the bed.

'Come on, Mrs Walker, you've got to sit up now.'

You'd've refused point blank if you could've remembered where your tongue was.

'Up you come.'

Something was staring at her from the side of a metal jug. She put a hand up to her head.

'Don't you worry about that now, it'll soon grow.'

It was a silly thing to cry about, but cry she did, and the young nurse, startled out of her professional sympathy, leaned over and caught her tears on the back of her hand.

Ten days later, they sent her home. 'You're a lucky woman,' the doctor said. There was no brain damage, no reason why her recovery should not be quick and complete. The scar would be with her for the rest of her life, but the fuzz of hair that now irritated her would grow long enough to cover it.

'Mind how you go,' the Sister said, as they reached the top of the steps.

They'd done her up, the nurses, as best they could, but she looked grotesque, and knew it, with her bald patch and her pleated lip, into which the carefully applied lipstick bled. They were all there, waving and wishing her well. She smiled with her newly stiff upper lip and tried not to cover her mouth with her hand when she said goodbye.

She started to shuffle down the steps, in her slippers, because Bill, who'd remembered everything else, had forgotten to bring her shoes. As she reached the car she turned and looked back, almost with regret. In that short time the hospital had become home, a place of safety at least, and now that the moment had come she was reluctant to leave it.

Bill had brought a blanket with him and tucked it round her, before getting into the driver's seat. It wasn't going to be easy. She guessed he was a little shy with her, as she was of him, because in the hospital they'd never really been alone. Now the silence seemed to stretch ahead of them full of things demanding to be said.

'Nice day,' she said.

'Yes, isn't it? Mind, we can do with it after all that rain.'

On the pavement people without holes in their heads were walking along, doing their shopping and enjoying what they hoped was spring. Maggie touched the window with her five fingers, delicately, as if needing to be reassured that only glass separated her from them.

'Our Moira wants you to go and stop with her for the first week.'

She was horrified. 'Aw, no,' she said. 'It'd be far too much for her. And anyway I couldn't stand the racket of the bairn.'

Besides, you needed to get back in the house as you needed to get back inside your own mind, to ferret about in corners and find out what, if anything, was left.

'Well, I just thought I'd warn you, because she's there now, and you know what she's like.'

The street must've known she was coming. More than one curtain twitched as they drove along, and Mrs Bulmer, who'd discovered that her front window needed cleaning, almost toppled off the step-ladder in her eagerness to see.

'Serve the nosy old bugger right if she had,' said Bill.

Moira was in the kitchen when they arrived. As soon as she heard the front door open she come running out, 'Oh, Mam . . .'

Maggie hugged her hard for a minute, then pushed her away. 'Now then,' she said, 'we've had enough of that. You'll be setting me off.' She looked round the living-room. 'You have kept it nice,' she said.

'What d'y' expect?' said Bill. 'A padding can?'

'Oh, I don't know. I just thought it might've changed.'

She laughed as she said it, to take any strangeness off the words, but she still wasn't sure. When she thought they weren't looking, she stroked the arm of her chair.

But it wasn't the house that had changed, it was Moira. There she was, bustling in and out of the kitchen, backside on her like a house-end, and somehow the girl you'd brought up had turned into this stocky, determined

393

woman. Who obviously had no doubt she knew what was right.

'You're coming to me, Mam,' she said.

'I'm bloody not, you know. You've got that bairn to look after, and besides, you're not over the birth yourself yet.'

'I was over that three hours after I had him.'

'Aye, big-head. You do too much now, you pay later. Believe me, I *know*. Anyway, I don't need looking after.'

'It's not that, Mam. It's when Dad goes back to work. You'll be stuck in here on your own.'

'Well, what of it? My God, you'll be going to the lavatory with me next. I've been on me own before.'

'I just thought you might get brooding, that's all.'

'What over?' She saw them look at each other; they were together over this, it wasn't just Moira. 'I didn't brood in the hospital, did I?' She hadn't. As soon as she got pulled round a bit she'd been quite cheerful. 'Well, I'm not going to brood now neither. It's over, I won't say I couldn't've done without it, but it's *past*. All I want now is to get home, get well, and get back to work.'

The rest of that day, and all weekend, people came. Relatives, neighbours, Renee and Sandra from the factory. Apparently, the women on the Mammy shift were going to have a bus to take them home. 'And about bloody time,' said Renee. 'They're only doing that because they know they'd all hand in their notices if they didn't.'

'It's daft really,' said Sandra. 'She's not on the Mammy shift.'

'Well, I wasn't leaving work anyway, was I? I was on me way home from the pub.'

But it was painful to talk about it. She was glad when they went.

There was a big gathering for Sunday tea. When, finally, Bill finished the washing up and came back into the living room, he said, 'You look wore out.'

'They mean well.'

'Last we'll see of some of 'em.'

Maggie shrugged. 'That's families, isn't it? You notice our Ivy wasn't there?'

'Now be fair. She told me she'd come round after the vultures had been.'

'It's Sarah she can't stand.' Maggie lowered her head carefully till it rested on the back of her chair. 'What did Sarah mean about the police being on at you?'

Bill looked away. 'You know Sarah. She's only got to open her gob for her brain to leak.'

There was something she wasn't being told, but she was too tired, perhaps too frightened, to pursue it. 'You couldn't give our Ivy a ring, could you? Tomorrow, before you go to work?'

'Oh, I reckon I might manage that.' He came across and looked at her. 'Howay, Maggie, get yourself to bed.'

Their own bedroom. She knew every mark on the wallpaper, every creak of the floorboards, every bump and sag in the mattress. It ought to've been completely safe, but it wasn't. She found herself listening for Bill's footsteps on the stairs.

This was something she couldn't understand. As long as she could *see* Bill, as long as he was in the same room with her, she was alright. But if he was behind her, or in a different part of the house, she started to worry. It wasn't fear exactly, but she needed to know what he was doing.

There were his footsteps now. She waited, and as soon as he reappeared, carrying two cups of hot chocolate in his hands, she relaxed.

But she was left with a feeling that the road back to 'normal' might be longer than she had wanted to believe.

She was pinning a lot of faith on Ivy.

'She says she'll be round about eleven,' Bill said. 'Oh and tell her not to bother with the shopping. I can do that on me way home.'

After he'd gone she sat down and looked round the room. Caught like that in a shaft of sunlight, the vase of daffodils made everything else look grey. Even the backs of her hands looked grey. She put her hand to her head and felt the ridge of half-healed flesh; then, because whatever happened you musn't think, you got up and got busy, inventing jobs to do since Bill and Moira had left you none.

But she did get tired easily. She had to admit that. By ten o'clock she was glad to sit down and, though she told herself it was only a five-minute break, she quickly went to sleep.

There was a bell ringing. The door bell. Trailing behind her the shreds of a nightmare, she stumbled to answer it and almost fell into Ivy's arms.

As soon as they were back in the living-room Ivy looked her up and down. 'Bill said you were doing alright.'

'I'm smashing.' She gestured round the room. 'I've been doing a bit.'

'*Over*-doing it. You're supposed to rest.'

'I'm supposed to get back to normal as soon as I can. The doctor said so.'

'Yes, well, he doesn't know "normal" means rushing round like a blue-arsed fly.'

She ought to've remembered they argued. They couldn't even agree on who was going to put the kettle on.

'I hope you don't think I've come to be waited on,' said Ivy. 'You'll have had enough of that.' She popped her head back round the kitchen door. 'I suppose Sarah was here?'

'Yes.'

'I thought so. Bloody vulture, that woman. You never meet her without she's either at a funeral or on her way to one.'

'Well, she wasn't yesterday. Least I hope not.'

'Aw, I shouldn't worry, you look as if you're stopping.' She brought the tea in. 'More than you did when I first saw you.'

'All *you* did was sit and talk to the bloody cleaner!'

'Well, I could get some sense out of her, there was none out of you.'

When they'd finished the tea Ivy said, 'Now, what do you want me to do?'

'Wash me hair. I don't think I could manage it on me own.' Bill would have helped, and gladly. But then you'd be crouched over the sink with your back to him and your eyes closed.

'Do you think we should?'

'I'm bloody sure we should. It's acky.'

Maggie rested her forehead on her knuckles while the warm water cascaded down. It was a comforting feeling, like being a child again. The warm moist smell of Ivy's armpits might've been their mother's smell.

'Do you know,' she said, 'the police thought I was a pro? And that was just because I'd been out drinking without Bill. They did. They knew I was working like, but they thought I was making a few bob on the side as well. At the finish I says, "*Look*, whatever I've had in this life I've had to work for, and I mean *work*," I says, "I don't mean lying on me back. And as for going out drinking, if your wife was stuck in that place eight hours a day, five days a week, shoving chicken legs up their arses she'd mebbe fancy a drink 'n' all." Mind, it did the trick, that Inspector was different altogether after that. Not that he was nasty before like, it was just you could tell what he was thinking.'

Ivy didn't say anything, she was too busy keeping the shampoo away from the scar. After she'd got it rinsed off she said, 'Did you know what come into me mind the other day? That time you were sent home from the Infants for swearing and me mam went down.' Another voice came into the kitchen. " '*My daughter Margaret said that?*" '

Maggie joined in. " '*But wherever can she have heard it?*" '

Ivy laughed. 'Eh, she could put it on when she wanted, couldn't she?'

'Yeah, and cuss. Do you remember that time me dad brought the parrot back from the pub, said he'd won it in a raffle? My God, the air was blue that night.'

'Yeah, and than the parrot started.' Ivy shook her head. 'She met her match in that parrot.'

'If she'd thought a bit quicker she could've blamed the parrot for me. Where d'y'suppose he got it? He can't've won it . . .

'Why, no! He'd bought it off a sailor, I expect. He was always buying daft things and saying he'd won them in raffles. She had a lot to put up with, you know.'

'Aye, but he worshipped her. That meks up for a lot.'

'Have you got any little rollers, Maggie? I was thinking if I could get this lot fluffed up a bit you could mebbe brush it over that side.'

'They're upstairs. First drawer on the left in the dressing table.'

'Right, but let's get you back on the sofa first, you look awful.'

Felt it too. It was a relief to lie down.

'You know what you could do with?' Ivy said, as she come back down the stairs, 'A woolly hat. I don't suppose you've got one, have you?'

'You know I've never wore a hat.'

'Well, you've never had a bald patch before either. I'll look you one out when I get home. Now let's see what we can do with this.'

After she'd gone Maggie got up and looked in the mirror, hoping that clean hair, even in rollers, might have brought about a transformation.

And looked away.

Teeth were the thing. That was what you told yourself. You couldn't be expected to look anything with your mouth sunk in like that. First thing tomorrow she'd get Bill to phone up about her teeth.

Teeth stuck in with dental fixative, Ivy's woolly hat pulled low about her ears, she ventured out for the first time.

'Now don't overdo it,' Bill said, 'If you'd only wait till this evening I could come with you.'

But she wanted to be on her own, to test out the tentative feeling of normality, to bare her newly recovered teeth at the world.

So out she went, smiling at people who looked at her and seemed to recognize what they saw. Some of them came up to her and said words and she replied with other words and nobody seemed to find anything odd. Though her voice still had a lispy quality. She would have to get used to speaking with the teeth in, just as in the hospital she'd had to get used to speaking with them out.

The supermarket. She stood at the deep-freeze counter,

trying to remember what it was that she'd persuaded herself she wanted to buy. She reached out for a packet of fish-fingers and there, coming towards her, slummocking her stomach along the edge of the counter, was a woman she knew, or half-remembered, who clearly knew *her*, because she stopped and said, 'Oh, hello. You're better.'

It was high-heels, though now you saw more of her than her feet you realized you knew her from way back.

'Oh, yes, I'm lot better, thanks.' In a minute, it'd come. She could see the other woman groping too.

Then it clicked. They said together, '*Annie Braithwaite.*'

'That's right,' Maggie said, 'You used to work next to her. I remember because you started the week after me, didn't you, and I used to watch the chickens piling up in front of you and I used to think, Well, at least I'm not the only one.'

'Annie used to do some of mine, you know. Eh, she was a good woman. I've missed her.'

The pleasure faded a little from their faces as they remembered that Annie was dead.

'Renee's still there.'

'She's not, is she? She must be well past sixty.'

'She's not, you know. She has another two year to do.'

'I haven't seen her in years. I don't suppose I'd know her now.'

'Oh, I think you would. She doesn't change much.'

There was an awkward pause as each looked back over the years between.

'I don't know how you've stuck it as long as you have.'

It was on the tip of Maggie's tongue to say there were worse jobs, but she checked herself. 'I want to thank you for what you did that night.'

Brenda looked uncomfortable. 'It was only what anybody would've done.'

But that wasn't true. Maggie knew from talking to the police that some of the people who heard her scream had walked the other way. This woman, clattering down Blind Lane in her high heels, had put him off the kill.

'I just wanted you to know that I appreciate it.'

Her words, though, couldn't restore the warmth that had

already leaked away, vanishing among the packets of fish-fingers and the tins of marrowfat peas.

'It was lucky I happened to be there.'

Though where the luck was, God knew. She'd *happened* to be there every night for years.

At that moment, steaming round the corner, came Mrs Bulmer, pushing lesser shoppers out of her way with the end of a well-laden trolley.

'Maggie Walker,' she said. 'You've never come out?'

Not a lot of point denying it. 'Yes.'

'Well, I think you need your . . .'

Head examining.

'. . . you could've asked *me*. What have you come for?'

What indeed? 'Fish-fingers,' she said, and picked a packet up.

Brenda touched her on the arm. 'Well, it's been nice seeing you,' she said, and moved away.

Maggie tried to call her back, and realized she couldn't remember her name.

'Hey, isn't that the woman in Melbourne Terrace? She's . . .' Mrs Bulmer waggled her fingers.

'No,' said Maggie. 'She works at the chicken factory.' Renee'd know. She'd ask Renee when she got back.

'Is that all you want?'

'Yes,' said Maggie, incautiously.

'Oh well, we can walk back together then. I only want a loaf of bread.'

It didn't feel like walking together, it felt more like being escorted.

'Well, you look a lot better than I thought you'd look.'

Maggie kept her head down, feeling Mrs Bulmer's eyes on the side of her face. The look was one of frank curiosity, she knew because she'd caught the tail-end of such glances before. They read the papers, they tried to read *between* the lines, and the same questions were there. *What does he do to them? How much did he do to her?* It was all very exciting, having a victim living in the same street. Oh, she didn't doubt the sympathy, but they were enjoying it too. Some of them hadn't had such a good time since Lesley Turner went into labour half way down the aisle. No use complaining, it was human nature. But even as she thought this, the smell of blood reached her nostrils, the feathers stirred.

She looked at Mrs Bulmer, at the avid mouth, and no longer saw a well-meaning woman. She listened, since she could do nothing else, and prayed for the safety of her home. Because now she was talking about Bill, and try as you might, you couldn't keep the meaning of the words out.

'Ted said they had him fifteen hours at the police station, taking it in turns, you know, going over and over the same ground. And everybody who'd been in the club with him, they went and saw them. "What time did he leave?" Well, as if anybody knew. You're not sat there looking at your watch, are you? Ted says, if Bill said ten o'clock it was ten o'clock, but then the barmaid turned round and said, it wasn't, it was earlier. And it's not as if he saw anybody on his way home, you see. He was handicapped. It was just like *his* word.'

She, waited for a response, but there was none.

'They even went to Mr Hutchinson and said, "Well, do you hear them rowing?" I says to Ted, "I think that's awful." But as he says, you couldn't fault them on it, they were only doing their job.'

Maggie tried to shut the voice out, but it went on drilling into her head. The dark shapes that had pursued her for so long suddenly closed in around her. She tried to switch her thoughts off, but across her mind's eye moved a line of faces, all women, young, old, fat, thin, smiling, serious. She knew who they were: she'd seen them in the papers, as everybody had, but then it had been just a story, something that had happened to somebody else, always to somebody else. But now it was real because it had happened to her. The image faded and was replaced by a line of chickens waiting to be killed. In each eye the same passive uncomprehending terror. Mrs Bulmer's voice went on, and on. You thought evil was simple. No, more than that, you *made* it simple, you froze it into a single shape, the shape of a man waiting in the shadows. But it wasn't simple. This woman, this wheezy middle-aged woman, with her corrugated-iron hair and her glasses that flashed when she looked sideways to see how you were taking it, she knew what she was doing. And she was enjoying it. You couldn't put evil into a single, recognizable shape.

When at last Maggie sat down again in her own armchair she knew that something irrevocable had happened. The abyss was at her feet, and she could do nothing except stare into it, while the fish-fingers thawed through and wetted the arm of her chair.

CHAPTER TWENTY

'If you'd wanted to know anything, Maggie, you'd only to ask.'

Maggie turned her face slowly towards her sister. There were some mornings now when even the effort of moving her head was too much.

'I don't know,' said Ivy. 'If you go on like this we'll just have to get the doctor.'

Maggie's mouth formed the single word, 'Nerves.'

'Well, he could give you nerve pills then! My God, you need something.'

But not pills.

'I suppose we did wrong keeping it from you, but then they said you hadn't to be upset, and you hadn't to be worried. I mean what was I supposed to say? "The police think Bill did it, but don't worry"? You were in no state for anything like that.'

'You could've told me later.'

'There was nothing to *tell*. Well, nothing much. Look, they come to the door, right? And of course Bill took one look at the uniform and he jumped to the conclusion you'd been run over. He says, "My God, where is she?" And he was ever so good, he broke it to Moira and he sent Neil over to get me, and he was . . . he was smashing. Then he looked at you, and mind, you did, you looked awful, and he just seemed to crumple. We were sat in the waiting room, because the doctor was examining you and then he come in and he says, "Mr Walker?" And Bill says, "Yes." Anyway he started on about the injuries, what they were and all that. "But," he says, "she hasn't been sexually assaulted." Well, Bill just stared at him. I don't think he took in a word the man said. And when he started on about sexual assault, Bill just shook his head, he didn't seem as if he could grasp that at all. Well, then the police started, and I heard a lot of that because I was in the next room. Bill kept saying, "The accident." Oh and they didn't half weigh into him. *"Accident?"* they said. *"There's been no bloody accident."* You know for all they'd told him you'd been attacked I think in his mind it was still a car. You'd been run over.

'Anyway the next day he was round the police station and they made him sign this statement, going back over all your married life and everything, and afterwards he come round our house and I'm not kidding you, Maggie, he sat on our sofa and he cried. He says, "It sounded awful. It sounded as if we were living a cat-and-dog life, and," he says, "you know, Ivy, we weren't." But they asked him daft questions, like do you ever have rows? I says, you should've said, who doesn't?'

'Anyway, that was the last he heard. They come round two days after and they as good as told him they wouldn't be bothering him again. You see, they'd checked the times out by then. There was no way he could've got there. And, he says, their faces had dropped a mile. Then as they were going he heard one of them say, "Well, it looks as if that's another one for the list." I says, "What did he mean?" "Oh," he says, "they think it's the same one that killed the prostitutes."'

Maggie seemed to be trying to say something. Ivy waited. When it came, it was an infinitely dry whisper. 'It doesn't matter who it was.'

'Catching the bugger matters!'

But Maggie had already turned away.

The mornings were the worst time. On a bad day Bill would come in from work at dinner-time and find her still sitting

404

in the same position as she'd been in when he left, arms along the arms of the chair, eyes staring straight ahead as if there was no hope of altering the direction of their gaze. They had to get the doctor to her in the end. He came and prescribed pills which she at first took, and then rebelled against, as she felt them begin to undermine the little resistance she had left.

Over and over again she was forced to relive the events of that day, from the moment in the plucking room when she had felt the feathers stir, to the moment at the entry to Blind Lane when a man had passed her, and said goodnight, and meant it to be forever. She could remember nothing after that. The three minutes she spent in Blind Lane had vanished from her memory as completely as if she'd never lived them.

It would have been difficult to say what she thought about at these times, though her mind was certainly not blank. But it seemed to think mainly in images, images that grew out of one another, with the fertility of a dream. By contrast, her worded thoughts were like dead leaves on a river, able to reveal the direction of the current, but neither its depth nor its power, and, taken together, might have amounted to no more — or less — than the single word, *Why?*

One morning, feeling a little better, she forced herself out of the house, slipping along the back lanes until she was far enough away from Lawson Street for nobody to recognize her. At first she thought it was a mistake, for there, all round her, were the hurrying crowds, housewives, children, married couples, gangs of lads and lasses, an old man who walked out into the centre of the road without looking. Even that little dog trotting along the pavement seemed to know where it was going. None of this had anything to do with her. She caught glimpses of herself, flitting along between the shop windows, a skimpy little woman in her ridiculous red tea-cosy of a hat. She became tired very quickly too. After a while she sat down on a church wall to rest, and then, thinking that inside it would be dark and quiet, she wandered in.

It *was* quiet, though not dark. Dust motes sifted about in shafts of coloured light. She listened to the silence, and then went to look at the window above the main altar. A rose window, she thought it was called. At any rate round, with swirls of red and gold and purple light all leading in towards the centre, where sat the tiny figure of Christ in Majesty, one arm raised. She knelt down and tried to pray, but it was no use. She hadn't prayed for years.

She wandered to the back of the church, smelling that smell you always thought was mice, though probably it wasn't, and there, tucked away, was a tiny chapel, hardly more than a cupboard. Very dark. She went in.

Her first thought was, No wonder they've got that tucked away, because it was, it was ugly. Not like the pictures of Christ you see blessing children, Christ in a meadow with long white robes and a lily in his hand. This Christ was dead.

She stared at his green mouth, and then her gaze moved down, and her attention quickened. The whole chest was deformed by the stretched-back arms and lolling head. The lower ribs flared out to a point where they seemed hardly to be human at all. There were marks all over his skin, from the flogging, she supposed, and here and there a thorn had escaped from the crown and embedded itself in the flesh of hip or breast. She had seen such marks before. They were like, no, *were*, the marks left when the spine of a feather is pulled out. That was it, and that was where she had seen the flaring ribs before. Though even as she identified the memory her perception shifted again and she was once more looking at tortured human flesh. She had never seen a death that looked less like sleep.

She went back to the main altar, though this time she didn't try to pray, but merely to clear her mind of its accumulated rubble, to still the surface chatter of a lifetime. Again, nothing. The chicken Christ on his cross might claim her as his own, but the risen Christ, Christ in Majesty, pain sloughed off behind him like an outworn skin, had nothing to say.

406

On Sundays the family gathered, though after the first hectic weekend they took it in turns to come, and Maggie was grateful, because a roomful of people made her headaches start.

This weekend it was Moira, which was what she liked best, especially since this time she brought the baby with her instead of leaving him with Neil's mam.

'Hello, Mam,' she said, coming in with the carefully wrapped bundle in her arms.

Neil followed, carrying a bouncing chair, a changing mat, a bottle, and a carrier bag full of nappies.

'They don't travel light, do they?' said Bill.

Neil laughed, and looked around for a space to put it all.

Maggie had pushed aside the folds of the blanket, and was looking at Ben.

'Isn't he a smasher?' she said, and took him into her own arms.

'Here, sit down, Mam.'

'I'm not gunna drop him, you know. I never dropped you.'

She sat nursing the baby, which stared back at her with smoky, unfocused eyes. There was a little scratch on his right cheek. 'Hey, our Moira, he's scratched hisself. You want to get his fingernails cut.'

'I daren't go near him with the scissors.'

'Scissors! You use your teeth. You can't feel where you are with scissors.'

She nursed the baby all afternoon. 'You want to put him down, Mam,' Moira said. 'He'll be heavy.'

'You leave her alone,' said Bill. 'She's happy.'

She was, too. Though she had a bad night after it, awake at two, and then again at four. She thought sometimes that if only she could have a long, deep, natural sleep she would be better, but there seemed to be no hope of that. Still, she was getting better. It had been a good day.

CHAPTER TWENTY-ONE

As she grew stronger she wanted to get away from the city. But on foot this seemed to be impossible because, however far she walked, the grey, twisting streets turned in on themselves, like the convolutions of a brain.

She took a bus and there was the country at last, a green, moist, safe place, but even then hard to get into. The road ran tidily between ploughed fields, dotted here and there with seagulls all facing the same way into the wind. But there was no way into the fields. She walked for hours along the road until her legs ached, but there was none of the magic she had half-expected. She didn't know what she *had* expected. Some revelation of good to balance the evil? If so, she was disappointed. The countryside stretched ahead of her, grey-green and featureless.

She didn't mention the walk to Bill. She was surprised at herself, keeping it from him, because normally she reported all the events of her day, needing to convince him, or perhaps it was herself, that she had made progress.

She *had* made progress. She did all the shopping now, except for the meat and the potatoes, they were a bit heavy, but all the supermarket stuff she did. She walked all the way to Finefare, rather than go to the Co-op and risk meeting somebody she knew. It was silly, it was wrong, she knew that, but it was the way she felt. The family you couldn't avoid, though neither could you respond to their too-insistent kindness. At last she said, 'You know, Bill, it's very nice them all rallying round like this, but do you think we could have a weekend to ourselves?'

Somehow he managed it, without offending any of them, and it was much better because Bill was content to sit in silence and there weren't the jarring insistent voices pulling you away from your thoughts.

Sometimes she looked at him and wondered what he was thinking, but she never asked. They were like two animals of different species caged together, each sunk in its own misery, neither able to reach out and comfort the other. Though he would have comforted her if he could. She was the one who had withdrawn.

It was a relief when the weekend was over and she could get out of the house again.

She walked every day now and her walks took her further and further away from the city. If she had to stay at home because of bad weather or for some other reason she was restless and miserable until she could get out again. Yet it was difficult to say what benefit she got from the walks. Often she had nothing to show for them but mud-splashed trousers and aching feet. She couldn't even claim they made her sleep. Only the pills did that.

She tried, on these walks, to keep her mind clear: not think, not question, not remember. Sometimes she succeeded and then she brought back images of another reality. Black, untidy birds, rooks, she thought, or they might have been crows, she was too far away to tell, blown across the sky like scraps of burnt paper. The purplish haze on an elm tree that resolved itself as she got closer into a million tiny flowers. Dry stalks of cow parsley chafing in the wind.

More often though, she failed, and then she was back with the blood-sodden feathers on the plucking room floor; with the face of the murdered prostitute, Kath Robson, that had hung for so many months outside the chicken factory until one day they came and covered it up with an advertisement for Guinness; with herself, stretched out on the cobbles in Blind Lane. These images no longer terrified her — she had got beyond fear — but they haunted her, draining her days and nights, sapping her will to live.

On one of these walks something happened that at first threatened to deepen the darkness in which she lived. She came out into a clearing, on a bright, cold day, and there in front of her was a fox, his coat the colour of last year's bracken, the still-twitching body of a rabbit clamped in his jaws. Perhaps he was confused because the wind blew her scent away from him, or perhaps hunger at the end of this long winter had made him reckless. At any rate, he neither dropped his prey nor fled, but stared steadily at her. Then, slowly, very slowly, he turned away, holding the rabbit high to keep it clear of the ground. You could see his neck muscles tauten as he took the strain. A second or two later and he was gone, disappearing into the dead bracken, gold into gold. He had left nothing behind except his own heavy smell and a few drops of blood on a small stone.

Maggie stared at the blood. This then was the country. This was the green, moist safe place of her childhood. And yet what she felt was neither disgust nor pity, but respect for this life that was lived apart from man. She walked home thoughtfully, and the image of the plucking room did not return.

She had to go back to the hospital. She got herself all keyed up about it, had a bad night, and ended up looking worse than she'd looked for weeks.

Bill took time off to go with her and they sat on spindly plastic chairs reading brochures about holidays in Majorca and the Costa Brava.

'You'd think they'd get a few decent magazines in, wouldn't you?' said Maggie.

'That's what you could do with,' said Bill, 'a couple of weeks in the sun.'

Maggie's name was called. She gave Bill a frightened look before she went in, because although she'd tried not to think too much about this visit in fact she'd been imagining all kinds of things, perhaps even another go inside that thing that went round and round. But there was nothing like that. He had a young man with him this time, he must be a student or something. Maggie stared at the gap between his trousers and his socks: he had the hairiest legs she'd ever seen. Meanwhile the questions had started. Was she eating? Was she sleeping? Did she still get the headaches? How often? Whereabouts was the pain? How bad was it? Sickness with it? Visual disturbances? Was she depressed? Was she taking the pills? Did she find herself getting bad-tempered more often? Impatient? 'I don't know,' she said, 'You'll have to ask me husband.'

And that was that.

Bill looked up as Maggie walked towards him. 'Are you alright?' he said.

'Signed off.'

'Never.'

'I am. He just says, "Come back if the headaches get worse."' But she had trouble believing it herself. 'I suppose I'd better phone the factory and tell them I'm coming back.'

'You're never going back to work, are you?'

'Well, of course I am. You can't stop off if you're not bad.'

He was more than put out, he was really angry. 'I think you want looking at,' he said.

'Look, Bill, you've never sat staring at four walls. You don't know what it's like.'

'You don't do much staring at them, Maggie. I don't know where you get to, but you certainly don't stop in.'

Maggie said nothing. This was something she couldn't share, even with Bill. Whatever was happening needed darkness and silence for its growth. And time. Above all, time. She felt cheated. It was as if her body in healing itself so quickly and so efficiently had abandoned her, had left her as naked and defenceless as a seed.

She wasn't ready to be well.

CHAPTER TWENTY-TWO

When they got home Ivy was waiting for them, with the fire on and a hot meal ready. Maggie told her the doctor had signed her off and that she was going back to work. She saw Bill and Ivy look at each other, but they said nothing. And she was too tired to care what they thought.

She washed and ironed the clothes she wore for work. She rang the chicken factory and told them she was coming back. She went to the hairdresser and had her hair restyled, choosing a shop so far away from home that nobody would know her. She told the girls she'd slipped on the ice and cracked her head open on the back door step. They all went '*Ugh!*' when they saw the dent in her head, but they seemed to believe her. Why do I lie about it? she thought. It was almost as if *she* had reason to be ashamed.

Soon everything would be back to normal. She would go back to work and the water would close over this disturbance, seamlessly, as if it had never been. And that was what she wanted: normal, unreflecting daily life, herself back with the flock, in no way different from the others, in no way changed. Only she wished it might happen quickly. It was the waiting that made doubts crowd into her mind.

As the final days of freedom passed she became more and more restless, until at last, one dank, cold day, more like November than spring, she was almost driven out of the house. She cut through the back streets to Northgate and waited for the bus that would take her into the country. Rain clouds massing over the viaduct bound in the smoke and smells of the city. The air tasted metallic.

She kept her face pressed to the window as the bus jolted along, rubbing away the mist of her own breath, seeing the long lines of houses and factories spread out, like a skin disease, to cover the green.

On previous walks she'd kept more or less to signposted paths, but now she struck out boldly across the ploughed fields. She walked quickly with her head down. Only once did she stop and look back at the city and then it was blurred by veils of rain drifting slowly across the middle ground.

All the while there was this pressure of desperation because she had to go back, back to normal life, back to the chicken factory. There was no choice now. She had left herself no choice.

The drizzle thickened to a downpour. Icy sheets of rain plastered the thin hair flat against her skull. Ahead of her on the brow of a hill was a clump of trees which might provide some shelter. She tried to run towards it, but the mud sucked at her feet, making every step a separate struggle. In the end she toiled to the top of the hill, head bent into the wind, enduring the wet as cows and horses do, subdued to the elements they live in.

The hill rose to a crest. There was a scraped out, stony hollow beneath and here she stopped, sheltered at least from the wind, though the trees, still leafless, gave little protection from the rain. She looked back the way she had come and saw the whole countryside smudged in the rain, yellow and green and brown all running together into grey, like the colours of a child's painting after the water has been knocked over. She closed her eyes and let her mind go blank, while drops of rain dripped steadily onto her head and neck, and ran down under the collar of her shirt.

She would have liked this rain to last forever, to close her eyes and not open them again, sealed off in the privacy and intimacy of the wood. It would have been easy to die here. She thought of the bodies of small animals she'd seen on

413

her walks, shrews and voles, how they seemed not to rot but rather to fade into the leaves and grass, growing a little fainter day by day, like the after images you see when a light is switched off. That kind of death held no terror. She would almost have welcomed it. But her body inside the stiff case of wet clothes was growing warm again, and the rain had begun to ease off.

She got up and walked to the top of the hill from where she could see the whole city spread out before her. Rain and mist together bound in the columns of yellow smoke, the clouds of steam from cooling towers. Even the tall flames of the burners could scarcely penetrate the haze. But then, as she watched, the ridge of black cloud lifted a little, and suddenly there were rays of light, or rather great shafts of golden light, falling onto the city, which looked now like an island raised up out of the sea, for there were still inlets of rain and mist in the surrounding fields.

This was not the city she knew: back streets, boarded-up houses, the smell of blood in a factory yard. And yet it was the same city. She watched the columns of light move over it, until the cloud thickened and the veils of rain closed round it once again.

She got back home only a few minutes before Bill was due in from work. The fire had gone out, but she was too tired to re-light it. Instead she went upstairs, took off her coat and shoes and then lay on the bed, just as she was, in her wet clothes. After a few minutes she started to shiver and pulled the quilt over her.

The skirt she'd got ready for work on Monday hung over the back of her chair. I won't be needing that now, she thought, and was surprised because she couldn't remember when she'd made up her mind. She'd seen the city raised up like an island out of the sea, awash with rain and light. A moment only. Then the long trek back through the mud. But at some stage on that journey home, without consciously thinking about the chicken factory at all, she'd taken the decision: she would not go back.

When she closed her eyes and tried to remember, her mind filled with the soft sound of the wind hushing and lulling through the wood. Nothing more.

She felt rather than saw Bill come in.

'Hello,' he said. A dark shape until he bent down and switched on the light.

She shielded her eyes.

'My God,' he said. 'What happened to you?'

'I got caught in the rain.'

'Fell in the river more like. Howay.' He pulled her up and started unbuttoning her shirt. 'Let's get these wet things off.'

She sat on the edge of the bed, like a little girl, and let him undress her.

'You're cold, aren't you?'

'I'm alright.'

The rain had gone all the way through. Even her underwear was wet. Bill shook his head and went to get a towel. Then, while she hung onto his waist for support, he started to rub her down. First her hair, then, very gently, the small drooping breasts, the puckered skin of her belly, the thin legs, until at last he reached her feet which he cradled, one by one, in his lap.

'There,' he said when he'd finished, but he didn't get up. Instead he looked at her and said, 'Oh, Maggie, Maggie May, why have you gone away?'

She didn't know what to say. All the things she'd believed hidden, the fear when he came up behind her, the nights she'd lain awake, afraid he might want to make love, the times she'd looked at his hands and felt the doubts, the awful possibilities, crowd into her mind, all these things were known. What could she say? 'I'm trying to come back'? No. In the end she said nothing, simply reached out for his hand and held it fast.

There is a moment in every evening when the streets of the city are dark although the sky is still light, almost as if the darkness is exhaled as a vapour from the pavements and cannot reach the sky. At this moment the starlings come. At first a solitary black dot against clear translucent turquoise, then later, as the sun sinks beneath the level of the bridges, in a great black wave swelling and breaking over the city. They swarm above its streets, they descend on its buildings, covering every ledge and gutter thickly, wing to wing. But however many come down the sky remains full and the people of the city walk home through air that tingles with the starlings' cries.

The sky flames. Then, gradually, as the birds continue to descend, the red gentles through purple and gold to rose, until at last every bird is lodged, and the singing dies away.

Above the hurrying people, above the lighted windows, above the sodium orange of the street lamps, they hump, black and silent; unnoticed, unless some stranger to the city should happen to look up, and be amazed.